RINGWORLD REDUX

Ten years after the publication of Ring-world, Larry Niven, winner of the Hugo and Nebula awards and author of one of the true popular classics of modern science fiction, has at last satisfied the call of his many fans and written a sequel —a return voyage to that astonishing world, with even more remarkable adventures and surprises, and a solution to that tantalizing question left from the earlier book: how was the Ringworld built and by whom?

"For new readers, there's fascinating adventure in plenitude. For old fans of Niven's *Known Space* series, or of the original volume, there are all the fine, characteristic touches that delight us Niven fans, and which support his reputation for uncommon wittiness and fast narrative pace."
—*Chicago Sun-Times*

Also by Larry Niven
Available now from Ballantine Books:

ALL THE MYRIAD WAYS

CONVERGENT SERIES

FLIGHT OF THE HORSE

THE FLYING SORCERERS
  (with David Gerrold)

A GIFT FROM EARTH

A HOLE IN SPACE

THE LONG <u>ARM</u> OF GIL HAMILTON

NEUTRON STAR

PROTECTOR

RINGWORLD

TALES OF KNOWN SPACE:
  The Universe of Larry Niven

WORLD OF PTAVVS

A WORLD OUT OF TIME

THE RINGWORLD ENGINEERS

Larry Niven

A Del Rey Book

BALLANTINE BOOKS • NEW YORK

A Del Rey Book
Published by Ballantine Books

Library of Congress Catalog Card Number: 79-18992

ISBN 0-345-26009-0

Hardcover edition published by Holt, Rinehart and Winston:
March 1980

Manufactured in the United States of America

First Ballantine Books Edition: March 1981
Fourth Printing: May 1981

Cover art by Dale Gustafson

Map by Diane Duane

Dedication

Ringworld is ten years old; and I have never stopped getting letters about it. People have been commenting on the assumptions, overt and hidden, and the mathematics and the ecology and the philosophical implications, precisely as if the Ringworld were a proposed engineering project and they were being paid for the work.

A man in Washington, D.C., sent me a full proofreading job on the first edition of *Ringworld*, with the title "The Niven-McArthur Papers, Vol. I." It was of enormous help to me. (If you own a first paperback edition of *Ringworld*, it's the one with the mistakes in it. It's worth money.)

A Florida high school class determined the need for the spillpipe system.

From a Cambridge professor came an estimate for the minimum tensile strength of *scrith*.

Freeman Dyson (Freeman Dyson!) has no trouble believing in the Ringworld (!), but can't see why the engineers wouldn't have built a lot of little ones instead. Wouldn't it be safer. I hope the answer I've given in this book is satisfactory.

Of course there are no petrochemicals on the Ringworld. Frank Gasperik pointed out that any civilization at our level would be based on alcohol. The Machine People would be able to use the vegetable sludge for other purposes, up to and including a plastics industry.

During a speech in Boston someone in the audience pointed out that, mathematically, the Ringworld can be treated as a suspension bridge with no endpoints. Simple in concept; harder to build.

From all directions came news of the need for attitude jets. (During the 1971 World Science Fiction Convention, MIT students were chanting in the hotel hallways: THE RINGWORLD IS UNSTABLE!) but it took Ctein and Dan Alderson, working independently, several years to quantify the instability. Ctein also worked out data on *moving* the Ringworld.

Dan Alderson was kind enough to work out the parameters for the Ringworld meteor defense for me . . . and that was the *only* piece of information I actually solicited.

You who did all that work and wrote all those letters: be warned that this book would not exist without your unsolicited help. I hadn't the slightest intention of writing a sequel to *Ringworld*. I dedicate this book to you.

Contents

PART THREE

CHAPTER

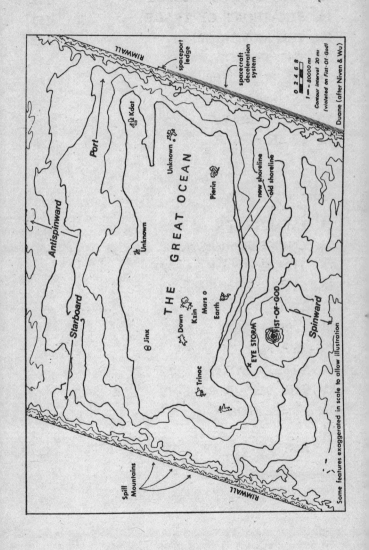

RIMWALL

spaceport ledge

spacecraft
deceleration
system

Kdat

Port

Unknown

Antispinward

Pierin

new shoreline
old shoreline

Unknown

Starboard

THE   GREAT   OCEAN

Jinx

Down

Kzin

Mars o

Earth

EYE STORM

FIST-OF-GOD

Trinoc

Spinward

Spill
Mountains

RIMWALL

Some features exaggerated in scale to allow illustration

0 2 4 6 8
1 = 80000 m
Contour interval 20 m
(violated on Fist-Of-God)

Duane (after Niven & Wu)

PART ONE

CHAPTER 1

Under the Wire

Louis Wu was under the wire when two men came to invade his privacy.

He was in full lotus position on the lush yellow indoor-grass carpet. His smile was blissful, dreamy. The apartment was small, just one big room. He could see both doors. But, lost in the joy that only a wirehead knows, he never saw them arrive. Suddenly they were there: two pale youths, both over seven feet tall, studying Louis with contemptuous smiles. One snorted and dropped something weapon-shaped in his pocket. They were stepping forward as Louis stood up.

It wasn't just the happy smile that fooled them. It was the fist-sized droud that protruded like a black plastic canker from the crown of Louis Wu's head. They were dealing with a current addict, and they knew what to expect. For years the man must have had no thought but for the wire trickling current into the pleasure center of his brain. He would be near starvation from self-neglect. He was small, a foot and a half shorter than either of the invaders. He—

As they reached for him Louis bent far sideways, for balance, and kicked once, twice, thrice. One of the invaders was down, curled around himself and not breathing, before the other found the wit to back away.

Louis came after him.

What held the youth half paralyzed was the abstracted bliss with which Louis came to kill him. Too late, he reached for the stunner he'd pocketed. Louis kicked it out of his hand. He ducked a massive fist and kicked at kneecap, kneecap (the pale giant stopped moving), groin, heart (the giant bent far forward, with a whistling scream), throat (the scream stopped suddenly).

The other invader was on hands and knees, breathing in sips. Louis chopped at his neck, twice.

The invaders lay still in the lush yellow grass.

Louis Wu went to lock his door. At no time had the blissful smile left his face, and it did not change when he found his door fully locked and alarmed. He checked the door to the balcony: bolted and alarmed.

How in the world had they gotten in?

Bemused, he settled where he was, in lotus position, and did not move again for over an hour.

Presently a timer clicked and switched off the droud.

Current addiction is the youngest of mankind's sins. At some time in their histories, most of the cultures of human space have seen the habit as a major scourge. It takes users from the labor market and leaves them to die of self-neglect.

Times change. Generations later, these same cultures usually see current addiction as a mixed blessing. Older sins—alcoholism and drug addiction and compulsive gambling—cannot compete. People who can be hooked by drugs are happier with the wire. They take longer to die, and they tend not to have children.

It costs almost nothing. An ecstasy peddler can raise the price of the operation, but for what? The user isn't a wirehead until the wire has been embedded in the pleasure center of his brain. Then the peddler has no hold over him, for the user gets his kicks from house current.

And the joy comes pure, with no overtones and no hangover.

So that by Louis Wu's time, those who could be enslaved by the wire or by any lesser means of self-destruction had been breeding themselves out of the human race for eight hundred years.

Today there are even devices that can tickle a victim's pleasure center from a distance. Tasps are illegal on most worlds, and expensive to make, but they are used. (A dour stranger wanders past, rage or misery written in the sour lines of his face. From behind a tree you make his day. Plink! His face lights up. For a moment he's got no worries at all . . .) They don't generally ruin lives. Most people can take it.

The timer clicked and switched off the droud.

Louis seemed to sag in upon himself. He reached across his smooth scalp to the base of the long black braid, and pulled the droud from its socket beneath the hair. He held it in his hand, considering; then, as always, he dropped it into a drawer and locked it. The drawer disappeared. The desk, which seemed a massive wooden antique, was actually paper-thin hullmetal, with endless room for secret compartments.

It was always a temptation to reset the timer. He'd done it routinely in the early years of his addiction. Neglect had made of him a skeletal rag doll, constantly dirty. Finally he had gathered what remained of his ancient dogged determination, and he had built a timer that took twenty minutes of nitpicking concentration to reset. On its present setting it would give him fifteen hours of current and twelve hours for sleep and for what he called maintenance.

The corpses were still there. Louis had no idea what to do about that. If he'd called the police immediately, it would still have attracted unwanted attention . . . but what could he tell them now, an hour and a half late? That he'd been knocked unconscious? They'd want to deep-radar his head for fractures!

This he knew: in the black depression that always followed his time under the wire, he simply couldn't make decisions. He followed his maintenance routine like a robot. Even his dinner was preprogrammed.

He drank a full glass of water. He set the kitchen. He went to the bathroom. He did ten minutes of exercise, pushing himself hard, fighting depression with exhaustion. He avoided looking at the stiffening corpses. Dinner was ready when he finished. He ate without tasting . . . and remembered that once he had eaten and exer-

cised and made every move with the droud set in his
skull, delivering a tenth of normal current to the pleasure center. For a time he had lived with a woman who
was also a wirehead. They had made love under the wire
. . . and played war games and held pun contests . . .
until she had lost interest in everything but the current
itself. By then Louis had regained enough of his natural
caution to flee Earth.

He thought now that it would be easier to flee this
world than to dispose of two large, conspicuous corpses.
But if he were already being watched?

They didn't look like ARM agents. Large, soft in the
muscle, pale from a sunlight more orange than yellow,
they were certainly low-gravity types, probably Canyonites. They hadn't fought like ARMs . . . but they had
bypassed his alarms. These men could be ARM hire-
lings, with friends waiting.

Louis Wu disarmed his balcony door and stepped
out.

Canyon does not quite follow the usual rules for
planets.

The planet is not much bigger than Mars. Until a few
hundred years ago its atmosphere was just dense
enough to support photosynthesis-using plants. The air
held oxygen, but was too thin for human or kzinti life.
The native life was as primitive and hardy as lichen.
Animals had never developed at all.

But there were magnetic monopoles in the cometary
halo around Canyon's orange-yellow sun, and radioac-
tives on the planet itself. The Kzinti Empire swallowed
the planet and staffed it with the aid of domes and
compressors. They called it Warhead, for its proximity
to the unconquered Pierin worlds.

A thousand years later the expanding Kzinti Empire
met human space.

The Man-Kzin wars were long over when Louis Wu
was born. Men won them all. The kzinti have always
had a tendency to attack before they are quite ready.
Civilization on Canyon is a legacy of the Third Man-

Kzin War, when the human world Wunderland developed a taste for esoteric weapons.

The Wunderland Treatymaker was used only once. It was a gigantic version of what is commonly a mining tool: a disintegrator that fires a beam to suppress the charge on the electron. Where a disintegrator beam falls, solid matter is rendered suddenly and violently positive. It tears itself into a fog of monatomic particles.

Wunderland built, and transported into the Warhead system, an enormous disintegrator firing in parallel with a similar beam to suppress the charge on the proton.

The two beams touched down thirty miles apart on Canyon's surface. Rock and kzinti factories and housing spewed away as dust, and a solid bar of lightning flowed between the two points. The weapon chewed twelve miles deep into the planet, exposing magma throughout a region the size and shape of Baja California on Earth, and running roughly east and west. The kzinti industrial complex vanished. The few domes protected by stasis fields were swallowed by magma, magma that welled higher in the center of the great gash before the rock congealed.

The eventual result was a sea surrounded by sheer cliffs many miles high, surrounding in turn a long, narrow island.

Other human worlds may doubt that the Wunderland Treatymaker ended the war. The Kzinti Patriarchy is not normally terrified by sheer magnitude. Wunderlanders have no such doubts.

Warhead was annexed after the Third Man-Kzin War, and became Canyon. Canyon's native life suffered, of course, from the gigatons of dust that dropped on its surface, and from the loss of water that precipitated within the canyon itself to form the sea. In the canyon there is comfortable air pressure and a thriving pocket-sized civilization.

Louis Wu's apartment was twelve stories up the side of the north face of the canyon. Night shadowed the canyon floor as he stepped outside, but the southern face still glowed with daylight. Hanging gardens of native lichen dripped from the rim. Old elevators were silver threads standing miles high against the cut stone. Transfer booths had made these obsolete for travel, but tourists still used them for the view.

The balcony overlooked the belt of parkland that ran down the center of the island. The vegetation had the wild look of a kzinti hunting park, with pink and orange blended into the imported terrestrial biosphere. Kzinti life was common throughout the canyon.

There were as many kzinti as human tourists down there. The kzinti males looked like fat orange cats walking on their hind legs . . . almost. But their ears flared like pink Chinese parasols, and their tails were nude and pink, and their straight legs and big hands marked them as toolmakers. They stood eight feet tall, and though they scrupulously avoided bumping human tourists, carefully tended claws slid out above black fingertips if a human passed too close. Reflex. Maybe.

Sometimes Louis wondered what impulse brought them back to a world once theirs. Some might have ancestors here, alive in frozen time in the domes buried beneath this lava island. One day they'd have to be dug up . . .

There were so many things he hadn't done on Canyon, because the wire was always calling. Men and kzinti had climbed those sheer cliffs for sport, in the low gravity.

Well, he would have one last chance to try that. It was one of his three routes out. The second was the elevators; the third, a transfer booth to the Lichen Gardens. He'd never seen them.

Then overland in a pressure suit light enough to fold into a large briefcase.

On the surface of Canyon there were mines, and there was a large, indifferently tended preserve for the surviving varieties of Canyon lichen. But most of the world was barren moonscape. A careful man could land a spacecraft undetected, and could hide it where only a deep-radar search would find it. A careful man had. For these past nineteen years Louis Wu's ship had been waiting, hidden in a cave in the northward-facing cliff of a mountain of low-grade metal ore: a hole hidden within permanent shadow on Canyon's airless surface.

Transfer booths or elevators or cliff-climbing. Let Louis Wu get to the surface and he was home free. But the ARM could be watching all three exits.

Or he could be playing paranoid games with himself. How could Earth's police force have found him? He had changed his face, his hair style, his way of life. The things he loved best were just the things he had given up. He used a bed instead of sleeping plates, he avoided cheese as if it were spoiled milk, and his apartment was furnished with mass-produced retractables. The only clothes he owned were of expensive natural fiber, with no optical effects at all.

He had left Earth as an emaciated and dreamy-eyed wirehead. Since then he had forced a rational diet on himself; he had tortured himself with exercise and a weekly course in martial arts (mildly illegal, and the local police would register him if they caught him, but not as Louis Wu!) until today he was an adequate facsimile of glowing health, with the hard muscles a younger Louis Wu had never bothered to attain. How could the ARM recognize him?

And *how had they got in*? No common burglar could have passed Louis's alarms.

They lay dead in the grass, and soon the smell would overpower the air conditioning. Now, a bit late, he felt the shame of the man-killer. But they had invaded his territory, and there is no guilt under the wire. Even pain is a spice added to joy, and joy—like the basic human joy of killing a thief in the act—becomes hugely intensified. They had known what he was, and that was both sufficient warning and a direct affront to Louis Wu.

The kzinti and human tourists and natives milling in the street below looked innocent enough, and probably were. If an ARM was watching him now, it would be through binoculars, from a window in one of those black-eyed buildings. None of the tourists were looking up . . . but Louis Wu's eyes found a kzin, and locked.

Eight feet tall, three feet broad, thick orange fur turning gray in spots: he was very like the dozens of kzinti about him. What caught Louis's eye was the way the fur grew. It was tufted, patchy, and whitened over more than half the alien's body, as if the skin below were extensively scarred. There were black markings around his eyes, and the eyes weren't looking at scenery. They were searching the faces of passing humans.

Louis wrenched himself free of the urge to gape and stare. He turned and went inside, in no obvious haste. He locked his balcony doors and reset the alarms, and then he dug his droud out of its hiding place in the table. His hands trembled.

It was Speaker-To-Animals he had seen, for the first time in twenty years. Speaker-To-Animals, once an ambassador to human space; Speaker, who with Louis Wu and a Pierson's puppeteer and a very odd human girl had explored a minuscule section of the enormous structure called the Ringworld; who had earned his full name from the Patriarch of Kzin for the treasure he brought back. You could die, now, for calling him by a profession, but what *was* his new name? Something that started with a cough, like a German *ch*, or like the warning cough a lion might give: *Chmeee*, that was it. But what could he be doing here? With a true name and land and a harem already mostly pregnant, Chmeee had had no intention of leaving Kzin ever again. The idea of his playing tourist on an annexed human world was ridiculous.

Could he possibly know that Louis Wu was in the canyon?

He had to get out, now. Up the canyon wall to his ship.

And that was why Louis Wu was playing with the timer in his droud, squinting as he used tiny instruments on tiny settings. His hands trembled irritatingly . . . The timing would have to be changed anyway, now that he was leaving Canyon's twenty-seven-hour day.

He knew his target. There was another world in human space whose surface was largely barren moonscape. He could land a ship undetected in the vacuum at the West End of Jinx . . . and set the timing on the droud *now* . . . and take a few hours under the wire *now* to nerve himself. It all made perfect sense. He gave himself two hours.

Almost two hours passed before the next invader came. Rapt in the joy of the wire, Louis would not have been disturbed in any case. He found the invader something of a relief.

The creature stood solidly braced on a single hind leg and two wide-spaced forelegs. Between the shoulders rose a thick hump: the braincase, covered by a rich golden mane curled into ringlets and glittering with jewels. Two long, sinuous necks rose from either side of the braincase, ending in flat heads. Those loose-lipped mouths had served the puppeteers as hands for all of their history. One mouth clutched a stunner of human make, a long, forked tongue curled around the trigger.

Louis Wu had not seen a Pierson's puppeteer in twenty-two years. He thought it quite lovely.

And it had appeared from nowhere. This time Louis had seen it blink into existence in the middle of his yellow grass rug. He had worried needlessly; the ARM had not been involved at all. The problem of the Canyonite burglars was solved.

"Stepping discs!" Louis cried joyfully. He launched himself at the alien. This would be easy, puppeteers were cowards—

The stunner glowed orange. Louis Wu spilled onto the carpet, every muscle limp. His heart labored. Black spots formed before his eyes.

The puppeteer stepped delicately around the two dead men. It looked down at him from two directions; and then it reached for him. Two sets of flat-topped teeth clamped on his wrists, not hard enough to hurt. The puppeteer dragged him backward across the rug and set him down.

The apartment vanished.

It could not be said that Louis Wu was worried. He felt no such unpleasant sensation. Dispassionately (for the uniform joy in the wire allows an abstraction of thought normally impossible to mortals) he was readjusting his world picture.

He had seen the system of stepping discs on the Pierson's puppeteers' home world. It was an open teleportation system, far superior to the closed transfer booths used on the human worlds.

Apparently a puppeteer had had stepping discs installed in Louis's apartment; had sent two Canyonites to fetch him; when that failed, had come himself. The puppeteers must want him badly.

That was doubly reassuring. The ARM was not involved at all. And puppeteers had a million years of tradition to back their philosophy of enlightened cowardice. They could hardly want his life; they could have had it more cheaply, with less risk. He should find it easy to cow them.

He was still lying on a patch of yellow grass and binding mat. It must have been sitting on the stepping disc. There was a huge orange fur pillow across the room from him . . . no, it was a kzin slumped with his eyes open, asleep or paralyzed or dead—and in fact it was Speaker. Louis was glad to see him.

They were in a spacecraft, a General Products hull. Beyond the transparent walls space-bright sunlight glared off sharp-edged lunar rocks. A patch of green-and-violet lichen told him he was still on Canyon.

But he wasn't worried.

The puppeteer released his wrists. Ornaments glittered in its mane: not natural jewels, but something like black opals. One flat brainless head bent and pulled the droud out of the plug in Louis's skull. The puppeteer stepped onto a rectangular plate and vanished, with the droud.

CHAPTER 2

Press Gang

The kzin's eyes had been watching him for some time. Now the paralyzed kzin cleared his throat experimentally and rumbled, "Loo-ee Woo."

"Uh," said Louis. He had been thinking of killing himself, but there was no way. He could barely wiggle his fingers.

"Louis, urr you wirehead?"

"Ungle," said Louis, to buy time. It worked. The kzin gave up the effort. And Louis—whose only real concern was for his missing droud—Louis followed an old reflex. He looked around him to learn just how bad his situation was.

The hexagon of indoor grass under him marked the stepping-disc receiver. A black circle beyond would be the transmitter. Otherwise the floor was transparent, as were the portside hull and the aft wall.

The hyperdrive shunt ran nearly the length of the ship, beneath the floor. Louis had to recognize the machinery from first principles. It was not of human manufacture; it had the half-melted look of most puppeteer construction. So: the ship had faster-than-light capability. It seemed he was slated for a long trip.

Through the aft wall Louis could see into a cargo hold with a curved hatch in the side. The hold was nearly filled by a skewed cone thirty feet tall and twice that long. The peak was a turret with ports for weapons and/or sensing instruments. Below the turret, a wraparound window. Lower still, a hatch that would drop to form a ramp.

It was a lander, an exploration vehicle. Human-built,

Louis thought, and custom-built. It had none of that half-melted look. Beyond the lander he glimpsed a silver wall, probably a fuel tank.

He had not yet seen a door into his own compartment.

With some effort Louis flopped his head to the other side. Now he was looking forward into the ship's flight deck. A big section of the ship was opaque green wall, but he could see past it to a curved array of screens, dials with tiny close-set numbers, knobs shaped to a puppeteer's jaws. The pilot's control couch was a padded bench with crash webbing and indentations for the hip and shoulders of a Pierson's puppeteer. There was no door in that wall.

To starboard—well, their cell was at least fairly large. He saw a shower, a pair of sleeping plates, and an expanse of rich fur covering what might be a kzin's water bed, and between them a bulky structure Louis recognized as a food recycler and dispenser, of Wunderland make. Beyond the beds was more green wall and no airlock, and that took care of that. They were in a box with no openings.

The ship was puppeteer-built: a General Products #3 hull, a cylinder flattened along the belly and rounded at the ends. The puppeteer trading empire had sold millions of such ships. They were advertised as invulnerable to any threat save gravity and visible light. About the time Louis Wu was being born, the puppeteer species had fled known space on a dash for the Clouds of Magellan. Now, two hundred odd years later, you still saw General Products hulls everywhere. Some had had a dozen generations of owners.

Twenty-three years ago, the puppeteer-built spacecraft *Liar* had crashed into the Ringworld surface at seven hundred and seventy miles per second. A stasis field had protected Louis and the other passengers—and the hull wasn't even scratched.

"You're a kzin warrior," Louis said. His lips were thick and numb. "Can you batter your way through a General Products hull?"

"No," said Speaker. (*Not* Speaker. *Chmeee!*)

"It was worth asking. Chmeee, what are you doing on Canyon?"

"I was sent a message. Louis Wu is in the gash on Warhead, living under the wire. There were holograms for proof. Do you know what you look like under the wire? A marine plant, with fronds stirring at the whim of the current."

Louis found there were tears dripping down his nose. "Tanj. Tanj for torment. Why did you come?"

"I wanted to tell you what a worthless thing you are."

"Who sent that message?"

"I didn't know. It must have been the puppeteer. It wanted us both. Louis, is your brain so ruined that you did not notice that the puppeteer—"

"Isn't Nessus. Right. But did you see the way it keeps its mane? That ornate hair style must cost it an hour a day, easy. If I'd seen it on the puppeteer world, I'd think its rank was high."

"Well?"

"No sane puppeteer would risk its life to interstellar travel. The puppeteers took their entire world with them, not to mention four farming worlds; they're going hundreds of thousands of years at sublight speeds, just because they don't trust spaceships. Whoever this one is, it's crazy, just like any puppeteer ever seen by humans. I don't know what to expect from it," said Louis Wu. "But it's back."

The puppeteer was on the flight deck, on a hexagonal stepping disc, watching them through the wall. It spoke in a woman's voice, a lovely contralto. "Can you hear me?"

Chmeee lurched away from the wall, held his feet for an instant, then dropped to all fours and charged. He thudded hard against the wall. Any puppeteer should have flinched, but this one didn't. It said, "Our expedition is almost assembled. We lack only one member of our crew."

Louis found he could roll over, and he did. He said,

"Back up and start from the beginning. You've got us in a box, you don't have to hide anything. Who are you?"

"You may choose any name for me that pleases you."

"*What* are you? What do you need from us?"

The puppeteer hesitated. Then, "I was Hindmost to my world. I was mate to the one you knew as Nessus. Now I am neither. I need you as crew for a return expedition to the Ringworld, to restore my status."

Chmeee said, "We will not serve you."

Louis asked, "Is Nessus all right?"

"I thank you for your concern. Nessus is healthy in mind and body. The shock he suffered on the Ringworld was just what was needed to restore his sanity. He is at home taking care of our two children."

What Nessus had suffered, Louis thought, would have shocked anybody. Ringworld natives had cut off one of his heads. If Louis and Teela had not thought of using a tourniquet on the alien's throat, Nessus would have bled to death. "I take it you transplanted a new head onto him."

"Of course."

Chmeee said, "You would not be here if you were not insane. Why would your trillion puppeteers elect a damaged mind to rule them?"

"I do not consider myself insane." The puppeteer's hind leg flexed restlessly. (Its faces, if they showed any expression at all, showed only loose-lipped idiocy.) "Please do not refer to this again. I served my species well, and four Hindmosts served well before me, before the Conservative faction found power to replace my faction. They are wrong. I will prove it. We will go to the Ringworld and find treasure beyond their puny understanding."

"To kidnap a kzin," Chmeee rumbled, "is probably a mistake." His long claws were extended.

The puppeteer looked at them through the wall. "You would not have come. Louis would not have come. You had your status and your name. Louis had his droud. Our fourth member was a prisoner. My agents inform me that she has been freed and is on her way to us."

Louis laughed bitterly. All humor was bitter without the droud. "You really don't have much imagination, do you? It's just like the first expedition. Me, Chmeee, a puppeteer, and a woman. Who's the woman? Another Teela Brown?"

"No! Nessus was terrified of Teela Brown—with reason, I believe. I've stolen Halrloprillalar from the mouths of the ARM. We will have a Ringworld native guide. As for the character of our expedition, why would I discard a winning strategy? You *did* escape the Ringworld."

"All but Teela."

"Teela stayed of her own choice."

The kzin said, "We were paid for our efforts. We brought home a spacecraft capable of crossing a light-year in one point two five minutes. That ship bought me my name and my status. What can you offer us now, to compare with that?"

"Many things. Can you move now, Chmeee?"

The kzin stood up. He seemed to have shaken off most of the effects of the stunner. Louis was still dizzy and numb in the extremities.

"Are you in health? Is there dizziness or ache or nausea?"

"Why so anxious, root-eater? You left me in an autodoc for over an hour. I lack coordination and I am hungry, nothing worse."

"Good. We were able to test the substance only so far. Very well, Chmeee, you have your payment. Boosterspice is the medicine that has kept Louis Wu young and strong for two hundred and twenty-three years. My people have developed an analogue for kzinti. You may take the formula home to the Kzinti Patriarchy when our mission is complete."

Chmeee seemed nonplussed. "I will grow young? This muck is in me already?"

"Yes."

"We could have developed such a thing ourselves. We did not want it."

"I need you young and strong. Chmeee, there is no great danger in our mission! I don't plan to land on the Ringworld itself, only on the spaceport ledge! You may share any knowledge we find, and so will you, Louis. As for your immediate reward—"

What appeared on the stepping disc was Louis Wu's droud. The casing had been opened and resealed. Louis's heart leaped.

"Don't use it yet," Chmeee said, and it was an order.

"All right. Hindmost, how long were you watching me?"

"Fifteen years ago I found you in the canyon. My agents were already at work on Earth, trying to free Halrloprillalar. They were having little success. I installed stepping discs in your apartment and waited for the proper time. I go now to enlist our native guide." The puppeteer mouthed something in the array of controls, walked forward, and was gone.

"Do not use the droud," Chmeee said.

"Whatever you say." Louis turned his back. He would know he'd gone crazy when his need for the wire impelled him to attack a kzin. At least one good thing might come out of this . . . and he clung hard to that thought.

He'd been able to do nothing for Halrloprillalar.

Halrloprillalar had been thousands of years old when she joined Louis and Nessus and Speaker-To-Animals in their search for a way off the Ringworld. The natives who lived beneath her floating police station had been treating her as a sky-living goddess. The whole team had played that game—living as gods to the natives, with Halrloprillalar's help—while they wended their way back to the wrecked *Liar*. And she and Louis had been in love.

The Ringworld natives, the three forms that the team had met, had all been related to humanity, but not quite human. Halrloprillalar was nearly bald, and had lips no more everted than a monkey's. Sometimes the very old

seek nothing but variety in their love affairs. Louis had
wondered if that was happening to him. He could see
character flaws in Prill . . . but, tanj! He had his own
collection.

And he owed Halrloprillalar. They had needed her
help, and Nessus had used a puppeteer's peculiar brand
of force on her. Nessus had conditioned her with a tasp.
Louis had let him do it.

She had returned with Louis to human space. She
had gone with him into the UN offices in Berlin, and
had never come out. If the Hindmost could break her
loose and return her to her home, it was more than
Louis Wu could do for her.

Chmeee said, "I think the puppeteer must be lying.
Delusions of grandeur. Why would puppeteers allow
one of unsound mind to rule them?"

"They won't try it themselves. Risk. Uneasy sits the
butt that bears the boss. For puppeteers it makes a kind
of sense, picking the brightest of a tiny percentage of
megalomaniacs . . . Or look at it from the other side: a
line of Hindmost teaching the rest of the population to
keep their heads down—don't try for too much power,
it isn't safe. It could work either way."

"You think he told the truth?"

"I don't know enough. What if he is lying? He's got
us."

"He's got you," said the kzin. "He's got you by the
wire. Why aren't you ashamed?"

Louis was ashamed. He was fighting to keep the
shame from crippling his mind, locking him in black
despair. He had no way out of this physical box: walls
and floor and ceiling were part of a General Products
hull. But there were elements . . .

"If you're still thinking about breaking out," he said,
"you'd better think about this. You'll be getting young.
He wouldn't have lied about that; there wouldn't be any
point. What happens when you get young?"

"Bigger appetite. More stamina. A tendency to fight,
and you'd better worry about that, Louis."

Chmeee had gained bulk as he aged. The black

"spectacle" marks around his eyes were nearly all gray, and there was some gray elsewhere. Hard muscle showed when he moved; no sensible younger kzin would fight him. But what mattered were the scars. The fur and a good deal of skin had been burned off over more than half of Chmeee's body the last time Chmeee had seen the Ringworld. Twenty-three years later the fur had grown back, but it grew in ragged tufts above the scar tissue.

"Boosterspice heals scars," Louis said. "Your fur will grow out smooth. No white in it either."

"Well, then, I will be prettier." The tail slashed air. "I must kill the leaf-eater. Scars are like memories. We do not have them removed."

"How are you going to prove you're Chmeee?"

The tail froze. Chmeee looked at him.

"He's got me by the wire." Louis had reservations regarding that remark, but he could be speaking for a microphone. A puppeteer would not ignore the possibility of mutiny. "He's got you by the harem, and the land, and the privileges, and the name that belongs to Chmeee the aging hero. The Patriarch may not believe your story, not unless you've got kzinti boosterspice and the Hindmost's word to back you up."

"Be silent."

It was all suddenly too much for Louis Wu. He reached for the droud, and the kzin pounced. Chmeee turned the black plastic case in a black-and-orange hand.

"As you like," Louis said. He flopped on his back. He was short of sleep anyway . . .

"How did you come to be a wirehead? How?"

"I," said Louis, and "What you've got to understand," and "Remember the last time we met?"

"Yes. Few humans have been invited to Kzin itself. You deserved the honor, then."

"Maybe. Maybe I did. Do you remember showing me the House of the Patriarch's Past?"

"I do. You tried to tell me that we could improve interspecies relationships. All we need do was let a team of human reporters go through the museum with holo cameras."

Louis smiled, remembering. "So I did."

"I had my doubts."

The House of the Patriarch's Past had been both grand and grandiose: a huge, sprawling building formed from thick slabs of volcanic rock fused at the edges. It was all angles, and there were laser cannon mounted in four tall towers. The rooms went on and on. It had taken Chmeee and Louis two days to go through it.

The Patriarch's official past went a long way back. Louis had seen ancient sthondat thighbones with grips worked into them, clubs used by primitive kzinti. He'd seen weapons that could have been classed as hand cannons; few humans could have lifted them. He'd seen silver-plated armor as thick as a safe door, and a two-handed ax that might have chopped down a mature redwood. He'd been talking about letting a human reporter tour the place when they came upon Harvey Mossbauer.

Harvey Mossbauer's family had been killed and eaten during the Fourth Man-Kzin War. Many years after the truce and after a good deal of monomaniacal preparation, Mossbauer had landed alone and armed on Kzin. He had killed four kzinti males and set off a bomb in the harem of the Patriarch before the guards managed to kill him. They were hampered, Chmeee had explained, by their wish to get his hide intact.

"You call that intact?"

"But he fought. How he fought! There are tapes. We know how to honor a brave and powerful enemy, Louis."

The stuffed skin was so scarred that you had to look twice to tell its species; but it was on a tall pedestal with a hullmetal plaque, and there was nothing around it but floor. Your average human reporter might have misunderstood, but Louis got the point. "I wonder if I can make you understand," he said, twenty years later, a wirehead kidnapped and robbed of his droud, "how good it felt, then, to know that Harvey Mossbauer was human."

"It is good to reminisce, but we were talking of current addiction," Chmeee reminded him.

"Happy people don't become current addicts. You have to actually go and get the plug implanted. I felt good that day. I felt like a hero. Do you know where Halrloprillalar was at that time?"

"Where was she?"

"The government had her. The ARM. They had lots of questions, and there wasn't a tanj thing I could do about it. She was under my protection. I took her back to Earth with me—"

"She had you by the glands, Louis. It's good that kzinti females aren't sentient. You would have done anything she asked. She asked to see human space."

"Sure, with me as native guide. It just didn't happen. Chmeee, we took the Long Shot and Halrloprillalar home, and we turned them over to a Kzin and Earth coalition, and that's the last we've seen of either one. We couldn't even talk about it to anyone."

"The second quantum hyperdrive motor became a Patriarch's Secret."

"It's Top Secret to the United Nations, too. I don't think they even told the other governments of human space, and they made it tanj clear I'd better not talk. And of course the Ringworld was part of the secret, because how could we have got there without the Long Shot? Which makes me wonder," Louis said, "how the Hindmost expects to reach the Ringworld. Two hundred light-years from Earth—more, from Canyon—at three days to the light-year if he uses this ship. Do you think he's got another Long Shot hovering somewhere?"

"You will not distract me. Why did you have a wire implanted?" Chmeee crouched, claws extended. Maybe it was a reflex, beyond conscious control—maybe.

"I left Kzin and went home," Louis said. "I couldn't get the ARM to let me see Prill. If I could have got a Ringworld expedition together, she would have had to go as native guide, but, tanj! I couldn't even talk about it except to the government . . . and you. You weren't interested."

"How could I leave? I had land and a name and children coming. Kzinti females are very dependent. They need care and attention."

"What's happening to them now?"

"My eldest son will administer my holdings. If I leave him too long he will fight me to keep them. If— *Louis! Why did you become a wirehead?*"

"Some clown hit me with a tasp!"

"Urrr?"

"I was wandering through a museum in Rio when somebody made my day from behind a pillar."

"But Nessus took a tasp to the Ringworld, to control his crew. He used it on both of us."

"Right. How very like a Pierson's puppeteer, to do us good by way of controlling us! The Hindmost is using the same approach now. Look, he's got my droud under remote control, and he's given you eternal youth, and what's the result? We'll do anything he tells us to, that's what."

"Nessus used the tasp on me, but I am not a wirehead."

"I didn't turn wirehead either, then. But I remembered. I was feeling like a louse, thinking about Prill— thinking about taking a sabbatical. I used to do that, take off alone in a ship and head for the edge of known space until I could stand people again. Until I could stand myself again. But it would have been running out on Prill. Then some clown made my day. He didn't give me much of a jolt, but it reminded me of that tasp Nessus carried, and that was *ten times* as powerful. I . . . held off for almost a year, and then I went and got a plug put in my head."

"I should rip that wire out of your brain."

"There turn out to be undesirable side effects."

"How did you come to the gash on Warhead?"

"Oh, that. Maybe I was paranoid, but look: Halrloprillalar vanished into the ARM building and never came out. Here Louis Wu was turning wirehead, and no telling whom the silly flatlander might tell secrets to. I thought I'd better run. Canyon's easy to land a ship on without being noticed."

"I expect the Hindmost found it so."

"Chmeee, give me the droud or let me sleep or kill me. I'm fresh out of motivation."

"Sleep, then."

CHAPTER 3

Ghost among the Crew

It was good to wake floating between sleeping plates
. . . until Louis remembered.

Chmeee was tearing at a joint of raw red meat.
Wunderland often made these food recyclers to serve
more than one species. The kzin stopped eating long
enough to say, "Every piece of equipment aboard was
built by humans, or could have been built by humans.
Even the hull could have been bought on any human
world."

Like a baby in its womb, Louis floated in free fall,
his eyes closed and his knees drawn up. But there was
no way to forget where he was. He said, "I thought the
big lander had a Jinxian look. Made to order, but on
Jinx. What about your bed? Kzinti?"

"Artificial fiber. Made to resemble the pelt of a kzin,
and sold in secret, no doubt, to humans with an odd
sense of humor. I would find pleasure in hunting down
the manufacturer."

Louis reached out and tripped the field control
switch. The sleeping field collapsed, lowering him gently
to the floor.

It was night outside: sharp white stars overhead and
a landscape that was formless velvet black. Even if they
could get to spacesuits, the canyon could be halfway
around the planet. Or just beyond that black ridge pro-
jecting into the starscape; but how would he know?

The recycler kitchen had two keyboards, one with
directions in Interworld and one in the Hero's Tongue.
And two toilets on opposite sides. Louis would have

preferred a less explicit arrangement. He dialed for a breakfast that would test the kitchen's repertoire.

The kzin snarled, "Does the situation interest you at all, Louis?"

"Look beneath your feet."

The kzin knelt. "Urrr . . . yes. Puppeteers built the hyperdrive shunt. This is the ship in which the Hindmost fled from the Fleet of Worlds."

"You forgot the stepping discs, too. The puppeteers don't use them anywhere but on their own world. Now we find the Hindmost sending human agents to get me, on stepping discs."

"The Hindmost must have stolen them and the ship and little else. His funds may have been owed to General Products and never claimed. Louis, I do not believe the Hindmost has puppeteer support. We should try to reach the puppeteer fleet."

"Chmeee, there are bound to be microphones in here."

"Should I watch my speech for this *leaf-eater*?"

"All right, let's look at it." The depression he was feeling came out as bitter sarcasm, and why not? Chmeee had his droud. "A puppeteer has indulged a whim for kidnapping men and kzinti. Naturally the honest puppeteers will be horrified. Are they really going to let us run home and tell the Patriarch? Who has no doubt been doing his best to build more *Long Shots*, which could reach the puppeteer fleet in just over four hours plus acceleration time to match velocities— say, three months at three gravities—"

"*Enough*, Louis!"

"Tanj, if you wanted to start a war you had your chance! According to Nessus, the puppeteers meddled in the First Man-Kzin War, in our favor. Now *hold* it. Do *not* tell me whether you told anyone else."

"Drop the subject now."

"Sure. Only, it just hit me—" and because the conversation might be recorded, Louis spoke partly for the Hindmost's benefit. "You and I and the Hindmost are the only ones in known space who know what the puppeteers have been doing, besides anyone either of us might have told."

"If we should be lost on the Ringworld, would the Hindmost mourn forever? I see your point. But the Hindmost might not even know that Nessus was indiscreet."

He'll know if he plays this back, Louis thought. My fault. I should watch my speech for a leaf-eater? He attacked his meal with some ferocity.

He had chosen for both simplicity and complexity: half a grapefruit, a chocolate soufflé, broiled moa breast, Jamaica Blue Mountain coffee topped with whipped cream. Most of it was good; only the whipped cream was unconvincing. But what could you say about the moa? A twenty-fourth-century geneticist had re-created the moa, or so he'd claimed, and the recycler kitchen produced an imitation of *that*. It had a good texture and tasted like rich bird meat.

It was nothing like being under the wire.

He had learned to live with this part-time depression. It existed only by contrast with the wire; Louis believed that it was the normal state of being for humanity. Being imprisoned by a mad alien for peculiar purposes didn't make it *that* much worse. What made the black morning so terrible was that Louis Wu was going to have to give up the droud.

Finished, he dumped the dirty dishes into the toilet. He asked, "What will you take for the droud?"

Chmeee snorted. "What do you have for trade?"

"Promises made on my word of honor. And a good set of informal pajamas."

Chmeee's tail slashed at the air. "You were a useful companion once. What will you be if I give you the droud? A browsing beast. I will keep the droud."

Louis began his exercises.

One-hand push-ups were easy in half a gravity. One hundred on each hand were not. The dorsal curve of the hull was too low for some of his routines. Two hundred scissors jumps, touching extended fingers to extended toes—

Chmeee watched curiously. Presently he said, "I wonder why the Hindmost lost his honors."

Louis didn't answer. Suspended horizontally with toes under the bottom sleeping-field plate and a platter under his calves, he was doing very slow sit-ups.

"And what he expects to find on the spaceport ledge. What did we find? The deceleration rings are too big to move. Could he want something from a Ringworlder spacecraft?"

Louis dialed for a pair of moa drumsticks. He wiped them of grease and began juggling them: oversized Indian clubs. Sweat formed in big droplets before reluctantly moving down his face and torso.

Chmeee's tail lashed. His large pink ears folded back, offering no purchase to an enemy. Chmeee was angry. That was *his* problem.

The puppeteer flicked into existence, one impervious wall away. It had changed the style of its mane, substituting points of light for the opals . . . and it was alone. It studied the situation for a moment. It said, "Use the droud, Louis."

"I don't have that option." Louis discarded the weights. "Where's Prill?"

The puppeteer said, "Chmeee, give Louis the droud."

"Where's Halrloprillalar?"

A tremendous furry arm enclosed Louis's throat. Louis kicked backward, putting his whole body into it. The kzin grunted. With curious gentleness he inserted the droud into its socket.

"All right," Louis said. The kzin let him go and he sat down. He'd guessed already, and so had the kzin, of course. Louis began to realize how much he had wanted to see Prill . . . to see her free of the ARM . . . to *see* her.

"Halrloprillalar is dead. My agents cheated me," the puppeteer said. "They have known that the Ringworld native was dead for eighteen standard years. I could stay to root them out wherever they have hidden, but it might take another eighteen years. Or eighteen hundred! Human space is too big. Let them keep their stolen money."

Louis nodded, smiling, knowing that this was going to hurt when he removed the droud. He heard Chmeee ask, "How did she die?"

"She could not tolerate boosterspice. The United Nations now believes that she was not quite human. She aged very rapidly. A year and five months after reaching Earth, she was dead."

"Already dead," Louis mused. "When I was on Kzin . . ." But there was a puzzle here. "She had her own longevity drug. Better than boosterspice. We brought a cryoflask home with us."

"It was stolen. I know nothing more."

Stolen? But Prill had never walked the streets of Earth, to meet common thieves. United Nations scientists might have opened the flask to analyze the stuff, but they wouldn't need more than a microgram . . . He might never know. And afterward they had kept her, to take her knowledge before she died.

This was definitely going to hurt. But not yet.

"We need not delay longer." The puppeteer settled itself in its padded bench. "You will travel in stasis, to conserve resources. I have an auxiliary fuel tank to be dropped before we enter hyperspace. We will arrive fully fueled. Chmeee, would you name our ship?"

Chmeee demanded, "Do you propose to explore blindly, then?"

"Only the spaceport ledge, and no further. Would you name our ship?"

"I name it *Hot Needle of Inquiry*."

Louis smiled and wondered if the puppeteer recognized the term. Their ship was now named for a kzinti instrument of torture. The puppeteer mouthed two knobs and brought them together.

CHAPTER 4

Off Center

Louis sagged as his weight suddenly doubled. The black Canyonscape was gone. It must be invisible in the starscape now, a changed starscape in which one star, directly underfoot, shone brighter than all the rest. The Hindmost disengaged itself from crash web and pilot's bench. The puppeteer had changed too. It moved as if tired, and its mane—differently styled now—seemed not to have been set for some time.

Current didn't deaden the brain. Louis could see the obvious: that he and Chmeee must have spent two years in stasis, while the puppeteer flew *Needle* alone through hyperspace; that known space, a bubble of explored star systems some forty light-years in radius, must be far behind them; that *Hot Needle of Inquiry* was built to be flown by a Pierson's puppeteer, with all other passengers in stasis, and only a puppeteer's mercy would ever return them. That he had seen a human being for the last time, and Halrloprillalar was dead of Louis Wu's carelessness, and he was going to feel terribly lonely when the droud came out of his head, which would be soon. None of that mattered while the tiny current still trickled into his brain.

He saw no drive flame. *Hot Needle of Inquiry* must be moving on reactionless thrusters alone.

Liar's designers had mounted the ship's motors on its great delta wing. Something like a tremendous laser blast had fired on them as they passed above the Ringworld, and the motors had been burned off. The Hindmost would not have repeated *that* mistake, Louis

30

thought. *Needle*'s thrusters would be mounted inside the impervious hull.

Chmeee asked, "How long until we can land?"

"We can be ready to dock in five days. I was unable to take advanced drive systems from the Fleet of Worlds. With human-built machinery we can decelerate only at twenty gravities. Do you find the cabin gravity comfortable?"

"A bit light. One Earth gravity?"

"One Ringworld gravity, point nine nine two Earth gravity."

"Leave it as it is. Hindmost, you gave us no instruments. I would like to study the Ringworld."

The puppeteer pondered the point. "Your lander vehicle includes a telescope, but it would not point straight down. Wait several moments." The puppeteer turned to its instrument board. One head turned back and spoke in the hissing-spitting-snarling accents of the Hero's Tongue.

Chmeee said, "Use Interworld. Let Louis listen, at least."

The puppeteer did. "It is good to speak again in any language. I was lonely. There, I give you a projection from *Needle*'s telescope."

An image appeared below Louis Wu's feet: a rectangle, with no borderlines, in which the Ringworld sun and the stars around it were suddenly far larger. Louis blocked the sun with his hand and searched. The Ringworld was there: a thread of baby blue forming a half-circle.

Picture fifty feet of baby-blue Christmas ribbon one inch wide. String it in a circle, on edge on the floor, and put a candle in the middle. Now expand the scale:

The Ringworld was a ribbon of unreasonably strong material, a million miles wide and six hundred million miles long, strung in a circle ninety-five million miles in radius with a sun at the center. The ring spun at seven hundred and seventy miles per second, fast enough to produce one gravity of centrifugal force outward. The unknown Ringworld engineers had layered the inner surface with soil and oceans and an atmosphere. They had raised walls a thousand miles high at each rim to hold the air inside. Presumably air leaked over the rim walls anyway, but not quickly. An inner ring of twenty rectangular shadow squares, occupying what would have been the orbit of Mercury in Sol system, gave a thirty-hour day and night cycle to the Ringworld.

The Ringworld was six hundred million million square miles of habitable planet. Three million times the area of the Earth.

Louis and Speaker-To-Animals and Nessus and Teela Brown had traveled across the Ringworld for almost a year: two hundred thousand miles across the width, then back to the point where *Liar* had crashed. A fifth of the width. It hardly made them experts. Could any thinking being ever have claimed to be an expert on the Ringworld?

But they had examined one of the spaceport ledges on the outside of the rim wall. If the Hindmost spoke the truth, they would need no more. Land on the spaceport ledge, pick up whatever the Hindmost expected to find, and go. Fast! Because—

Because within the rectangular telescope image that the Hindmost had set before them, it was painfully obvious. The baby-blue arc of Ringworld—the color of three million Earthlike worlds, too far away for detail to show, but banded with midnight blue from the shadow squares—was well off center from its sun.

"We didn't know this," Chmeee said. "We spent a Kzin year on the structure and did not know this. How could we not?"

The puppeteer said, "The Ringworld could not have been off center when you were here. It was twenty-three years ago."

Louis nodded. To speak would be distracting. Only the joy of the wire now held away horror for the fate of the Ringworld natives, fear and guilt for himself. The

Hindmost continued, "The Ringworld structure is unstable in the plane of its orbit. Surely you knew?"

"No!"

Louis said, "I didn't know myself till after I was back on Earth. I did some research then."

Both aliens were looking at him. He hadn't really wanted that much of their attention. Oh, well. "It's easy enough to show that the Ringworld is unstable. Stable along the axis, but unstable in the plane. There must have been something to keep the sun on the axis."

"But it's off center *now*!"

"Whatever it was stopped working."

Chmeee clawed at the invisible floor. "But then they must die! Billions of them, tens of billions—trillions?" He turned to Louis. "I tire of your fatuous smile. Would you talk better without the droud?"

"I can talk fine."

"Talk, then. Why is the Ringworld unstable? Is it not in orbit?"

"No, of course not. It has to be rigid. That terrific spin would pull it rigid. If you nudge the Ringworld off center it'll fall further off center. But the equations are pretty hairy. I played around with a computer and I got numbers I'm not sure I believe."

The Hindmost said, "At one time we thought we might build our own Ringworld. The instability is too great. Even a strong solar flare would exert enough pressure on the structure to throw it off balance. Five years later it would grind against its sun."

"That's the same figure I got," Louis said. "That must be what happened here."

Chmeee was clawing the floor again. "Attitude jets! The Ringworld engineers would have mounted attitude jets!"

"Maybe. We know they had Bussard ramjets. They used them to drive their starships. Okay, a lot of big Bussard ramjets on the rim walls would be enough to keep the Ringworld centered. The motors would fuse the hydrogen in the solar wind. They'd never run out of fuel."

"We saw nothing. Think how huge the motors would have to be!"

Louis chuckled. "What do you call huge? On the Ringworld? We missed them, that's all." But he couldn't like the way Chmeee stood above him with claws extended.

"You accept it all so easily? There may be enough Ringworld natives to crowd the worlds of known space thousands of times over. They are more nearly your kind than mine."

"You're a ruthless, merciless carnivore. Try to remember," Louis told the kzin. "Look: it'll bother me. It'll bother me a *lot* after the Hindmost turns off my droud. But it won't kill me, because I'll be a little bit used to it by then. Can you think of anything we can do to help them? *Anything*?"

The kzin turned away. "Hindmost, how much time do they have left?"

"I will attempt to find out."

The sun was well off center to the Ringworld. Louis guessed it might be, oh, seventy million miles from the near side, which would put it a hundred and twenty million miles from the far side. The near side would be getting nearly three times as much sunlight as the far side, and the structure rotated in seven and a half thirty-hour days. There would be weather. Plants that couldn't take the changes would be dying. And animals. And men.

The Hindmost had finished its work at the telescope. Now it worked at the computer, out of sight behind the solid green wall. Louis wondered what else was concealed in that hidden part of the ship.

The puppeteer trotted into view. "One year and five months from now, the Ringworld will graze its sun. I expect it will disintegrate then. Given their rotational velocity, the fragments would all recede into interstellar space."

"Shadow squares," Louis murmured.

"What? Yes, the shadow squares would impact before the sun. Still, we should have at least a year. Plenty of time for us," the Hindmost said briskly. "We will not touch the Ringworld surface at all. Your expedition examined the spaceport ledge, from some tens of thousands of miles away, without being fired on by the Ringworld meteor defenses. I believe the spaceport has been abandoned. We can land in safety."

Chmeee asked, "What do you expect to find?"

"I'm surprised you haven't remembered." The Hindmost turned to its control board. "Louis, you've had enough time."

"Wait—"

The wire in his brain went dead.

CHAPTER 5

Withdrawal Symptoms

Louis watched through the wall as the puppeteer worked on his droud. He thought of death in mind-stunning numbers, and death as his own very personal experience, and death for aliens who monitored the current to his brain.

Flat heads poised and shifted and nosed the small black casing as if nibbling at a dubious meal. Long tongues and sensitive lips worked inside the casing. In a few minutes the puppeteer had reset the timer to a thirty-hour day, and cut the current by half.

The next day it was pure joy unfiltered by human sense, and nothing could actually bother him, but . . . Louis had trouble defining his own feelings. When the current cut off too soon that evening, depression dropped over him like thick saffron smog.

Then Chmeee stooped above Louis Wu, pulled the droud from his scalp, and set it on the stepping disc to be flicked to the flight deck. For resetting. Again.

Louis screamed and leaped. He scrambled up the kzin's broad back via fur handholds and tried to tear his ears off. The kzin whirled. Louis found himself clinging to a great arm, found the arm slinging him across the room. He fetched up against a wall. Half stunned, with blood streaming down his torn arm, Louis turned to the attack.

He turned in time to see Chmeee leap onto the stepping disc just as the Hindmost mouthed the controls.

Chmeee crouched on the black disc, looking dangerous and foolish.

The Hindmost said, "Nothing so massive may be

flicked to these discs. Do you judge me an idiot, to flick
a kzin onto my own flight deck?"

Chmeee snarled, "How much intelligence does it
take to sneak up on a leaf?" He flipped the droud to
Louis and shambled toward his water bed.

A diversion. Chmeee had snatched the droud from
Louis's scalp just after it switched off, solely to drive
Louis Wu into berserker rage, to distract the puppeteer's
attention.

The Hindmost said, "When next I alter your droud I
will do it just before you plug in. Does that make you
happy?"

"You know tanj well what makes me happy!" Louis
held the droud tightly. It was dead, of course—dead
until the timer made it live again.

"You are nearly as long-lived as we are. This is so
temporary," the Hindmost wheedled him. "You will be
wealthy beyond dreams! The Ringworld spacecraft
used a method of cheap, large-scale transmutation, the
same that they must have used to build the Ringworld
itself!"

Louis looked up, startled.

"I wish we knew the mass and bulk of the machine,"
the puppeteer continued. "The Ringworld spacecraft
are tremendous things. But we need not transport it. If
necessary, a hologram taken by deep-radar, and holograms of the mechanism in action, should be enough to
convince my subjects. Then we need only send a General Products #4 craft to pick it up."

The alien would not expect a man deep in current
withdrawal to respond to every little comment. Of
course not. But from under his brows Louis watched
Chmeee, to see how he would handle it.

The kzin was admirable. For a moment he froze.
Then, "How did you come to lose your prerogatives?"

"The tale is complex."

"We entered Ringworld system with eleven billion
miles to fall and a velocity of fifty-two thousand miles
per second to be shed. Only a day has passed. We have
time."

"So we do, and no other useful work. You must know, then, that Conservative and Experimentalist factions are old among us. Usually the Conservatives rule. But when our world suffered from heat pollution due to too much use of industrial power, Experimentalists moved our world outward into the cometary halo. An Experimentalist regime altered and then seeded two farming worlds. A later regime moved two more worlds inward from where they had formed as moons of distant ice giants . . ."

And Chmeee had gained time to lose his agitation and think what he would say next. Good! Maybe the kzin had earned the position he once held: Speaker-To-Animals, a junior ambassador to humanity.

". . . we do the necessary things, then are deposed. It is the general rule. Experimentalists came into power when our probes learned of the Kzinti Empire. I believe Nessus told you how we handled that."

"You aided humanity." Chmeee was peculiarly still. Louis would have expected him to be tearing up the walls. "The four Wars With Men killed four generations of our mightiest fighters so that the more docile among us might reproduce their kind."

"We hoped you would become able to deal amicably with other species. My faction also established a trading empire in this region. Despite our successes, we were losing our authority. Then it was discovered that the core of our galaxy has exploded. The shock wave will arrive in twenty thousand years. Our faction stayed in power, to arrange the exodus of the Fleet of Worlds."

"How fortunate for you. Yet they deposed you after all."

"Yes."

"Why?"

The puppeteer didn't answer for a time. Then: "Some of my decisions were not popular. I meddled with human and kzinti destiny. Somehow you learned our secret, how we had tampered with the Fertility Laws on Earth in an attempt to breed lucky humans, and with the course of the First War With Men, to produce reasonable kzinti. My predecessor established General Products, the interstellar trading empire. It was said that he had made a virtue of madness, since only the mad among us will risk their lives in space. When I arranged your expedition to explore the Ringworld, I was called mad, to risk contact with so advanced a technology. But one does not hide one's sight from danger!"

"So they deposed you."

"It may have been . . . a convenient excuse." The Hindmost paced restlessly: clopclopclop, clopclopclop. "You know that I agreed to take Nessus as mate if he returned from the Ringworld. He demanded this concession. And he returned, and we mated. Then we did it again, for love. Nessus was mad, and the Hindmost has often been mad, and . . . they deposed me."

Louis suddenly asked, "Which of you is male?"

"I wonder why you did not ask that of Nessus. But he would not have told you, would he? Nessus is shy on certain subjects. We have two kinds of male, Louis. My kind implants its sperm in the female's flesh, and Nessus's kind implants its egg in the female with a most similar organ."

Chmeee asked, "You have three sets of genes?"

"No, two only. The female contributes none. In fact, females mate among themselves in another way to make more females. They are not properly of our species, though they have been symbiotic with us for all history."

Louis winced. The puppeteers bred like digger wasps: their progeny ate the flesh of a helpless host. Nessus had refused to talk about sex. Nessus was right. This was ugly.

"I was right," said the Hindmost. "I was right to send a mission to the Ringworld, and we will prove it. Five days in, and no more than ten on the spaceport ledges, and five more to reach flat space where we may escape by hyperdrive. We need never board the Ringworld at all. Halrloprillalar told Nessus that the Ringworld ships carried lead, for compactness, and transmuted it into air and water and fuel during the journey. A Conservative government could not deal with the ramifications of such a technology. They will reinstate me."

Current-withdrawal depression left Louis no urge to laugh. Still, it was all very funny, and funnier still because it was his own fault from the beginning.

The next morning the aliens cut the droud's current flow in half again, and left it alone thereafter. It shouldn't have made that much difference. Under the wire he was still content. But for years he had suffered through the depression when the timer stopped, knowing what he would feel when the current resumed. His depressions were worse now, and there was no security. The aliens could cut the current at any time . . . and even if they didn't, he would still have to give it up.

What the aliens talked about during those four days he didn't know. He tried to concentrate on the ecstasy in the wire. Vaguely he remembered them calling up holograms from the computer. There were the faces of Ringworld natives: the small ones completely covered with golden hair (and one, a priest, was shaven); and the tremendous wire sculpture in the sky castle (stub of a nose, bald head, knife-slash lips); and Halrloprillalar (probably of the same race); and Seeker, the wanderer who had taken Teela under his protection (almost human, but muscled like a Jinxian, and beardless). There were cities ruined by time and by floating buildings that had fallen when their power died. There were holograms of *Liar*'s approach to a shadow square, and of a city nestled in a smoke cloud of fallen shadow-square wire.

The sun grew from a point to a black dot with a bright rim around it, its brightness blocked by flare shielding on *Needle*'s inner hull. The blue halo around the sun expanded.

In dreams Louis returned to the Ringworld. In a great floating prison he hung head down from his burned-out flycycle, ninety feet above a hard floor

strewn with the bones of earlier captives. Nessus's voice
beat in his ears, promising rescue that never came.

When awake he took refuge in routine . . . until on
the evening of the fourth day he looked at his dinner,
then dumped it and dialed for bread and a selection of
cheeses. Four days to realize that he was forever beyond the reach of the ARM. He could eat cheese again!

What's good besides the wire? Louis asked himself.
*Cheese. Sleeping plates. Love (impractical). Wild skin
dye jobs. Freedom, security, self-respect. Winning as
opposed to losing. Tanj, I've almost forgotten how to
think like this, and I've lost it all. Freedom, security,
self-respect. A little patience and I can take the first
step. What else is good? Brandy poured in coffee.
Movies.*

Twenty-three years earlier, Speaker-To-Animals had
brought the spacecraft *Lying Bastard* close to the Ringworld's edge. Now Chmeee and the Hindmost watched
recordings of that event.

Seen from that close, the Ringworld became straight
lines meeting at a vanishing point. From out of the
point where the checkered blue inner surface dropped
to meet the top and bottom edges of the rim wall, the
rings of the spacecraft decelerator system seemed to fly
straight into the camera, over and over, in infrared and
visible and ultraviolet light and deep-radar images. Or
they crept past in slow motion, huge electromagnets, all
identical.

But Louis Wu watched the entire eight hours of the
Changeling Earth fantasy epic while getting soddenly
drunk. Brandy in coffee, then brandy and soda, then
brandy alone. It was a movie he watched, not a sensual:
it used live actors and only two of the human senses.
He was at two removes from reality.

At one point he tried to engage Chmeee in a discussion of Saberhagen's use of impossible visual effects.
He retained just enough wit to desist at once. He dared
not talk to Chmeee while drunk. *The puppeteers have
hidden ears, hidden ears—*

The Ringworld grew large.

For two days it had been a finely etched blue ring, narrow, flimsy-looking, off center to its sun, growing as the black circle of its sun grew. Gross detail appeared. An inner ring of black rectangles, the shadow squares. A rim wall, a mere thousand miles high, but growing to block their view of the Ringworld's inner surface. By evening of the fifth day *Hot Needle of Inquiry* had lost most of its velocity, and the rim wall was a great black wall across the stars.

Louis was not under the wire. Today he'd forced himself to skip it; and *then* the Hindmost had told him that he would send no current until they had landed safely. Louis had shrugged. Soon, now—

"The sun is flaring," the Hindmost said.

Louis looked up. Meteor shielding blocked the sun. He saw only the solar corona, a circle of flame enclosing a black disc. "Give us a picture," he said.

Darkened and expanded in the rectangular "window," the sun became a huge, patterned disc. This sun was slightly smaller and cooler than Sol. There were no sunspots, no blemishes, except for a patch of glaring brightness at the center. "Our vantage is not good," the Hindmost said. "We see the flare head on."

Chmeee said, "Perhaps the sun has become unstable recently. This could explain why the Ringworld is off center."

"It may be. *Lying Bastard*'s records show a flare during your approach to the Ringworld, but for most of that year the sun was quiet." The Hindmost's heads poised above his instrument board. "Odd. The magnetic patterns—"

The black disc slid behind the black edge of the rim wall.

"The magnetic patterns of that star are most unusual," the Hindmost continued.

Louis said, "So go back for another look."

"Our mission does not permit the collection of random data."

"No curiosity?"

"No."

From under ten thousand miles away, the black wall seemed straight as a ruled line. Darkness and speed blurred all detail. The Hindmost had the telescope screen set for infrared light, but it did little good . . . or did it? There were shadows along the bottom of the rim wall, triangles of coolness thirty to forty miles tall, as if something on the inner side of the thousand-mile-high wall was reflecting sunlight away. And here came a darker, cooler line along the bottom, moving left to right.

Chmeee asked politely, "Are we boarding or merely hovering?"

"Hovering, to assess the situation."

"The treasure is yours. You may leave without it if it pleases you."

The Hindmost was restless. His legs gripped the pilot's bench hard. Muscles twitched in his back. Chmeee was relaxed; he seemed pleased with himself. He said, "Nessus had a kzin for his pilot. There were times when he could give way to total fear. You dare not. Can the automatics land *Needle* for you while you hide in stasis?"

"What if an emergency developed? No. I did not anticipate this."

"You must land us yourself. Do it, Hindmost."

Needle turned nose down and accelerated.

It took nearly two hours to accelerate to the Ringworld's seven hundred and seventy miles per second. By then, hundreds of thousands of miles of the dark line had raced past them. The Hindmost began to ease them closer—slowly, so slowly that Louis wondered if he would back out. He watched without impatience. He wasn't under the wire, and by his own choice. Nothing else could be that important.

But where was Chmeee's patience coming from? Was Chmeee feeling his oncoming youth? A human reaching his first century could feel that he had all the time in the world, for anything. Would a kzin react that way? Or . . . Chmeee was a trained diplomat. Perhaps he could hide his feelings.

Needle balanced on belly thrusters. .992 gravities of thrust warped its path into the Ringworld's curve; left to itself, the ship would have flung itself outward toward interstellar space. Louis watched the puppeteer's heads darting and weaving to check the dials and meters and screens around him. Louis couldn't read them.

The dark line had become a row of rings set well apart, each ring a hundred miles across, drifting past. During the first expedition, an old recording had shown them how ships would position themselves fifty miles from the rim wall and wait for the rings to sweep them up and accelerate them from free fall to Ringworld rotational speed and then dump them at the far end, on the spaceport ledge.

To left and right the black wall converged at vanishing points. It was close now, a few thousand miles away. The Hindmost tilted *Needle* to coast along the linear accelerator. Hundreds of thousands of miles of rings . . . but the Ringworlders had lacked gravity generators. Their ships and crews would not tolerate high accelerations.

"The rings are inactive. I find not even sensors for incoming ships," a puppeteer head turned to tell them, and then turned quickly back to work.

Here came the spaceport ledge.

It was seventy miles across. There were tall cranes built in beautiful curves, and rounded buildings, and low, wide flatbed trucks. There were ships: four flat-nosed cylinders, of which three had been damaged, the curve of the hulls broken.

"I hope you brought lights," Chmeee said.

"I do not want to be noticed yet."

"Do you find any sign of awareness? Will you land us without lights?"

"No and no," said the Hindmost. The spotlight flared

from *Needle*'s nose, tremendously powerful: an auxiliary weapon, of course.

The ships were vast. An open airlock was a mere black speck. Thousands of windows glittered on the cylinders precisely like candy flecks sprinkled on a cake. One ship seemed intact. The others had been torn open and cannibalized in varying degrees, their guts opened to vacuum and prying alien eyes.

"Nothing attacks, nothing warns us," the puppeteer said. "The temperature of the buildings and machinery is as that of the ledge and the ships, 174° Absolute. This place is long abandoned."

A pair of massive toroids, copper-colored, ringed the waist of the intact ship. They must have been a third the mass of the ship itself, or more. Louis pointed them out. "Ramscoop generators, maybe. I studied the history of spaceflight once. A Bussard ramjet generates an electromagnetic field to scoop up interstellar hydrogen and guide it into a constriction zone for fusion. Infinite fuel supply. But you need an inboard tank and rocket motor for when you're moving too slow for the ramscoop. There." Tanks were visible within two of the rifled ships.

And on all three of the rifled ships, the massive toroids were missing. That puzzled Louis. But Bussard ramjets commonly used magnetic monopoles, and monopoles could be valuable in other contexts.

Something else was bothering the Hindmost.

"Tanks to carry the lead? But why not simply plate it around the ship, where it would serve as shielding before it need be transmuted into fuel?"

Louis was silent. There had been no lead.

"Availability," Chmeee said. "Perhaps they had to fight battles. Lead could be boiled from the hull, leaving the ship without fuel. Land us, Hindmost, and we will seek answers in the unharmed ship."

Needle hovered.

"Easy to depart," Chmeee insinuated. "Ease us off the ledge and turn off the thrusters. We fall to flat space, activate the hyperdrive and rush for safety."

Needle settled on the spaceport ledge. The Hindmost said, "Take your place on the stepping discs."

Chmeee did. He was . . . not chuckling, but purring as he vanished. Louis stepped after him and was elsewhere.

CHAPTER 6

"Now Here's My Plan..."

The room felt familiar. He'd never seen one exactly like it, but it looked like the flight deck on any small interplanetary spacecraft. You always needed cabin gravity, a ship's computer, thrust controls, attitude jets, a mass detector. The three control chairs were recliners equipped with crash webs, controls in the arms, urinal tubes, and slots for food and drink. One chair was much larger than the others, that was all. Louis felt he could fly the lander blindfolded.

There was a broad strip of wraparound window above a semicircle of screens and dials. Through the window Louis watched a section of *Needle*'s hull swing out and up. The hanger was open to space.

Chmeee glanced over the larger knobs and switches set before his own chair. "We have weapons," he said softly.

A screen blinked and showed a foreshortened puppeteer head, which said, "Descend the steps to reach your vacuum equipment."

The lander's stairs were broad and shallow, made for a kzin's tread. Below was a much larger area, living space, with a water bed and sleeping plates and a kitchen the duplicate of the one in their cell. There was an autodoc big enough for a kzin, with an elaborate control console. Louis had been an experimental surgeon once. Perhaps the Hindmost knew it.

Chmeee had found the vacuum equipment behind one of an array of locker doors. He encased himself in what looked like an assortment of transparent balloons. He was edgy with impatience. "Louis! Gear yourself!"

47

Louis pulled on a flexible one-piece suit, skintight, and attached the fishbowl helmet and backpack. It was standard equipment; the suit would pass sweat, letting the body be its own cooling system. Louis added a loose oversuit lined in silver. It would be cold out there.

The airlock was built for three. Good: Louis could picture times when he wouldn't want to wait outside while an airlock cycled for someone else. If the Hindmost wasn't expecting emergencies, he had prepared for them anyway. As air was replaced by vacuum, Louis's chest expanded. He pulled shut the "girdle," the wide elastic band around his middle that would help him exhale.

Chmeee strode out of the lander, out of *Needle*, into the night. Louis picked up a tool kit and followed at an easy jog.

The sense of freedom was heady, dangerous. Louis reminded himself that his suit's communication link included the Hindmost. Things had to be said, and soon, but not in the puppeteer's hearing.

Proportions were wrong here. The half-disassembled ships were too big. The horizon was too close and too sharp. An infinite black wall cut the brilliant, half-familiar starscape in half. Seen through vacuum, the shapes of distant objects remained sharp and clear up to hundreds of thousands of miles away.

The nearest Ringworld ship, the intact one, looked to be half a mile distant. It was more like a mile. On the last voyage he had constantly misjudged the scale of things, and twenty-three years hadn't cured him.

He arrived puffing beneath the huge ship, to find an escalator built into one landing leg. The ancient machinery wasn't working, of course. He trudged up.

Chmeee was trying to work the controls of a big airlock. He fished a grippy out of the kit Louis carried. "Best not to burn through doors yet," he said. "There is power." He pried a cover off and worked at the innards.

The outer door closed. The inner door opened on vacuum and darkness. Chmeee turned on his flashlight-laser.

Louis was a little daunted. This ship would probably carry enough people to fill a small town. Easy to get lost here. "We want inspection tubes," he said. "I'd like to get the ship pressurized. With that big helmet you couldn't get into an access tube built for men."

They turned into a corridor that curved with the curve of the hull. There were doors just taller than Louis's head. Louis opened some of the doors. He found small living cubicles with bunks and pull-down chairs for humanoids his own size and smaller.

"I'd say Halrloprillalar's people built these ships."

Chmeee said, "We knew that. Her people built the Ringworld."

"That they did not do," said Louis. "I wondered if they built the ships or took them over from someone else."

The Hindmost spoke in their helmets. "Louis? Halrloprillalar told you her people built the Ringworld. Do you think she lied?"

"Yes."

"Why?"

She'd lied about other things. Louis didn't say so. He said, "Style. We know they built the cities. All those floating buildings, they're the kind of thing you put up to show off your wealth and power. Remember the sky castle, the floating building with the map room in it? Nessus took back tapes."

"I studied them," said the puppeteer.

"And it had a raised throne and a wire sculpture of someone's head that was as big as a house! If you could build a Ringworld, would you bother with a sky castle? I don't believe it. I never believed it."

"Chmeee?"

The kzin said, "We must accept Louis's judgment on human matters."

They turned right into a radial corridor. Here were more sleeping rooms. Louis inspected one in detail. The pressure suit was interesting. It was mounted against a wall like a hunter's trophy hide: one piece, crisscrossed with zippers, all open. Instantly accessible in case of vacuum.

The kzin waited impatiently while Louis zipped it shut and stepped back to study the effect.

The joints bulged. Knees and shoulders and elbows like cantaloupes, hands like a fistful of walnuts strung together. The face jutted forward; there were power and air-reserve gauges set below the faceplate.

The kzin growled, "Well?"

"Nope, I need more proof. Let's go."

"More proof of what?"

"I think I know who built the Ringworld . . . and why the natives are so much like humans. But why would they build something they couldn't defend? It doesn't make sense."

"If we discussed it—"

"Nope, not yet. Come on."

At the ship's axis they found pay dirt. Half a dozen radial corridors converged, and a tube with a ladder led up and down. There were diagrams covering four sections of wall, with labels that were tiny, detailed pictograms.

"How convenient," said Louis. "It's almost as if they had us in mind."

"Languages change," said the kzin. "These people rode the winds of relativity; their crews might be born a century apart. They would have needed such aids. We held our empire together with similar aids, before the Wars With Men. Louis, I find no weaponry section."

"There was nothing guarding the spaceport either. Nothing obvious, anyway." Louis's finger traced the diagrams. "Galley, hospital, living area—we're here in the living area. Three control centers; seems excessive."

"One for the Bussard ramjet and interstellar space. One for fusion drive and maneuvering in an occupied system, and weapons control, if any. One for life support: this one, that shows wind blowing through a corridor."

The Hindmost spoke. "With transmutation, they would use a total conversion drive."

"Oh, not necessarily. A blast of radiation that powerful would play merry hell in an inhabited system," said
Louis. "Hah! There are our access tubes, going to . . .
ramscoop generators, fusion motor, fuel feed. We want
the life-support controls first. Two flights up and *that*
way."

The control room was small: a padded bench facing
three walls of dials and switches. A touchpoint in the
doorjamb caused the walls to glow yellow-white, and
set the dials glowing too. They were unreadable, of
course. Pictograms segregated the controls into clusters
governing entertainment, spin, water, sewage, food, air.

Louis began flipping switches. The ones most often
used would be large and easy to reach. He stopped
when he heard a whistling sound.

The pressure dial at his chin rose gradually.

There was low pressure at 40 percent oxygen. Hu-
midity was low but not absent. No detectable noxious
substances.

Chmeee had deflated his suit and was stripping it off.
Louis removed his helmet, dropped the backpack, and
peeled his suit away, all in unseemly haste. The air was
dry and faintly stale.

Chmeee said, "I think we may start with the access
tube to the fuel feed. Shall I lead?"

"Fine." Louis heard in his voice the tension and
eagerness he'd tried to repress. With luck the Hindmost
would miss it. Soon, now. He followed the kzin's
orange back.

Out the door, turn right into a radius, follow to the
ship's axis and down a ladder, and a great furry hand
engulfed Louis's upper arm and pulled him into a corridor.

"We must talk," the kzin rumbled.

"Yah, and about time too! If he can hear us now, we
might as well give up. Listen—"

"The Hindmost will not hear us. Louis, we must
capture *Hot Needle of Inquiry*. Have you given thought
to this?"

"I have. It can't be done. You made a nice try, but what the futz were you going to do next? You can't fly *Needle*. You saw the controls."

"I can make the Hindmost fly it."

Louis shook his head. "Even if you could stand guard over him for two years, I think the life-support system would break down, trying to keep you both alive that long. That's the way he planned it."

"You would surrender?"

Louis sighed. "All right, let's look at it in detail. We can offer the Hindmost a credible bribe or a credible threat, or we can kill him if we think we can fly *Needle* afterward."

"Yes."

"We can't bribe him with a magic transmutation device. There isn't any."

"I dreaded that you would blurt out the truth."

"No way. Once he knows we aren't needed, we're dead. And we don't have any other bribes." Louis continued, "We can't get to the flight deck. There may be stepping discs that would take us there, somewhere aboard *Needle*, but where are they and how do we get the Hindmost to turn them on? We can't attack him either. Projectiles won't go through a GP hull. There's flare shielding on the hull, and probably more flare shielding between our cell and the flight deck. A puppeteer wouldn't have ignored that. So we can't fire a laser at him because the walls would turn mirror-colored and bounce the beam back at us. What's left? Sonics? He just turns off the microphones. Have I left anything out?"

"Antimatter. You need not remind me that we have none."

"So we can't threaten him, we can't hurt him, and we can't reach the flight deck anyway."

The kzin clawed thoughtfully at the ruff around his neck.

"It just occurred to me," Louis said. "Maybe *Needle* can't get back to known space at all."

"I don't see what you mean."

"We know too much. We're very bad publicity for the puppeteers. Odds are the Hindmost never planned to take us home. Well, why would he go himself? The place he wants to reach is the Fleet of Worlds, which is twenty or thirty light-years from here by now, in the opposite direction. Even if we could fly *Needle*, we probably don't have the life support to reach known space."

"Shall we steal a Ringworld ship, then? This one?"

Louis shook his head. "We can look it over. But even if it's in good shape, we probably can't fly it. Halrloprillalar's people took crews of a thousand, and *they* never went that far, according to Prill . . . though the Ringworld engineers probably did."

The kzin stood peculiarly still, as if afraid to release the energy bottled inside him. Louis began to realize how angry Chmeee was. "Do you counsel me to surrender, then? Is there not even vengeance for us?"

Louis had thought this through, over and over, while under the wire. He tried to remember the optimism he'd felt then, but it was gone. "We stall. We search the spaceport ledges. When we don't find anything, we search the Ringworld itself. We're equipped for that. We don't let the Hindmost give up till we find our own answer. Whatever it might be."

"This situation is entirely your fault."

"I know. That's what makes it so funny."

"Laugh, then."

"Give me my droud and I'll laugh."

"Your foolish speculations have left us slave to a mad root-eater. Must you always pretend to more knowledge than is yours?"

Louis sat down with his back to a yellow-glowing wall. "It seemed so reasonable. Tanj, it *was* reasonable. Look: the puppeteers were studying the Ringworld years before we came on the scene. They knew its spin and its size and its mass, which is just more than the mass of Jupiter. And there's nothing else in the system. Every planet, every moon, every asteroid, gone. It seemed so obvious. The Ringworld engineers took a Jupiter-style planet and made it into building materials, and they used the rest of the planetary garbage, too, and they built it all into a Ringworld. The mass of, say, Sol system would be just about right."

"It was only speculation."

"I convinced you both. Remember that. And gas giant planets," Louis continued doggedly, "are mostly hydrogen. The Ringworld engineers would have had to convert hydrogen into Ringworld floor material—*whatever* that stuff is; it's like nothing *we* ever built. They would have had to transmute material at a rate that would outstrip a supernova. Listen, Chmeee, I'd *seen the Ringworld*. I was ready to believe anything."

"And so was Nessus." The kzin snorted, forgetting that he too had believed. "And Nessus asked Halrloprillalar about transmutation. And she thought our two-headed companion was charmingly gullible. She told him a tale of Ringworld starships carrying lead to transmute into fuel. Lead! Why not iron? Iron would bulk more, but its structural strength would be greater."

Louis laughed. "She didn't think of it."

"Did you ever tell her that transmutation was your hypothesis?"

"What do you think? She'd have laughed herself to death. And it was too late to tell Nessus. By then Nessus was in the autodoc with one head missing."

"Uurrr."

Louis rubbed his aching shoulders. "One of us should have known better. I told you I did some math after we got back. Do you know how much energy it takes to spin the mass of the Ringworld up to seven hundred and seventy miles per second?"

"Why do you ask?"

"It takes a *lot*. Thousands of times the yearly energy output of this kind of sun. Where would the Ringworld engineers get all that energy? What they had to do was disassemble a *dozen* Jupiters, or a superjovian planet a dozen times Jupiter's mass. All mostly hydrogen, remember. They'd use some of the hydrogen in fusion for the energy to run that project, and reserve more of it in magnetic bottles. After they made the Ringworld from the solid residues, they'd have fuel for fusion rockets to spin it up to speed."

"Hindsight is so wonderful." Chmeee prowled back and forth along the corridor, on his hind legs, like a man, deep in thought. "So we are slaved to a mad alien searching for a magical machine that never was. What do you hope will happen in the year left to us?"

It was difficult to be optimistic without current. "We explore. Transmutation or not, there's got to be *something* valuable on the Ringworld. Maybe we'll find it. Maybe there's a United Nations ship already here. Maybe we'll find a thousand-year-old Ringworld spaceship crew. Maybe the Hindmost will get lonely and let us join him on the flight deck."

The kzin paced, his tail switching back and forth. "Can I trust you? The Hindmost controls the current flow to your brain."

"I'll kick the habit."

The kzin snorted.

"Finagle's festering testicles! Chmeee, I'm two and a quarter centuries old. I've been *everything*. I've been a master chef. I helped build and operate a wheel city above Down. I settled on Home for a while and lived like a colonist. Now I'm a wirehead. Nothing lasts. You can't do any one thing for two hundred years. A marriage, a career, a hobby—they're good for twenty years, and maybe you go through a phase more than once. I did some experimental medicine. I wrote a big chunk of that documentary on the Trinoc culture that won a—"

"Current addiction involves the brain directly. It's different, Louis."

"Yah. Yah, it's different." Louis felt the depression like a wall of black jelly sagging inward, crushing him down. "It's all black or all white. The wire is sending or it isn't. There's no variety. I'm sick of it. I was sick of it before the Hindmost took over my current flow."

"But you did not give up the droud."

"I want the Hindmost to think I can't."

"You want me to think you can."

"Yah."

"What of the Hindmost? Never have I heard of a puppeteer who behaved so strangely."

"I know. It makes me wonder if all the mad traders were Nessus's sex. If the . . . call them sperm-carrying males . . . are the dominant ones."

"Urrr—"

"It doesn't have to be that way. The kind of madness that sends a puppeteer to Earth because he can't deal with other puppeteers, that's not the same as the madness that makes a Joseph Stalin. What do you want from me, Chmeee? I don't know how he'll act. If we give him some credit for brains, then he'll use General Products trading techniques. It's the only way he knows to deal with *us*."

The canned air tasted cool and metallic. There was too much metal in these ships, Louis thought. It seemed queer that Halrloprillalar's people hadn't used more advanced materials. Making a Bussard ramjet was no task for primitives.

The air smelled funny, and the yellow-white glow in the walls dimmed and brightened irregularly. Best get back to their pressure suits, soon.

Chmeee said, "There is the lander. It would function as a spacecraft."

"What do you call a spacecraft? It must have interplanetary capability. It'd need that to get around on the Ringworld. I wouldn't think we could reach another star with it."

"I was thinking of ramming *Needle*. If there is no escape, we may take vengeance."

"That'd be fun to watch. You ramming a General Products hull."

The kzin loomed over him. "Do not be too amusing, Louis. What would I be on the Ringworld, with no mate, no land, no name, and a year to live?"

"We'd be buying time. Time to find a way off. In the meantime"—Louis stood up—"officially, we're still searching for a magic transmutation machine. Let's make at least a token search."

CHAPTER 7

Decision Point

Louis woke ravenous. He dialed a Cheddar cheese soufflé and Irish coffee and blood-oranges and ate his way through it all.

Chmeee slept curled protectively around himself. He looked different somehow. Neater—yes, neater, because the scar tissue under his fur had disappeared and the new fur was growing out.

His stamina was impressive. They had searched every one of the four Ringworlder ships, then moved on to a long, narrow building at the very lip of infinity, which proved to be the guidance center for the spacecraft accelerator system. At the last, Louis was moving in a fog of exhaustion. He knew he should have been examining *Needle* for details of construction, weak points, routes into the flight deck. Instead he had watched Chmeee, with hatred. The kzin never stopped to rest.

The Hindmost appeared from somewhere, from behind or within the green-painted private sector. His mane was combed and fluffy, dressed with crystals that changed their spectral color as he moved. Louis was intrigued. The puppeteer had been scruffy while he was flying *Needle* alone. Did he dress to impress his alien prisoners with his elegance?

He asked, "Louis, do you want the droud?"

Louis did, but—"Not yet."

"You slept eleven hours."

"Maybe I'm adjusting to Ringworld time. Did you get anything done?"

"I took laser spectrograms of the ships' hulls. They

58

are largely iron alloys. I have deep-radar scans, two views each for the four ships; I moved *Needle* while you slept. There are two more spaceport ledges one hundred and twenty degrees around the Ringworld. I located eleven more ships by their hull composition. I could not learn detail at this distance."

Chmeee woke, stretched, and joined Louis at the transparent wall. "We learn only to ask more questions," he said. "One ship was left intact, three were stripped. Why?"

"Perhaps Halrloprillalar could have told us," the Hindmost said. "Let us deal with the only urgent question. Where is the transmutation device?"

"We have no instruments here. Flick us to the lander, Hindmost. We will use the screens on the flight deck."

Eight screens glowed around the horseshoe curve of the lander's instrument board. Chmeee and Louis studied ghostly schematics of the Bussard ramjet ships, generated by the computer from the deep-radar scans.

"It looks to me," Louis said, "like one team did the entire looting job. They had three ships to work with, and they took what they wanted most first. They kept working till something stopped them: they ran out of air or something. The fourth ship came later. Mmm . . . but why didn't the fourth crew loot their own ship?"

"Trivialities. We seek only the transmuter. Where is it?"

Chmeee said, "We could not identify it."

Louis studied the deep-radar ghosts of four ships. "Let's be methodical. What *isn't* a transmutation system?" He traced lines on the image of the one intact ship, using a light-pointer. "Here, these paired toroids circling the hull have to be the ramscoop field generators. Fuel tanks here. Access tubes here, here, here . . ." As he pointed them out, the Hindmost obliged by removing sections of ship from the screen. "Fusion reaction motor, this whole section. Motors for the landing legs. Take out the legs too. Attitude jets here, here, here, all fed by tubes along here carrying plasma from the one small fusion generator, here. Battery. This thing with the snout, pointing out of the middle of the hull—what did Prill call it?"

"*Cziltang brone*," Chmeee sneezed. "It softens the Ringworld floor material temporarily, for penetration. They used it instead of airlocks."

"Right." Louis continued, with enthusiasm and hidden glee. "Now, they probably wouldn't keep the magic transmuter in the living quarters, but . . . sleeping rooms here, control rooms here, here, here, the kitchen—"

"Could that be—?"

"No, we thought of that. It's just an automated chemistry lab."

"Proceed."

"Garden area here. Sewage treatment feeds in. Airlocks . . ."

When Louis had finished, the ship was gone from the screen. The Hindmost patiently restored it. "What did we overlook? Even if the transmuter was dismounted, removed, there would be space for it."

This was getting to be fun. "Hey, if they really kept their fuel outside—lead, molded around the hull—then this isn't really an inboard hydrogen tank, is it? Maybe they kept the magic transmuter in there. It needed heavy padding or heavy insulation . . . or cooling by liquid hydrogen."

Chmeee asked, before the Hindmost could, "How would they remove it?"

"Maybe with the *cziltang brone* from another ship. Were all the fuel tanks empty?" He looked at the ghosts of the other ships. "Yah. Okay, we'll find the transmuters on the Ringworld . . . and they won't be working. The plague will have got to them."

"Halrloprillalar's tale of the bacterium that eats superconductor is in our records," the Hindmost said.

"Well, she really couldn't tell us all that much," said Louis. "Her ship left on a long tour. When it came back, there was no more Ringworld civilization. Everything that used superconductors had stopped." He had wondered how much to believe of Prill's tale of the Fall of the Cities. But *something* had destroyed the Ringworld's ruling civilization. "Superconductor is almost too wonderful. You end up using it in everything."

"Then we can repair the transmuters," said the Hindmost.

"Oh?"

"You will find superconducting wire and fabric stored aboard the lander. It is not the same superconductor the Ringworld used. The bacterium will not touch it. I thought we might need trade goods."

Louis kept his poker face intact, but the Hindmost had made a startling statement. How did puppeteers come to know so much about a mutant plague that killed Ringworld machines? Suddenly Louis didn't doubt the bacterium at all.

Chmeee hadn't caught it. "We want to know what the thieves used for transportation. If the rim-wall transport system failed, then our transmuters may be just the other side of the rim wall, abandoned there because they stopped working."

Louis nodded. "Failing that, we've got a lot of territory to search. I think we should be looking for a Repair Center."

"Louis?"

"There has to be a control and maintenance center somewhere. The Ringworld can't run itself forever. There's meteor defense, meteor repair, the attitude jets . . . the ecology could go haywire—it all has to be watched. Of course the Repair Center could be anywhere. But it's got to be big. We shouldn't have that much trouble finding it. And we'll probably find that it's been abandoned, because if anyone had been minding the store, he wouldn't have let the Ringworld slide off center."

The Hindmost said, "You have been putting your mind to this."

"We didn't do too well the first time we came here. We came to explore, remember? Some kind of laser weapon shot us down, and we spent the rest of our time trying to get off alive. We covered maybe a fifth of the *width*, and learned just about nothing. It's the Repair Center we should have been looking for. That's where the miracles are."

"I had not expected such ambition from a current addict."

"We'll start cautiously." Cautiously for humans, Louis told himself; not for puppeteers. "Chmeee's right: the machines could have been dumped as soon as they were through the rim wall, when the bacterium got to them."

Chmeee said, "We should not try to take the lander through the rim wall. I have no faith in an alien machine a thousand years old. We must go over."

The Hindmost asked, "How would you avoid the meteor defense?"

"We must try to outguess it. Louis, do you still believe that what fired on us was merely an automated defense against meteors?"

"I thought so at the time. It all happened so tanj fast." *Falling sunward, all a little edgy, daunted by the reality of the Ringworld. All but Teela, of course. A momentary flash of violet-white; then* Liar *was embedded in tenuous violet-glowing gas. Teela had looked out through the hull. "The wing's gone," she'd said.*

"It didn't fire on us till we were on a course to intersect the Ringworld surface. It's got to be automated. I told you why I think there's nobody in the Repair Center."

"Nobody to fire on us deliberately. Very well, Louis. Automatics would not be set to fire on the rim transport system, would they?"

"Chmeee, we don't know who built the rim transport system. Maybe it wasn't the Ringworld engineers; maybe it was added later, by Prill's people—"

"It was," said the Hindmost.

His crew turned to look at the puppeteer's image on the screen.

"Did I tell you that I spent some time at the telescope? I have learned that the rim transport system is only partly finished. It runs along 40 percent of this rim wall, and does not include the section we occupy now. On the portward rim wall the system is only 15 percent complete. The Ringworld engineers would not have left so minor a subsystem half built, would they? Their own mode of transport may have been the same spacecraft used to supervise construction."

"Prill's people came later," Louis said. "Maybe a lot later. Maybe the rim transport system got too expensive. Maybe they never actually completed their conquest of the Ringworld . . . but then why were they building starships? Oh, futz, we may never know. Where does this leave us?"

"It leaves us trying to outthink the meteor defense," Chmeee said.

"Yah. And you were right. If the meteor defense made a habit of firing on the rim wall, nobody would have built anything there." Louis chewed it a moment longer. There would be holes in his assumptions . . . but the alternative was to go through the wall via an ancient *cziltang brone* of unknown dependability. "Okay. We fly over the rim wall."

The puppeteer said, "You suggest a fearful risk. I prepared as best I could, but I was forced to use human technology. Suppose the lander should fail? I hesitate to risk any of my resources. You would be stranded. The Ringworld is doomed."

"I hadn't forgotten," Louis said.

"First we must search all of the spaceport ledges. There are eleven more ships on this rim wall, and an unknown number on the portward rim—"

And it would be weeks before the Hindmost satisfied himself that no transmutation system was to be found on those ships. Oh, well—

"We should go now," Chmeee said. "The secret may be nearly within our grip!"

"We have fuel and supplies. We can afford to wait."

Chmeee reached out and tapped controls. He must have planned this sequence in detail; he must have studied the lander minutely while Louis was dopey with fatigue. The small conical craft lifted a foot from the floor, spun ninety degrees, and the blast of a fusion motor filled the docking chamber with white fire.

"You are being foolish," the Hindmost's liquid contralto reproved them. "I can turn off your drive."

The lander slid clear of the curved docking hatch and lifted at a brutal four gees. When the Hindmost finished speaking, a fall would already have killed them. Louis cursed himself for not foreseeing this. Chmeee's blood was bubbling with youth. Half the kzinti never grew up—they died in fights . . .

And Louis Wu, too engrossed in himself and his current-withdrawal depression, had let his options slip by him.

He asked coolly, "Have you decided to do your own exploring, Hindmost?"

The puppeteer's heads quivered indecisively above his control board.

"No? Then we'll do it our way, thank you very much." Louis turned to Chmeee and said "Try landing on the rim wall" before he noticed the kzin's peculiarly rigid attitude, blank eyes, and exposed claws. Rage? Would the kzin actually try to ram *Hot Needle of Inquiry*?

The kzin howled in the Hero's Tongue.

The puppeteer answered in the voice of a kzin; changed his mind and repeated in Interworld. "Two fusion rockets, one mounted aft and one beneath. No thrusters. You need never fire the fusion motors on the ground except for defense. You may lift with repulsers, which repel the Ringworld floor material. You may fly as if using a negative gravity generator, but the repulsers are simpler in design, easier to repair and maintain. Do not use them now. They would repel the rim wall and thrust you into space."

That explained Chmeee's apparent panic. He was having trouble flying the lander. Not reassuring. But the spaceport ledge was far below, and an unnerving wobble at takeoff had almost disappeared. There was steady four-gee thrust under him . . . which suddenly cut off. Louis said "Wuff!" as the lander went into free fall.

"We must not rise too far above the rim wall. Search the lockers, Louis. Inventory our equipment."

"You'll warn me before you do that again?"

"I will."

Louis disengaged the crash web and floated down the stairwell.

Here was living space surrounded by lockers and an airlock. Louis began opening doors. The biggest locker held what must have been a square mile of fine, silky black cloth, and hundreds of miles of black thread on twenty-mile spools. Another locker held modified flying belts, with repulsers over the shoulders and a small thruster. Two small and one large. One for Halrloprillalar, of course. Louis found flashlight-lasers and hand-held sonic stunners and a heavy two-handed disintegrator. He found boxes the size of Chmeee's fist, with a shirt clip and a microphone grid, and earplugs (two small and one large) in the same compartment. Those would be translators, with compact computers included. If they worked through the onboard computer they would have been less bulky.

There were large rectangular repulsion plates—for towing cargo through the air? Spools of Sinclair molecule chain, like very thin, very strong thread. Small bars of gold: for trade? Binocular goggles with a light-amplification setting. Impact armor. Louis muttered, "He's thought of everything."

"Thank you." The Hindmost spoke from a screen Louis hadn't noticed. "I had many years to prepare."

Louis was getting tired of finding the Hindmost wherever he went. Funny: he could hear the sounds of a cat fight drifting down from the flight deck. The Hindmost must be holding two conversations at once, instructing Chmeee on the lander's controls. He heard the expression for "attitude jets"—

Chmeee's voice roared without benefit of microphone. "Louis, take your place!"

Louis glided up the stairwell. He was barely into his chair when Chmeee lit the fusion motors. The lander slowed and hovered just at the edge of the rim wall.

The top of the rim wall was broad enough for the lander, but not much more than that. And how was the Ringworld meteor defense taking all this?

They had been within the arc of the Ringworld, falling toward the inner ring of shadow squares, when violet light bathed the spacecraft Lying Bastard. Liar's *hull had instantly enclosed itself in a bubble of no-time. When time began again, the hull and its occupants had suffered no damage. But* Liar's *delta wing, with its thrusters and fusion motors and pods of sensing instruments, had become ionized vapor. And the hull was falling toward the Ringworld.*

They had speculated, later, that the violet laser was no more than an automated meteor defense. They had guessed that it might be based on the shadow squares. It was all guesswork; they had never learned anything about the Ringworld weapon.

The rim transport system was a late addition. The Ringworld engineers would not have taken it into account when programming the meteor defense. But Louis had seen old recordings of it in action, in a building abandoned by Halrloprillalar's species. It had worked; the meteor defense had *not* fired on the linear accelerator loops or the ships they enclosed. And Louis gripped his chair arms hard, waiting for violet flame, as Chmeee settled the lander on the rim wall.

But it didn't come.

CHAPTER 8

Ringworld

From a thousand miles above the Earth—from, say, a space station in a two-hour orbit—the Earth is a great sphere. The kingdoms of the world revolve below. Details disappear around the horizon's curve; other, hidden features rotate into view. At night, glowing cities outline the continents.

But from a thousand miles above the Ringworld, the world is flat, and the kingdoms thereof are all there at once.

The rim wall was of the same stuff as the Ringworld floor. Louis had walked on it, in places where eroded landscape let it show through. It had been grayish, translucent, and terribly slippery. Here the surface had been roughened for traction. But the pressure suit and backpack made Chmeee and Louis top-heavy. They moved with care. That first step would be a beauty.

At the bottom of a thousand miles of glassy cliff were broken layers of cloud, and seas: bodies of water from ten thousand to a couple of million square miles in area, spread more or less uniformly across the land, and linked by networks of rivers. As Louis raised his eyes, the seas grew smaller with distance . . . smaller and a little hazy . . . too small to see, until sea and fertile land and desert and cloud all blended into a blue knife-edge against black space.

To left and right it was the same, until the eye found a blue band swooping up from the infinity beyond the horizon. The Arch rose and narrowed and curved over and above itself, baby blue checked with midnight blue, to where a narrow ribbon of Arch lost itself behind a shrunken sun.

This part of the Ringworld had just passed its maximum distance from the sun, but a Sol-type star could still burn your eyes out. Louis blinked and shook his head, his eyes and mind dazzled. Those distances could grab your mind and hold it, leave you looking into infinity for hours or days. You could lose your soul to those distances. What was one man when set against an artifact so huge?

He was Louis Wu. There was nothing like him on all the Ringworld. He held to that. Forget the infinities: concentrate on detail.

There, thirty-five degrees up the Arch: a faintly bluer patch.

Louis worked the magnification on his goggles. They locked onto the faceplate, but you had to hold your head very still. The patch was all ocean, an ellipse stretching nearly across the Ringworld, with clusters of islands showing through cloud cover.

He found the other Great Ocean higher up on the other branch of the Arch. It was a ragged four-pointed star, dotted with similar clusters of tiny islands—tiny at this distance, at which the Earth would be a naked-eye object, barely.

It was getting to him again. Deliberately he looked down, studying the near distance.

Almost below, a couple of hundred miles to spinward, a half-cone of mountain leaned drunkenly against the rim wall. It seemed oddly regular. It was layered in half-circles: a bare, dirt-colored peak; far below, a band of white, probably snow and ice; then green spreading down and out into foothills.

The mountain was quite isolated. In the spinward direction the rim wall was a flat vertical cliff out to the limit of the binocular goggles—almost. If that bump at the very limit of vision was another such mountain, it was a futz of a long way away. At the distance you could almost see the Ringworld starting to curve upward.

There was another such bump in the antispinward direction. Louis scowled. *File for future study.*

Far to port (ahead) and a bit to spinward (right) was a region of glittering white, brighter than land, brighter than sea. A midnight-blue edge of night was sweeping toward it. Salt, was Louis's first thought. It was big. It had engulfed a couple of dozen Ringworld seas, and those seas varied in size from Lake Huron to the Mediterranean. Brighter points came and went like ripples . . .

Ah. "Sunflower patch."

Chmeee looked. "The one that burned me was bigger."

Slaver sunflowers were as old as the Slaver Empire, which had died more than a billion years ago. The Slavers seemed to have planted sunflowers around their estates, for defense. You still found these plants on some of the worlds of known space. Cleaning them out was a difficult business. You couldn't just burn them out with laser cannon. The silver blossoms would throw the beam back at you.

What sunflowers were doing on the Ringworld was a mystery. But Speaker-To-Animals had been flying above a Ringworld landscape when a rift in the clouds exposed him to the plants beneath. The scars were almost gone . . .

Louis raised the magnification on his goggles. A smoothly curved borderline marked off the blue-green-brown of an Earthlike world from the silver sunflower patch. The border curved inward to half enclose one of the larger seas.

"Louis? Look for a short black line, just beyond the sunflowers and a bit to antispinward."

"I see it." A black dash on the infinite noonday landscape, perhaps a hundred thousand miles from where they stood. Now, what would that be? A vast tar pit? No, petrochemicals would never form on the Ringworld. A shadow? What could cast a shadow in the Ringworld's permanent noon?

"Chmeee, I think it's a floating city."

"Yes . . . At worst it will be a center of civilization. We should consult them."

They had found floating buildings in some of the old cities. Why not a floating city? They'd be seeing it edge on, of course. "What we should do," Louis said, "is touch down a fair distance away and ask the natives about them. I'd hate to come on them cold. If they're good enough to keep that city going, they could be tough. Say we touch down near the edge of the sunflower patch—"

"Why there?"

"The sunflowers would be fouling up the ecology. Maybe the locals could use some help. We'd be surer of our welcome. Hindmost, what do you think?"

There was no answer.

"Hindmost? Calling the Hindmost . . . Chmeee, I think he can't hear us. The rim wall's blocking his signals."

Chmeee said, "We will not remain free long. I saw a pair of probes mounted in the cargo bay, behind the lander. The puppeteer will use them as relays. Is there anything you would like to say during this temporary freedom?"

"I'd say we covered it all last night."

"Not quite. Our motives are not quite the same, Louis. I take it that you are eager to save your life. Beyond that you want free access to current. For myself, I want my life and my freedom, but I also want satisfaction. The Hindmost has kidnapped a kzin. He must be made to regret it."

"I can buy that. He kidnapped me too."

"What does a wirehead know of thwarted honor? Do not let me find you blocking my path, Louis."

"I'm just going to diffidently remind you," Louis said, "that I got you off the Ringworld. Without me you would never have taken the *Long Shot* home to earn your name."

"You were not a current addict then."

"I am not a current addict now. And *don't you call me a liar*."

"I am not ac—"

"Hold it." Louis pointed. The corner of his eye had caught something moving against the stars. A moment later the voice of the Hindmost spoke in their ears.

"Please forgive the hiatus. What have you decided to do?"

"Explore," Chmeee said curtly. He turned back to the lander.

"Give me details. I am not happy about risking one of my probes merely to maintain communications. The primary purpose of these probes was to refuel *Needle*."

"Return your probe to safety," Chmeee told the puppeteer. "When we return we will report in full."

The probe settled onto the rim wall on several small jets. It was a lumpy cylinder twenty feet long. The Hindmost said, "You speak frivolously. It is my landing craft you risk. Do you plan to search the base of the rim wall?"

That thrilling contralto, that lovely woman's voice, was the same that every puppeteer trader had learned from his predecessor. Possibly they learned another to influence women. To men it was a voice that pushed buttons, and Louis resented that. He said, "There are cameras on the lander, aren't there? Just watch."

"I have your droud. Explain."

Neither Louis nor Chmeee bothered to answer.

"Very well. I have locked open the stepping-disc link between the lander and *Needle*. The probe will function as a relay for this, too. As for your droud, Louis, you may have it when you learn to obey."

And that, thought Louis, defined his problem nicely.

Chmeee said, "It is good to know that we can flee our mistakes. Are there range limits to stepping discs?"

"Energy limits. The stepping-disc system can absorb only a limited kinetic energy difference. *Needle* and the lander should have no relative velocity when you flick across. You are advised to stay directly to port of *Needle*."

"This fits our plans."

"But if you abandon the lander, I still control your

means of escape from the Ringworld. Do you hear me, Chmeee, Louis? The Ringworld will impact the shadow squares in just more than Earth's year."

Chmeee lifted the lander on puppeteer-developed repulsers. A burst from the aft fusion motor edged the craft forward and off the edge.

Flying on Ringworld-floor-material repulsers was *not* like using antigravity, Louis noted. Repelled by both the rim wall and the landscape, the lander fell in a swooping curve. Chmeee stopped their descent at forty miles.

Louis displayed a telescope view on one of the screens. Floating on repulsers alone, above most of the atmosphere, the lander was very steady and utterly quiet: a good telescope mount.

Rocky soil lapped up in foothills to the base of the rim wall. Louis ran the telescope slowly along that border, at high magnification. Barren brown soil against glassy gray. An anomaly would be easy to spot.

"What do you expect to find?" Chmeee asked.

Louis didn't mention the watching puppeteer, who thought they were searching for an abandoned transmutation device. "A spacecraft crew would have come through from the spaceport ledge about here. But I don't see anything *big* in the way of abandoned machinery. We aren't really interested in little stuff, are we? They wouldn't have left anything valuable unless it was just too tanj big to move, and then they'd have left almost everything they had."

He stopped the telescope. "What do you make of that?"

It stood thirty miles tall against the base of the rim wall: a half-cone, with a weathered look, as if smoothed by a hundred million years of wind. Ice glittered in a broad belt around its lower slope. The ice was thick and showed the flow patterns of glaciers.

"The Ringworld imitates the topography of Earthlike worlds," said Chmeee. "From what I know of Earthlike worlds, this mountain doesn't fit the pattern."

"Yah. It's inartistic. Mountains come in chains, and they aren't this regular. But, you know, it's worse than that. Everything on the Ringworld is contoured in. Remember when we took the *Liar* underneath? Sea bottoms bulging, dents for mountains and gullies for mountain ranges, riverbeds like veins in a weight lifter's arm? Even the river deltas are carved into the structure. The Ringworld isn't thick enough to let the landscape carve itself."

"There are no tectonic processes to do the carving, for that matter."

"Then we should have seen that mountain from the back, from the spaceport. I didn't. Did you?"

"I'll take us closer."

That turned out to be difficult. The closer the lander came to the rim wall, the more fusion thrust was needed to hold it there . . . or to lift the lander if the repulsers were turned off.

They came within fifty miles, and that was close enough to find the city. Great gray rocks protruded through the ice floes, and some of these showed myriad black-shadowed doors and windows. Focus closer and the doorways had balconies and awnings, and hundreds of slender suspension bridges ran up, down, and sideways. Stairways were hacked into the rock; they ran in strange branching curves, half a mile tall and more. One dipped all the way to the foothills, to the tree line.

A fortuitous flat space in the center of the city, half rock and half permafrost, had become a public square; the hordes that thronged it were pale golden flecks just big enough to see. Golden clothing or golden fur? Louis wondered. A great boulder at the back of the square had been carved with the face of a hairy, chubby, jovial baboon.

Louis said, "Don't try to get closer. We'll scare them away if we try to land on fusion drive, and there isn't any other way."

A vertical city with a population of ten thousand, at a guess. Deep-radar showed that they had not dug deep into the rock. In fact, those rocks riddled with rooms looked like dirty permafrost.

"Surely we want to question them regarding their peculiar mountain?"

"I'd love to talk to them," Louis said, and he meant it. "But look at the spectrograph and deep-radar. They don't use metals or plastics, let alone single-crystal stuff. I hate to think what those bridges are made of. They're primitives. They'll think they're living on a mountain."

"I agree. Too much trouble to reach them. Where next? The floating city?"

"Yah, by way of the sunflower patch."

A shadow square was sliding across the sun's disc.

Chmeee lit the aft motor again and ran their speed to ten thousand miles per hour, then coasted. Not too fast for detail, but fast enough to get them where they were going in about ten hours. Louis studied the racing landscape.

In principle the Ringworld should have been an endless garden. It was not a randomly evolved world, after all, but a made thing.

What they had seen on their first visit could not be considered typical. They had spent most of their time between two big meteoroid punctures: between the eye storm, which was spewing air through a puncture in the Ringworld floor, and the stretched and raised landscape around Fist-of-God Mountain. Of *course* the ecology was damaged. The engineers' carefully planned wind patterns must have been ruined.

But here? Louis looked in vain for the pattern of an eye storm, a hurricane turned on its side and flattened. There were no meteoroid punctures here. Yet there were patches of desert, Sahara-size and larger. On the ridges of mountain ranges he found the pearly gleam of naked Ringworld foundation. Winds had stripped away the covering rock.

Had the weather patterns grown this bad, this fast? Or did the Ringworld engineers *like* deserts? It struck Louis that the Repair Center must have been deserted

for a very long time. Halrloprillalar's people might
never have found it at all, after the Ringworld engineers
vanished. As they had to have vanished, if Louis's
guess was right.

"I want three hours' sleep," Chmeee said. "Can you
fly the lander if something happens?"

Louis shrugged. "Sure, but what could happen?
We're too low for the meteor defense. Even if it's based
on the rim wall, it'd be firing on settled land. We'll just
cruise awhile."

"Yes. Wake me in three hours." Chmeee reclined his
chair and slept.

Louis turned to the fore and aft telescopes for amuse-
ment and instruction. Night had covered the sunflower
region. He ran the view up along the Arch to the nearer
of the Great Oceans.

There, to spinward of the ocean and almost on the
Ringworld median line: that tilted mock volcano was
Fist-of-God Mountain, in a patch of Mars-colored
desert much bigger than Mars. Farther to port, a reaching bay of the Great Ocean, itself bigger than worlds.

They had reached the shore of that bay and turned
back, last time.

The islands were scattered in clusters across the blue
ellipse. One was a single island, disc-shaped, desert-
colored. One was a disc with a channel cut through it.
Strange. But the others were islands in a vast sea . . .
there, he had found the map of Earth: America, Greenland, Eurasiafrica, Australia, Antarctica, all splayed
out from the glare-white North Pole, just as he had seen
it in the sky castle long ago.

Were they *all* maps of real worlds? Prill wouldn't
have known. The maps must have been made long before her species came on the scene.

He had left Teela and Seeker somewhere in there.
They must still be in the area. Given Ringworld distance and native technology, they could not have gone
far in twenty-three years. They were thirty-five degrees
up the curve of the Arch—fifty-eight million miles
away.

Louis really didn't want to meet Teela again.

Three hours had passed. Louis reached out and shook Chmeee's shoulder, gently.

A great arm lashed out. Louis threw himself backward, not far enough.

Chmeee blinked at him. "Louis, never wake me like that. Do you want the autodoc?"

There were two deep gashes just behind his shoulder. He could feel blood seeping into his shirt. "In a minute. Look." He pointed at the map of Earth, tiny islands well separated from the other clusters.

Chmeee looked. "Kzin."

"What?"

"A map of Kzin. There. Louis, I think we were wrong when we assumed that these were miniature maps. They are full size, one-to-one scale."

Half a million miles from the map of Earth was another cluster. As with the Earth map, the oceans were distorted by the polar projection, but the continents were not. "That *is* Kzin," Louis said. "Why didn't I notice? And that disc with a channel cut through it—that's Jinx. The smaller red-orange blob must be Mars." Louis blinked away dizziness. His shirt was wet with blood. "We can take this up later. Help me down to the autodoc."

CHAPTER 9

The Herdsmen

He slept in the autodoc.

Four hours later—with a trace of tightness behind and below his shoulder to remind him never to touch a sleeping kzin—Louis took his seat.

It was still night outside. Chmeee had the Great Ocean on the screen. He asked, "How are you?"

"Restored to health, thanks be to modern medicine."

"You were not distracted by your wounds. Yet there must have been pain and shock."

"Oh, I suppose Louis Wu at fifty would have gone into hysterics, but futz, I knew the autodoc was right there. Why?"

"It seemed to me at first that you must have the courage of a kzin. Then I wondered if current addiction has left you unable to respond to any lesser stimulus."

"We'll just assume it's courage, okay? How are you making out?"

"Well enough." The kzin pointed. "Earth. Kzin. Jinx; the two peaks rise right out of the atmosphere, as do the East and West Poles of Jinx. So does the Map of Mars. This is Kdat, the slave planet—"

"Not any more."

"The kdatlyno were our slaves. So were the pierin, and this is their world, I think. Here, you would know: is this the home world of the Trinocs?"

"Yah, and they'd settled this one next to it, I think. We can ask the Hindmost if he's got maps."

"We can be sure enough."

"Granted. Okay, what is it? It's *not* a roster of Earthlike worlds. And there are half a dozen I can't identify at all."

Chmeee snorted. "Obvious to the meanest intelligence, Louis. It is a roster of potential enemies, intelligent or near-intelligent beings who may one day threaten the Ringworld. Pierin, kzinti, martians, human, Trinoc."

"But where does Jinx fit in? *Oh*. Chmeee, they couldn't have thought the bandersnatchi might come at them with warships. They're big as dinosaurs, and handless. And Down has intelligent natives, too. So where is it?"

"There."

"Yah. That's kind of impressive. The Grogs aren't all that obvious a menace. They spend their whole lives sitting on one rock."

"The Ringworld engineers found all of these species, and left the Maps as a message for their descendants. Are we agreed? But they did not find the puppeteer world."

"Oh?"

"And we know they landed on Jinx. We found a bandersnatch skeleton during the first expedition."

"So we did. They may have visited all these worlds."

The quality of the light changed, and Louis saw the shadow of night receding to antispinward. He said, "Nearly time to land."

"Where do you suggest?"

The sunflower field ahead was brightening with sunlight. "Turn us left. Follow the terminator line. Keep going till you see real dirt. We want to be down before dawn."

Chmeee bent their path in a great curve. Louis pointed. "Do you see where the border dips toward us, where the sunflowers are spreading around both sides of a sea? I think the sunflowers must have trouble crossing water. Land us on the far shore."

The lander dipped into atmosphere. Flame built up before and around the lander, throwing a white glaze over the view. Chmeee held the lander high, shedding their velocity slowly, dipping lower when he could. The sea fled beneath them. Like all Ringworld seas, it was built for convenience, with a highly convoluted shoreline, forming bays and beaches, and a gentle offshore slope to a uniform depth. There were seaweed forests and numerous islands and beaches of clean white sand. A vast grassy plain ran to antispinward.

The sunflower plague reached two arms around to engulf the sea. A river meandered in S-curves through the sunflowers to the delta where it entered the sea. To port the sunflowers were edging up against a swampy outflow river. Louis could sense the frozen motion, slow as the march of glaciers.

The sunflowers noticed the lander.

Light exploded from below. The window darkened instantly, leaving Chmeee and Louis dazzled.

"Fear not," Chmeee said. "We can't hit anything at this height."

"The stupid plants probably took us for a bird. Can you see yet?"

"I can see the instruments."

"Drop us to five miles. Put them behind us."

The window cleared a few minutes later. Behind them the horizon blazed; the sunflowers were still trying. Ahead . . . yah. "Village."

Chmeee dropped for a closer look. The village was a closed double ring of huts. "Land in the center?"

"I wouldn't. Land at the edge, and I wish I knew what they consider crops."

"I won't burn anything."

A mile above the village, Chmeee braked the lander with the fusion drive. He settled on the tall grassy stuff that covered the plain. At the last moment Louis saw the grass move—saw three things like green dwarf elephants stand up, raise short, flattened trunks to bleat warning, and begin running.

"The natives must be herders," Louis said. "We've started a stampede." More green beasts were joining the exodus. "Well, good flight, Captain."

The instruments showed Earthlike atmosphere.

Hardly surprising. Louis and Chmeee donned impact armor: leathery stuff, not unpleasantly stiff, which would go rigid as steel under impact from spear, arrow, or bullet. They added sonic stunners, translators, binocular goggles. The ramp carried them down into waist-high grass.

The huts were close together and joined by fences. The sun was right overhead . . . of course. It was dawn, and the natives ought to be just stirring. No windows on the outsides of the huts—except for one twice the height of the others, and that one had a balcony. Perhaps they'd been seen already.

As Chmeee and Louis came near, the natives stirred.

They came over the fence in a bounding swarm, screaming at each other in falsetto. They were small and red and human-shaped, and they ran like demons. They carried nets and spears. Louis saw Chmeee draw his stunner, and drew his own. The red humanoids darted past Louis and Chmeee and kept going.

Chmeee asked, "Have we been insulted?"

"No, they're off to turn the stampede, of course. I can't even fault their sense of proportion. Let's go in. Maybe somebody's home."

Somebody was. A couple of dozen red-skinned children watched them from behind the fences as they approached. They were thin; even the babies were lean as greyhound puppies. Louis stopped at the fence and smiled at them. They paid him scant attention. Most of them clustered around Chmeee.

The compound within the circle of huts was bare earth. A border of rocks marked a burnt-out campfire. A one-legged red man came out of one building and approached, using a crutch, moving at a pace Louis would have considered jogging. He wore a kilt of cured hide marked with decorative lacing. His ears were large and stood out from his head, and one had been torn, long ago. His teeth were filed . . . were they? The children were all smiling and laughing, and *their* teeth were filed, even those of the babies. Nope. They must grow that way.

The old man stopped at the fence. He smiled and asked a question.

"I don't speak your language yet," Louis said.

The old man nodded. He gestured with an upward sweep of his arm: invitation?

One of the older children found the courage to leap. He (she; the children wore no kilts) landed on Chmeee's shoulder, settled herself comfortably in the fur, and began to explore. Chmeee stood very still. He asked, "What should I do now?"

"She isn't armed. Don't tell her how dangerous you are." Louis climbed over the fence. The old man stood back for him. Chmeee followed, carefully, with the girl still on his shoulder, clinging to the thick fur around his neck.

They settled near the fireplace, Louis and Chmeee and the one-legged red man, surrounded by children. They began to teach the native language to the translating widgets. For Louis it was routine. Oddly, it also seemed routine to the old man; even the voices of the translators didn't surprise him.

His name was Shivith hooki-Furlaree something. His voice was high and piping. His first intelligible question was "What do you eat? You don't have to say."

"I eat plants and sea life and meat treated with fire. Chmeee eats meat without fire," Louis said, and that seemed sufficient.

"We eat meat without fire too. Chmeee, you are an unusual visitor." Shivith hesitated. "I have to tell you this. We do not do *rishathra*. Don't be angry." At the word *rishathra* the translator only beeped.

Chmeee asked, "What is *rishathra*?"

The old man was surprised. "We thought that the word was the same everywhere." He began to explain. Chmeee was oddly silent as they delved into the subject, working around the unknown words:

Rishathra was sex outside of one's own species.

Everyone knew the word. Many species practiced it.

For some, it could be a means of mutual birth control; for others, the first move in a trade agreement. For some it was taboo. The People didn't need a taboo. They just couldn't do it. The sexual signals were wrong; it might be a matter of distinct pheromones. "You must come from far away, not to know this," the old man said.

Louis spoke of himself, how he had come from the stars beyond the Arch. No, neither he nor Chmeee had ever practiced *rishathra*, though there was great variety among his species. (He remembered a Wunderland girl a foot taller and fifteen pounds lighter than himself, a feather in his arms.) He spoke of the variety of worlds and of intelligent life, but he skirted the subject of wars and weaponry.

The tribes of the People herded many kinds of animals. They liked variety, but they didn't like starving, and it was not usually possible to keep herds of different animals at the same time. Tribes of the People kept track of each other, to trade feasts. Sometimes they traded herds. It was like trading entire life styles: you could spend half a *falan* in mutual instruction before parting. (A *falan* was ten turns, ten Ringworld rotations, seventy-five days of thirty hours each.)

Would the herders worry that there were strangers in the village? Shivith said they wouldn't. Two strangers were no threat.

When would they return? At midday, Shivith said. They had had to hurry; there had been a stampede. Otherwise they would have stopped to talk.

Louis asked, "Do you need to eat meat right after it's been killed?"

Shivith smiled. "No. Half a day is okay. A day and a night is too long."

"Do you ever—"

Chmeee stood up suddenly. He set the girl down gently and turned off his translator. "Louis, I need exercise and solitude. This time of confinement has threatened my sanity! Do you need me?"

"No. Hey—"

Chmeee was already over the fence. He turned.

"Don't take off your clothes. At a distance there's no way to tell you're intelligent. Don't kill any of the green elephants."

Chmeee waved and bounded off into the green grass.

"Your friend is fast," said Shivith.

"I should go too. I have a project in mind."

Survival and escape had been their concerns during their first visit to the Ringworld. Only later, in the safe and familiar surroundings of Resht on Earth, had Louis Wu's conscience become active. Then he remembered destroying a city.

The shadow squares formed a ring concentric to the Ringworld. There were twenty of them held face-on to the sun by invisibly thin wire. The wire stayed taut because the shadow squares rotated at greater than orbital speed.

Liar, falling free with its drive motors burned away, had struck one of the shadow square wires and torn it loose. The wire, a single strand tens of thousands of miles long, had settled like a smoke cloud over an occupied city.

Louis had needed it to tow the grounded *Liar*.

They had found an endpoint and moored it to their makeshift vehicle—Halrloprillalar's floating jail—and towed it behind them. Louis couldn't know exactly what had happened to the city, but he could guess. The stuff was as fine as gossamer and strong enough to cut hullmetal. It must have cut the buildings into gravel as its loops contracted.

This time the natives would not suffer because Louis Wu had arrived. He was in current-addiction withdrawal; he didn't need guilt too. His first act on this visit was to start a stampede. He was going to fix that.

It was hard physical work.

He took a break at one point and went up on the flight deck. He was worried about the kzin. Even a human being—a flatlander of five hundred years ago, say, a successful man in middle age—might have been

disconcerted to find himself suddenly eighteen years
old, his smooth progression toward death interrupted,
his blood flowing with powerful and unfamiliar juices,
his very identity in question: hair thickening and changing color, scars disappearing . . .

Well, where was Chmeee?

The grass was strange. Here in the vicinity of the
camp, it was waist-high. To spinward was a vast area
cropped almost to the ground. Louis could see the herd
moving along the edge, guided by small red humanoids,
leaving a swath that was almost dirt-colored.

Give 'em this: the little green elephants were efficient. The red men must have to shift camp fairly fre-
quently.

Louis saw motion in the grass nearby. He watched
patiently until it moved again . . . and suddenly it was
an orange streak. Louis never saw Chmeee's prey.
There were no humanoids around, and that was good
enough. He went back to work.

The herdsmen returned to find a feast.

They came in a band, chattering among themselves.
They paused to examine the lander without coming too
close. Some of them surrounded one of the green elephants. (Lunch?) It may have been coincidence that
the spearmen led the rest as they entered the circle of
huts.

They stopped in surprise, confronting Louis, and
Chmeee with a different girl on his shoulder, and half a
ton of dressed meat laid on clean leather.

Shivith introduced the aliens, with a short and fairly
accurate account of their claims. Louis was prepared to
be called a liar, but it never happened. He met the
chief: a woman four feet and a few inches tall, Ginjerofer by name, who bowed and smiled with disconcert-
ingly sharp teeth. Louis tried to bow in the same
fashion.

"Shivith told us you like variety in meat," Louis said,
and gestured toward what he had taken from the lander's kitchen. Three of the natives turned the green ele-

phant around, aimed it at where the rest of the herd was grazing, and prodded its butt with spear hafts to get it going. The tribe converged on lunch. Others came to join them, out of huts Louis had assumed were empty: a dozen very old men and women. Louis had thought Shivith was old. He was not used to seeing people with wrinkled skin and arthritic joints and old scars. He wondered why they had hidden, and surmised that arrows had been aimed at him and Chmeee while they talked with Shivith and the children.

In a few minutes the natives reduced the meal to bones. They did no talking; they seemed to have no order of precedence. They ate, in fact, like kzinti. Chmeee accepted a gestured offer to join them. He ate most of the moa, which the natives ignored; they preferred red meat.

Louis had carried it in several loads on one of the big repulsion plates. His muscles ached from the strain of moving it. He watched the natives tearing into the feast. He felt good. There was no droud in his head, but he felt good.

Most of the natives left then, to tend the herd. Shivith and Ginjerofer and some of the older ones stayed. Chmeee asked Louis, "Is this moa an artifact or a bird? The Patriarch might want such birds for his hunting parks."

"There's a real bird," Louis said. "Ginjerofer, this should make us even for the stampede."

"We thank you," she said. There was blood on her lips and chin. Her lips were full, and redder than her skin. "Forget the stampede. Life is more than not being hungry. We love to meet people who are different. Are your worlds really so much smaller than ours? And round?"

"Round like balls. If mine were far up the Arch, you would see only a white point."

"Will you go back to these small places to tell of us?"

The translators must be feeding to recorders aboard *Needle*. Louis said, "One day."

"You will have questions."

"Yah. Do the sunflowers ruin your grazing ground?"

He had to point before she understood. "The brightness to spinward? We know nothing of it."

"Did you ever wonder? Ever send scouts?"

She frowned. "This is the way of it. My fathers and mothers tell that we have been moving to antispinward since they were little. They remember that they had to go around a great sea, but they did not come too close, because the beasts would not eat the plants that grow around the shore. There was a brightness to spinward then, but it is stronger now. As for scouts—a party of the young went to see for themselves. They met giants. The giants killed their beasts. They had to return quickly then. They had no meat."

"It sounds like the sunflowers are moving faster than you are."

"Okay. We can move faster than we do."

"What do you know about the floating city?"

Ginjerofer had seen it all her life. It was a landmark, like the Arch itself. Sometimes when the night was cloud-covered, one could still find the yellow glow of the city, but that was all she knew. The city was too far even for rumor.

"But we hear tales from large distances, if they are worth telling. They may be garbled. We hear of the people of the spill mountains, who live between the cold white level and the foothills, where air is too dense. They fly between the spill mountains. They use sky sleds when they can get them, but there are no new sky sleds, so that for hundreds of years they must use balloons. Will your seeing-things see that far?"

Louis put the binocular goggles on her and showed her the enlargement dial. "Why did you call them spill mountains? Is that the same word you use when you spill water?"

"Yes. I don't know why we call them that. Your eyepiece only shows me larger mountains . . ." She turned to spinward. The goggles almost covered her small face. "I can see the shore, and a glare across."

"What else do you hear from travelers?"

"When we meet we talk most of dangers. There are brainless meat-eaters to antispinward that kill people. They look something like us, but smaller, and they are black and hunt at night. And there are . . ." She frowned. "We don't know the truth of this. There are mindless things that urge one to do *rishathra* with them. One does not live through the act."

"But you can't do *rishathra*. They can't be dangerous to you."

"Even to us, we are told."

"What about diseases? Parasites?"

None of the natives knew what he meant! Fleas, hookworm, mosquitoes, measles, gangrene: there was nothing like that on the Ringworld. Of course he should have guessed that. The Ringworld engineers just hadn't brought them. He was startled nonetheless. He wondered if he might have brought disease to the Ringworld for the first time . . . and decided that he had not. The autodoc would have cured him of anything dangerous.

But the natives were that much like civilized humans. They grew old, but not sick.

CHAPTER 10

The God Gambit

Hours before nightfall, Louis was exhausted.

Ginjerofer offered them the use of a hut, but Chmeee and Louis elected to sleep in the lander. Louis fell between the sleeping plates while Chmeee was still setting up defenses.

He woke in the dead of night.

Chmeee had activated the image amplifier before he went to sleep. The landscape glowed bright as a rainy day. The daylit rectangles of the Arch were like ceiling light panels: too bright to do more than glance at. But most of the nearer Great Ocean was in shadow.

The Great Oceans lured him. They were flamboyant. They should not have been. If Louis was right about the Ringworld engineers, flamboyance was not their style. They built with simplicity and efficiency, and they planned in very long time spans, and they fought wars.

But the Ringworld was flamboyant in its own way, and impossible to defend. Why hadn't they built a lot of little Ringworlds instead? And why the Great Oceans? They didn't fit either.

He could be wrong from the start. That had happened before! Yet the evidence—

Was there something moving in the grass?

Louis activated the infrared scanner.

They glowed by their own heat. They were bigger than dogs, like a blend of human and jackal: horrid supernatural things in this unnatural light. Louis spent a moment locating the sonic stun cannon in the lander's turret and another swinging it toward the interlopers. Four of them, moving on all fours through the grass.

They stopped not far from the huts. They were there for some minutes. Then they moved off, and now they were hunched half erect. Louis turned off the infrared scanner.

In augmented Archlight it was clear: they were carrying the day's garbage, the remains of the feast. Ghouls. The meat probably wasn't ripe enough for them yet.

Yellow eyes in his peripheral vision: Chmeee was wide-awake. Louis said, "The Ringworld's old. A hundred thousand years at least."

"What makes you say that?"

"The Ringworld engineers wouldn't have brought jackals. There's been time enough for some branch of the hominids to fit that niche in the ecology."

"A hundred thousand years wouldn't be enough," said Chmeee.

"It might. I wonder what else the engineers didn't bring. They didn't bring mosquitoes."

"You are facetious. But they would not have brought bloodsuckers of any kind."

"No. Or sharks, or cougars." Louis laughed. "Or skunks. What else? Venomous snakes? Mammals couldn't live like snakes. I don't think any mammals secrete poison in their mouths."

"Louis, it would take millions of years for hominids to evolve in so many directions. We must consider whether they evolved on the Ringworld at all!"

"They did, unless I'm *completely* wrong. As for how long it took, there's a small matter of mathematics. If we assume they started evolving a hundred thousand years ago, from a base popu . . ." Louis let the sentence trail off.

A good distance away—moving at fair speed, considering their burdens—the jackal-hominids suddenly stopped, turned back, seemed to pose for a moment, then dropped into the grass and vanished. A touch of the infrared sensor showed four glowing spots fanning out and away.

"Company to spinward," Chmeee said quietly.

The newcomers were big. They were Chmeee's size, and they weren't trying to hide. Forty bearded giants marched through the night as if they owned it. They were armed and armored. They moved in a wedge formation, with bowmen on the forward arms of the triangle and swordsmen inside, and the one fully armored man at the point. Others had plates of thick leather to guard arms and torsos, but that one, the biggest of the giants, wore metal: a gleaming shell that bulged at elbows, knuckles, shoulders, knees, hips. The forward-jutting mask was open, with a pale beard and wide nose showing inside.

"I was right. I was right all along. But why a Ringworld? Why did they build a Ringworld? How in Finagle's Name did they expect to defend it?"

Chmeee finished swinging the stun cannon around. "Louis, what *are* you talking about?"

"The armor. Look at the armor. Haven't you ever been in the Smithsonian Institute? And you saw the pressure suits in the Ringworlder spaceship."

"Uurrr . . . yes. We have a more immediate problem."

"Don't shoot yet. I want to see . . . Yah, I was right. They're going past the village."

"Would you say that the little red ones are our allies? It was only coincidence that we met them first."

"I'd say they are. Tentatively."

The microphone picked up a high-pitched scream, interrupted by a bellow. The archers drew arrows simultaneously, fitted them to bows. Two small red sentries were bounding toward the huts at impressive speed. They were ignored.

"Fire," Louis said softly.

The arrows went wild. The giants crumpled. Two or three green elephants bellowed and tried to get to their feet, paused, then settled back. One had a couple of arrows in its flank.

"They were after the herd," Chmeee said.

"Yah. We don't really want them slaughtered, do

we? Tell you what, you stay here with the stun cannon
and I'll go out and negotiate."

"I don't take your orders, Louis."

"Do you have other suggestions?"

"No. Save at least one giant to answer questions."

This one had fallen on his back. He was not just
bearded, he was *maned*: only his eyes and nose showed
in a mass of golden hair that spilled over face and head
and shoulders. Ginjerofer squatted and forced his
mouth open with two small hands. The warrior's jaw
was massive. His teeth were flat-topped molars, well
worn down. *All* of them.

"See," Ginjerofer said, "a plant-eater. They wanted
to kill the herd, to take their grass."

Louis shook his head. "I wouldn't have thought the
competition would be so fierce."

"We didn't know. But they come from spinward,
where our herds have cropped the grass close. Thank
you for killing them, Louis. We must have a great
feast."

Louis's stomach lurched. "They're only sleeping.
And they've got minds, like you, like me."

She looked at him curiously. "Their minds were
turned to our destruction."

"We shot them. We ask you to let them live."

"How? What would they do to us if we let them
wake up?"

It was a problem. Louis temporized. "If I solve that,
will you let them live? Remember, it was our sleep-
gun." And that should suggest to Ginjerofer that
Chmeee could use the gun again.

"We will confer," said Ginjerofer.

Louis waited, and thought. No way would forty giant
herbivores fit in the lander. They could be disarmed, of
course . . . Louis grinned suddenly at the sword in the
giant's big, broad-fingered hand. The long, curved blade
would work as a scythe.

Ginjerofer came back. "They may live if we never
see their tribe again. Can you promise that?"

"You're a bright woman. Yah, they could have relatives with a vengeance tradition. And yah, I can promise you'll never see this tribe again."

Chmeee spoke in his ear. "Louis? You may have to exterminate them!"

"No. It could cost us some time, but tanj, look at them! Peasants. They can't fight us. At worst I'll make them build a big raft and we'll tow it with the lander. The sunflowers haven't crossed the downstream river yet. We'll let them off a good way away, where there's grass."

"For what? A delay of weeks!"

"For information." Louis turned back to Ginjerofer. "I want the one in the armor, and I want all their weapons. Leave them not so much as a knife. Keep what you want, but I want most of it piled in the lander."

She looked dubiously at the armored giant. "How shall we move him?"

"I'll get a repulser plate. You tie the rest up after we're gone. Let them loose in pairs. Tell them the situation. Send them to spinward in daylight. If they come back to attack you with no weapons, they're yours. But they won't. They'll cross that plain damn fast, with no weapons and no grass over an inch tall."

She considered. "It seems safe enough. It will be done."

"We'll be at their camp, wherever it is, long before they arrive. We'll wait for them, Ginjerofer."

"They will not be hurt. My promise is for the People," she said coldly.

The armored giant woke shortly after dawn.

His eyes opened, blinked, and focused on a looming orange wall of fur, and yellow eyes, and long claws. He held quite still while his eyes roved . . . seeing the weapons of thirty comrades piled around him . . . seeing the airlock, with both doors open. Seeing horizon slide past; feeling the wind of the lander's speed.

He tried to roll over.

Louis grinned. He was watching via a scanner in the rec-room ceiling while he steered the lander. The giant's armor was soldered to the deck at knees, heels, wrists, and shoulders. A little heat would free him, but rolling around wouldn't.

The giant made demands and threats. He did not plead. Louis paid scant attention. When the computer's translating program started getting sense out of that, he'd notice. At the moment he was more concerned with his view of the giants' camp.

He was a mile up, and fifty miles from the red carnivores' huts. He slowed. The grass hereabouts had had time to grow back, but the giants had left another great bare region behind them, toward the sea and the sunflower gleam beyond. They were out in the grass: thousands of them scattered widely across the veldt. Louis caught points of light glittering from scythe-swords.

No giants were near the camp itself. There were wagons parked near the center of camp, and no sign of draft beasts. The giants must pull the wagons themselves. Or they might have motors left from the event Halrloprillalar had called the Fall of the Cities, a thousand years ago.

The one thing Louis couldn't see was the central building. He saw only a black spot on his window, a black rectangle overloaded by too much light. Louis grinned. The giants had enlisted the enemy.

A screen lighted. A seductive contralto said, "Louis."

"Here."

"I return your droud," the puppeteer said.

Louis turned. The small black thing was sitting on the stepping disc. Louis turned away as one turns one's back on an enemy, remembering that the enemy is still there.

He said, "There's something I want you to investigate. There are mountains along the base of the rim wall. The natives—"

"For the risks of exploring I selected you and Chmeee."

"Can you understand that I might want to minimize those risks?"

"Certainly."

"Then hear me out. I think we'll want to investigate the spill mountains. Before we do, there are just a *lot* of things we need to know about the rim wall. All you have to—"

"Louis, why did you call them spill mountains?"

"The natives call them that. I don't know why, and neither do they. Suggestive, eh? And they don't show from the back. Why not? Most of the Ringworld is like the mask of a world, with seas and mountains molded into it. But there's *volume* to the spill mountains."

"Suggestive, yes. You must learn the answers yourselves. I am called Hindmost, as any leader may be called Hindmost," the puppeteer said, "because he directs his people from safety, because safety is his prerogative and his duty, because his death or injury would be disaster for all. Louis, you've dealt with my kind before!"

"Tanj, I'm only asking you to risk a probe, not your valuable hide! All we need is a running hologram taken along the rim wall. Put the probe in the rim transport loops and decelerate it to solar orbital speed. You'll be using the system just as it's meant to be used. The meteor defense won't fire on the rim wall—"

"Louis, you are trying to outguess a weapon programmed hundreds of thousands of years ago by your reckoning. What if something has blocked the rim transport system? What if the laser targeting system has become faulty?"

"Even at worst, what have you lost?"

"Half my refueling capability," said the puppeteer. "I planted stepping-disc transmitters in the probes, behind a filter that will pass only deuterium. The receiver is in the fuel tank. To refuel I need only drop a probe in a Ringworld sea. But if I lose my probes, how will I leave the Ringworld? And why should I take that risk?"

Louis held tight to his temper. "The volume, Hindmost! What's inside the spill mountains? There must be hundreds of thousands of those half-cones thirty to forty miles tall, and the backs are flat! One could be the control and maintenance center, or a whole string of them. I don't think they are, but I want to know before I go anywhere near them. Aside from that, there must be attitude jets for the Ringworld, and the best place for them is the rim wall. Where are they, and why aren't they working?"

"Are you quite sure they must be rocket motors? There are other solutions. Gravity generators would serve for attitude control."

"I don't believe it. The Ringworld engineers wouldn't need to spin the Ringworld if they had gravity generators. It'd make for a much simpler engineering problem."

"Control of magnetic effects, then, in the sun and the Ringworld floor."

"Mmm . . . maybe. Tanj, I'm *not* sure. I want you to find out!"

"How can you dare to bargain with me?" The puppeteer seemed more puzzled than angry. "At my whim you remain until the Ringworld grinds against the shadow squares. At my whim you will never taste current again."

The translator was finally speaking. "Butt out," Louis said. He'd been given no volume control for the Hindmost's voice, but the Hindmost stopped talking.

The translator said, "Docile? Because I eat plants, must I be docile? Take me out of my armor and I will fight you naked, you ball of orange hair. My space in the longhouse needs a fine new rug."

"And what," Chmeee asked, "of these?" He showed polished black claws.

"Give me one tiny dagger against your eight. Or give me none, I will fight without."

Louis was chortling. He used the intercom. "Chmeee, haven't you ever seen a bullfight? And this one must be the Patriarch of the herd, the king giant!"

The giant asked, "Who or what was that?"

"That was Louis." Chmeee's voice dropped. "There is

danger for you. I urge you to be respectful. Louis is . . . fearsome."

Louis was a little startled. What was this? A reverse God Gambit, with the Voice of Louis Wu as guest star? It could work, if Chmeee the ferocious kzin was clearly afraid of an unseen voice . . . Louis said, "King of Plant Eaters, tell me why you attacked my worshippers."

"Their beasts ate our forage," said the giant.

"Was there forage elsewhere, that you could avoid risking my anger?"

Among the males of a herd of cattle or buffalo, one either dominates or submits. There is no middle ground. The giant's eyes rolled, seeking escape, but there was none. If he couldn't dominate Chmeee, how could he cow an unseen voice?

"We had no choice," he said. "To spinward are the fire plants. To port are the Machine People. To starboard is a high ridge of exposed *scrith*. Nothing will grow on *scrith*, and it is too slippery to climb. To antispinward is grass, and nothing to stop us but small savages, until you came! What is your power, Louis? Are my men alive?"

"I let your men live. In"—fifty miles, running naked and hungry— ". . . in two days they will be with you. But I can kill you all with a motion of my finger."

The giant's eyes searched the ceiling, pleading. "If you can kill the fire plants, we will worship you."

Louis settled back to think. Suddenly it was no longer fun.

He heard the giant begging Chmeee for information on Louis; he heard Chmeee lying outrageously. They'd played such games before. The God Gambit had kept them alive during their long return to the *Liar*; Speaker-To-Animals's reputation as a war god, and the natives' offerings, had kept them from starvation. Louis hadn't realized that Speaker/Chmeee enjoyed it.

Sure, Chmeee was having fun. But the giant was pleading for help, and what could Louis do against sunflowers? Actually, it was hardly a problem. The giants had offended him, hadn't they? Gods in general were not noted for forgiveness. So Louis opened his mouth, and closed it again, and thought some more, and said, "For your life and the lives of your people, tell me the truth. Can you eat the fire plants if they do not burn you first?"

The giant answered eagerly. "Yes, Louis. We forage along the border at night, when we grow hungry enough. But we must be far away by dawn! The plants can find us miles away, and they burn anything that moves! They all turn at once, they turn the glare of the sun on us, and we burn!"

"But you can eat them when the sun isn't shining."

"Yes."

"How do the winds blow in this region?"

"Winds? . . . In these parts they blow to spinward. For great distances around, they blow only into the realm of fire plants."

"Because the plants heat the air?"

"Am I a god, to know that?"

After all, the sunflowers only got a certain amount of sunlight. The way they worked. they'd heat the air around and above them, but the sunlight would never pass the silver blossoms to reach the roots. Dew would condense on the cool soil The plants would get their moisture that way. And rising hot air would bring a steady wind from the borders of the sunflower patch.

And the plants burned anything that moved, to turn plant-eating beasts and birds into fertilizer.

He could do it. He could.

"You will do most of the work yourself," Louis said. "The tribe is yours and you will save them. Afterward, you and they will turn toward the dying fire plants. Eat them, or plow them under and plant whatever you like to eat." Louis grinned at Chmeee's bewilderment, and continued, "You will never disturb my worshippers, the red people."

The armored giant was gloriously happy. "All of this is most welcome news. Our worship is yours. We must seal the covenant by *rishathra*."

"You're kidding."

"What? No, I spoke of this earlier, but Chmeee did not understand. Bargains must be sealed by *rishathra*, even between men and gods. Chmeee, this is no problem. You are even of proper size for my women."

"I am stranger than you think," Chmeee said.

From Louis's ceiling viewpoint it looked like Chmeee was exposing himself to the giant. Certainly something had caused the giant's startled expression. Louis couldn't have cared less. *Tanj dammit!* he thought. *I actually thought of an answer! And now this. What do I have to do to—*

Yah. "I will make for you a servant," Louis said. "Because I am hurried, he will be dwarf, and mute in your language. Call him Wu. Chmeee, we must confer."

CHAPTER 11

The Grass Giants

The lander touched down in a malevolent glare of white light. The glare from the longhouse persisted for a minute after the lander stopped moving. then died. Presently the ramp descended. The king giant, fully armored, let it carry him to the ground. He raised his head and bellowed. The sound must have carried for many miles.

Giants began jogging toward the lander.

Chmeee descended, then Wu. Wu was small, partly hairless, and harmless-looking. He smiled a lot; he looked about him with charming enthusiasm, as if seeing the world for the first time . . .

The longhouse was a fair distance away. It was mud and grass, reinforced with vertical members. The row of sunflowers planted on the roof shifted restlessly, now turning their concave mirror faces and green photosynthetic nodes to the sun, now flashing at the giants converging from all directions.

Chmeee was asking. "What if an enemy attacked in the daytime? How can you reach the longhouse? Or do you store your weapons elsewhere?"

The giant considered before giving away secrets of defense. But Chmeee served Louis, and it was well not to offend him . . . "See you the pile of brush to antispinward of the longhouse? If danger threatens, a man must approach from behind that pile and wave a sheet. The sunflowers fire the damp wood. Under cover of smoke we may then enter and take weapons." He glanced at the lander and added, "An enemy fast enough to reach us before we can reach weapons is too

99

strong for us anyway. Perhaps the sunflowers would surprise him."

"May Wu choose his own mate?"

"Does he have that much volition? I had thought to lend him my wife Reeth, who has practiced *rishathra* before. She is small, and the Machine People are not so different from Wu."

"Acceptable," Chmeee said without a glance at Wu.

A hundred of the giants surrounded them now. No more seemed to be coming. The kzin asked, "Are these all?"

"These and my warriors are all of my tribe. There are twenty-six tribes on the veldt. We stay together when we can, but none speaks for all," the king giant said.

Of the hundred or so, eight were males, and all of the eight were markedly scarred; three were actual cripples. None but the king giant showed the wrinkles and whitening hair of age.

The rest were females . . . rather, they were women. They stood six and a half to seven feet tall, small next to their men: brown-skinned, dignified, naked. Their hair was golden and spilled in wealth down their backs; it was generally a mass of tangles. None bore any kind of decoration. Their legs were thick, their feet large and hard. A few of the women were white-haired. Their heavy breasts gave a good indication of their relative ages. They examined their guests with pleasure and wonder while the armored giant told what he knew of them.

And Chmeee, with his translator off, spoke low. "If you prefer one or another female, I must say so now."

"No, they're all about equally . . . attractive."

"We can still end this situation. You must be mad to make such a promise!"

"I can do it. Hey, don't you want revenge for your burnt pelt?"

"Revenge on a *plant*? You are mad. Our time is precious, and in just over a year they will all be dead—sunflowers, giants, little red carnivores, and all!"

"Yah . . ."

"Your help is no help at all, if they knew it. How long will your project take? A day? A month? You hurt our own project."

"Maybe I am mad. Chmeee, I have to carry this through. In all the time since I left the Ringworld I haven't . . . had reason to be proud of myself. I have to prove—"

The king giant was saying, "Louis himself will tell you that the threat of the fire plants is over for us. He will tell us our part—"

Wu, self-effacing, as was his nature, stepped behind the great kzin; and none of the giants particularly noticed that he was talking to his hand. Half a minute later the time-delayed Voice of Louis boomed from the lander, saying, "Hear me, for your day has come to make the places of the fire plants clean for all the breeds of men. My work will go before you as a cloud. You must gather the seeds of what you wish to grow where fire plants grow now . . ."

In the first light of dawn, when the sun shone overhead as a mere splinter of light at the edge of a shadow square, the giants were up and moving.

They liked to sleep touching each other. The king giant was the center of a circle of women, with Wu at its edge, his small, half-bald head pillowed on a woman's shoulder, his legs hooked over a man's long bony legs. The dirt floor was covered in flesh and hair.

Waking, they moved in order, those nearest the door untangling themselves and picking up bags and sickle-swords and moving out, then those farther in. Wu moved out with them.

Outside the distant lander, a one-armed giant with a marred face said a quick farewell to Chmeee and came jogging toward the longhouse. Last night's guards would be sleeping inside during the day, and some older women had stayed too.

The giants turned and stared openly when Wu began climbing the wall.

The grass and mud surface was crumbly, but the roof was only twelve feet high. Louis pulled himself up between two sunflowers.

The plants stood a foot tall on knobbly green stalks. Each had a single oval blossom, mirror-surfaced, nine to twelve inches across. A short stalk poked from the mirror's center and ended in a dark-green bulb. The back of the blossom was stringy. laced with some vegetable analogue of muscle fibers. And all of the blossoms were throwing sunlight at Louis Wu; but there wasn't enough sunlight to hurt him yet.

Louis wrapped his hands around a thick sunflower stalk and rocked it gently. There was no give; the roots were dug deep into the roof. He took off his shirt and held it between the blossom and the sun. The mirror-blossom wavered and rippled in indecision, then folded forward to enclose the green bulb.

Mindful of his audience, Wu climbed down with some attention to style. A white glare followed him as he went to join Chmeee.

The kzin said, "I spent part of this night talking to a guard."

"Learn anything?"

"He has the utmost confidence in you, Louis. They're gullible."

"So were the carnivores. I wondered if it was just good manners."

"I think not. The carnivores and the herbivores expect anything at all to walk in from the horizon at any moment. They know that there are people with strange shapes and godlike powers. They made me wonder what *we* may meet next. Uurrr, and the sentry knew that we are not of the race that built the Ringworld. Is this significant?"

"Maybe. What else?"

"There will be no problem with the other tribes. Cattle they may be, but with minds. Those who stay on the veldt will collect seeds for those who choose to invade sunflower territory. They will give women to the young

adult men if they go. Perhaps a third of them will leave
when you have worked your magic. The rest will have
enough grass. They will not need to move toward the
red people."

"Okay."

"I asked about long-term weather."

"Good! Well?"

"The guard is an old man," Chmeee said. "When he
was young and had both legs—before something
marred him; the translator said 'ogre'—the sun was
always the same brightness and the days were always
the same length. Now the sun seems sometimes brighter
and sometimes dimmer, and when the sun is bright, the
days seem too short, and vice versa. Louis, he remembers how it started. Twelve *falans* ago, which would
be one hundred and twenty rotations of the constella-
tions, there was a time of dark. Dawn never came for
what would have been two or three days. They saw the
stars, and a ghost-flame spreading overhead. Then all
was as it should be for some *falans*. When the uneven
days came, it was long before they noticed; they don't
have clocks."

"Seems predictable enough. Except—"

"But the long night, Louis. What does that sound
like?"

Louis nodded. "The sun flared up. The shadow
square ring closed somehow. Maybe the wire that holds
it together can be reeled in by automatics."

"Then the flare jet pushed the Ringworld off center.
Now the days grow more uneven. It frightens all of the
races the giants trade with."

"And well it should."

"I wish there were something we could do." The
kzin's tail lashed once. "But we battle sunflowers instead. Did you enjoy yourself this night?"

"Yah."

"Then you should be smiling."

"If you really wanted to know, you could have
watched. Everyone else did. There aren't any walls in

that big building; they all crowd in together. Anyway, they like watching."

"I can't tolerate the smell."

Louis laughed. "It's strong. Not bad, just strong. And I had to stand on a stool. And the women were . . . docile."

"Females should be docile."

"Not human females! They're not even stupid. I couldn't talk, of course, but I listened." Louis's forefinger tapped the knob in his ear. "I listened to Reeth organizing the clean-up squad. She's good. Hey, you were right, they're organized just like a herd of cattle! The females are all wives of the king giant. None of the other males ever gets laid, except that sometimes the king giant declares a holiday and then goes away so he won't have to watch. Fun's over when he comes back, and officially nothing happened. Everyone's a little miffed because we brought him back from the raid two days early."

"What are human females supposed to be like?"

"Oh . . . orgasm. The males of all the mammals have orgasms. The females generally don't. But human women do. But the giant women, they just accept. They don't, ah, participate."

"You didn't enjoy it?"

"Of course I enjoyed it. It's sex, isn't it? But it takes a little getting used to, that I couldn't make Reeth enjoy it like I did, that she *can't*."

"My sympathy is all that it should be," Chmeee said, "considering that my nearest wife is two hundred light-years away. What must we do next?"

"Wait for the king giant. He may be a little groggy. He spent a lot of last night getting reacquainted with his wives. In fact, the only way he had to tell me how was by demonstration. He's awesome," Louis said. "He . . . serviced? He serviced a dozen women, and I tried like tanj to keep up with him, but it didn't help my ego that . . . Skip it." *Now* Louis was grinning.

"Louis?"

"My reproductive set isn't built to the same scale."

"The guard said that the females of other species stand in awe of the giant males. The males practice *rishathra* whenever they can. They enjoy peace conferences immensely. The guard was annoyed that Louis did not make you female."

"Louis was in a hurry," Wu said, and he went in.

Last night the gatherers' big bags had disgorged a great heap of cut grass some distance from the long-house. Guards and the king giant had eaten most of the pile; the gatherers must have been eating as they worked. Now Louis watched as the king giant, loping toward the lander, stopped to finish the pile off.

Herbivores spent too much of their lives eating, Louis mused. How had the humanoids kept their intelligence? Chmeee was right—you didn't need intelligence to sneak up on a blade of grass. Maybe it took intelligence to avoid being eaten. Or . . . it took considerable cunning to sneak up on a sunflower.

Louis felt himself being watched.

He turned. Nothing.

It would be embarrassing at best if the king giant learned he'd been duped. Yet Louis was all alone on the flight deck, if you ignored the Hindmost's spy-eyes. Why this tingling at the back of his neck? He turned again, and who was he kidding? It was the droud. The black plastic case was staring at him from the stepping disc.

A touch of the wire would really make him feel like a god. It would really louse up his act, too! He remembered that Chmeee had seen him under the wire. "Like a mindless marine plant . . ." He turned away.

The king giant came without armor today. As he and Chmeee entered the rec room the kzin raised his hands to the ceiling, palms together, and intoned, "Louis." The giant imitated him.

"Find me one of the repulser plates," Louis said without preamble. "Set it out on the floor. Good. Now get some of the superconductor cloth. It's three doors down, the big locker. Good. Wrap the cloth around the repulser plate. Cover it completely, but leave a fold so you can reach the settings. Chmeee, how strong is that cloth?"

"A moment, Louis . . . See, it cuts with a knife. I don't think I could rip it."

"Good. Now get me twenty miles of the superconducting wire. Wrap one end around the repulser plate. Tie it well; use a lot of loops. Be lavish. Good enough. Now coil the rest of the wire so it won't tangle when you let it out. I need the other end. Chmeee, you do that. King of the Grass Eaters, I need the biggest rock you can carry. You know this territory. Find it and bring it."

The king giant stared . . . and dropped his eyes and went. Chmeee said, "It sours my stomach to take your orders so meekly."

"But you thought of it, and besides that, you're dying to find out what I'm planning. But—"

"I could make you tell."

"I can make you a better offer than that. Come up here, please."

Chmeee bounded up through the hatch. Louis asked, "What do you see on the stepping disc?"

Chmeee picked up the droud.

Louis's voice was jagged in his throat. "Break it."

The kzin instantly stiff-armed the small instrument into a wall. It didn't dent. He pried at the casing, got it open, and jabbed at the inside with the hullmetal blade of the knife he'd been using. At last he said, "It's beyond repair."

"Good."

"I will wait below."

"No, I'll come with you. I want to check your work. And I want breakfast." He was feeling twitchy. He wasn't sure how he felt. *Rishathra* hadn't quite lived up to his expectations, and the pure joy of the wire was over forever. But . . . cheese fondue? Right. And freedom, and pride. In a couple of hours he was going to wipe out a sunflower invasion and shock tanj out of Chmeee. Louis Wu, ex-wirehead, whose brain hopefully had not turned to oatmeal after all.

The king giant came back hugging a boulder and moving very slowly. Chmeee started to take it from him, hesitated an instant as he saw its size, and finished the motion. He turned with it in his arms and, with strain just showing in his voice, said, "What must I do with it, Louis?"

It was tempting. *Oh, there are so many possibilities . . . Give me a minute to think it over . . .* But gods don't dither, and he couldn't let Chmeee drop it with the giant watching.

"Set it on superconductor cloth and wrap it up. Tie it with superconductor wire. Take a lot of turns around the rock, and be lavish with the knots, too. Okay, now I want some stronger wire that'll stand up to heat."

"We have Sinclair molecule chain."

"Less than twenty miles of that. I want it shorter than the superconductor wire." Louis was glad he'd made the inspection. He had overlooked the chance that the superconductor wire wouldn't be strong enough to hold the cloth-wrapped repulser plate, once the plate reached altitude. But Sinclair chain was fantastic stuff. It ought to hold.

CHAPTER 12

Sunflowers

Louis flew high and fast to spinward. The veldt showed too much brown: grass cropped first by green elephants and then by giants was having trouble growing back. Ahead, the white line of sunflowers glared across the sea.

The king giant watched through the transparent airlock doors. "It may be I should have brought armor," he said.

Chmeee snorted. "To fight sunflowers? Metal grows hot."

"Where," Louis asked, "did you get the armor?"

"We made a road for the Machine People. They made us free of the grasslands the road was to go through, and afterward they made armor for the kings of the tribes. We kept moving. We didn't like their air."

"What's wrong with it?"

"It tastes wrong and smells wrong, Louis. It smells like what they drink sometimes. They pour the same stuff in their machines, but without mixing it with anything."

Chmeee asked, "I wondered about the shape of your armor. It is not quite your own shape. I wondered why."

"The shape is meant to awe and frighten. Did you not find it so?"

"No," said Chmeee. "Is it the shape of those who built the Ringworld?"

"Who knows?"

"I do," Louis said. The giant's eyes flicked nervously upward.

The grass, grown tall again, abruptly gave way to

forest. The sunflowers had grown bright. Louis dropped the lander to a hundred feet and slowed drastically.

The forest ended in a long white beach. Louis slowed further and eased the lander down, down, until he was almost skimming the water. The sunflowers lost interest.

He flew on toward the diminished glare. The sea was calm, rippled by a breeze from astern. The sky was blue and cloudless. Islands went by, small and medium-sized, with beaches and convoluted shores and peaks charred black. Two had been commandeered by sunflowers.

Fifty miles offshore, the sunflowers were taking an interest again. Louis brought the lander to a halt. "They can't hope to use us for fertilizer," he said. "We're too far away and flying too low."

"Brainless plants." Chmeee coughed contempt.

The king giant said, "They are clever. They start brush fires. When only ashen ground is left, the fire plants spread their seed."

But they were over water! . . . Skip it. "King of the Grass Giants, this is your hour. Drop the rock overboard. Don't snag the wire." Louis opened the airlock and lowered the ramp. The king giant went forth into the ominous glare. The boulder fell twenty feet into the water, trailing black and silver wires.

Spotlights seemed to wink at them from the far shore as clusters of the plants tried to burn the lander, then lost interest. They sought motion, but they wouldn't fire on running water, would they? On a waterfall, say? The plants did best on half-arid worlds . . . "Chmeee. Take the repulser plate outside. Set it for, oh, eighteen miles. See that the wires don't foul."

The black rectangle rose. Wire trailed, black and silver. The thread of Sinclair chain should have been invisibly thin, but it glowed silver, and a bright nimbus glowed around the dwindling repulser plate. The plate was a black dot now, harder to see than the bright halo around it. At that altitude it was a target for hordes of sunflower blossoms.

A superconductor will pass an electric current with

no resistance whatever. It is this property that makes it so valuable to industry. But superconductors have another property. A superconductor is always the same temperature throughout.

Air and dust particles, and Sinclair wire, glowed by sunflower light. But the superconductor cloth and wire remained black. Good. Louis blinked away the dazzle and looked down at the water. "King of the Grass People," he said, "come inside before you're hurt."

Where the two wires entered the water, the water boiled. A streamer of steam blew into the white glare to spinward. Louis set the lander drifting to starboard. Already a fair patch of water was steaming.

The Ringworld engineers had built only two deep oceans, the Great Oceans, counterbalanced opposite each other. The rest of the Ringworld's seas were twenty-five feet deep throughout. Like humans, they apparently used only the top of a sea. That was to Louis's advantage. It was making it easier to boil a sea.

The steam cloud reached for shore.

Gods don't gloat. That was a pity. "We will watch until you are satisfied," he told the king giant.

"Uurrr," said Chmeee.

"I begin to see," the king giant said, "but . . ."

"Speak."

"The fire plants burn away clouds."

Louis swallowed uneasiness. "We will watch. Chmeee, you may offer our guest lettuce. It may be that you will want to eat with a door between you."

They were fifty miles to starboard of the anchored wire, on the port side of a tall, bare island. The island blocked half the glare of those sunflowers still interested in cremating the lander . . . but most of the sunflowers were distracted anyway. Some of the glare focused on the hovering black rectangle; some, on the steam cloud.

For the water was steaming for a couple of square

miles around the wire and submerged boulder. The steam ran in a spreading cloud across the sea, fifty miles to shore, and there it caught fire. Five miles inland it ran, burning like a firestorm, and then it was gone.

Louis focused the telescope on the patch of steam. He could see water boiling. Plants would be starting to die. A five-mile strip of plants was getting no sunlight; plants around them were wasting their light on a steam cloud instead of making sugar with it. But a five-mile strip was nothing, nothing. The patch was half the size of a world.

He saw something else that made him swing the view straight upward.

The silver wire was falling, drifting to spinward in the wind. The sunflowers had burned through Sinclair molecule chain. Louis softly spoke a one-syllable word meaning impotence. But the thread of superconductor was still black.

It would hold. Sure it would.

It would be no hotter than boiling water, and everywhere the same temperature. More light from the plants wouldn't change that; it would only boil the water faster. And this was a big sea. And water vapor doesn't just vanish. Heat it and it rises.

"God eats well," the king giant said. He was munching on a head of Boston butter lettuce: his twentieth or maybe thirtieth. He stood beside Chmeee, watching, and like Chmeee he did not speculate on what was happening outside.

Sea water boiled merrily. The sunflowers were sure as tanj determined to knock down that bit of potential fertilizer, that possible sunflower-eating bird. They couldn't judge altitude or distance. Evolution wouldn't let them keep that up until they starved. Time off for each blossom to focus on the green photosynthetic node, while others took turns.

Quietly Chmeee said, "Louis. The island."

Something large and black stood waist-deep in the

water offshore. It was not human and not otter, but a little of both. It waited patiently, watching the lander with large brown eyes.

Louis spoke calmly, but with effort. "Is this sea peopled?"

"We did not know it," said the king giant.

Louis slid the lander toward the beach. The humanoid waited without fear. He was covered with short, oily black fur, and nicely streamlined: thick neck, drastically sloping shoulders, a broad nose flattened against his chinless face.

Louis activated the microphones. "Do you use the speech of the Grass Giants?"

"I can use it. Talk slowly. What are you doing there?"

Louis sighed. "Heating the sea."

The creature's self-possession was remarkable. The idea of heating a sea didn't faze him. He asked the mobile building, "How hot?"

"Very hot at this end. How many are you?"

"Thirty-four of us now," said the amphibian. "We were eighteen when we came here fifty-one *falans* past. Will the starboard part of the sea grow hot?"

Louis sagged with relief. He'd had visions of hundreds of thousands of people cooked because Louis Wu had played god. He croaked, "You tell me. The river inlet's at that end. How much warmth can you stand?"

"Some. We will eat better; fish like warmth. It is polite to ask before you destroy even part of a home. Why are you doing this?"

"To kill off the fire plants."

The amphibian considered. "Good. If the fire plants die, we can send a messenger upstream to Fuboobish's Son's Sea. They must think us long dead." He added, "I forget my manners. *Rishathra* is acceptable to us if you will state your sex, and if you can function underwater."

Louis needed a moment to regain his voice. "None of us mate in water."

"Few do," said the amphibian, with no obvious disappointment.

"How did you come here?"

"We were exploring downstream. Rapids carried us into the realm of the fire plants. We could not go ashore, to walk. We must let the river carry us to this place, which I named Tuppugop's Sea, for myself. It is a good place, though one must be wary of the fire plants. Can you really kill them with fog?"

"I think so."

"I must move my people," the amphibian said. He disappeared without a splash.

"I thought you would kill him," Chmeee told the ceiling, "for his impudence."

"It's his home," said Louis. He turned off the intercom. He was weary of the game. I'm boiling someone's *home*, he thought, and I don't even know it'll *work*! He wanted the droud. Nothing else could help, nothing but the vegetable happiness of current running in his brain; nothing else would stop the black rage that had him pounding the arms of his chair and making animal noises with his eyes squeezed tightly shut.

That, and time. Time passed, and the spell passed, and he opened his eyes.

Now he could see neither the black wire nor the boiling of the water. It was all a vast fog bank drifting to spinward, catching fire as it reached shore, ten miles inward and gone. Then only the flare of sunflowers . . . and a pair of parallel lines at the horizon.

White line above, black below, across fifty degrees of horizon.

Water vapor doesn't just disappear. Heated, it had gone up, and recondensed in the stratosphere. White edge of cloud, blazing under sunflower attack; black shadow across a tremendous patch of sunflowers. It must be five hundred to a thousand miles away, to be seen so near to its own shadow, and hundreds of miles across. And it was spreading—excruciatingly slowly, but it was spreading.

In the stratosphere the air would be forced *outward* from the center of the sunflower patch. Some of the cloud would rain out, but some water vapor would meet the steam from the boiling sea and flow inward, recirculating.

His arms hurt. Louis realized that he had a death grip on the chair arms. He let go. He turned on the intercom.

"Louis has kept his promise," the king giant was saying, "but the dying plants may be out of our reach. I don't know—"

"We'll spend the night here," Louis told them. "In the morning we'll know better."

He set the lander on the antispinward side of the island. Seaweed had washed ashore in great heaps. Chmeee and the king giant spent an hour stuffing seaweed into a hatch in the lander's hull, feeding the converter-kitchen with raw material. Louis took the opportunity to call *Hot Needle of Inquiry*.

The Hindmost was not on the flight deck. He must be in the hidden part of *Needle*. "You have broken your droud," he said.

"I know it. Have you done anything—"

"I have a replacement."

"I don't care if you've got a dozen. I quit. Do you still want the Ringworld engineers' transmuter?"

"Of course."

"Then let's cooperate a little. The Ringworld control center has to be somewhere. *If* it's been built into one of the spill mountains, then the transmuters that came off the ships on the spaceport ledge *have* to be there. I want to know everything about the situation before I go into it."

The Hindmost thought it through.

Behind his flat weaving hands, massive buildings glowed with light. A wide street, with stepping discs at intersections, dwindled to a vanishing point. The street swarmed with puppeteers. Their coiffeured manes glowed in glorious variety; they seemed always to move in groups. In a sliver of sky between buildings, two farming worlds hovered, each surrounded by orbiting points of light. There was a background sound like alien music, or like a million puppeteers holding conversations too far away to be heard clearly.

The Hindmost had a piece of his lost civilization here: tapes and a holo wall and, probably, the smell of his own kind constantly in the air. His furniture was all soft curves, with no sharp corners to bump a knee on. An oddly shaped indentation in the floor was probably a bed..

"The back of the rim wall is quite flat," the Hindmost said abruptly. "My deep-radar won't penetrate it. I can afford to risk one of my probes. It will still serve as a relay between *Needle* and the lander; in fact, it will serve better as it rises higher. Accordingly I will place a probe in the rim wall transport system."

"Good enough."

"Do you really think the repair center is—"

"No, not really, but we'll find enough surprises to keep us entertained. It should be checked out."

"One day we must decide who rules this expedition," the puppeteer said. He disappeared from the screen.

There were no stars that night.

Morning was a brightening of chaos. From the flight deck nothing showed but a formless pearly glow: no sky, no sea, no beach. Louis was tempted to re-create Wu, just to step out and see if the world was still there.

Instead he took the lander up. There was sunlight at three hundred feet. Below was nothing but white cloud, growing brighter at the spinward horizon. The fog had spread a long way inland.

The repulser plate was still in place, a black dot just overhead.

Two hours after dawn, a wind swept the fog away. Louis dropped the lander to sea level before the edge reached shore. Minutes later a bright nimbus formed around the repulser plate.

The king giant had been at the airlock doors all morning, watching, absently stuffing his face with lettuce. Chmeee too had been almost silent. They turned toward the ceiling when Louis spoke.

"It will work," he said, and finally he believed it. "Soon you will find an alley of dead sunflowers leading to a much bigger patch of them under a permanent cloud deck. Sow your seeds. If you'd rather eat live fire plants, forage at night on both sides of the streamer of fog. You may want a base on some island in this sea. You'll want boats."

"We can make our own plans now," the king giant said. "It will help to have Sea People near, even so few. They trade service for metal tools. They can build our boats. Will grass grow in all this rain?"

"I don't know. You'd better seed the burned-off islands too."

"Good . . . For our special heroes we carve their likeness on a rock, with a few words. We are migratory; we can't carry large statues with us. Is this adequate?"

"Certainly."

"What is your likeness?"

"I'm a little bigger than Chmeee, with more hair around the shoulders, and the hair is your own color. Carnivore teeth, with fangs. No external ears. Don't go to too much trouble. Where shall we take you now?"

"To our camp. Then I think I must take a few women and scout the edges of the sea."

"We can do that now."

The king giant laughed. "Our thanks, Louis, but my warriors will be in an ugly mood when they return. Naked, hungry, defeated. It may go better for them when they learn that I am gone for a few days. I am no god. A hero must have warriors happy with his rule. He cannot be fighting every waking hour."

PART TWO

CHAPTER 13

Origins

The lander cruised five miles up at just under sonic speed.

Thirteen thousand miles was no great distance for the lander. Louis's caution irked the kzin. "Two hours and we can be dropping onto the floating city, or rising from underneath! One hour, without serious discomfort!"

"Sure. We'd have to go out of the atmosphere with the fusion drive blazing like a star, but sure. Remember how we reached Halrloprillalar's floating jail? Upside down in midair, with the motors burned out of our flycycles?"

Chmeee's tail thumped the back of his chair. He remembered.

"We don't want to be noticed by any old machinery. The superconductor plague doesn't seem to have got it all."

Grassland gave way to patterns of cultivation, then to a watery jungle. Vertical sunlight reflected back at them from between the trunks of flowering trees.

Louis was feeling wonderful. He wouldn't let himself see the futility of his war on the sunflower patch. It had *worked*. He had set himself a task; he had accomplished it with intelligence and the tools at hand.

The swamp seemed to go on forever. Once Chmeee pointed out a small city. It was difficult to see, with water half drowning the buildings, and vines and trees trying to pull them down. The architectural style was strange. Every wall and roof and door bulged outward

119

a little, leaving the streets narrow in the center. *Not* built by Halrloprillalar's people.

By midday the lander had traveled further than Ginjerofer or the king giant would travel in their lifetimes. Louis had been foolish to question savages. They were as far from the floating city as any two points on Earth.

The Hindmost called.

Today his mane was a swirling rainbow, dyed in streamers of primary colors. Behind him puppeteers flickered along lines of stepping discs, clustered at shop windows, brushed against each other without apology or resentment, all in a murmur of music with flutes and clarinets predominating: puppeteer language. The Hindmost asked, "What have you learned?"

"Little," said Chmeee. "We have wasted time. There was certainly a great solar flare seventeen *falans* ago— about three and a half years—but we guessed that much. The shadow squares closed to protect the surface. Their guidance system must operate independently of the Ringworld's."

"We could guess that too. No more?"

"Louis's hypothetical Repair Center is certainly inactive. This swamp below us was not designed. I imagine a major river silted up to block the outflow of a sea. We find a variety of hominids, some intelligent, some not. Of those who built the Ringworld we find no trace, unless they were Halrloprillalar's ancestors. I am inclined to think they were."

Louis opened his mouth . . . and glanced down at a threshold pain in his leg. He found four kzinti claws just resting on his thigh. He shut his mouth. Chmeee continued, "We have not met any of Halrloprillalar's species. Perhaps they were never a dense population. We hear rumors of another race, the Machine People, who may rise to replace them. We go to seek them."

"The Repair Center is inactive, yes," the Hindmost said briskly. "I have learned much. I have put a probe to work—"

"You have two probes," Chmeee said. "Use both."

"I hold one in reserve, to refuel *Needle*. With the

other I have learned the secret of the spill mountains. See—"

The far right screen showed a probe's-eye view. It raced along the rim wall; passed something, too quick for detail; slowed, turned, moved back.

"Louis advised me to explore the rim wall. The probe had barely started its deceleration routine when it found this. I thought it worth investigating."

There was a swelling on the rim wall—a tube hooked over the lip. It was molded, flattened against the rim wall, and was made of the same translucent gray *scrith*. The probe eased toward it until the camera was looking up into a pipe a quarter-mile across.

"Much of the Ringworld's design shows a brute-force approach," the Hindmost was saying. And the probe moved alongside the pipe, over the lip, and down the outer face of the rim wall to where the pipe disappeared into the foamed material that formed a meteor shield for the Ringworld's underside.

"I see," Louis said. "And it wasn't working?"

"No. I tried to trace the pipe and had some success."

The scene jumped. Now it showed dark racing motion as the probe cruised a good distance outward from the Ringworld. Inverted landscape passed above, seen by infrared light. The probe slowed, stopped, moved upward.

If a meteor struck the Ringworld, it had to fall first from interstellar space; and it struck with that velocity plus the Ringworld's own seven hundred and seventy miles per second. A meteor had struck here. The plasma cloud had drawn a savage gouge across hundreds of miles of sea bottom, vaporizing the protective foam. There in the gouge was a length of pipe a few hundred feet in diameter. It led up into the sea bottom.

"A recycling system," Louis murmured.

The puppeteer said, "Without some counterbalance to erosion, the Ringworld's topsoil would all be in the sea bottoms in a few thousand years. I expect the pipes run from the sea bottoms along the underside and up over the rim wall. They deposit sea-bottom sludge on

the spill mountains. Much of the water would boil away
in the near vacuum at the peak, thirty miles high. The
mountain gradually collapses under its own weight.
Material moves from the rim walls inward, carried by
winds and rivers."

Chmeee said, "Mere supposition, but plausible. Hindmost, where is your probe now?"

"I intend to bring it out from under the Ringworld
and reinsert it into the rim transport system."

"Do that. Does the probe have deep-radar?"

"Yes, but the range is short."

"Deep-radar the spill mountains. The spill mountains
are . . . perhaps twenty to thirty thousand miles apart?
Thus we may find on the order of fifty thousand spill
mountains along both rim walls. A handful of those
would make a fine hiding place for the Repair Center."

"But why should the Repair Center be hidden?"

Chmeee made a rude noise. "What if the subject
races should revolt? What of an invasion? Of course the
Repair Center is hidden, and fortified too. Search every
spill mountain."

"Very well. I will scan the starboard rim wall in one
Ringworld rotation."

"Scan the other rim afterward."

Louis said, "Keep the cameras going too. We're still
looking for attitude jets . . . though I'm starting to think
they had something else going."

The Hindmost clicked off. Louis turned to the window. It had been tickling at his attention all along: a
pale thread that curved along the edge of the swamp,
straighter than a river. Now he pointed out the barely
visible pair of dots moving along its length. "I think we
need a closer look at that. Why don't you take us
down?"

It was a road. From a hundred feet up it was rough-
surfaced, stony stuff: white stone poured in a stream.
Louis said, "The Machine People, I presume. Shall we
track those vehicles?"

"Let us wait until we are closer to the floating city."

Giving up a present opportunity seemed silly, but Louis was afraid to object. The kzin's tension was thick enough to smell.

The road avoided the low, wet areas. It seemed in good repair. Chmeee followed it at low speed, a hundred feet up.

Once they passed a handful of buildings, the biggest of which seemed to be a chemical plant. Several times they watched boxy vehicles pass below them. They were seen only once. A box stopped suddenly, and humanoid shapes spilled out, ran in circles, then produced sticks which they pointed at the lander. A moment later they were out of sight.

There were great pale shapes in the wet jungle. They couldn't be glacier-scoured boulders; not here. Louis wondered if they might be tremendous fungi. He stopped wondering when he saw one move. He tried to point it out to Chmeee. The kzin ignored him.

The road curved away to antispinward as it approached a range of craggy mountains; it jogged through a notch in the range, rather than carving its own path, then jogged right to run alongside the swamp again.

But Chmeee swerved left and accelerated. The lander streaked along the portward side of the range, trailing a plume of fire. Abruptly the kzin spun the lander around, braked, and set down at the foot of a granite cliff.

He said, "Let us step outside."

The *scrith* shell of the mountain would block the Hindmost's microphones, but they'd feel still safer outside the lander. Louis followed the kzin.

The day was bright and sunny—too bright, as this arc of the Ringworld approached its nearest point to the sun. A stiff warm wind was blowing. The kzin asked, "Louis, were you about to tell the Hindmost of the Ringworld engineers?"

"Probably. Why not?"

"I assume we've come to the same conclusion."

"Doubtful. What would a kzin know of Pak protectors?"

"I know everything in the records of the Smithsonian Institute, what little there is. I have studied the testimony of the asteroid belt miner, Jack Brennan, and holos of the mummified remains of the alien Phssthpok and of the cargo pod from his ship."

"Chmeee, how did you get hold of that stuff?"

"Does it matter? I was a diplomat, The existence of the Pak has been a Patriarch's Secret for generations, but any kzin who must deal with humans is required to study the records. We learn to know our enemy. I may know more of your ancestry than you do. And I surmise that the Ringworld was built by Pak."

Six hundred years before Louis Wu's birth, a Pak protector arrived in Sol system on a mission of mercy. It was through this Phssthpok, via the Belter Jack Brennan, that historians learned the rest of the story.

The Pak were native to a world in the galactic core. They lived their lives in three stages: child, breeder, protector. The adults or breeders were just intelligent enough to swing a club or throw a stone.

In middle age, if they lived long enough, Pak breeders developed a compulsion to gorge on the plant called tree-of-life. A symbiotic virus in the plant triggered the change. The breeder lost its gonads and teeth. Its skull and brain expanded. Lips and gums fused into a hard, blunt beak. Its skin wrinkled and thickened and hardened. Its joints became enlarged, offering a larger moment arm to the muscles, increasing their strength. A two-chambered heart developed in the groin.

Phssthpok came tracking a Pak colony ship that had reached Earth more than two million years earlier.

The Pak were in a constant state of war. Previous colonies to nearby worlds in the galactic core had always been overrun by subsequent waves of ships. Perhaps that was the reason this ship had come so far.

The colony was large and well-equipped, and guided by beings tougher and smarter than humans. It had failed nonetheless. Tree-of-life grew in Earth's soil, but the virus didn't. The protectors had died out, leaving a

lost population of Pak breeders to fend for themselves
. . . and leaving records of a cry for help that had
crossed thirty thousand light-years to the Pak home
world.

Phssthpok found those records in an ancient Pak
library. And Phssthpok crossed thirty thousand light-
years, all alone in a slower-than-light craft, seeking Sol
system. The resources that built that craft, in knowledge and minds and materials, were resources Phssthpok
had conquered and held by war. His cargo pod was
jammed with tree-of-life roots and seeds, and bags of
thallium oxide. His own research had discovered the
need for that unusual soil additive.

It might have occurred to him that the breeders
would mutate.

Among the Pak a mutant stood no chance. If the
children smelled wrong to their protector forefathers,
they were killed. On Earth—perhaps Phssthpok
counted on a lower mutation rate, this far from the
savage cosmic-ray density among the core suns. Perhaps he took his chances.

The breeders had mutated. By Phssthpok's time they
showed little resemblance to the Pak breeder—barring
certain changes at middle age, when the production of
eggs stopped in females, and when both sexes showed
wrinkling of skin, lost teeth, swelling of joints, and a
restlessness and dissatisfaction that was all that remained of the hunger for tree-of-life. Later in life, heart
attacks would result from the lack of the second heart.

Phssthpok learned none of this. The rescuer died
almost painlessly, with no more than a suspicion that
those he intended to rescue had become monsters, and
had no need of him at all.

Such was the tale that Jack Brennan told to United
Nations representatives before his disappearance. But
Phssthpok was dead by then, and Jack Brennan's testimony was doubtful. He had eaten tree-of-life. He had
become a monster; his braincase in particular was expanded and distorted. Perhaps he had become mad too.

* * *

It was as if a load of spinach noodles had been spilled all over this rocky area. Strips of greenery, fuzzy to the touch, hugged the ground in places where dirt had packed itself between the boulders. Clouds of insects buzzed around their ankles, staying within inches of the ground.

"Pak protectors," said Louis. "That's what I thought, but I've been having trouble making myself believe it."

Chmeee said, "The vacuum suits and the Grass Giant's armor show their shape: humanoid, but with enlarged joints and a face pushed forward. There is more proof. We've met so many hominids, all different. They had to be derived from a common ancestor: your own ancestor, the Pak breeder."

"Sure. It'd also tell us how Prill died."

"Does it?"

"Boosterspice was tailored for the metabolism of *Homo sapiens.* Halrloprillalar couldn't use it. She had her own longevity drug, and it could be used by a number of species. It struck me that Prill's people might have made it from tree-of-life."

"Why?"

"Well, the protectors lived thousands of years. Some factor of tree-of-life, or a subcritical dose of it, might trigger just enough of the change to do that for a hominid. And the Hindmost says Prill's supply was stolen."

Chmeee was nodding. "I remember. One of your asteroid mining craft boarded the abandoned Pak spacecraft. The oldest man in the crew smelled tree-of-life and went mad. He ate beyond the capacity of his belly, and died. His crewmates could not restrain him."

"Yah. Now, is it too much to expect that the same thing happened to some UN lab assistant? Prill walks into the UN building carrying a flask of Ringworld longevity drug. The UN wants a sample. A kid barely too young for his first dose of boosterspice—forty, forty-five—opens the flask. He's got the eyedropper all ready. Then he gets a whiff. He drinks it all."

Chmeee's tail lashed air. "I would not go so far as to say that I liked Halrloprillalar. Still, she was an ally."

"I liked her."

The hot wind blew around them, filled with dust. Louis felt harried. They wouldn't get another chance to talk in privacy. The probe that relayed signals to and from *Needle* would soon be too high up the Arch for this kind of trick to work.

"Can you think like a Pak for me, Chmeee?"

"I can try."

"They put maps all over the Great Oceans. Instead of mapping Kzin and Down and Mars and Jinx, can you tell me why Pak protectors wouldn't just exterminate the kzinti and Grogs and martians and bandersnatchi?"

"Uurrr. Why not? The Pak would not flinch at exterminating alien species, according to Brennan."

Chmeee paced as he mulled the problem. He said, "Perhaps they expected to be followed. What if they lost a war; what if they expected the winners to come hunting them? To the Pak, a dozen burnt-out worlds within a dozen light-years of one another might indicate the presence of Pak."

"Mmm . . . maybe. Now tell me why they'd build a Ringworld in the first place. How the futz did they expect to defend it?"

"I would not attempt to defend a structure so vulnerable. Perhaps we will learn. I have also wondered why Pak would come to this region of space in the first place. Coincidence?"

"No! Too far."

"Well?"

"Oh . . . we can guess. Suppose a lot of Pak wanted to run as fast and as far as they could. Again, say they lost a war. Got kicked off the Pak world. Well, there was one safe route out into the galactic arms, and it was mapped. The first expedition, the one that settled Earth, got to Sol system without running into any danger they couldn't handle. They sent back directions. So the losers followed them. Then they set up shop a good safe distance from Sol system."

Chmeee mulled that. Presently he said, "However they came here, the Pak were intelligent and warlike xenophobes. That has implications. The weapon that vaporized half of *Liar*, the weapon you and Teela persisted in calling a meteor defense, was almost certainly programmed to fire on invading ships. It will fire on *Hot Needle of Inquiry* or the lander, given the chance. My second point is that the Hindmost must not learn who built the Ringworld."

Louis shook his head. "They must be long gone. According to Brennan, a protector's only motivation is to protect his descendants. They wouldn't have let mutations develop. They'd never have let the Ringworld start sliding into the sun."

"Louis—"

"In fact they must have been gone hundreds of thousands of years. Look at the variety of hominids we've found."

"I would say millions of years. They must have departed soon after the first ship called for help, and died soon after completing the structure. How else would all of these varieties have had time to develop? But—"

"Chmeee, look: suppose they finished the Ringworld a mere half million years ago. Give the breeders a quarter of a million years to spread out, with the protectors fighting no wars because the territory's virtually unlimited. Then let the protectors die off."

"From what?"

"Insufficient data."

"Accepted. Well?"

"Let the protectors die off a quarter of a million years ago. Give the breeders a tenth the time it took humans to evolve on Earth. A tenth of the time, and a lot of nice gaps in the ecology because the protectors didn't bring anything to prey on the breeders, and a base population in the *trillions*.

"See? On Earth there were maybe half a million breeders when the protectors died out. On the Ringworld, three million times the room, and plenty of time to spread out before the protectors died. The mutants would have it all their own way."

"I don't accept that you're right," Chmeee said quietly. "I do feel that you've missed a point. Granted that the protectors are almost certainly gone. Almost certainly. What if the Hindmost learns that this was their property, their home?"

"Oops. He'd run. With or without us."

"Officially we have not penetrated the secret of the Ringworld's construction. Agreed?"

"Yah."

"Are we still looking for the Repair Center? The smell of tree-of-life might be deadly to you. You are too old to become a protector."

"I wouldn't want to. Is there a spectroscope in the lander?"

"Yes."

"Tree-of-life doesn't grow right without a soil additive: thallium oxide. Thallium must be more common in the galactic core than it is out here. Wherever the protectors spent a lot of their time, we'll find thallium oxide for the plants. That's how we'll find the repair center. We'll go in in pressure suits, if we ever get that far."

CHAPTER 14

The Scent of Death

The Hindmost's voice exploded at them as they reached the road. " . . . LANDER! CHMEEE, LOUIS, WHAT ARE YOU HIDING? HINDMOST CALLING THE LAND—"

"Stop! Tanj dammit, turn down the volume, you'll blow our ears out!"

"Can you still hear me?"

"We can hear you fine," said Louis. Chmeee's ears had folded into pockets of fur. Louis was wishing he could do that. "The mountains must have blocked us."

"And what was it you discussed while we were cut off?"

"Mutiny. We decided against it."

A momentary pause; then "Very wise," said the Hindmost. "I want your interpretation of this hologram."

One of the screens showed a kind of bracket poking out from the rim wall. The picture was slightly blurred, and oddly lit: taken in vacuum, in sunlight and light reflected from the Ringworld landscape on the right. The bracket seemed to be of a piece with the rim wall itself, as if *scrith* had been stretched like taffy. The bracket held a pair of washers or doughnuts separated by their own diameter. Nothing else showed save the top of the rim wall. It was impossible to guess the scale.

"This was taken from the probe," the puppeteer said. "I have inserted the probe into the rim transport system, as advised. It is accelerating to antispinward."

"Yah. What do you think, Chmeee?"

"It might be a Ringworld attitude jet. It would not be firing yet."

"Maybe. There are a lot of ways to design a Bussard ramjet. Hindmost, do you get anything in the way of magnetic effects?"

"No, Louis, the machine seems dormant."

"The superconductor plague wouldn't have touched it in vacuum. It doesn't *look* damaged. The controls could be somewhere else, though. On the surface. Maybe they can be repaired."

"You would have to find them first. In the Repair Center?"

"Yah."

The road ran between swampland and stony highlands. They passed what looked like another chemical plant. They must have been seen; there was a deep-throated foghorn sound and a blast of steam from what might have been a chimney. Chmeee didn't slow down.

They saw no more of the boxy vehicles.

Louis had seen pale glimmers passing slowly among the trees, far into the swamp. They moved as slowly as mist on water, or as ocean liners docking. Now, far ahead, a white shape moved free of the trees and toward the road.

From a vast white bulk the beast's sense-cluster rose on a slender neck. Its jaw was at ground level; it dropped like a shovel blade, scooping up swamp water and vegetation as the beast cruised uphill on rippling belly muscles. It was bigger than the biggest dinosaur.

"Bandersnatch," Louis said. What *were* they doing here? Bandersnatchi were native to Jinx. "Slow down, Chmeee, it wants to talk to us."

"What of it?"

"They've got long memories."

"What would they remember? Swamp dwellers, muck-eaters, without hands to make weapons. No."

"Why not? Maybe they could tell us what bander-snatchi are doing on the Ringworld in the first place."

"That is no mystery. The protectors must have

stocked their maps in the Great Ocean with samples of
the species they considered potentially dangerous."

Chmeee was playing dominance games, and Louis
didn't like it. "What's the matter with you? We could at
least ask!"

The bandersnatch dwindled behind them. Chmeee
snarled, "You avoid confrontation like a Pierson's
puppeteer. Questioning muck-eaters and savages! Killing sunflowers! The Hindmost brought us to this doomed
structure against our wills, and you delay our vengeance to kill sunflowers. Will it matter to the Ringworld natives a year from now that Louis the God
paused in his passing to pull weeds?"

"I'd save them if I could."

"We can do nothing. It is the road builders we want.
Too primitive to threaten us, advanced enough to know
answers to questions. We will find an isolated vehicle
and swoop down on it."

In midafternoon Louis took over the flying.

The swamp became a river that arched away to spinward, wide of its original bed. The crude road followed
the new river. The original bed ran more nearly to port,
in careful S-curves, with an occasional stretch of rapids
or waterfall. It was dry as bone, running into bone-dry
desert. The swamp must have been a sea before it silted
up.

Louis dithered, then followed the original bed.

"I think we've got the timing right," he told Chmeee.
"Prill's people evolved long after the engineers were
gone. Of all the intelligent races here, they were the
most ambitious. They built the big, grand cities. Then
that odd plague knocked out most of their machinery.
Now we've got the Machine People, and they *could* be
the same species. The Machine People built the road.
They did it after the swamp formed. But I think the
swamp formed after Prill's people's empire collapsed.

"So what I'm doing is looking for an old Prill People
city. We could get lucky and find an old library or a
map room."

They had found cities scarce during the first expedition. Today they traveled for some hours without seeing anything except, twice, a cluster of tents, and once, a sandstorm the size of a continent.

The floating city was still ahead of them, edge on, hiding detail. A score of towers reared around the edge; inverted towers dropped from nearer the center.

The dry river ended in a dry sea. Louis cruised along the shore, twenty miles up. The sea bed was strange. It was quite flat, except where artfully spaced islands with fluted edges rose from the bottom.

Chmeee called, "Louis! Set us on autopilot!"

"What have you found?"

"A dredge."

Louis joined Chmeee at the telescope.

He had taken it for part of one of the bigger islands. It was huge and flat, disc-shaped, the color of sea-bottom mud. Its top would have been below sea level. Its seamless rim was angled like the blade of a wood planer. The machine had stalled up against the island it had dredged from the sea bottom.

So this was how the Ringworld engineers had kept the sludge flowing into the spillpipes. It wouldn't flow of itself; the sea bottoms were too shallow. "The pipe blocked," Louis speculated. "The dredge kept going till it broke down, or till something cut the power—something like the superconductor plague. Shall I call the Hindmost?"

"Yes. Keep him satisfied . . ."

But the Hindmost had bigger news.

"Observe," he said. He ran a quick succession of holograms on one of the screens. A bracket poked up and out from the rim wall, with a pair of toroids mounted at its tip. Another bracket, seen from farther away; and in this picture a spill mountain showed at the foot of the rim wall. The spill mountain was half the size of the bracket. A third bracket showed. A fourth, with structures next to it. A fifth— "Hold it!" Louis cried. "Go back!"

The fifth bracket stayed on the screen for a moment.

Its tip held nothing at all. Then the Hindmost flipped back to the fourth hologram.

It was somewhat blurred by the probe's velocity. There was heavy lifting machinery anchored to the rim wall next to the bracket: a crude fusion generator; a powered winch; a drum and a hook floating unsupported below it. The cable depending from the drum must be invisibly thin, Louis thought. It could be shadow square wire.

"A repair team already at work? Uurrr. Are they mounting attitude jets or dismounting them? How many are mounted?"

"The probe will tell us," the Hindmost said. "I direct your attention to another problem. Recall to your mind those toroids that circle the waist of the one intact Ringworld spacecraft. We surmise that they generate the electromagnetic scoop fields for Bussard ramjets."

Chmeee studied the screen. "The Ringworld ships were all of the same design. I wondered why. You may be right."

Louis said, "I don't understand. What has—"

Two one-eyed snakes looked out of a screen at him. "Halrloprillalar's species built part of a transportation system that would give them endless room to colonize and explore. Why didn't they continue? All of the Ringworld was theirs through the rim transport system. Why would they make the effort to reach the stars?"

It made an ugly pattern. Louis didn't want to believe it, but it fit too well. "They got the motors for free. They dismounted a few of the Ringworld attitude jets, built ships around them, and reached the stars. And nothing went obviously wrong. So they dismounted a few more. I wonder how many they used."

"The probe will tell us in time," the puppeteer said. "They seem to have left a few motors still mounted. Why did they not move the Ringworld back into position before the instability grew so great? Chmeee's question is a good one. Are motors being remounted, or stolen to be used in ships so that a few more of Halrloprillalar's race may escape?"

Louis's laugh was bitter. "How does this sound? They left a few jets in place. Then came a plague that killed off most of their machinery. Some of them panicked. They took all the ships they had, and they built more ships in a hurry and dismounted most of the attitude jets to do it. They're still at it. They're leaving the Ringworld to its fate."

Chmeee said, "Fools. They did it to themselves."

"Did they? I wonder."

"But this is just the possibility I find ominous," said the puppeteer. "Would they not have taken as much of their civilization as they could move? Certainly they would have taken transmutation machinery."

Oddly, Louis was not even tempted to laugh. But what answer could he make?

The kzin found an answer. "They would take all they could reach. Anything near the spaceport ledges. Anything near the rim wall, where the rim transport system was available. We must search inward, and we must search out the Repair Center. Any of Prill's people found there would have been trying to save the Ringworld, not leave it."

"Perhaps."

Louis said, "It would help if we knew just when the plague started eating their superconductors."

If he thought the Hindmost would flinch, he was wrong. The puppeteer said, "You will likely learn that before I do."

"I think you know already."

"Call me if you learn anything." The snaky heads disappeared.

Chmeee was looking at him strangely, but he said nothing. Louis returned to the flight controls.

The terminator line was a vast shadow encroaching from spinward when Chmeee spotted the city. They had followed a sand-filled riverbed to port of the dry sea. The river forked here, and the city nestled in the fork.

Prill's people had built tall even where there was no obvious need. The city had not been wide, but it had been tall, until floating buildings smashed down into the lesser structures below. One slender tower still stood, but at a slant. It had driven itself like a spear into the lower levels. A road ran from port, along the outer edge of one branch of the dry river, then across a bridge so massively braced that it had to belong to the Machine People. Halrloprillalar's people would have used stronger materials or would have floated it.

Chmeee said, "The city will have been looted."

"Well, yes, given that someone built a road to do the looting. Why don't you take us down anyway?"

"Your monkey curiosity?"

"Maybe. Just circle the tanj thing, give us a closer look."

Chmeee dropped the lander fast enough to put them in free fall. The kzin's fur was almost all grown out, a glossy and handsome orange coat, and a reminder of Chmeee's new youth. Adolescence wasn't helping his temper. Four Man-Kzin wars, plus a few "incidents" . . . Louis kept his mouth shut.

The lander surged under them. Louis waited until the savage weight left him, then began adjusting the views through the outside cameras. He saw it almost instantly.

A boxlike vehicle was parked beside the tilted tower. It could have held up to a dozen passengers. The motor housing at its rear should have been enough to lift a spacecraft . . . but this was a primitive people. He couldn't guess what they'd be using to move the vehicle. He pointed and said, "We find an isolated vehicle and swoop down on it, right?"

"Right." Chmeee let the lander settle. As he did, Louis studied the situation:

The tower had speared down into a squarish building; had smashed through the roof and three stories and possibly into a basement. It was the shell of the lesser building that held it upright. White puffs of steam or smoke jetted irregularly from two tower windows. Pale human shapes were dancing before the lower building's big front entrance—dancing, or holding sprinting contests—and two were resting prone, though in unrestful positions . . .

Just before the single remaining wall of a collapsed building rose to block Louis's view, it all jumped into his mind's focus. The pale ones were trying to reach the entrance across a rubble-covered street. Someone in the tower was shooting at them.

The lander settled. Chmeee stood and stretched. "You seem to have your own luck, Louis. We can take the ones with the guns to be the Machine People. Our strategy will be to come to their aid."

It seemed reasonable. "Do you know anything about projectile weapons?"

"If we assume chemical propellants, a portable weapon will not penetrate impact armor. We can enter the tower via flying belts. Carry stunners. We would not want to kill our future allies."

They emerged into full night. Clouds had closed over the sky. Even so, Archlight glowed through in a faint broad band, and the floating city was a tight star-cluster to port. You couldn't get lost.

Louis Wu was not comfortable. The impact armor was too stiff; the hood covered most of his face. The padded straps of the flying belt constricted his breathing, and his feet dangled. But nothing was ever again going to feel like an hour under the wire, and that was that. At least he felt relatively safe.

He hung in the sky and used light-amplified binocular goggles.

The attackers didn't seem that formidable. They were quite naked and weaponless. Their hair was silver; their skin was very white. They were slender and pretty; even the men were more pretty than handsome, and beardless.

They kept to the shadows and the cover provided by fragments of broken buildings, except when one or two would sprint for the great doorway, zigzagging. Louis had counted twenty, eleven of them women. Five more

were dead in the street. There might be others already
in the building.

The defenders had stopped firing now. Perhaps they
had run out of ammunition. They had been using two
windows in the downward-slanting face of the tower,
perhaps six stories up. Every window in the tower was
broken.

He eased close to the larger floating shape of Chmeee.
"We go in the other side, with lights at low intensity
and wide aperture. I go first because I'm human.
Right?"

"Right," said Chmeee.

The belts lifted by *scrith* repulsion, like the lander.
There were small thrusters in back. Louis circled round,
checked to see Chmeee following, and floated in one
of the windows at what he hoped was the right level.

It was one big room, and it was empty. The smell
made him want to sneeze. There was web furniture with
the webbing rotted away, and a long glass table, shattered. At the bottom of the sloping floor, a shapeless
thing proved to be a pack with shoulder straps. So: they
had been here. And the smell—

"Cordite," Chmeee said. "Chemical propulsives. If
they shoot at us, cover your eyes." He moved toward a
door. He flattened himself against the wall and flung the
door suddenly open. A toilet, empty.

A bigger door hung open with the slant of the floor.
With stunner in one hand and flashlight-laser in the
other, Louis moved toward it. He felt a driving excitement drowning the fear.

Beyond the ornately carved wooden door, a broad
circular staircase wound down into darkness. Louis
shined his light down along loops of railing to where
the spiral of stairs and the bottom of the building all
crumpled in on itself. The light picked out a two-
handed weapon with a shoulder butt, and a box that
had spilled tiny golden cylinders; another weapon further down; a coat equipped with straps; more scraps of
clothing on the lower stair; a human shape crumpled in

the crushed bottom of the stairway—a naked man, seeming darker and more muscular than the attackers.

Louis's excitement was growing unbearable. Was this really what he had needed all along? Not the droud and wire, but the risk of his life to prove its value! Louis adjusted his flying belt and dropped over the railing.

He fell slowly. There was nothing human on the stairs, but things had been dropped: anonymous clothing, weapons, boots, another shoulder pack. Louis continued dropping . . . and suddenly knew he'd found the right level. Quick adjustments to his flying belt sent him slamming through a doorway in pursuit of a smell radically different from what Chmeee had called *cordite*.

He was outside the tower. He barely avoided smashing into a wall; he was still inside the lower, crushed building. Somehow he'd dropped his light. He flicked up the amplification in the binocular goggles and turned right, toward light.

There was a dead woman in the great doorway: one of the attackers. Blood had pooled beneath a projectile wound in her chest. Louis felt a great sadness for her . . . and a driving urgency that made him fly right over her, through the doors and out.

The amplified Archlight was bright even through cloud cover. He had found the attackers, and the defenders too. They were paired off, pale, slender forms with shorter, darker ones who still wore bits of clothing, a boot or a head covering or a shirt ripped open. In the fury of their mating they ignored the flying man.

But one was not paired with anyone. As Louis stopped his flight she reached up and grasped his ankle, without insistence and without fear. She was silverhaired and very pale, and her finely chiseled face was beautiful beyond words.

Louis turned off the flying belt and dropped beside her. He took her in his arms. Her hands ran over his strange clothing, questing. Louis dropped the stunner, pulled off his vest and flying belt—his fingers were clumsy—his impact armor, his undersuit. He took her without finesse. His urgency was greater than any consideration for her. But she was as eager as he.

He was not aware of anything but himself and her. Certainly he didn't know that Chmeee had joined them. He knew that, joltingly, when the kzin rapped his new love hard across the head with his laser. The furry alien hand sank its claws in her silver hair and pulled her head back, and pulled her teeth loose from Louis Wu's throat.

CHAPTER 15

The Machine People

The wind blew dust up Louis Wu's nostrils; it whipped his hair in a storm around his face. Louis brushed it back and opened his eyes. The light was blinding-bright. His fumbling hands found a plastic patch on his neck, then binocular goggles covering his face. He pulled them loose.

He rolled away from the woman and sat up.

Now it was dim. Almost dawn: the terminator line split the world into light and dark. Louis ached in every muscle. He felt as if he'd been beaten. Paradoxically, he felt wonderful. For too many years he had used sex only rarely, and only as cover, because wireheads traditionally have no interest in such things. Last night his whole soul had been involved.

The woman? She was about Louis's height, and on the stocky side of pretty. Not flat-chested, but not busty either. Her black hair was bound in a long braid, and there was a disconcerting fringe of beard along her jaw. She slept the sleep of exhaustion, and she'd earned it. They both had. Now he was beginning to remember. But his memories didn't make much sense.

He'd been making love—no, he'd been head over heels in love with the pale, slender woman with the red lips. Seeing his blood on her mouth, feeling the sting in his neck, had left him only with a terrible sense of loss. He'd howled when Chmeee twisted her head around until her neck snapped. He'd fought when the kzin plucked him off the dead woman. The kzin had tucked him under one arm; he was still raging, still fighting, while Chmeee fished the medkit out of Louis's vest and

141

slapped a patch on his neck and tucked the medkit away again.

Then Chmeee had killed them, all the pretty silver-haired men and women, spearing them accurately through their heads with the brilliant ruby needle of his flashlight-laser. Louis remembered trying to stop him, and being thrown rolling across the broken pavement. He'd staggered to his feet, and seen someone else moving, and moved toward her. Her, the dark-haired woman, the only defender left alive. They'd moved into each other's arms.

Why had he done that? And Chmeee had tried to get his attention . . . hadn't he? Louis remembered a shrieking as of tigers at war.

"Pheromones," he said. "And they looked so harmless!" He stood up and looked about him in sheer horror. The dead were all around him: the dark ones with wounded necks, the pale ones with blood on their mouths and black char marks in their silver hair.

The guns hadn't been enough. What the vampires had was worse than a tasp. They put out a superstimulus cloud of pheromones, human scent-signals of sexual readiness. One of the vampires, or a pair, must have reached the tower. And the defenders had come out, running, shedding guns and clothing in a haste that sent one over the banister to his death.

But why, with the vampires dead, had he and the dark-haired woman . . . ?

The wind tossed at Louis's hair. *Yah.* The vampires were dead, but he and the dark-haired woman were still in a cloud of pheromones. They'd mated in frenzy . . . "If the wind hadn't come up we'd still be Doing It. Yah. Now, where the tanj did I leave . . . everything?"

He found the impact armor and the flying belt. The undersuit was torn to shreds. What about the vest? He saw that the woman's eyes were open. She sat up suddenly, with a horror in her eyes that Louis could well understand. He said to her, "I've got to have the vest because the translator's in it. I hope Chmeee doesn't frighten you off before I can—"

Chmeee. How had this looked to *him*?

Chmeee's great hand engulfed Louis's skull and twisted it backward. Louis clung to the woman with his body and his mind, and thrust, thrust; but his eyes were filled with that orange beast-face, and his ears with screaming insults. It was distracting . . .

Chmeee wasn't in sight. Louis found the vest a good distance away, gripped in a vampire's dead hand. He couldn't find the stunner. By now he was really worried. Something ugly was thrusting out of his memory. He was running when he reached the place where they'd grounded the lander.

A chunk of rock too big for three men to lift was holding down a generous pile of black superconductor cloth. Chmeee's parting gift. The lander was gone.

I'll have to get over this sooner or later, Louis thought. *Why not now?* A friend had taught him this cantrip, this bit of magic for recovering from shock or grief. Sometimes it worked.

He was sitting on what had been a porch railing, though the porch now sat alone in a sand-covered walkway. He had donned his impact armor and the vest with all the pockets. He had put clothing between himself and a vast and lonely world. Not modesty, but fear.

That had used up all his ambition. Now he sat. Thoughts drifted aimlessly. He thought of a working droud as far away as the Earth from its moon, and a two-headed ally who would not risk landing here even to save Louis Wu. He thought of the Ringworld engineers and their idealized ecology, which had included nothing like mosquitoes or vampire bats; and his lips quirked into the beginning of a smile, then settled into a dead man's expression, which is no expression at all.

He knew where Chmeee had gone. He smiled again to think how little good it did him. Had Chmeee told him that? No matter. Survival or the mating urge or vengeance on the Hindmost would all drive Chmeee in

the same direction. But would any of these motives
bring him back to rescue Louis Wu?

And he thought how little one death mattered, with
the Ringworld's trillions all doomed to intimate contact
with their sun.

Well, Chmeee might return. Louis ought to get off his
butt and do something about reaching the floating city.
They'd been headed there; Chmeee would expect to
find him there, if some whim brought the kzin back for
the ally who had failed him so badly. Or Louis might
actually learn something valuable. Or . . . he'd have to
survive somewhere in the year or two left to him. *I'll
have to get over this sometime. Why not now?*

Somebody yelled.

The black-haired woman had dressed herself in
shorts and shirt and a backpack. She held a projectile
weapon at her side, pointed at Louis Wu. With her
other arm she gestured and yelled again.

Vacation was over. Louis became acutely aware that
his hood was around his neck. If she tried a head shot
—well, she might just give him time to pull the hood
over his face, and then it wouldn't matter if she fired
or not. The impact suit would stop the projectiles
while he ran. What he really needed was the flying belt.
Or did he?

"Okay," said Louis, and he smiled and raised his
hands to the sides. What he really needed was an ally.
With one hand he reached slowly into his vest, withdrew the translator, clipped it just under his throat.
"This will talk for us, as soon as it learns to."

She motioned with the gun: *Go ahead of me.*

Louis walked as far as the flying belt, then stooped
and picked it up, without jerky motions. Thunder
cracked. A stone six inches from Louis Wu's foot
jumped wildly away. He dropped the harness and
stepped back.

Tanj, she wasn't talking! She'd decided he couldn't
speak her language, and that was that. How would the
translator learn anything?

With his hands in the air, he watched her fiddle one-handed with the flying belt while she kept the gun more or less on him. If she touched the wrong controls, he'd lose the belt and the cloth too. But she set the belt down, studied Louis's face a moment, then stepped back and gestured.

Louis picked up the flying belt. When she gestured toward her vehicle, he shook his head. He went to where Chmeee had left an acre or so of superconductor cloth, weighted down by a boulder far too heavy to move.

The gun never left him as he strapped the harness around the rock and activated the flying belt. He wrapped his arms around the rock—and the harness, for fear it would slip—and lifted. The rock came up. He turned full around and let go. It settled slowly to the ground.

Was that respect in her eyes? Was it for his technology or his strength? He turned off the belt, picked up it and the superconductor cloth, and moved ahead of her to her vehicle. She opened double doors in its side. He set his burden down and looked around.

Couches around three sides; a tiny stove in the center, and a hatch in the roof for a smoke hole. Stacks of baggage behind the rear seat. Another couch in front, facing forward.

He backed out. He turned back toward the tower, took one step forward, and looked at her. She got the idea. She dithered, then gestured him on.

The dead were beginning to smell. He wondered if she would bury or burn them. But she walked among the bodies without stopping. It was Louis who stopped, to probe with his fingers in a woman's silver hair.

There was too much hair, too little skull. Beautiful she was, but her brain was smaller than a human brain. He sighed and went on.

The woman followed him through the shell of the lower building, into the tower's spiral staircase, and down. A dead man of her species lay broken in the

crushed basement, and the flashlight-laser was next to
him. When he glanced back at the woman, he saw tears
in her eyes.

He reached for the flashlight-laser and she fired past
him. The ricochet thumped him on the hip, and he
shied violently inside the suddenly rigid shell. He backed
against the shattered wall while she picked up the
device.

She found the switch, and light jumped around them
in a wide beam. She found the focus; the beam narrowed. She nodded and dropped the device in her
pocket.

On their walk back to the vehicle Louis casually
pulled the impact-suit hood over his face, as if the sunlight were too bright. She might have all she wanted
from Louis Wu, or she might be short of water, or she
might not want his company.

She didn't shoot him. She climbed into the car and
locked the doors, with a key. For an instant Louis saw
himself marooned with no water and no tools. But she
gestured him close to the right-hand window, where the
driving controls were. She began to show him how to
drive.

It was the breakthrough Louis had hoped for. He
repeated the words she called through the window, and
added his own words. "Steering ring. Turn. Activator.
Key. Throttle. Retrothrottle." She was pretty good with
gestures. A hand zipping through air plus a finger tracing a needle's path were "airspeed gauge."

It startled her when the translator began talking back
to her. She let the language lesson continue for a bit.
Then she unlocked the door, backed across the seat
with the gun ready, and said, "Get in. Drive."

The machine was noisy and balky. It translated every
little bump directly to the driver's couch until Louis
learned to steer around cracks in the road, rubble, or
drifts of sand. The woman watched him silently. Did
she have no curiosity? It occurred to him that she had

lost a dozen companions to the vampires. Under the circumstances she was functioning well enough.

Presently she said, "I am Valavirgillin."

"I am Louis Wu."

"Your devices are strange. The speaker, the lifter, the variable light—what more have you?"

"Tanj dammit! I left the eyepieces."

She pulled the binocular goggles out of a pocket. "I found these."

She may have found the stunner too. Louis didn't ask. "Good. Put them on and I'll show you how they work."

She smiled and shook her head. She must be afraid he'd jump her. She asked, "What were you doing in the old city? Where did you find these things?"

"They are mine. I brought them from a far star."

"Do not mock me, Louis Wu."

Louis looked at her. "Did the people who built the cities have such things?"

"They had things that speak. They could raise buildings in the air; why not themselves?"

"What of my companion? Have you found *his* like on the Ringworld?"

"He seemed monstrous." She flushed. "I had no chance to study him."

No, she'd been distracted. Nuts. "Why do you point a gun at me? The desert is enemy to both of us. We should help each other."

"I have no reason to trust you. Now I wonder if you are mad. Only the City Builders traveled between the stars."

"You are mistaken."

She shrugged. "Must you drive so slowly?"

"I need practice."

But Louis was getting the hang of it. The road was straight and not too rough, and there was nothing coming at him. There were drifts of sand across the road. Valavirgillin had told him not to slow for these.

And he was moving at a fair clip toward his destination. He asked, "What can you tell me about the floating city?"

"I have never been there. The children of the City Builders use it. They no longer build, nor do they rule, but our custom is that they keep the city. They have many visitors."

"Tourists? People who go only to see the city?"

She smiled. "For that and other reasons. One must be invited. Why must you know these things?"

"I have to get to the floating city. How far may I drive with you?"

Now she laughed. "I think that you will not be invited there. You are not famous nor powerful."

"I'll think of something."

"I go as far as the school at River's Return. There I must tell them what happened."

"What did happen? What were you doing there in the desert?"

She told him. It wasn't easy. There were gaps in the translator's vocabulary. They worked around the gaps and filled them in.

The Machine People ruled a mighty empire.

Traditionally an empire is a cluster of nearly independent kingdoms. The various kingdoms must pay taxes, and they follow the emperor's commands as regards war, banditry control, maintenance of communication, and sometimes an official religion. Otherwise they follow their own customs.

And that was doubly true within the Machine Empire, where, for instance, the way of life of a herd-keeping carnivore was in competition with the life style of the Grass People; was useful to the traders, who bought the carnivores' tooled leather goods; and was irrelevant to the ghouls. In some territories many species worked in cooperation, and all allowed free passage to the ghouls. The various species followed their own customs because they were built to.

Ghoul was Louis Wu's word. Valavirgillin called them something like *Night People*. They were the garbage collectors and the morticians too, which was why Valavirgillin had not buried her dead. The ghouls had speech. They could be taught to give last rites in the local hominid religions. They formed an information source for the Machine People. Legend said that they had done the same for the City Builders when the City Builders ruled.

According to Valavirgillin, the Machine Empire was an empire of trade, and it taxed only its own merchants. The more she talked, the more exceptions Louis found. The kingdoms maintained the roads that linked the empire, if their people were capable of it, which (for instance) the tree-living Hanging People were not. The roads marked the borders between territories held by different species of hominid. Wars of conquest across the roads were forbidden; and so the roads prevented wars (sometimes!) merely by existing.

The empire had the power to draft armies to battle bandits and thieves. The large patches of land the empire took for trading posts tended to become full colonies. Because roads and vehicles linked the empire, the kingdoms thereof were required to distill chemical fuel and hold it available. The empire purchased mines (by forced sale?), mined its own ore, and leased the right to manufacture machinery according to the empire's specifications.

There were schools for traders. Valavirgillin and her companions were students and a teacher from the school at River's Return. They had set out on a field trip to a trade center bordering the jungle lands of the Hanging People—brachiators, Louis gathered, who traded in nuts and dried fruit—and the Herders, carnivores who dealt in leather goods and handicrafts. (No, they were not small and red. A different species.) They had veered for a side trip to an ancient desert city.

They had not expected vampires. Where would vampires find water in this desert? How would they get there? Vampires were almost extinct except for—

"Except for what? I missed something."

Valavirgillin blushed. "Some older people keep tooth-less vampires for—for the purpose of *rishathra*. That may be how it happened. A tame pair escaped some-how, or a pregnant female."

"Vala, that's disgusting."

"It is," she agreed coolly. "I never heard anyone admit to keeping vampires himself. Where you come from, is there nothing that some do that others find shameful?"

That shot struck home. "I'll tell you about current addiction sometime. Not now."

She studied him over the metal snout of her weapon. Despite that fringe of black beard along her jaw, she looked human enough . . . but widened. Her face was almost perfectly square. Louis was having trouble read-ing her face. That was predictable; the human face has evolved as a signaling device, and Vala's evolution di-verged from his.

He asked, "What will you do next?"

"I must report the deaths . . . and give over the artifacts from the desert city. There is a bounty, but the empire claims City Builder artifacts."

"I tell you again that they are mine."

"Drive."

The desert was showing patches of greenery, and a shadow square sliced the sun, when Valavirgillin bade him stop. He was glad to. He was exhausted with the battering of the road and the endless task of keeping the vehicle aimed.

Vala said, "You will —— dinner."

They were used to gaps in the translation. "I missed that word."

"You contrive to heat food until it can be eaten. Louis, can't you ——?"

"Cook." She wasn't likely to have frictionless pans and a microwave oven, was she? Or measuring cups, refined sugar, butter, any spice he could recognize—

"No."

"I will cook. Make me a fire. What do you eat?"

"Meat, some plants, fruit, eggs, fish. Fruit I can eat not cooked."

"Just like my people, except for fish. Good. Step out and wait."

She locked him out of the vehicle, then crawled into the back. Louis stretched aching muscles. The sun was a blazing sliver, still dangerous to look at, but the desert was growing dark. A broad band of worldscape blazed to antispinward. There was brownish scrub grass around him now, and a clump of tall, dry trees. One tree was white and dead-looking.

She crawled out into the air. She tossed a heavy thing at Louis's feet. "Cut wood and build a fire."

Louis picked it up: a length of wood with a wedge of crude iron fixed to one end. "I hate to sound stupid, but what is it?"

She named it. "You swing the sharp edge against the trunk till the tree falls down. See?"

"Ax." Louis remembered the war axes in the museum on Kzin. He looked at the ax, then the dead tree . . . and suddenly he'd had enough. He said, "It's getting dark."

"Do you have trouble seeing at night? Here." She tossed him the flashlight-laser.

"That dead tree good enough?"

She turned, giving him a nice profile, the gun turning with her. Louis adjusted the light to narrow beam, high intensity. He flipped it on. A bright thread of light licked past her. Louis flicked it across her weapon. The weapon spurted flame and fell apart.

She stood there with her mouth open and the two pieces in her hands.

"I am perfectly willing to take suggestions from a friend and ally," he told her. "I'm sick of taking orders. I got plenty of that from my furry companion. Let's be friends."

She dropped what she was holding and raised her hands.

"You've got more bullets and more guns in the back of the vehicle. Arm yourself." Louis turned away. He sliced his beam down the dead tree in zigzag fashion. A dozen logs fell burning. Louis strolled over and kicked the logs into a tighter pile around the stump. He played the laser into their midst and watched the fire catch.

Something thumped him between the shoulder blades. For an instant the impact suit went stiff. He heard a single crack of thunder.

Louis waited for a bit, but the second shot didn't come. He turned and walked back to the vehicle and Vala. He said to her, "Don't you ever, ever, ever do that again."

She looked pale and frightened. "No. I won't."

"Shall I help you carry your cooking things?"

"No, I can . . . Did I miss you?"

"No."

"Then *how*?"

"One of my tools saved me. I brought it a thousand times the distance light travels in a *falan*, and it's *mine*."

She made a kind of arm-flapping gesture and turned away.

CHAPTER 16

Strategies of Trade

There was a plant that grew along the ground like so many links of green-and-yellow-striped sausage, with rootlets sprouting between the links. Valavirgillin sliced some of these into a pot. She added water, then some seed pods from a sack in the vehicle. She set the pot on the burning logs.

Tanj, Louis could have done that himself. Dinner was going to be crude.

The sun was entirely gone now. A tight cluster of stars to port must be the floating city. The Arch swooped up the black sky in horizontal bands of glowing blue and white. Louis felt that he was on some tremendous toy.

"I wish I had some meat," Vala said.

Louis said, "Give me the goggles."

He turned away from the fire before he put the goggles on. He turned up the light amplification. The pairs of eyes that had been watching from beyond the reach of the firelight resolved. Louis was glad he hadn't fired at random. Two large shapes and a smaller one were a family of ghouls.

But one bright-eyed shadow was small and furry. Louis snipped it headless with the long bright thread from his flashlight-laser. The ghouls flinched. They whispered among themselves. The female started toward the dead animal, but stopped to give Louis precedence. Louis picked up the body and watched her back away.

The ghouls seemed diffident enough. But their place in the ecology was very secure. Vala had told him what

happened when a people went to the great effort of
burying or burning their dead. The ghouls attacked the
living. They owned the night. With magic gleaned from
scores of local religions, they were said to be able to
turn invisible. Even Vala half believed it.

But they weren't bothering Louis. Why would they?
Louis would eat the furry beast, and one day Louis
himself would die, and the ghouls would claim their
due.

While they watched him, he examined the creature:
rabbitlike, but with a long, flat-ended tail and no fore-
paws at all. Not a hominid. Good.

When he looked up, there was a faintly glowing violet flame far to port.

Holding his breath, holding himself very still, Louis
raised both the light amplification and the magnification. Even his pulse in his temples was blurring the
picture now, but he knew what he saw. The magnified
flame was eye-hurting violet, and it fanned out like a
rocket firing in vacuum. Its bottom was clipped off by a
straight black line: the edge of the portward rim wall.

He lifted the goggles. Even after his eyes adjusted,
the violet flame was barely visible, but it was still there.
Tenuous . . . and tremendous.

Louis returned to the fire and dropped the beast at
Vala's feet. He walked into the darkness to starboard
and donned the goggles again.

The flame to starboard showed much larger, but of
course that rim wall was much closer.

Vala skinned the little furry beast and dropped it into
the pot without removing the entrails. When she had
finished, Louis led her by the arm into the darkness.
"Wait a little, then tell me if you see a blue flame far
away."

"Yes, I see it."

"Do you know what it is?"

"No, but I think my father does. There was something he wouldn't talk about, the last time he came
back from the city. There are more. Turn your eyes to
the base of the Arch to spinward."

A daylit blue-and-white horizontal stripe was bright enough to make him squint. Louis covered it with the edge of his hand . . . and now, with the goggles to help, he could make out two small candle flames on the rims of the Arch, and two above them, tinier yet.

Valavirgillin said, "The first appeared seven *falans* ago, near the base of the spinward Arch. Then more to spinward, and these large flames to port and starboard, then more small ones on the antispinward Arch. Now there are twenty-one. They only show for two days each turn, when the sun is brightest."

Louis heaved a gusty sigh of relief.

"Louis, I don't know what it means when you do that. Are you angry or frightened or relieved?"

"I don't know either. Let's say relieved. We've got more time than I thought."

"Time for what?"

Louis laughed. "Haven't you had enough of my madness yet?"

She bridled. "After all, I can choose whether to believe you or not!"

Louis got mad. He didn't hate Valavirgillin, but she was a thorny character, and she had already tried to kill him once. "Fine. If this ring-shaped structure you live on is left to itself, it will brush against the shadow squares—the objects that cover the sun when night comes—in five or six *falans*. That will kill everything. There won't be anything left alive when you brush against the sun itself—"

She screamed, "And you sigh with relief?"

"Easy, take it easy. The Ringworld is *not* being left alone. Those flames are motors for moving it. We're almost at the closest point to the sun, and they're using braking thrust—they're firing inward, sunward. Like this." He sketched the situation for her in the dirt with a pointed stick. "See? They're holding us back."

"You say now that we will *not* die?"

"The motors may not be strong enough for that. But they'll hold us back. We could have ten or fifteen *falans*."

"I do hope you are mad, Louis. You know too much. You know that the world is a ring, and that is secret." She shrugged as one shifts a heavy weight. "Yes, I have had enough of it. Will you tell me why you have not suggested *rishathra*?"

He was surprised. "I would have thought you'd had enough of *rishathra* to last a lifetime."

"That is not funny. *Rishathra* is the way to seal a truce!"

"Oh. All right. Back to the fire?"

"Of course, we need light."

She pulled the pot a little back from the flame, to cook more slowly. "We must discuss terms. Will you agree not to harm me?" She sat down across from him on the ground.

"I agree not to harm you unless I am attacked."

"I make you the same concession. What else do you want from me?"

She was brisk and matter-of-fact, and Louis fell into the spirit of the thing. "You will transport me as far as you can, subject to your own needs. I expect that's as far as, ah, River's Return. You will treat the artifacts as mine. You will not turn them or me over to any authority. You will give me advice, to the best of your knowledge and ability, that will get me into the floating city."

"What can you offer in return?"

Here now, wasn't this woman utterly at Louis Wu's mercy? Well, never mind. "I will attempt to find out if I can save the Ringworld," he said, and was somewhat astonished to realize that it was what he most desired. "If I can, I will, no matter what the cost. If I decide the Ringworld can't be saved, I will try to save myself, and you if it's convenient."

She stood. "A promise empty of meaning. You offer me your madness as if it held real value!"

"Vala, haven't you dealt with madmen before?" Louis was amused.

"I have never dealt with even sane aliens! I am only a student!"

"Calm down. What else can I offer you? Knowledge?

I'll share my knowledge freely, such as it is. I know how the City Builders' machines failed, and who caused it." It seemed safe to assume that the City Builders were Halrloprillalar's species.

"More madness?"

"You'll have to decide that for yourself. And . . . I can give you my flying belt and eyepieces when I'm through with them."

"When is *that* likely to be?"

"When and if my companion returns." The lander held another flying belt and set of goggles, intended for Halrloprillalar. "Or let them be yours when I die. And I can give you half my store of cloth now. Strips of it would let you repair some of the City Builders' old machines."

Vala thought it over. "I wish I were more skilled. Well, then, I agree to all of your requirements."

"I agree to yours."

She began to take off her clothes and jewelry. Slowly, seemingly titillatingly . . . until Louis saw what she was doing: stripping herself of all possible weapons. He waited until she was quite naked, then imitated her, dropping the flashlight-laser and goggles and the pieces of impact armor some distance from her, adding even his chronometer.

They made love, then, but it wasn't love. The madness of last night was gone with the vampires. She asked his preferred technique, then insisted, and he chose the missionary position. It was too much a formality. Perhaps it was meant to be. Afterward, when she went to stir the cooking pot, he was careful that she didn't get between him and his weapons. It felt like that kind of situation.

She came back to him, and he explained that his kind could make love more than once.

He sat cross-legged with Vala in his lap, her legs closed tight around his hips. They stroked each other, aroused each other, learned each other. She liked having her back scratched. Her back was muscular, her torso wider than his own. A strip of her hair ran all the way down her spine. She had fine control of the muscles of her vagina. The fringe of beard was very soft, very fine.

And Louis Wu had a plastic disc under the hair at the crown of his head.

They lay in each other's arms, and she waited.

"Even if you don't have electricity, you must know about it," Louis said. "The City Builders used it to run their machines."

"Yes. We can make electricity from the flow of a river. Tales tell that endless electricity came from the sky before the fall of the City Builders."

Which was accurate enough. There were solar power generators on the shadow squares, and they beamed the power to collectors on the Ringworld. Naturally the collectors used superconducting cables, and naturally they had failed.

"Well, then. If I let a very fine wire down into my brain in the right place—which I did—then a very little bit of electric power will tickle the nerves that register pleasure."

"What is it like?"

"Like getting drunk without the hangover or the dizziness. Like *rishathra*, or real mating, without needing to love anyone but yourself and without needing to stop. But I stopped."

"Why?"

"An alien had my electric source. He wanted to give me orders. But I was ashamed before that."

"The City Builders never had wires in their skulls. We would have found them when we searched the ruined cities. Where is this custom practiced?" she asked. Then she rolled away from him and stared at him in horror.

It was the sin he regretted most often: not keeping his mouth shut. He said, "I'm sorry."

"You said strips of that cloth would— *What is that cloth?*"

"It conducts electric current and magnetic fields with no loss. Superconductor, we call it."

"Yes, that was what failed the City Builders. The . . . superconductor rotted. Your cloth will rot too, will it not? How long?"

"No. It's a different kind."

She screamed it at him. *"How do you know that, Louis Wu?"*

"The Hindmost told me. The Hindmost is an alien who brought us here against our will. He left us with no way home."

"This Hindmost, he took you as slaves?"

"He tried to. Humans and kzinti, we make poor slaves."

"Is his word good?"

Louis grimaced. "No. And he took the superconductor cloth and wire when he fled his world. He didn't have time to make it. He must have known where it was, in storage. Like the other things he brought, the stepping discs: it must have been readily available." And he knew instantly that something was wrong, but it took him a moment to know what it was.

The translator had stopped speaking too soon.

Then it spoke with a very different voice. "Louis, is it wise to tell her these things?"

"She guessed part of it," Louis said. "She was about to blame *me* for the Fall of the Cities. Give me back my translator."

"Can I allow you this ugly suspicion? Why would my people perform so malicious an act?"

"Suspicion? You son of a bitch." Vala knelt watching him with big eyes, listening to him talk to himself in gibberish. She couldn't hear the Hindmost's voice in his earphones. Louis said, "They kicked you out as Hindmost and you ran. You grabbed what you could and ran. Stepping discs and superconductor cloth and wire and a ship. Discs were easy. You must make them by the million. But where would you find superconductor cloth just waiting for you? And you *knew* it wouldn't rot on the Ringworld!"

"Louis, why would we do such a thing?"

"Trade advantage. Give me back my translator!"

Valavirgillin got up. She pulled the pot a little out from the fire, stirred it, tasted. She disappeared toward the vehicle and returned with two wooden bowls, which she filled with a dipper.

Louis waited uneasily. The Hindmost could leave him stranded, with no translator. Louis wasn't good with languages . . .

"All right, Louis. It wasn't planned this way, and it happened before my time. We were searching for a way to expand our territory with minimal risk. The Outsiders sold us the location of the Ringworld."

The Outsiders were cold, fragile beings who roamed throughout the galaxy in slower-than-light craft. They traded in knowledge. They might well have known of the Ringworld, and sold the information to puppeteers, but . . . "Wait a minute. Puppeteers are afraid of spaceflight."

"I overcame that fear. If the Ringworld had proved suitable, then one spaceflight in an individual's lifetime is no great risk. We would have flown in stasis, of course. From what the Outsiders told us, and from what we learned via telescopes and automatic probes, the Ringworld seemed ideal. We had to investigate."

"An Experimentalist faction?"

"Of course. Still, we hesitated to contact so powerful a civilization. But we analyzed Ringworld superconductors through laser spectroscopy. We made a bacterium that could feed on it. Probes seeded the superconductor plague across the Ringworld. You guessed as much?"

"That much, yah."

"We were to follow with trading ships. Our traders would come opportunely to the rescue. They would learn all we needed to know, and gain allies too." Clear and musical, the puppeteer's voice held no trace of guilt, nor even embarrassment.

Vala set the bowls down and knelt across from him. Her face was in shadow. From her viewpoint the translation could not have ended at a worse moment.

Louis said, "Then the Conservatives won an election, I take it."

"Inevitable. A probe found attitude jets. We knew of the Ringworld's instability, of course, but we hoped for some more sophisticated means of dealing with it. When the pictures were made public, the government fell. We have had no chance to return to the Ringworld until—"

"When? When did you spread the plague?"

"Eleven hundred and forty years ago by Earth time. The Conservatives ruled for six hundred years. Then the threat of the kzinti put Experimentalists back in power. When the time seemed opportune, I sent Nessus and his team to the Ringworld. If the structure had survived for eleven hundred years after the fall of the culture that kept it in repair, it would have been worth investigating. I could have sent a trade and rescue team. Unfortunately—"

Valavirgillin had the flashlight-laser in her lap, pointed at Louis Wu.

"—unfortunately the structure was damaged. You found meteor holes and landscape eroded down to the *scrith*. It now seems—"

"This is an emergency. This is an emergency." Louis held his voice steady. How had she *done* that? He'd watched her kneel with a steaming bowl of stew in each hand. Could the thing have been taped to her back? Skip it. At least she hadn't fired yet.

"I hear you," said the Hindmost.

"Can you turn off the flashlight-lasers by remote control?"

"I can do better than that. I can explode it, killing him who holds it."

"Can't you just turn it off?"

"No."

"Then give me back my translator function tanj quick. Testing—"

The box spoke Machine People speech. Vala answered immediately. "Whom or what were you talking to?"

"To the Hindmost, the being who brought me here. May I assume that I have not yet been attacked?"

She hesitated before answering. "Yes."

"Then our agreements are still in force, and I'm still gathering data with intent to save the world. Do you have reason to doubt that?" The night was warm, but Louis felt very naked.

The dead eye of the flashlight-laser remained dead. Vala asked, "Did the Hindmost's race cause the Fall of the Cities?"

"Yes."

"Break off negotiation," Vala ordered.

"He's got most of our data-gathering instruments."

Vala thought it through, and Louis remained still. Two pairs of eyes glowed close behind her in the dark. Louis wondered how much the ghouls heard with those goblin ears, and how much they understood.

"Use them, then. But I want to hear what he says," said Vala. "I have not even heard his voice. He may be only your imagination."

"Hindmost, you heard?"

"I did." Louis's earplugs were speaking Interworld, but the box at his throat spoke Valavirgillin's own tongue. Well and good. "I heard your promise to the woman. If you can find a way to stabilize this structure, do so."

"Sure, your people could use the room."

"If you should stabilize the Ringworld with help from my equipment, I want credit. I may want to ask a reward."

Valavirgillin snarled and choked off a reply. Louis said quickly, "You'll get the credit you deserve."

"It was my government, under my leadership, that tried to bring aid to the Ringworld eleven hundred years after the damage was done. You will vouch for that."

"I will, with reservations." Louis was speaking for Vala's benefit. He told her, "By our agreements, you regard what you're holding as my property."

She flipped him the flashlight-laser. He set it aside, and felt himself sagging with relief, or fatigue, or hunger. *No time.* "Hindmost, tell us about the attitude jets."

"Bussard ramjets mounted on brackets on the rim wall, regularly spaced, three million miles apart. We should find two hundred mountings on each rim wall. In operation each would collect the solar wind over a four- to five-thousand-mile radius, compress it electromagnetically until it undergoes fusion, and blast it back in rocket fashion, in braking mode."

"We can see some of them firing. Vala says there are . . . twenty-one operating?" Vala nodded. "That's 95 percent of them missing. Futz."

"It seems likely. I have holos of forty mountings since we last spoke, and all were empty. Shall I compute the thrust delivered with all jets firing?"

"Good."

"I expect there are not enough jets mounted to save the structure."

"Yah."

"Would the Ringworld engineers have installed an independently operating stabilizing system?"

Pak protectors didn't think that way, did they? They tended to have too much confidence in their ability to improvise. "Not likely, but we'll keep looking. Hindmost, I'm hungry and sleepy."

"Is there more that must be said?"

"Keep a watch on the attitude jets. See what's functional and get their thrust."

"I will."

"Try to contact the floating city. Tell—"

"Louis, I can send no message through the rim wall." Of course not, it was pure *scrith*. "Move the ship."

"It would not be safe."

"What about the probe?"

"The orbiting probe is too distant to send on random frequencies." With vast reluctance the Hindmost added, "I can send messages via the remaining probe. I should send it over the rim wall in any case, to refuel."

"Yah. First set it on the rim wall for a relay station. Try to reach the floating city."

"Louis, I had trouble homing on your translator. I

trace the lander nearly twenty-five degrees to antispin-ward of your position. Why?"

"Chmeee and I split our efforts. I'm headed for the floating city. He's headed for the Great Ocean." It should be safe to say that much.

"Chmeee doesn't answer my broadcasts."

"Kzinti make poor slaves. Hindmost, I'm tired. Call me in twelve hours."

Louis took up his bowl and ate. Valavirgillin had used nothing in the way of spices. The boiled meat and roots didn't excite his taste buds. He didn't care. He licked the bowl clean and retained just enough sense to take an allergy pill. They crawled into the vehicle to sleep.

CHAPTER 17

The Moving Sun

The padded bench was a poor substitute for sleeping plates, and it was jolting under him. Louis was still tired. He slept and was shaken awake, slept and was shaken awake . . .

But this time it was Valavirgillin shaking his shoulders. Her voice was silkily sarcastic. "Your servant dares to break your well-earned rest, Louis."

"Uh. Okay. Why?"

"We have come a good distance, but here there are bandits of the Runner breed. One of us must ride as gunner."

"Do Machine People eat after waking?"

She was disconcerted. "There is nothing to eat. I am sorry. We eat one meal, then sleep."

Louis donned impact armor and vest. Together he and Vala manhandled a metal cover into place over the stove. Louis stood on it and found that his head and armpits rose through the smoke hole. He called down, "What do Runners look like?"

"Longer legs than mine, big chests, long fingers. They may carry guns stolen from us."

The vehicle lurched into motion.

They were driving through mountainous country, through dry scrub vegetation, chaparral. The Arch was visible by daylight, if you remembered to look; otherwise it faded into the blue of the sky. In the haze of distance Louis could make out a city floating on air in fairy-tale fashion.

It all looked so real, he thought. Two or three years

from now it might as well have been some madman's daydream.

He fished the translator out of his vest. "Calling the Hindmost. Calling the Hindmost . . ."

"Here, Louis. Your voice holds an odd tremor."

"Bumpy ride. Any news for me?"

"Chmeee still does not answer calls, nor do the citizens of the floating city. I have landed the second probe in a small sea, without incident. I doubt that anyone will discover it on a sea bottom. In a few days *Hot Needle of Inquiry* will have full tanks."

Louis declined to tell the Hindmost about the Sea People. The safer the puppeteer felt, the less likely he was to abandon his project, the Ringworld, and his passengers. "I meant to ask. You've got stepping discs on the probes. If you sent a probe for me, I could just step through to *Needle*. Right?"

"No, Louis. Those stepping discs connect only to *Needle*'s fuel tank, through a filter that passes only deuterium atoms."

"If you took off the filter, would they pass a man?"

"You would still end in the fuel tank. Why do you ask? At best you might save Chmeee a week of travel."

"That could be worth doing. Something might come up." Now, why was Louis Wu hiding the rogue kzin's defection? Louis had to admit that he found the incident embarrassing. He really didn't want to talk about it . . . and it might make a puppeteer nervous. "See if you can work out an emergency procedure, just in case we need it."

"I will. Louis, I locate the lander a day short of reaching the Great Ocean. What does Chmeee expect to find there?"

"Signs and wonders. Things new and different. Tanj, he wouldn't have to *go* if we knew what was there."

"But of course," the puppeteer said skeptically. He clicked off, and Louis pocketed the translator. He was grinning. What did Chmeee expect to find at the Great Ocean? Love and an army! If the map of Jinx had been stocked with bandersnatchi, then what of the map of Kzin?

Sex urge or self-defense or vengeance—any one of these would have driven Chmeee to the map of Kzin. For Chmeee safety and vengeance went together. Unless Chmeee could dominate the Hindmost, how could he return to known space?

But even with an army of kzinti, what could Chmeee expect to do against the Hindmost? Did he think they'd have spacecraft? Louis thought he was in for a disappointment.

But there would certainly be female kzinti.

There *was* something Chmeee could do about the Hindmost. But Chmeee probably wouldn't think of it, and Louis couldn't tell him now. He wasn't sure he wanted to, yet. It was too drastic.

Louis frowned. The puppeteer's skeptical tone was worrying. How much had he guessed? The alien was a superb linguist; but because he was an alien, such nuances would never *creep* into his voice. They had to be *put* there.

Time would tell. Meanwhile, the dwarf forest had grown thick enough to hide crouching men. Louis kept his eyes moving, searching clumps and folds of hillside ahead. His impact armor would stop a sniper's bullet, but what if a bandit shot at the driver? Louis could be trapped in mangled metal and burning fuel.

He kept his full attention on the landscape.

And presently he saw that it was beautiful. Straight trunks five feet tall sprouted enormous blossoms at their tips. Louis watched a tremendous bird settle into a blossom, a bird similar to a great eagle except for the long, slender spear of a beak. Elbow root, a larger breed than he'd seen on his first visit, some ninety million miles from here, flourished in a tangle of randomly placed fences. Here grew the sausage plant they'd eaten last night. There, a sudden cloud of butterflies, at this distance looking much like Earth's butterflies.

It all looked so real. Pak protectors wouldn't build

anything *flimsy*, would they? But the Pak had had vast
faith in their works, and in their ability to repair *anything*, or even to create new widgets from scratch.

And all of his speculation was based on the word of
a man seven hundred years dead: Jack Brennan the
Belter, who had known the Pak only through one individual. The tree-of-life had turned Brennan himself
into a protector-stage human—armored skin, second
heart, expanded braincase, and all. That might have left
him insane. Or Phssthpok might have been atypical.
And Louis Wu, armed with Jack Brennan's opinions on
Phssthpok the Pak, was trying to think like something
admittedly more intelligent than himself.

But there *had* to be a way to save all this.

Chaparral gave way to sausage-plant plantations to
spinward, rolling hills to antispinward. Presently Louis
saw his first refueling station ahead. It was a major
operation, a chemical factory with the beginnings of a
town growing around it.

Vala called him down from his perch. She said,
"Close the smoke hole. Stay in the van and do not be
seen."

"Am I illegal?"

"You are uncustomary. There are exceptions, but I
would need to explain why you are my passenger. I
have no good explanation."

They pulled up along the windowless wall of the factory. Through the window Louis watched Vala dicker-
ing with long-legged, big-chested people. The women
were impressive, with large mammaries on large chests,
but Louis wouldn't have called them beautiful. Each
woman had long, dark hair covering her forehead and
cheeks, enclosing a tiny T-shaped face.

Louis crouched behind the front seat while Vala
stowed packages through the passenger's door. Soon
they were moving again.

An hour later, far from any habitation, Vala pulled
off the road. Louis climbed down from his gunner's

perch. He was ravenous. Vala had bought food: a large smoked bird and nectar from the giant blossoms. Louis tore into the bird. Presently he asked, "You're not eating?"

Vala smiled. "Not till night. But I will drink with you." She took the colored glass bottle around to the back of the vehicle and ran clear fluid into the nectar. She drank, then passed the bottle. Louis drank.

Alcohol, of course. You couldn't have oil wells on the Ringworld, could you? But you could build alcohol distilleries anywhere there were plants for fermenting. "Vala, don't some of the, ah, subject races get to like this stuff too much?"

"Sometimes."

"What do you do about it?"

The question surprised her. "They learn. Some become useless from drinking. They supervise each other if they must."

It was the wirehead problem in miniature, with the same solution: time and natural selection. It didn't seem to bother Vala . . . and Louis couldn't afford to let it bother him. He asked, "How far is it to the city?"

"Three or four hours to the air road, but we would be stopped there. Louis, I have given thought to your problem. Why can't you just fly up?"

"You tell me. I'm for it if nobody shoots at me. What do you think—would somebody shoot at a flying man, or would they let him talk?"

She sipped from the bottle of fuel and nectar. "The rules are strict. None but the City Builder species may come unless invited. But none have flown to the city either!"

She passed him the bottle. The nectar was sweet: like watered grenadine syrup, with a terrific kick from what must be 200 proof alcohol. He set it down and turned his goggles on the city.

It was vertical towers in a lily-pad-shaped clump, in a jarring variety of styles: blocks, needles tapered at top and bottom, translucent slabs, polyhedral cylinders, a slender cone moored tip down. Some buildings were all window; some were all balconies. Gracefully looping bridges or broad, straight ramps linked them at unpredictable levels. Granted that the builders weren't quite human, Louis still couldn't believe that anyone would build such a thing on purpose. It was grotesque.

"They must have come from thousands of miles around," he said. "When the power stopped, there were buildings with independent power supplies. They all got together. Prill's people mushed them all up into one city. That's what happened, isn't it?"

"Nobody knows. But, Louis, you speak as if you watched it happen!"

"You've lived with it all your life. You don't see it the way I do." He kept looking.

There was a bridge. From a low, windowless building at the top of a nearby hill, it rose in a graceful curve to touch the bottom of a huge fluted pillar. A poured stone road switchbacked uphill to the hilltop building.

"I take it the invited guests have to go through that place at the top, then up the floating bridge."

"Of course."

"What happens in there?"

"They are searched for forbidden objects. They are questioned. If the City Builders are choosy about whom they let up, why, so are we! Dissidents have sometimes tried to smuggle bombs up. Mercenaries hired by the City Builders once tried to send them parts to repair their magic water collectors."

"What?"

Vala smiled. "Some still work. They collect water from the air. Not enough water. We pump water to the city from the river. If we argue over policy, they go thirsty, and we do without the information they gather, until a compromise is reached."

"Information? What have they got, telescopes?"

"My father told me about it once. They have a room that shows what happens in the world, better than your goggles. After all, Louis, they have height and a view."

"I should be asking your father all this. How—"

"That may not be a good idea. He is very . . . he does not see . . ."

"I'm the wrong shape and color?"

"Yes, he would not believe you can make things like the things you own. He would take them."

Tanj dammit. "What happens after they let the tourists through?"

"My father comes home with his left arm inscribed in a language only the City Builders know. The script gleams like silver wire. It does not wash off, but it fades in a *falan* or two."

That sounded less like a tattoo than like printed circuitry. The City Builders might have more control over their guests than their guests knew. "Okay. What do the guests do up there?"

"They discuss policy. They make gifts: large quantities of food and some tools. The City Builders show them wonders and do *rishathra* with them." Vala stood suddenly. "We should be moving."

They had left the threat of bandits behind. Louis rode in front, beside Vala. Noise was as much a problem as the bumping; they had to raise their voices. Louis shouted, "*Rishathra*?"

"Not now, I'm driving." Vala showed a wide expanse of teeth. "The City Builders are very good at *rishathra*. They can deal with almost any race. It helped them hold their ancient empire. We use *rishathra* for trading and for not having children until we want to mate and settle down, but the City Builders never give it up."

"Do you know anyone who could get me invited up as a guest? Say, because of my machines."

"Only my father. He wouldn't."

"Then I'll have to fly up. Okay, what's under the city? Can I just stroll underneath and float up?"

"Underneath is the shadow farm. You might pass for a farmer if you leave your tools behind. The farmers are of all races. It is a dirty job. The city sewer outlet is above, and sewage must be spread for the plants. The plants are all cave life, plants that grow in darkness."

"But . . . Oh, sure, I see it now. The sun never moves, so it's always dark under the city. Cave life, huh? Mushrooms?"

She was staring at him. "Louis, how can you expect the sun to move?"

"I forgot where I was." He grimaced. "Sorry."

"How can the sun move?"

"Well, of course it's the planet that moves. Our worlds are spinning balls, right? If you live on one point, the sun seems to go up one side of the sky and down the other; then there's night till it rises again. Why did you think the Ringworld engineers put up the shadow squares?"

The car began to weave. Vala was shaking, her face pale. Gently Louis asked, "Too much strangeness for you?"

"Not that." She made an odd barking sound. Agonized laughter? "The shadow squares. Obvious to the stupidest of people. The shadow squares mock the day and night cycle for spherical worlds. Louis, I really hoped you were mad. Louis, what can we *do*?"

He had to give her some kind of answer. He said, "I thought of punching a hole under one of the Great Oceans, just before it reaches the point closest to the sun. Let several Earth-masses of water spew into space. The reaction would push the Ringworld back where it belongs. Hindmost, are you listening?"

The too-perfect contralto said, "It does not seem feasible."

"Of course it's not feasible. For one thing, how would we plug the hole afterward? For another, the Ringworld would wobble. A wobble that big would probably kill everything on the Ringworld, and lose the atmosphere too. But I'm trying. Vala, I'm trying."

She made that odd barking sound and shook her head hard. "At least you do not think too small!"

"What would the Ringworld engineers have done?

What if some enemy shot away most of the attitude jets? They wouldn't have built the Ringworld without planning for something like this. I need to know more about them. Get me into the floating city, Vala!"

CHAPTER 18

The Shadow Farm

They began to pass other vehicles: large or small windowed boxes, each with a smaller box at the rear. The road widened and became smoother. Now the fueling stations were more frequent and were of sturdy, square Machine People architecture. There were more and more boxy vehicles, and Vala had to slow. Louis felt conspicuous.

The road topped a rise, and the city was beyond. Vala played tour director as they drove downhill through growing traffic.

River's Return had first seen life as a string of docks along the spinward shore of the broad brown Serpent River. That core region now had the look of a slum. The city had jumped the river via several bridges, and expanded into a circle with a piece bitten out of it. That missing piece was the shadow of the City Builders' floating city.

Moving boxes surrounded them now. The air was scented with alcohol. Vala slowed to a crawl. Louis hunched low. Other drivers had ample opportunity to peer in at the strangely built man from the stars.

But they didn't. They saw neither Louis nor each other; they seemed to see only other vehicles. And Vala drove on, into the center of town.

Here the houses crowded each other. Three and four stories tall, the houses were narrow, with no space between them. They pushed out above the street, cutting into the daylight. In marked contrast, public buildings were all low and sprawling and massive, situated on ample grounds. They competed for ground, not for height: never for height, with the floating city hovering over all.

Vala pointed out the merchants' school, a wide complex of prosperous stone buildings. A block later she pointed down a cross-street. "My home is that way, in pink poured stone. See?"

"Any point in going there?"

She shook her head. "I thought hard on this. No. My father would never believe you. He thinks that even the City Builders' claims are mostly boastful lies. I thought so too, once, but from what you tell me of this . . . Halrloprillalar . . ."

Louis laughed. "She *was* a liar. But her people did rule the Ringworld."

They left River's Return and continued to port. Vala drove several miles farther before crossing the last of the bridges. On the far, portward side of the great shadow, she left an almost invisible side road and parked.

They stepped out into too-bright sunlight. They worked almost in silence. Louis used the flying belt to lift a fair-sized boulder. Valavirgillin dug a pit where it had been. Into the pit went most of Louis's share of the fine black cloth. The dirt went back into the pit, and Louis lowered the boulder on it.

He put the flying belt into Vala's backpack and shouldered it. The pack already held his impact suit, vest, binoculars, flashlight-laser, and the flask of nectar. It was lumpy and heavy. Louis set the pack down, adjusted the flying belt to give him some lift. He set the translator box just under the cover and shouldered the pack again.

He was wearing a pair of Vala's shorts, with a length of rope to hold them up. They were too big for him. His depilated face would be taken as natural to his race. Nothing about him now suggested the star traveler, except the earplug for his translator. He'd risk that.

He could see almost nothing of where they were going. The day was too bright; the shadow, too extensive and too dark.

They walked from day into night.

Vala seemed to have no trouble picking her path. Louis followed her. His eyes adjusted, and he saw that there were narrow paths among the growths.

The fungi ranged from button-size to asymmetrical shapes as tall as Louis's head, with stalks as thick as his waist. Some were mushroom-shaped, some had no shape at all. A hint of corruption was in the air. Gaps in the sprawl of buildings overhead let through vertical pillars of sunlight, so bright that they looked solid.

Frilly yellow fungus fringed in scarlet half smothered an outcropping of gray slate. Medieval lances stood upright, white tipped with blood. Orange and yellow and black fur covered a dead log.

The people were almost as various as the fungi. Here were Runners using a two-handed saw to cut down a great elliptical mushroom fringed in orange. There, small, broad-faced people with big hands were filling baskets with white buttons. Grass giants carried the big baskets away. Vala kept up a whispered commentary. "Most species prefer to hire themselves in groups, to protect against culture shock. We keep separate housing."

There, a score of people were spreading manure and well-decayed garbage; Louis could smell it from a fair distance away. Were those of Vala's species? Yes, they were Machine People, but two stood aside and watched, and they held guns. "Who are those? Prisoners?"

"Prisoners convicted of minor crimes. For twenty or fifty *falans* they serve society in this—" She stopped. One of the guards was coming to meet them.

He greeted Vala. "Lady, you should not be here. These shit-handlers may find you too good a hostage."

Vala sounded exhausted. "My car died. I have to go to the school and tell them what happened. Please, may I cross the shadow farm? We were all killed. All killed by vampires. They have to know. Please."

The guard hesitated. "Cross, then, but let me give you an escort." He whistled a short snatch of music, then turned to Louis. "What of you?"

Vala answered for Louis. "I borrowed him to carry my pack."

The guard spoke slowly and distinctly. "You. Go with the lady as far as she likes, but stay in the shadow farm. Then go back to what you were doing. What were you doing?"

Louis was mute without the translator. He thought of the flashlight-laser buried in his pack. Somewhat at random he laid his hand on a lavender-fringed shelf fungus, then pointed to a sledge stacked with similar fungi.

"All right." The guard looked past Louis's shoulder. "Ah."

The smell told Louis before he turned. He waited, docile, while the guard instructed a pair of ghouls: "Take the lady and her porter to the far edge of the shadow farm. Guard them from harm."

They walked single file along the paths, tending toward the center of the shadow farm. The male ghoul led, the female trailed. The smell of corruption grew riper. Sledges of fertilizer passed them on other paths.

Blood and tanj! How was he going to get rid of the ghouls?

Louis looked back. The ghoul woman grinned at him. She certainly didn't mind the smell. Her teeth were big triangles, well designed for ripping, and her goblin ears were erect, alert. Like her mate, she wore a big purse on a shoulder strap, and nothing else; thick hair covered most of their bodies.

They reached a broad arc of cleared dirt. Beyond was a pit. Mist stood above the pit, hiding the far side. A pipe poured sewage into the pit. Louis's eyes followed the pipe up, up into the black, textured sky.

The ghoul woman spoke in his ear, and Louis jumped. She was using the Machine People speech. "What would the king giant think if he knew that Louis and Wu were one?"

Louis stared.

"Are you mute without your little box? Never mind. We are at your service."

The ghoul man was talking to Valavirgillin. She nodded. They moved off the path. Louis and the woman followed them around an extensive white shelf fungus, to huddle under its far lip.

Vala was edgy. The smell might be getting to her; it was certainly getting to Louis. "Kyeref says this is fresh sewage. In a *falan* it'll be ripe and they'll move the pipe and start hauling it away for fertilizer. Meanwhile nobody comes here."

She took the pack off Louis's back and spilled it out. Louis reached for the translator (the ghouls' ears came sharply alert as his hand neared the flashlight-laser) and turned up the volume. He asked, "How much do the Night People know?"

"More than we ever thought." Vala looked like she wanted to say more, but she didn't.

The male answered. "The world is doomed to fiery destruction in not many *falans*. Only Louis Wu can save us." He smiled, showed a daunting expanse of white wedge-shaped teeth. His breath was that of a basilisk.

"I can't tell if you're being sarcastic," Louis said. "Do you believe me?"

"Strange events can spark an urge to prophecy in the insane. We know that you carry tools not known elsewhere. Your race is not known either. But the world is large, and we do not know all of it. Your furry friend's race is stranger yet."

"That's not an answer."

"Save us! We dare not interfere." The ghoul lost a little of his grin, though his lips still didn't meet. (That would take a conscious effort. Those big teeth . . .) "Why should we care if you are insane? The activities of other species rarely interfere with our own lives. In the end they all belong to us."

"I wonder if you aren't the real rulers of the world." Louis said that for diplomatic relations, then wondered uneasily if it might be true.

The woman answered. "Many species may claim to rule the world, or their own part of it. Would we lay claim to the forest tops of the Hanging People? Or to the airless heights of the Spill Mountain People? And what species would want our domain?" She was laughing at him, that was certain.

Louis said, "There's a Repair Center for the world somewhere. Do you know where?"

"No doubt you are right," the male said, "but we do not know where it might be."

"What do you know about the rim wall? And the Great Oceans?"

"There are too many seas. I know not which you mean. There was activity along the rim wall before the great flames first appeared."

"*Was* there! What kind of activity?"

"Many lifting devices raised equipment beyond even the level of the Spill Mountain People. There were City Builders and Spill Mountain People in great number, many other species in lesser number. They worked right at the upper edge of the world. Perhaps you can tell us the meaning of it all."

Louis was dazed. "Tanj dammit. They must have been . . ." Remounting the attitude jets, and he probably didn't want to say so. So much power and ambition, so close, could be bad for a puppeteer's nerves. "That's a long way for carrion-eaters to pass messages."

"Light travels farther than that. Does this news affect your predictions of doom?"

"I'm afraid not." There might well be a repair crew in action somewhere, but they had almost run out of Bussard ramjets to be remounted. "But with the great flames acting, we should have more than the seven or eight *falans* I thought we had."

"Good news. What will you do now?"

For a moment Louis was tempted to abandon the floating city and deal strictly with the ghouls. But he'd come too far, and after all, there were ghouls everywhere. "I'll wait for night and then go up. Vala, your share of the cloth is in the vehicle. I'd be obliged if you don't show it to anyone or tell anyone about me for . . . a couple of turns should do it. My share you can dig up in a *falan* if nobody comes for it. And I've got this." He patted a vest pocket, where a square yard of super-conductor was folded into the bulk of a handkerchief.

"I wish you wouldn't take it to the city," Vala said.

"After all, they'll think it's just cloth unless I tell them different," Louis said. It was almost a lie. Louis intended to use the superconductor.

The ghouls stared when he took off his shorts—adding detail to his description, no doubt, to help them find his species' home on the Ringworld. He donned impact armor.

The female suddenly asked, "How did you convince a Machine People woman that you were sane?"

Vala told her, while Louis donned vest and goggles and pocketed the flashlight-laser. The ghouls almost lost their smiles. The woman asked, "Can you save the world?"

"Don't count on me. Try to find the Repair Center. Spread the word. Try questioning the bandersnatchi— the great white beasts who live in the great swamp to spinward."

"We know of them."

"Good. Vala—"

"I go now to tell how my companions died. We may not meet again, Louis." Valavirgillin picked up the empty pack and walked quickly away.

"We should escort her," the female ghoul said. They left.

They hadn't said *good luck*. Why? The way they lived . . they might all be fatalists. Luck would mean nothing to them.

Louis scanned the textured sky. He was tempted to go now, immediately. Better to wait for night. He spoke into the translator: "Hindmost, are you there?"

Apparently the puppeteer wasn't.

Louis stretched out under the shelf fungus. The air seemed cleaner near the ground. He sipped meditatively at the fuel-and-nectar bottle Vala had left him.

What *were* the ghouls? Their position in the ecology seemed very secure. How had they kept their intelligence? Why would they need intelligence? Perhaps they had to fight for their prerogatives on occasion. Or for respect. Complying with a thousand local religions could also require considerable verbal facility.

More to the point: how could they help him? Was there a ghoulish enclave somewhere that remembered the source of the immortality drug? Which, by hypothesis, was made from Pak tree-of-life root . . .

One thing at a time. Try the city first.

The pillars of light thinned, then faded out. Other lights appeared in the solid sky: hundreds of lighted windows. None showed directly above him. Who would occupy a basement above a garbage dump? (Someone who couldn't afford lighting?)

The shadow farm seemed deserted. Louis heard only the wind. Standing on the shelf fungus gave him a glimpse of distant windows flickering as if with firelight: housing for the farmers around the perimeter.

Louis touched the lift knob on his flying belt and went up.

CHAPTER 19

The Floating City

At something over a thousand feet the smell of fresh air became more pronounced, and the floating city was around him. He circled the blunt tip of an inverted tower: four levels of dark windows, and a garage below that. The big garage door was closed and locked. Louis circled, looking for a broken window. There weren't any.

These windows must have survived for eleven hundred years. Probably he couldn't break one if he tried. He didn't want to enter the city as a burglar anyway.

Instead, he let himself rise along the sewer pipe, hoping to gain privacy that way. There were ramps around him now, but no street lights anywhere. He guided himself to a walkway and settled on it. Now he felt less conspicuous.

There was nobody in sight. The broad ribbon of poured stone curved away among the buildings, left and right, up and down, putting out pseudopods at random. With a thousand feet of empty space below, there were no guardrails. Halrloprillalar's people must be closer to their brachiating past than Earth's people. Louis strolled toward the lights, keeping nervously to the center of the walk.

Where was everybody? The city had an insular look, Louis thought. There was housing in plenty, and ramps between the housing areas, but where were the shopping centers, the playhouses, the bars, the malls, parks, sidewalk cafés? Nothing advertised itself, and everything was behind walls.

Either he should find someone to introduce himself

to, or he should be hiding. What about that glass slab with the dark windows? If he entered from above, he could make *certain* it was deserted.

Someone came down the walk toward him.

Louis called, "Can you understand me?" and heard his words translated into the Machine People tongue.

The stranger answered in the same language. "You should not walk about the city in darkness. You might fall." He was closer now. His eyes were huge; he was not of the City Builder species. He carried a slender staff as long as himself. With the light behind him, Louis could see no more of him. "Show your arm," he said.

Louis bared his left arm. Of course it bore no tattoos. He said what he had planned to say from the beginning. "I can repair your water condensers."

The staff slashed at him.

It rapped his head glancingly as Louis threw himself backward. He rolled and was on his feet, crouching, trained reflexes working fine, with his arms coming up just too late to block the staff. It cracked against his skull. Lights flared behind his eyes and went out.

He was in free fall. Wind roared past him. Even to a man nearly unconscious, the connection was obvious. Louis thrashed in panic in the dark. *Blowout in a spacecraft! Where am I? Where are the meteor patches? My pressure suit? The alarm switch?*

Switch— He half remembered. His hands leaped to his chest, found flying-belt controls, twisted the lift knob hard over.

The belt lifted savagely and swung him around, feet down. Louis tried to shake the mists out of his head. He looked up. Through a gap in darkness he saw the solar corona glowing around a shadow square; he saw hard darkness descending to smash him. He twisted the lift knob to stop his rapid rise.

Safe.

His belly was churning and his head hurt. He needed time to think. Clearly his approach had been wrong.

But if the guard had rolled him off the walk . . . Louis patted his pockets; everything was there. Why hadn't the guard robbed him first?

Louis half remembered the answer: he'd jumped, missed the guard, rolled. And passed out in midair. That put a different face on the matter. It might even have been best to wait. Too late now.

So try the other approach.

He swam beneath the city, outward toward the rim. Not too far. There were too many lights along the perimeter. But near the center was a double cone with no lights showing at all. The lower tip was blunt: a carport with a poured-stone ledge protruding. Louis floated into the opening.

He raised the amplification of his goggles. It worried him that he hadn't done that earlier. Had the blow to his head left him stupid?

Prill's people, the City Builders, had had flying cars, he remembered. There was no car here. He found a rusted metal track along the floor, and a crude, armless chair at the far end, and bleachers: three rows of raised benches on either side of the track. The wood had aged, the metal was crumbly with rust.

He had to examine the chair before he understood. It was built to run down the track and to flop forward at the end. Louis had found an execution chamber, with provision for an audience.

Would he find courtrooms above? And a jail? Louis had about decided to try his luck elsewhere when a gravelly voice spoke out of the dark, in a speech he hadn't heard in twenty-three years. "Intruder, show your arm. Move slowly."

Again Louis said, "I can make your water condensers work," and heard his translator speak in Halrloprillalar's tongue. It must have been already in the translator, in storage.

The other stood in a doorway at the top of a flight of stairs. He was Louis's height, and his eyes glowed. He carried a weapon like Valavirgillin's. "Your arm is bare. How did you come here? You must have flown."

"Yes."

"Impressive. Is that a weapon?"

He must mean the flashlight-laser. "Yes. You see very well in the dark. What are you?"

"I am Mar Korssil, a female of the Night Hunters. Set down your weapon."

"I won't."

"I am reluctant to kill you. Your claim might be true—"

"It is."

"I am reluctant to wake my master, and I will not let you pass this door. Set down your weapon."

"No. I've already been attacked once tonight. Can you lock that door so that neither of us can open it?"

Mar Korssil tossed something through the door; it jingled as it struck. She closed the door behind her. "Fly for me," she said. Her voice was still a gravelly bass.

Louis lifted a few feet, then settled back.

"Impressive." Mar Korssil came down the stairs with her weapon at ready. "We have time to talk. In the morning we will be found. What do you offer, and what do you want?"

"Was I right in guessing that your water condenser doesn't work? Did it stop at the Fall of the Cities?"

"It has never worked to my knowledge. Who are you?"

"I am Louis Wu. Male. Call my species the Star People. I come from outside the world, from a star too dim to see. I have stuff to repair at least some of the water condensers in the city, and I have hidden much more. It may be that I can give you lighting too."

Mar Korssil studied him with blue eyes as big as goggles. She had formidable claws on her fingers, and buck teeth like axheads. What was she, a rodent-hunting carnivore? She said, "If you can repair our machines, that is good. As to repairing those of other buildings, my master will decide. What do you want?"

"A great deal of knowledge. Access to whatever the

city holds in the way of stored knowledge, maps, histories, tales—"

"You cannot expect us to send you to the Library. If your claim is true, you are too valuable. Our building is not wealthy, but we may buy knowledge from the Library if you have specific questions."

It was becoming obvious: the floating city was no more a city than Pericles' Greece had been a nation. The buildings were independent, and he was in the wrong building. "Which building is the library?" he asked.

"At the port-by-spinward perimeter, a cone moored tip down . . . Why do you ask?"

Louis touched his chest, rose, moved toward the outer night.

Mar Korssil fired. Louis fell sprawling. Flames blazed against his chest. He yelled and jerked the harness loose and rolled away. The flying-belt controls burned, a smoky yellow flame with blue-white flashes in it.

Louis found the flashlight-laser in his hand, pointed at Mar Korssil. The Night Hunter seemed not to notice. "Do not make me do that again," she said. "Are you wounded?"

Those words saved her life; but Louis had to kill *something*. "Drop the weapon or I slice you in half," he said, "like this." He waved the laser beam through the execution chair; it flamed and fell apart.

Mar Korssil didn't move.

"I only want to leave your building," Louis said. "You've marooned me. I'll have to enter your building, but I'll leave by the first ramp I find. Drop the weapon or die."

A woman's voice spoke from the stairway. "Drop the gun, Mar Korssil."

The Night Hunter did.

The woman came down the stairs. She was taller than Louis, and slender. Her nose was tiny, her lips invisibly thin. Her head was bald, but rich white hair flowed down her back from behind her ears and the back of her neck. Louis guessed that the white hair was a mark of age. She showed no fear of him. He asked, "Do you rule here?"

"I and my mate-of-record rule. I am Laliskareerlyar. Did you call yourself Luweewu?"

"Close enough."

She smiled. "There is a peephole. Mar Korssil signaled from the garage: an unusual act. I came to watch and listen. I am sorry about your flying device. There are none left in all the city."

"If I repair your water condenser, will you set me free? And I need advice."

"Consider your bargaining position. Can you resist my guards who wait outside?"

Louis had almost resigned himself to killing his way out. He made one more try. The floor seemed to be the usual poured stone. He ran the laser beam in a slow circle, and a patch of stone a yard across dropped into the night. Laliskareerlyar lost her smile. "Perhaps you can. It shall be as you say. Mar Korssil, come with us. Stop anyone who tries to interfere. Leave your gun where it lies."

They climbed a spiral escalator that no longer ran. Louis counted fourteen loops, fourteen stories. He wondered if he had been wrong about Laliskareerlyar's age. The City Builder woman climbed briskly and had breath left over for conversation. But her hands and face were wrinkled as if worn too long.

An unsettling sight. Louis wasn't used to that. Intellectually he knew what it was: the sign of age, and the sign of her ancestor, the Pak protector.

They climbed by the light of Louis's flashlight-laser. People appeared at doorways; Mar Korssil warned them back. Most were City Builders, but there were other species too.

These servants had served the Lyar family for many generations, Laliskareerlyar explained. The Mar family of night watchmen had been policemen serving a Lyar judge. The Machine People cooks had served almost as long. Servants and City Builder masters saw themselves as one family, bound by periodic *rishathra* and old loyalties. All told, Lyar Building held a thousand people, half of them interrelated City Builders.

Louis stopped to look through a window halfway up. A window, in a stairwell that ran through the core of a building? It was a hologram, a view along one of the rim walls, showing a vast stretch of Ringworld landscape. One of the last of the Lyar treasures, Laliskareerlyar told him with pride and regret. Others had been sold over hundreds of *falans* to pay water fees.

Louis found himself talking too. He was wary and angry and tired, but there was something about the old City Builder woman that drew him out. She knew about planets. She didn't question his veracity. She listened. She looked so much like Halrloprillalar that Louis found himself talking about her: about the ancient, immortal ship's whore who had lived as a half-mad goddess until Louis Wu and his motley crew arrived; how she had helped them, how she had left her ruined civilization with them, how she had died.

Laliskareerlyar asked, "Is that why you didn't kill Mar Korssil?"

The Night Hunter woman looked at him with great blue eyes.

Louis laughed. "Maybe." He told them of his conquest of the sunflower patch. He was skirting a dangerous subject, for he saw no point in telling Laliskareerlyar that the world was going to brush against its sun. "I want to leave the world knowing that I've done no damage. I've got more of that cloth buried near here . . . Tanj! I can't think of any way to reach it now."

They had reached the top of the spiral. Louis was huffing. Mar Korssil unlocked a door; there were more stairs beyond. Laliskareerlyar asked, "Are you nocturnal?"

"What? No."

"We had best wait for day. Mar Korssil, go and send us breakfast. Send Whil, with tools. Then go to sleep." As Mar Korssil trotted obediently downstairs, the old woman sat cross-legged on ancient carpet. "I expect we must work outside," she said. "I don't understand the risk you took. For what? Knowledge? What knowledge?"

It was difficult to lie to her, but the Hindmost might well be listening. "Do you know anything of a machine to change one kind of matter into another? Air into dirt, lead into gold?"

She was interested. "Ancient magicians were said to be able to turn glass into diamonds. But these were children's tales."

So much for that. "What of a Repair Center for the world? Are there legends about that? Telling its location?"

She stared. "As if the world were no more than a made thing, a larger version of the city?"

Louis laughed. "Much larger. Much much much larger. No?"

"No."

"What about an immortality drug? I *know* that's real. Halrloprillalar used it."

"Of course it was real. There is none left in the city, nor anywhere else that I know of. The tale is a favorite with"—the translator used an Interworld phrase—"con men."

"Does the tale tell where it might have come from?"

A young City Builder woman came puffing up the stairs carrying a shallow bowl. Louis's fears of poison disappeared at once. The stuff was lukewarm, something like oatmeal, and they ate with their hands from the one bowl.

"The youth drug comes from spinward," the old woman said, "but I know not how far to spinward. Is this the treasure of knowledge you came for?"

"Any of several treasures. That would be a good one." There would certainly have been tree-of-life in the Repair Center, Louis thought. I wonder how they'd handle it? Surely no human being would *want* to be a protector? But there might be hominids who would . . . Well, those puzzles could wait.

Whil was a burly hominid with a simian face, dressed in a sheet whose original color was lost to time. It was a mad god's rainbow now. Whil didn't talk much. His arms were short and thick and looked very strong. He led them up the last flight of steps, carrying his toolbox, and out into the dawn.

They were on the lip of a funnel, at the truncated tip of the double cone. The rim was only a foot across. Louis's breath caught in his throat. With his flying belt dead, he had reason to fear heights. Wind rushed past him, whipping Whil's sheet into a fluttering multi-colored flag.

Laliskareerlyar asked, "Well? Can you fix it?"

"Not from here. There must be machinery below."

There was, but it wasn't easy to reach. The crawl space was inches wider than Louis Wu. Whil crawled ahead of him, opening panels, as instructed.

The crawl space was doughnut-shaped, circling the machinery that must circle the funnel. And the water was supposed to precipitate on the funnel, no doubt. By refrigeration? Or had they something more sophisticated?

The widgetry concealed by the panels was tightly packed, and a total mystery to Louis Wu. It was sparkling clean, except for . . . yah. He peered closer, not breathing. A wire-thin worm trail of dust had fallen through the widgetry. Louis tried to guess where it had fallen from. He'd have to assume the rest of the machinery was still functional.

He backed out. From Whil he borrowed thick gloves and a pair of needle-nosed pliers. He cut a strip from the edge of the black cloth in his vest and twisted it. He strung it between two contacts and fastened them.

Nothing obvious happened. He continued around the circle, following Whil. In all he found six worm trails of dust. He fastened six twisted strips of superconductor where he thought they belonged.

He wriggled out of the crawl space. "Of course your power source could be long dead," he said.

"We must see," said the old woman. She went up the stairs to the roof. Louis and Whil followed.

The smooth face of the funnel seemed misted over. Louis knelt and reached to touch it. Wet. The water was warm. Already it was beading and flowing down-slope to the pipes. Louis nodded thoughtfully. Another good deed that wouldn't matter in fifteen *falans*.

CHAPTER 20

Economics in Lyar

Just below the thick waist of Lyar Building was what seemed to be a combination audience chamber and bedroom. A huge circular bed with a curtained canopy, couches and chairs around small and large tables, a picture-window wall facing the nearer edge of the shadow farm, a bar built to offer a wide variety of potables. That variety was gone. Laliskareerlyar poured from a crystal decanter into a two-handled goblet, sipped, and passed it across to Louis.

He asked, "Do you hold audiences in here?"

She smiled. "Of a sort. Family gatherings."

Orgies? Very likely, if *rishathra* was what held the Lyar family together. A family fallen on hard times. Louis sipped from the goblet, tasted nectar-and-fuel. The sharing of cups and food dishes—was fear of poison behind that? But she did it so naturally. And there were no diseases on the Ringworld.

"What you have done for us will increase our status and our funds," said Laliskareerlyar. "Ask."

"I need to reach the Library, enter it, and persuade the people who rule there to let me make free use of all their knowledge."

"That would be very expensive."

"Not impossible? Good."

She smiled. "Too expensive. The relationship among the buildings is complicated. The Ten rule the tourist trade—"

"Ten what?"

"Ten large buildings, Luweewu, the most powerful among us. Nine still have lights and water condensers.

Together they built the bridge to Sky Hill. Well, they rule the tourist trade, and they pay fees to the lesser buildings to cover hospitality for their alien guests, the use of all public places, and special fees for events in private buildings. They make all agreements with other species, as with the water the Machine People pump up to us. We pay fees to the Ten for water and for special concessions. Yours would be a very special concession . . . although we pay the Library a general fee for education."

"The Library is one of the Ten?"

"Yes. Luweewu, we do not have the money. Is there a chance that you can do the Library a service? Perhaps your research would help them."

"It's possible."

"They would return some of the fee for a service rendered. Even more than we gave, possibly. But we don't have it. Would you sell them your light weapon or the machine that talks for you?"

"I think I'd better not."

"Can you repair more water condensers?"

"Maybe. Did you say one of the Ten does *not* have a working water condenser? Then why are they one of the Ten?"

"Orlry Building has been among the Ten since the Fall of the Cities. Tradition."

"What were they when the cities fell?"

"A military installation, a storehouse for weapons." She ignored Louis's chortling. "They have a fondness for weapons. Your light-projector—"

"I'd be afraid to let it go. But maybe they'd like their water condenser fixed."

"I will learn what fee they ask to let you into Orlry Building."

"You're joking."

"No. You must be guarded, to prevent your carrying away weapons. You pay an entertainment fee to see the ancient weapons, and more if they are to be demonstrated. If you see their maintenance facilities, you may

learn weaknesses. I will ask." She stood. "Shall we indulge in *rishathra*?"

Louis had been expecting that, a little, and it wasn't
Laliskareerlyar's odd appearance that made him hesitate. It was the terror of taking off his armor and his
tools. He remembered an old sketch of a king brooding
on his throne. *I'm paranoid. But am I paranoid
enough?*

But he was far overdue for sleep! He was simply
going to have to trust the Lyars. "Good," he said. He
began to strip off his armor.

Age had treated Laliskareerlyar oddly. Louis knew
ancient literature, plays and novels that predated boosterspice. Age was a crippling disease . . . but this woman
wasn't crippled. Her skin was loose on her, and her
limbs didn't bend as far as Louis's. But she had an
endless interest in love, and in the strangeness of Louis's body and reflexes.

It was a long time before he slept. He had begged off
telling her about the plastic under his hair. He wished
she hadn't reminded him of that. The Hindmost had a
working droud . . . and he hated himself for wanting
it.

He was awakened near nightfall. The bed jolted
twice, and he blinked and rolled over. He faced Laliskareerlyar and a City Builder man who had also been
touched by age.

Laliskareerlyar introduced him as Fortaralisplyar,
her mate of record and Louis's host. He thanked Louis
for his work on the building's old machinery. Dinner
was already on one of the tables, and Louis was invited
to share it with them: a large bowl of stew, too bland
for Louis's taste. He ate.

"Orlry Building asks more than we have," Fortaralisplyar told Louis. "We have bought for you the
right to enter three of our neighbors' buildings. If you
succeed in repairing even one of their water condensers,
we can get you into Orlry Building. Is that satisfactory?"

"Excellent. I need machines that haven't worked in eleven hundred years, and haven't been tampered with either."

"My mate told me."

Louis left them to their sleep as dark was falling. They had invited him to join them, and the great bed was roomy enough, but Louis was slept out and restless.

The great building was like a tomb. From the upper floors Louis watched for activity in the maze of bridges. He saw nothing but an occasional big-eyed Night Hunter. It figured. If the City Builders slept ten hours out of thirty, it might as well be during the dark. He wondered if they were all asleep in the lighted buildings too.

"Calling the Hindmost," he said.

"Yes, Louis. Must we translate?"

"No need, we're alone. I'm in the floating city. It'll take me a day or two to get into the Library. I think I'm marooned here. My flying belt's ruined."

"Chmeee still will not answer."

Louis sighed. "What else is new?"

"In two days my first probe will complete its circuit of the rim wall. I can bring it to the floating city. Will you want me to negotiate directly with the inhabitants? We are good at that. At least I can lend credence to your tale."

"I'll let you know. What about the Ringworld attitude jets? Have you found any more mounted?"

"No. Of those you know of, all twenty-one are firing. Can you see them?"

"Not from here. Hindmost? Can you learn anything about the physical properties of *scrith,* Ringworld floor material? Strength, flexibility, magnetic properties?"

"I have been working on that. The rim wall is available to my instruments. *Scrith* is very much denser than lead. The *scrith* floor of the Ringworld is probably less than a hundred feet thick. I'll show you my data when you return."

"Good."

"Louis, I can give you transportation, if need be. It would be easier if I could send Chmeee."

"Great! What kind of transportation?"

"You will have to wait for my probe. I will give further instructions then."

He watched the nearly empty city for a while after the Hindmost hung up. He felt depressed. Alone in a gone-to-seed building in a gone-to-seed city, without his droud . . .

A voice behind his shoulder said, "You told my mistress that you are not nocturnal."

"Hello, Mar Korssil. We use electric lighting. Some of us keep strange hours. Anyway, I'm used to a shorter day." Louis turned around.

The big-eyed humanoid wasn't pointing her weapon at Louis, exactly. She said, "These past *falans*, the day has been changing its length. It is distressing."

"Yah."

"Whom did you speak to?"

"A two-headed monster."

Mar Korssil departed. Perhaps she was offended. Louis Wu remained at the window, free-associating through the memories of a long and eventful life. He had given up hope of returning to known space. He'd given up the droud. Perhaps it was time to give up . . . more.

Chkar Building was a poured-stone slab covered in balconies. Explosions had scarred one side of the building, exposing the metal skeleton in places. The water condenser was a trough along the top, slightly canted. An old explosion had sprayed metal droplets into the machinery below. Louis didn't expect his repairs to work, and they didn't.

"Mine is the blame," Laliskareerlyar said. "I had forgotten that Chkar Building fought with Orlry Building two thousand *falans* ago."

Panth Building was built like an onion standing on its tip. Louis guessed that the building had started life as a health club; he recognized pools, spas, hotboxes, massage tables, a gymnasium. The place seemed to have plenty of water. And a faint half-familiar smell tickled at his memory . . .

Panth had also fought with Orlry. There were craters. A bald young man named Arrivercompanth swore that the water condenser had never been damaged. Louis found the dust tracks in the machinery, and the contacts above them. When he had made his repairs, there were water droplets forming on the rounded roof and running into a gutter.

There was some difficulty about payment. Arrivercompanth and his people wanted to offer *rishathra* and promises. (And *then* Louis recognized the scent tickling his nose and hindbrain. He was in a house of ill repute, and there were vampires somewhere about.) Laliskareerlyar wanted cash *now*. Louis tried to follow her argument. He gathered that the Ten would be unhappy when Panth stopped buying water, and only too happy to levy a fine against them for fraud. Arrivercompanth paid.

Gisk had been a condominium, or something similar, at the Fall of the Cities. It was a cube with an air well down the center, and it was half empty. Judging by the smell of the place, Gisk had been restricting its use of water overmuch. Louis was learning the look of water-condensation machinery. He made his repairs quickly, and they worked. The Gisks paid at once. They fell at Laliskareerlyar's feet to express their thanks . . . ignoring her tool-wielding servant. Oh, well.

Fortaralisplyar was delighted. He packed a double-handful of metal coins into Louis's vest and explained the tricky etiquette of bribery. The face-saving language would strain his translator to the limits. "When in doubt, don't," Fortaralisplyar told him. "I will come with you to Orlry Building tomorrow. Let me do the bargaining."

Orlry Building was on the port side of the city. Louis and Fortaralisplyar took their time, sightseeing, walking the highest ramps to get a better view. Fortaralisplyar was proud of his city. "A bit of civilization remained even after the Fall," he said. He pointed out Rylo, a building that had been an emperor's castle. It was beautiful but scarred. The emperor had tried to claim the city for his own at about the time Orlry Building arrived. A fluted column shaped like a Greek pillar, supporting nothing but itself, was Chank, which had been a shopping center. Without the supplies aboard Chank—from markets, restaurants, clothing and bedding stores, even toy shops—for trading with the Machine People, the city would have died early. From the basement of Chank the air road spiraled down to Sky Hill.

Orlry Building was a disc forty feet thick and ten times that wide, built along the lines of a pie. The massive tower at one edge, elaborated with gun emplacements and railed platforms and a derrick, reminded Louis of the bridge of a great ship—a battleship. The walkway to Orlry was broad, but there was only one walkway and one entrance. Along the upper rim were hundreds of small projections. Louis guessed that they were cameras or other sensors, and that they no longer worked. Windows had been chopped into Orlry's sides after the building was raised. The glass in them fitted poorly.

Fortaralisplyar was dressed in yellow and scarlet robes of what appeared to be vegetable fiber: coarse by Louis's standards, but grand from a distance. Louis followed him into Orlry, into a large reception area. There was light, but it flickered: scores of alcohol lamps burning near the ceiling.

Eleven City Builder types of both sexes waited for them. They were dressed almost identically, in loose pants with tight cuffs and brightly colored capes. The edges of the capes were cut elaborately and without symmetry. Badges of rank? The white-haired man who came smiling to greet them wore the most elaborately cut cape and a shoulder gun.

He spoke to Fortaralisplyar. "I had to see him for

myself, this being who can give us water from machinery five thousand *falans* dead."

The handgun in his worn plastic shoulder holster was small, with clean, efficient lines; but even a gun couldn't make Filistranorlry look warlike. His small features showed happy curiosity as he examined Louis Wu. "He seems unusual enough, but . . . well. You have paid. We shall see." He gestured to the soldiers.

They searched Fortaralisplyar, then Louis. They found his flashlight, tested it, gave it back. They puzzled over his translator until Louis said, "That speaks for me."

Filistranorlry jumped. "So it does! Will you sell that?" He was speaking to Fortaralisplyar, who answered, "It is not mine."

Louis said, "I would be mute without it." Orlry's master seemed to accept this.

The water condenser was a dip in the center of Orlry's broad roof. The access tubes below were too small for Louis. Even if he took off his armor he wouldn't fit, and he didn't intend to do that. "What do you use for repairmen? Mice?"

"Hanging People," Filistranorlry said. "We must rent their services. Chilb Building was to have sent them by now. Do you see any other problems?"

"Yes." By now the machinery was familiar enough; Louis had repaired three buildings and failed at a fourth. He could see what ought to be a pair of contacts. He looked for the dust below them, and it wasn't there. "Were there earlier attempts at repair?"

"I assume so. How would we know, after five thousand *falans*?"

"We'll wait for the repairmen. I hope they can follow orders." Tanj! Somebody long dead had neatened things up by blowing the telltale dust tracks away. But Louis was sure he could get his arms in there . . .

Filistranorlry asked, "Would you care to see our museum? You've bought that right."

Louis had never been a weapons buff. He recognized some of the principles, if not the forms, behind the killing tools in the glass cases and behind the glass walls. Most of them used projectiles or explosions or both. Some would throw strings of tiny bullets that exploded like small firecrackers in enemy flesh. The few lasers were massive and cumbersome. Once they must have been mounted on tractors or floating platforms, but those had been scavenged for use elsewhere.

A City Builder arrived with half a dozen workmen. The Hanging People stood as high as Louis's floating ribs. Their heads seemed too large for their bodies; their toes were long and dexterous, and their fingers nearly brushed the floor. "This is probably a waste of time," one said.

"Do it right and you'll be paid anyway," Louis told him. The little man sneered.

They wore armless gowns covered in pockets, the pockets heavy with tools. When the soldiers wanted to search them, they stripped off the gowns and let the soldiers search those. Perhaps they didn't like to be touched.

So small. Louis whispered to Fortaralisplyar, "Does your species do *rishathra* with those?"

The City Builder chuckled. "Yes, but carefully."

The Hanging People clustered around Louis Wu's shoulders, peering, as he reached into the access tube. He wore the insulated gloves he'd borrowed from Mar Korssil. "These are what the contacts look like. Fasten the cloth strip thus . . . and thus. You should find six pairs of contacts. There may be a worm track of dust below."

After they had disappeared around the curve of the access tube, he told the masters of Orlry and Lyar, "We'll never know it if they make a mistake. I wish we could inspect their work." But he did not mention his other fear.

The Hanging People presently emerged. They all trooped up onto the roof: workers, soldiers, masters, and Louis Wu. There they watched as mist formed and condensed and water ran toward the center of the dip.

And six Hanging People now knew how to repair water condensers with strips of black cloth.

"I want to buy that black cloth," Filistranorlry said.

The Hanging People and their City Builder master were already disappearing down the stairwell. Filistranorlry and ten soldiers blocked Louis and Fortaralisplyar from that escape route.

"I don't intend to sell," Louis said.

The silver-haired soldier said, "I hope to keep you here until I can persuade you to sell. If pressed, I will insist that you sell the talking box too."

Louis had half expected this. "Fortaralisplyar, would Orlry Building keep you here by force?"

Lyar's master looked Orlry's master in the eye as he said, "No, Louis. The complications would be unpleasant. The lesser buildings would join to free me. The Ten would become the Nine rather than face a boycott on guests."

Filistranorlry laughed. "The lesser buildings would grow thirsty . . ." and his smile vanished as Fortaralisplyar's grew. Lyar Building now had water to give away.

"You could not hold me. Guests would be pushed from the ramps. The dramas in Chkar and the facilities in Panth would be closed to you—"

"Go, then."

"I take Louis."

"You do not."

Louis said, "Take the money and go. It'll make things easier for all concerned." His hand was in his pocket, on the flashlight-laser.

Filistranorlry held out a small bag. Fortaralisplyar took it, counted the contents. He walked through the soldiers and descended the stairway. When he was out of sight, Louis pulled the hood of the impact suit over his head.

"I offer a high price. Twelve ——" something untranslated. "You would not be cheated," Filistranorlry was saying. But Louis backed toward the edge of the roof. He saw Filistranorlry signal to the soldiers, and he ran.

The edge of the roof was a chest-high fence: zigzag iron spokes, carved to resemble elbow root. The shadow farm was far below. Louis ran along the fence toward the walkway. The soldiers were close, but Filistranorlry was standing back and firing his pistol. The roar was disconcerting, even terrifying. A slug slammed into Louis's ankle; the suit went rigid, and he rolled like a tumbled statue, picked himself up, and ran again. As two soldiers threw themselves at him, he swung over the fence and dropped.

Fortaralisplyar was on the walkway. He turned, startled.

Louis landed flat on his face, in an impact suit gone rigid as steel. The form-fitting coffin supported him, but he was still stunned. Hands helped him to his feet before he really wanted to get up. Fortaralisplyar put his shoulder under Louis's armpit and began walking them away.

"Get away. They might shoot," Louis gasped.

"They would not dare. Are you hurt? Your nose is bleeding."

"It was worth it."

CHAPTER 21

The Library

They entered the Library via a small vestibule in the bottom of the cone, the tip.

Behind a wide, massive desk, two librarians worked at reading screens: bulky machines, styled like a cluster of boxes, that used book tapes rolling through a reader. The librarians looked like a priest and priestess in identical blue robes with jaggedly cut collars. It was some minutes before the woman looked up.

Her hair was pure, clean white. Perhaps she'd been born with white hair, because she wasn't old. A woman of Earth would have been about to take her first shot of boosterspice. She was straight and slender, and pretty, Louis thought. Flat-chested, of course, but nicely built. Halrloprillalar had taught Louis to find a bald head and a well-shaped skull sexy. If she would smile . . . but even to Fortaralisplyar she was rude and imperious. "Yes?"

"I am Fortaralisplyar. Have you my contract?"

She tapped at the keyboard of the reading machine. "Yes. Is this the one?"

"He is."

Now she looked at Louis. "Luweewu, can you understand me?"

"I can, with the aid of this."

When the translator spoke, her calm cracked, but only for a moment. She said, "I am Harkabeeparolyn. Your master has purchased your right to unlimited research for three days, with an option to purchase an additional three days. You may roam the Library at will, barring the residential sections, the doors marked

in gold. You may use any machine unless it is marked
thus." She showed him: an orange tic-tac-toe grid. "To
use these, you need help. Come to me or to anyone
whose collar is cut like mine. You may use the dining
room. For sleep or a bath you must return to Lyar
Building."

"Good."

The librarian looked puzzled. Louis was a little startled himself. Why had he said that with such force? It
struck him that Lyar Building felt more like home to
him than the apartment on Canyon ever had.

Fortaralisplyar paid out silver coins, bowed to Louis,
and departed. The librarian turned back to her reading
screen. (Harkabeeparolyn. He was tired of six-syllable
names, but he'd better memorize it.) Harkabeeparolyn
glanced around when Louis said, "There's a place I'd
like to find."

"In the Library?"

"I hope so. I saw a place like it long ago. You stood
at the center of a circle, and the circle was the world.
The screen at the center turned, and you could make
any part of the world show big—"

"We have a map room. Climb the stairs all the way
up." She turned away.

A tight spiral of metal stairs wound up the Library's
axis. Anchored only at the top and bottom, it was
springy under his weight as he climbed. He passed
doors marked in gold, all closed. Higher up, arched
openings led to banks of reading screens with chairs.
Louis counted forty-six City Builders using reading
screens, and two elderly Machine People, and a compact, very hairy male you-name-it, and a ghoul woman
all alone in one room.

The top floor was the map room. He knew when he
had reached it.

They had found the first map room in an abandoned
floating palace. Its wall was a ring of blue mottled with
white. There had been globes of ten oxygen-atmosphere

worlds, and a screen that would show a magnified view. But the scenes it showed were thousands of years old. They showed a bustling Ringworld civilization: glowing cities; craft zipping through rectangular loops along the rim wall; aircraft as big as this library: spacecraft much bigger.

They had not been looking for a Repair Center then. They'd been looking for a way off the Ringworld. Clearly the old tapes had been almost useless.

They'd been in too much of a hurry. So: twenty-three years later, in another kind of desperation, we try again . . .

Louis Wu emerged from the stairwell with the Ringworld glowing around him. Where the sun would have been, there was Louis Wu's head. The map was two feet tall and almost four hundred feet in diameter. The shadow squares were the same height, but much closer in, hovering over a thousand square feet of jet black floor flecked with thousands of stars. The ceiling, too, was black spattered with stars.

Louis walked toward one of the shadow squares, and through it. Holograms, right, as with that earlier map room. But this time there were no globes of Earthlike worlds.

He turned to inspect the back of a shadow square. No detail showed: nothing but a dead-black rectangle, slightly curved.

The magnification screen was in use.

A three-foot-by-two-foot rectangular screen, with controls below, was mounted on a circular track that ran between the shadow squares and the Ringworld. The boy had an expanded view of one of the mounted Bussard ramjets. It showed as a glare of bluish light. The boy was trying to squint past it.

He must have just reached adolescence. Very fine brown hair covered his entire scalp, thickening at the back. He wore a librarian's blue robes. His collar was wide and square, almost a cape, with a single notch cut into it.

Louis asked, "May I look over your shoulder?"

The boy turned. His features were small and nearly unreadable, as with any City Builder. It made him look older. "Are you allowed such knowledge?"

"Lyar Building has purchased full privileges for me."

"Oh." The boy turned back. "We can't see anything anyway. In two days they'll turn off the flames."

"What are you watching?"

"The repair crew."

Louis squinted into the glare. A storm of blue-white light filled the screen, with darkness at its core. The attitude jet was a dim pinkish dot at the center of the darkness.

Electromagnetic lines of force gathered the hot hydrogen of the solar wind, guided and compressed it to fusion temperatures, and fired it back at the sun. Machinery strove with single-minded futility to hold the Ringworld against the gravity of its star. But this was all that showed: blue-white light and a pinkish dot on the line of the rim wall.

"They're almost finished," the boy said. "We thought they'd call us for help, but they never came." He sounded wistful.

"Maybe you don't have the tools to hear them calling." Louis tried to keep his voice calm. *Repair crew!* "They must be finished anyway. There aren't any more motors."

"No. Look." The boy set the view zipping along the rim wall. The view stopped, jarringly, well beyond the blue glare. Louis saw bits of metal falling along the rim wall.

He studied them until he was certain. Bars of metal, a great spool-shaped cylinder—those were the dismantled components of what he had seen through *Needle*'s telescope. That was the scaffolding for remounting the Ringworld's attitude jets.

The repair crew must have decelerated this equipment to solar orbital speed by using a segment of the rim transport system. But how did they plan to reverse the procedure? The machinery would have to be accelerated to Ringworld rotational speed at its destination.

By friction with the atmosphere? Those materials could be as durable as *scrith*. If so, heating would not be a problem.

"And here." The view skidded again, spinward along the rim wall to the spaceport ledge. The four great City Builder ships showed clear. *Hot Needle of Inquiry* was a speck. Louis would have missed it if he hadn't known just where to look: a mile from the only ship that still sported a Bussard ramjet around its waist.

"There, you see?" The boy pointed to the pair of copper-colored toroids. "There's only one motor left. When the repair crew mounts that, they'll be finished."

Megatons of construction equipment were falling down the rim wall, no doubt accompanied by hordes of construction men of unknown species, all aimed at *Needle*'s parking space. The Hindmost would not be pleased.

"Finished, yes," Louis said. "It won't be enough."

"Enough for what?"

"Never mind. How long have they been working, this repair team? Where did they come from?"

"Nobody wants to tell me anything," the boy said. "*Flup*. Odorous *flup*. What's everybody so excited about? Why am I asking you? You don't know either."

Louis let that pass. "Who are they? How did they find out about the danger?"

"Nobody knows. We didn't know anything about them till they started putting up the machines."

"How long ago?"

"Eight *falans*."

Fast work, Louis thought. Just over a year and a half, plus whatever time it took them to get ready. Who were they? Intelligent, quick, decisive, not overwhelmed by large projects and large numbers—they might almost be . . . but the protectors were long gone. They had to be.

"Have they done other repairs?"

"Teacher Wilp thinks they've been unblocking the spillpipes. We've seen fog around some of the spill mountains. Wouldn't that be a big thing, unblocking a spillpipe?"

Louis thought about it. "Big, all right. If you could get the sea-bottom dredges going again . . . you'd still have to heat the pipes. They run *under* the world. The sea-bottom ooze in a blocked pipe would freeze, I think."

"*Flup,*" said the boy.

"What?"

"The brown stuff that comes out of a spillpipe is called *flup.*"

"Oh."

"Where are you from?"

Louis grinned. "I came from the stars, in *this.*" He reached past the boy's shoulder to point out the speck that was *Hot Needle of Inquiry.* The boy's eyes grew big.

More clumsily than the boy had, Louis ran the view along the path the lander had taken since leaving the rim wall. He found a continent-sized expanse of white cloud where the sunflower patch had been. Farther to port was a wide green swamp, then a river that had cut itself a new bed, leaving the old as a twisting brown track through the yellow-brown desert. He followed the dry riverbed. He showed the boy the city of vampires; the boy nodded.

The boy *wanted* to believe. *Men from the stars, come to help us!* Yet he was afraid to look gullible. Louis grinned at him and continued.

The land turned green again. The Machine People road was easy to follow; in most places the land was clearly different to either side. Here the river curved back to join its old bed. He ran the scale up again and was looking down on the floating city. "Us," he said.

"I've seen that. Tell me about the vampires."

Louis hesitated. But after all, the boy's species were this world's experts at interspecies sex. "They can make you want to do *rishathra* with them. When you do, you get bitten on the neck." He showed the boy the healed wound in his throat. "Chmeee killed the vampire that, uh, attacked me."

"Why didn't the vampires get him?"

"Chmeee's like nothing in the world. He's as likely to be seduced by a sausage plant."

"We make perfume from vampires," the boy said.

"What?" Something wrong with the translator?

The boy smiled too wisely. "One day you'll see. I've got to go. Will you be here later?"

Louis nodded.

"What's your name? Mine's Kawaresksenjajok."

"Luweewu."

The boy left by the stairwell. Louis stood frowning at the screen.

Perfume? The smell of vampires in Panth Building . . . and now Louis remembered the night Halrloprillalar came to his bed, twenty-three years ago. She'd been trying to control him. She'd *said* so. Had she used vampire scent on him?

It couldn't matter now. "Calling the Hindmost," he said. "Calling the Hindmost."

Nothing.

The screen wasn't built to swivel. It faced always outward, away from the shadow squares. Annoying but informative: it could mean that the pictures were being beamed from the shadow squares themselves.

He reduced the scale on the screen. He sent the viewpoint swooping to spinward at impossible speed until he was looking down on a world of water. He dropped like an angel in a death dive. This was fun. The Library's facilities were considerably better than *Needle*'s telescope.

The Map of Earth was old. Half a million years had distorted the continents. Or more? A million? Two? A geologist would have known.

Louis shifted to starboard of antispinward until the Map of Kzin filled the screen: islands clustered around a plate of glare ice. And how old was this Map's togography? Chmeee might know.

Louis expanded the view. He hummed as he worked. He skimmed above yellow-and-orange jungle. His view crossed a broad silver band of river, and he followed it toward the sea. At the junctures of rivers there ought to be cities.

He almost skimmed past it. A delta where two rivers joined; a pale grid pattern imposed on jungle colors. Some human cities had "green belts," but in this kzinti city they must cover more territory than the buildings. At maximum magnification Louis could just make out patterns of streets.

The kzinti had never liked *big* cities. Their sense of smell was too acute. This city was almost as big as the Patriarch's seat of government on Kzin.

They had cities. What else? If they had any kind of industry, they'd need . . . seaports? Mining towns? Keep skimming.

Here the jungle was scrawny. The yellow-brown of barren soil showed through in a pattern that wasn't city-shaped at all. It looked like a melted archery target. At a guess, it was a very large and very old strip mine.

Half a million years ago, or more, a sampling of kzinti had been dropped here. Louis didn't expect to find mining towns. They'd be lucky to have anything left to mine. For half a million years they had been confined to one world, a world whose surface ended a few hundred feet down. But it seemed the kzinti had kept their civilization.

They had brains, these near-cats. They had ruled a respectable interstellar civilization. Tanj, it was kzinti who had taught humans to use gravity generators! And Chmeee must have reached the Map of Kzin hours ago, in his search for allies against the Hindmost.

Louis had followed the river to the sea. Now he skimmed his god's-eye view "south" along the shoreline of the Map's largest continent. He expected ports, though the kzinti didn't use ships much. They didn't like the sea. Their seaports were industrial cities; nobody lived there for pleasure.

But that was in the Kzinti Empire, where gravity

generators had been used for millennia. Louis found himself looking down on a seaport that would have rivalled New York harbor. It crawled with the wakes of ships barely large enough to see. The harbor had the nearly circular look of a meteor crater.

Louis lowered the magnification, backing his viewpoint into the sky, to get an overview.

He blinked. Had his miserable sense of scale betrayed him again? Or had he mishandled the controls?

There was a ship moored across the harbor. It made the harbor look bathtub-sized.

The wakes of tinier ships were still there. It was real, then. He was looking at a ship as big as a town. It nearly closed off the arc of the natural harbor.

They wouldn't move it often, Louis thought. The motors would chew up the sea bed something fierce. With the ship gone, the harbor's wave patterns would change. And how would the kzinti fuel something so big? How had they fueled it the first time? Where did they find the metals?

Why?

Louis had never seriously wondered if Chmeee would find what he sought on the Map of Kzin. Not until now.

He spun the magnification dial. His viewpoint receded into space until the Map of Kzin was a cluster of specks on a vast blue sea. Other Maps showed near the edges of the screen.

The nearest Map to the Map of Kzin was a round pink dot. Mars . . . and it was as far from Kzin as the Moon was from Earth.

How could such distances be conquered? Even a telescope wouldn't penetrate more than two hundred thousand miles of atmosphere. The idea of crossing that distance in a seagoing ship—even a ship the size of a small city—tanj!

"Calling the Hindmost. Louis Wu calling the Hindmost." Time was running out for Louis Wu as repairmen moved in on *Needle* and Chmeee culled the Map of Kzin for warriors. Louis didn't intend to mention any of this to the Hindmost. It would only upset the puppeteer.

What was the Hindmost *doing* that he couldn't answer a call?

Could a human even guess at the answer?

Continue the survey, then.

Louis ran the scale down until he could see both rim walls. He looked for Fist-of-God Mountain near the Ringworld's median line, to port of the Great Ocean. Not there. He expanded the scale. A patch of desert bigger than the Earth was still small against the Ringworld, but there it was, reddish and barren, and the pale dot near the center was . . . Fist-of-God, a thousand miles tall, capped with naked *scrith*.

He skimmed to port, tracing the path they had taken following *Liar*'s crash. Long before he was ready, he had reached water, a wide-flung arm of the Great Ocean. They had stopped within sight of that bay. Louis drifted back, looking for what would be an oblong of permanent cloud, seen from above.

But the eye storm wasn't there.

"Calling the Hindmost! In the names of Kdapt and Finagle and Allah I summon thee, God tanj it! Calling—"

"I am here, Louis."

"Okay! I'm in a library in the floating city. They've got a map room. Look up Nessus's records of the map room we—"

"I remember," the puppeteer said coolly.

"Well, that map room showed old tapes. This one is running on present time!"

"Are you safe?"

"Safe? Oh, safe enough. I've been using superconductor cloth to make friends and influence people. But I'm trapped here. Even if I could bribe my way out of the city, I'd still have to get past the Machine People station on Sky Hill. I'd rather not shoot my way out."

"Wise."

"What's new at your end?"

"Two data. First, I have holograms of both of the

other spaceports. All of the eleven ships have been rifled."

"The Bussard ramjets gone? All of them?"

"Yes, all."

"What else?"

"You cannot expect rescue from Chmeee. The lander has set down on the Map of Kzin in the Great Ocean," the puppeteer reported. "I should have guessed. The kzin has defected, taking the lander with him."

Louis cursed silently. He should have recognized that cool, emotionless tone. The puppeteer was badly upset; he was losing control of the finer nuances of human speech. "Where is he? What's he doing?"

"I watched through the lander's cameras as he circled the Map of Kzin. He found a capacious seagoing ship—"

"I found it too."

"Your conclusions?"

"They tried to explore or colonize the other Maps."

"Yes. In known space the kzinti eventually conquered other stellar systems. On the Map of Kzin they must have looked across the ocean. They were not likely to develop space travel, of course."

"No." The first step in learning space travel is to put something in orbit. On Kzin, low orbital velocity was around six miles per second. On the Map of Kzin, the equivalent was seven hundred and seventy miles per second. "They couldn't have built too many of these ships either. Where would they get the metals? And the voyages would take decades, at least. I wonder how they even knew there were other Maps."

"We may guess that they launched telescopic camera equipment aboard rockets. The instruments would have to perform quickly. A missile could not go into orbit. It would rise and fall back."

"I wonder if they reached the Map of Earth? It's another hundred thousand miles past Mars . . . and Mars wouldn't make a good staging area." What would kzinti have found on the Map of Earth? *Homo habilis* alone, or Pak protectors too? "There's the Map of

Down to starboard, and I don't know the world to antispinward."

"We know it. The natives are communal intelligences. We expect that they will never develop space travel. Their ships would need to support an entire hive."

"Hospitable?"

"No, they would have fought the kzinti. And the kzinti have clearly given up the conquest of the Great Ocean. They seem to be using the great ship to block off a harbor."

"Yah. I'd guess it's a seat of government too. You were telling me about Chmeee."

"After learning what he could by circling above the Map of Kzin, he hovered above the great ship. Aircraft rose and attacked him with explosive missiles. Chmeee allowed this, and the missiles did no harm. Then Chmeee destroyed four aircraft. The rest continued the attack until weapons and fuel were exhausted. When they returned to the ship, Chmeee followed them down. The lander presently rests on a landing platform on the great ship's conning tower. The attack continues. Louis, is he seeking allies against me?"

"If it's any comfort to you, he won't find anything that can go up against a General Products hull. They can't even hurt the lander."

Long pause; then "Perhaps you're right. The aircraft use hydrogen-burning jets and missiles propelled by chemical explosives. In any case, I must rescue you myself. You must expect the probe at dusk."

"Then what? There's still the rim wall. You told me stepping discs won't send through *scrith*."

"I used the second probe to place a pair of stepping discs on the rim wall as a relay."

"If you say so. I'm in a building shaped like a top, at the port-by-spinward perimeter. Set the probe to hover until we decide what to do with it. I'm not sure I want to leave yet."

"You must."

"But all the answers we need could be right here in the Library!"

"Have you made any progress?"

"Bits and pieces. Everything Halrloprillalar's people knew is somewhere in this building. I want to question the ghouls too. They're scavengers, and they seem to be everywhere."

"You only learn to ask more questions. Very well, Louis. You have several hours. I will bring the lander to you at dusk."

CHAPTER 22

Grand Theft

The cafeteria was halfway down the building. Louis gave thanks for a bit of luck: the City Builders were omnivores. The meat-and-mushroom stew could have used salt, but it filled the vacuum in his belly.

*Nobod*y used enough salt. And all the seas were fresh water, except for the Great Oceans. He might be the only hominid on the Ringworld who needed salt, and he couldn't live without it forever.

He ate quickly. Time pressed on the back of his neck. The puppeteer was already skittish. Surprising that he hadn't already fled, leaving Louis and the renegade Chmeee and the Ringworld to their similar fates. Louis could almost admire the puppeteer for waiting to rescue his press-ganged crewman.

But the puppeteer might change his mind when he saw the repair crew coming at him. Louis intended to be back aboard *Needle* before the Hindmost turned his telescope in that direction.

He went back to the upper rooms.

The reading screens he tried all gave unreadable script and no pictures and no voice. Finally, at one of a bank of screens, his eye caught a familiar collar.

"Harkabeeparolyn?"

The librarian turned. Small flat nose; lips like a slash; bald scalp and a fine, delicate skull; long, wavy white hair . . . and a nice flare to her hips, and fine legs. In human terms she'd have been about forty. City Builders might age more slowly than human beings, or faster; Louis didn't know.

"Yes?"

There was a snap in her voice. Louis jumped. He said, "I need a voice-programmed screen and a tape to tell me the characteristics of *scrith*."

She frowned. "I don't know what you mean. Voice-programmed?"

"I want the tape to read to me out loud."

Harkabeeparolyn stared, then laughed. She tried to strangle the laugh, and couldn't; and it was too late anyway. They were the center of attention. "There is no such thing. There never has been," she tried to whisper, but the giggle bubbled up and made her voice louder than she wanted. "Why, can't you read?"

Blood and tanj! Louis felt the heat rising in his ears and neck. Literacy was admirable, of course, and everybody learned to read sooner or later, at least in Interworld. But it was no life or death matter. Every world had voice boxes! Why, without a voice box, his translator would have nothing to work with!

"I need more help than I thought. I need someone to read to me."

"You need more than you paid for. Have your master renegotiate."

Louis wasn't prepared to risk bribing this embarrassed and hostile woman. "Will you help me find the tapes I need?"

"You've paid for that. You've even bought the right to interrupt my own researches. Tell me just what you want," she said briskly. She tapped at keys, and pages of strange script jumped on her screen. "Characteristics of *scrith*? Here's a physics text. There are chapters on the structure and dynamics of the world, including one on *scrith*. It may be too advanced for you."

"That, and a basic physics text."

She looked dubious. "All right." She tapped more keys. "An old tape for engineering students on the construction of the rim transport system. Historical interest only, but it might tell you something."

"I want it. Did your people ever go *under* the world?"

Harkabeeparolyn drew herself up. "I'm sure we must have. We ruled the world and the stars, with machines that would make the Machine People worship us if we had them now." She played with the keyboard again. "But we have no record of that event. What do you want with all this?"

"I don't quite know yet. Can you help me trace the origin of the old immortality drug?"

Harkabeeparolyn laughed, softly this time. "I don't think you can carry that many book spools. Those who made the drug never told their secret. Those who wrote books never found it. I can give you religious spools, police records, confidence games, records of expeditions to various parts of the world. Here's the tale of an immortal vampire who haunted the Grass Giants for a thousand *falans*, growing uncomfortably cunning with the years, until—"

"No."

"His hoard of the drug was never found. No? Let me see . . . Ktistek Building joined the Ten because the other buildings ran out of the drug before Ktistek did. A fascinating lesson in politics—"

"No, forget it. Do you know anything about the Great Ocean?"

"There are *two* Great Oceans," she informed him. "They're easy to pick out on the Arch at night. Some of the old stories say the immortality drug came from the antispinward Ocean."

"Uh-*huh*."

Harkabeeparolyn smirked. The small mouth could look prissy. "You are naive. One can pick out just two features on the Arch with the naked eye. If anything valuable came from far away and comes no more, somebody will say that it came from one of the Great Oceans. Who can deny it, or offer another origin?"

Louis sighed. "You're probably right."

"Luweewu, how can these questions possibly be connected?"

"Maybe they can't."

She got the spools he'd requested, and another: a book for children, tales of the Great Ocean. "I can't think what you'll do with these. You won't steal them. You'll be searched when you leave, and you can't carry a reading machine with you."

"Thank you for your help."

He needed someone to read to him.

He didn't have the nerve to ask random strangers. Perhaps a nonrandom stranger? There had been a ghoul in one of these rooms. If ghouls in the shadow farm knew of Louis Wu, perhaps this one did too.

But the ghoul was gone, leaving only her scent.

Louis dropped into a chair in front of a reading screen and closed his eyes. The useless spools bulged in two of his vest pockets. *I'm not licked yet,* he thought. *Maybe I can find the boy again. Maybe I can get Fortaralisplyar to read to me, or to send someone. It'll cost more, of course. Everything always costs more. And takes longer.*

The reading machine was a big, clumsy thing, moored to the wall by a thick cable. The manufacturer certainly hadn't had superconducting wire. Louis threaded a spool into it and glared at the meaningless script. The screen's definition was poor, and there was no place for a speaker grid. Harkabeeparolyn had told the truth.

I don't have time for this.

Louis stood up. He had no choices left.

The roof of the Library was an extensive garden. Walks spiraled out from the center, from the top of the spiral stairs. Giant nectar-producing flowers grew in the rich black soil between the walks. There were small dark-green cornucopias with tiny blue flowers in the mouths, and a patch of weenie plant in which most of the "sausages" had split to give birth to golden blossoms, and trees that dropped festoons of greenish-yellow spaghetti.

The couples on the scattered benches gave Louis his privacy. He saw a good many blue-robed librarians, and a tall male librarian escorting a noisy group of

Hanging People tourists. Nobody had the look of a guard. No ramps led away from the Library roof: there was nothing to guard, unless a thief could fly.

Louis intended a poor return for the hospitality he'd been given. True, he'd bought that hospitality . . . but it bothered him.

The water condenser rose from the roof's edge like a sculptured triangular sail. It drained into a crescent-shaped pond. The pond seethed with City Builder children. Louis heard his name, "Luweewu!" and turned in time to catch an inflated ball against his chest.

The brown-haired boy he'd met in the map room clapped and shouted for the ball's return.

Louis dithered. Warn him to leave the roof? The roof would soon be a dangerous place. But the kid was bright. He might be bright enough to see the implications and call for guards.

Louis threw the wet ball back at him, and waved, and moved away.

If only he could think of a way to clear the roof entirely!

There were no guardrails at the edge of the roof. Louis walked with care. Presently he circled a clump of small trees whose trunks seemed to have been wrung like washcloths, and found himself in a place of reasonable privacy. There he used his translator.

"Hindmost?"

"Speaking. Chmeee is still under attack. He has retaliated once, by melting one of the great ship's large swiveling projectile launchers. I cannot guess at his motives."

"He's probably letting them see how good his defenses are. Then he'll deal."

"What will he deal for?"

"Even he doesn't know that yet. I doubt they can do much for him except introduce him to a female or three. Hindmost, there's no way I can do any research here. I can't read the screens. I've got too much material anyway. It'd take me a week."

"What might Chmeee accomplish in a week? I dare not stay to find out."

"Yah. What I've got is some reading spools. They'll tell us most of what we want to know, if we can read them. Can you do anything with them?"

"I think it unlikely. Can you furnish me with one of their reading machines? With that I could play the tapes on the screen and photograph them for *Needle*'s computer."

"They're heavy. They've got thick cables that—"

"Cut the cables."

Louis sighed. "Okay. Then what?"

"Already I can see the floating city through the probe camera. I will guide the probe to you. You must remove the deuterium filter to expose the stepping disc. Have you a grippy?"

"I don't have any tools at all. What I've got is a flashlight-laser. You tell me where to slice."

"I hope this is worth losing half my fuel source. Very well. If you can secure a reading machine, and if it will pass through the opening to the stepping disc, well and good. Otherwise, bring the tapes. Perhaps there is something I can do."

Louis stood at the rim of the Library roof and looked down past his toes, into the textured dusk of the shadow farm. At the shadow's edge was noonday light. Rectangle-patterned farmland ran away from him. The Serpent River curled away to port and disappeared among low mountains. Beyond the mountains were seas, flatlands, a tiny mountain range, tinier seas, all bluing with distance . . and finally the Arch rising up and up. Half hypnotized, Louis waited beneath the bright sky. There was nothing else to be done. He was barely aware of time passing.

The probe came out of the sky on a breath of blue flame. Where the nearly invisible fire touched the rooftop, the plants and soil became an orange inferno. Small Hanging People and blue-robed librarians and wet children ran screaming for the stairwell.

The probe settled into the flame and toppled on its side, slowed by attitude jets. There were tiny jets all around the upper rim, and the big jet underneath. It was twenty feet long and ten feet thick, a cylinder made lumpy by cameras and other instruments.

Louis waited until the fires had mostly gone out. Then he waded through coals to the probe. The roof was empty, as far as he could tell—empty even of bodies. No dead. Good.

The voice of his translator guided him as he cut away the thick molecular sieve in the top of the probe. Presently he had exposed a stepping disc. He asked, "Now what?"

"I've reversed the action of the stepping disc in the other probe and removed the filter. Can you get a reading machine?"

"I'll try. I don't like any of this."

"In two years it won't matter. I give you thirty minutes. Then come, bringing whatever you have."

A score of blue-robed librarians had almost decided to come after him when Louis appeared in the stairwell. His hood was pulled over his face. The bits of heavy metal they fired at him bounced from his impact armor, and he came on in a jerky step-stop-step walk.

The fusillade slowed and stopped. They retreated before him.

When they had gone far enough, Louis sliced through the top of the stairway below him. The spiral staircase had been moored only at top and bottom. Now it compressed like a spring, ripping side ramps from doorsills. Librarians hung on for dear life. Louis had the top two floors to himself.

And when he turned to the nearest reading room, Harkabeeparolyn was blocking his path with an ax in her hands.

"Once again I need your help," Louis said.

She swung. Louis caught the ax as it rebounded from the join of his neck and shoulder. She thrashed, trying to wrench it from his grip.

"Watch," he said. He waved the laser beam through the cable that fed a reading machine. The cable spurted flame and fell apart, sparking.

Harkabeeparolyn screamed, "Lyar Building will pay dearly for this!"

"That can't be helped. I want you to help me carry a reading machine up to the roof. I thought I was going to have to cut through a wall. This is better."

"I won't!"

Louis waved the light through a reading machine. It burned after falling apart. The smell was horrible. "Say when."

"Vampire lover!"

The machine was heavy, and Louis wasn't about to let go of the laser. He backed up the stairs; most of the weight was in Harkabeeparolyn's arms. He told her, "If we drop it we'll have to go back for another one."

"Idiot! . . . You've already . . . ruined the cable!"

He didn't answer.

"Why are you doing this?"

"I'm trying to save the world from brushing against its sun."

She almost dropped it then. "But—but the motors! They're all back in place!"

"So you already knew that much! It's too little too late. Most of your spaceships never came back. There aren't enough motors. Keep moving."

As they reached the roof, the probe lifted and settled beside them on attitude jets. They set the machine down. It wasn't going to fit. Louis gritted his teeth and sliced the screen free of the rest of the machine. Now it would fit.

Harkabeeparolyn just looked at him. She was too exhausted to comment.

The screen went into the gap where the molecular filter had been, and vanished. What remained, the guts of the machine, was much heavier. Louis managed to heave one end into the gap. He lay down on his back and used his legs to push it inward until it too vanished.

"Lyar Building had nothing to do with this," he told

the librarian. "They didn't know what I had in mind. Here." He dropped a swatch of dull black cloth beside her. "Lyar Building can tell you how to fix water condensers and other old machines with this. You can make the whole city independent of the Machine People."

She watched him with eyes full of horror. It was hard to tell if she heard.

He eased himself feet first into the probe.

And out head first into *Needle*'s cargo hold.

PART THREE

CHAPTER 23

Final Offer

He was in a great echoing glass bottle, in near darkness. Twilight-shrouded, half-dismantled spacecraft showed through the transparent walls. The probe had been returned to clamps on the back wall of the cargo hold, eight feet off the gray-painted floor. And Louis nestled in the probe, in the gap where the deuterium filter had been, like an egg in an egg cup.

Louis swung out, hung by his hands, and dropped. He was tired to the bone. One last complication, now, and then he could rest. Safety was just the other side of an impenetrable wall. He could see the sleeping plates . . .

"Good." The Hindmost's voice spoke from somewhere near the ceiling. "Is that the reading screen? I expected nothing so bulky. Did you have to chop it in half?"

"Yah." He had also dropped the components eight feet to the floor. Fortunately puppeteers were good with tools . . . "I hope you've got a set of stepping discs in here."

"I anticipated emergencies. Glance toward the forward left . . . *Louis!*"

A moan of unearthly terror rose behind him. Louis spun around.

Harkabeeparolyn was nestled in the probe, where Louis had been a moment ago. Her hands strangled the stock of a projectile weapon. Her lips were skinned back from her teeth. Her eyes could not find rest. They flicked up, down, left, right, and found no comfort anywhere.

The Hindmost spoke in a monotone. "Louis, who is this that invades my spacecraft? Is it dangerous?"

"No, relax. It's just a confused librarian. Harka-beeparolyn, go back."

Her keening rose in pitch. Suddenly she wailed, "I know this place, I've seen it in the map room! It's the starship haven, outside the world! Luweewu, what *are* you?"

Louis pointed the flashlight-laser at her. "Go back."

"No! You've wrecked the stolen Library property. But if—if the world is threatened, I want to help!"

"Help how, you crazy woman? Look: you go back to the Library. Find out where the immortality drug came from before the Fall of the Cities. That's the place we're looking for. If there's any way to move the world without the big motors, that's where we'll find the controls."

She shook her head. "I don't . . . How can you know that?"

"It's their home base. The pro—the Ringworld engineers had to have certain plants growing somewhere close . . . Tanj . . . I'm guessing. I'm only guessing. Tanj dammit!" Louis held his head. It was throbbing like a big drum. "I didn't ask for any of this. I was kidnapped!"

Harkabeeparolyn swung herself out from the probe and dropped. Her coarse blue robe was damp with sweat. She looked a good deal like Halrloprillalar. "I can help. I can read to you."

"We've got a machine for that."

She came closer. The weapon drooped as if forgotten. "We did it to ourselves, didn't we? My people took the world's steering motors for our starships. Can I help set that right?"

The Hindmost said, "Louis, the woman cannot return. The stepping disc in the first probe is still a transmitter. Is that a weapon in her hands?"

"Harkabeeparolyn, give me that."

She did. Louis held the projectile weapon awkwardly. It looked to be of Machine People make.

The Hindmost told him, "Carry it to the forward left corner of the cargo bay. The transmitter is there."

"I don't see it."

"I painted it over. Set the weapon in the corner and step back. Woman, hold your place!"

Louis obeyed. The gun disappeared. Louis almost missed a flick of motion beyond the hull as the weapon dropped onto the spaceport ledge. The Hindmost had set a stepping-disc receiver on the outside of the hull.

Louis marveled. There were elements of Renaissance Italy in the puppeteer's paranoia.

"Good. Next— *Louis! Another!*"

A brown-fuzzed scalp poked out of the probe. It was the boy from the map room, stark naked and dripping wet and on the verge of toppling out as he stretched to look about him. His eyes were big with wonder. He was just the right age for confrontation with magic.

Louis bellowed, "*Hindmost! Turn off those stepping discs now!*"

"I have. I should have earlier. Who is this?"

"A librarian child. He's got a six-syllable name and I can't remember it."

"Kawaresksenjajok," the boy shouted, smiling. "Where are we, Luweewu? What are we doing here?"

"Finagle only knows."

"Louis! I will not have these aliens on my ship!"

"If you're thinking of spacing them, forget it. I won't allow it."

"Then they must stay in the cargo hold, and so will you. I think you planned this, you and Chmeee. I should never have trusted either of you."

"You never did."

"Repeat, please?"

"We'll starve in here."

There was a longish pause. Kawaresksenjajok dropped lithely from the probe. He and Harkabeeparo-lyn engaged in furious whispering.

"You may return to your cell," the Hindmost said suddenly. "They may stay here. I will leave a stepping-disc link open so that you may feed them. This may work out very well."

"How?"

"Louis, it is good that some Ringworld natives survive."

The Ringworlders weren't close enough to hear Louis's translator. He said, "You're not thinking of giving up now, are you? What's in these tapes could take us straight to the magic transmutation device."

"Yes, Louis. And the wealth from the Maps of several worlds may be in Chmeee's hands right now. We may count on distance to protect us for two or three days, no more. We must go soon."

The natives looked around at Louis's approach. He said, "Harkabeeparolyn, help me carry the reading machine."

Ten minutes later the spools and the reading machine and the severed screen were with the Hindmost on the flight deck. Harkabeeparolyn and Kawaresksenjajok awaited further orders.

"You'll have to stay here for a bit," Louis told them. "I don't know just what's going to happen. I'll send you food and bedding. Trust me." He could feel the guilt in his face as he turned quickly and stepped into the corner.

A moment later he was back in his cell—pressure suit, vest, and all.

Louis stripped himself and dialed for a set of informal pajamas. Already he felt better. He was tired, but Harkabeeparolyn and Kawaresksenjajok had to be provided for. The kitchen would not give him blankets. He dialed for four voluminous hooded ponchos and sent them through the stepping discs.

He reached back into his memory. What did Halrloprillalar like to eat? She was an omnivore, but she preferred fresh foods. He chose provisions for them. Through the wall he watched their dubious expressions as they examined it.

He dialed for walnuts and a pedigreed Burgundy for himself. Munching and sipping, he activated the sleeping field, tumbled into it, and stretched out in free fall to think.

Lyar Building would pay for his banditry. Had Harkabeeparolyn left the superconductor cloth behind in the Library, to help pay for the damage? He didn't even know that.

What was Valavirgillin doing now? Frightened for her whole species, for her whole world, and with no way to do anything about it, courtesy of Louis Wu. The woman and boy in the cargo hold must be just as frightened . . . and if Louis Wu died in the next few hours, they would not survive him long.

It was all part of the price. His own life was on the line too.

Step one: Get the flashlight-laser aboard *Needle*. Done.

Step two: Could the Ringworld be moved back into position? In the next few hours he *might* prove that it was *not* possible. It would depend on the magnetic properties of *scrith*.

If the Ringworld could not be saved, then flee.

If the Ringworld *could* be saved, then—

Step three: Make a decision. Was it possible for Chmeee and Louis Wu to return alive to known space? If not, then—

Step four: Mutiny.

He should have left that patch of superconductor cloth in Lyar Building itself. He should have reminded the Hindmost to disconnect the probe's stepping discs. The fact was that Louis Wu had been making some poor decisions lately. It bothered him. His next moves were going to be savagely important.

But for the moment, he would steal a few hours' sleep . . . to match his other thefts.

Voices, dimly heard. Louis stirred, and turned in free fall, and looked about him.

Beyond the aft wall, Harkabeeparolyn and Kawaresk-senjajok were in animated conversation with the ceiling. To Louis it was gibberish. He didn't have his translator. But the City Builders were pointing into a rectangular hologram floating outside the hull, blocking part of the spaceport ledge.

Through that "window" Louis could see the sunlit courtyard of a gray stone castle. Rough-hewn stone in big masses; lots of right angles. The only windows were vertical arrow slits. Some kind of ivy was crawling up one of the walls. Luxuriant pale-yellow ivy with scarlet veins.

Louis pushed himself out of the field.

The puppeteer was at his bench on the flight deck. Today his mane was a cloudy phosphorescent glow. He turned one head at Louis's approach. "Louis, I trust you are rested?"

"Yah, and I needed it, too. Any progress?"

"I was able to repair the reading machine. *Needle*'s computer doesn't know enough of the City Builder tongue to read tapes about physics. I hope to pick up a vocabulary by talking to the natives."

"How much longer? I've got some questions about the Ringworld's general design." Could the Ringworld floor, the whole six hundred million million square miles of it, be used to manipulate the Ringworld's position electromagnetically? If he could know for sure!

"Ten to twenty hours, I think. We all need to rest occasionally."

Too long, Louis thought, with the repair crew coming down their throats. Too bad. "Where's the picture coming from? The lander?"

"Yes."

"Can we get a message to Chmeee?"

"No."

"Why not? He must be carrying his translator."

"I made the mistake of turning the translator function off by way of coercion. He isn't carrying it."

"What happened?" Louis asked. *"What's he doing in a medieval castle?"*

The Hindmost said, "It has been twenty hours since Chmeee reached the Map of Kzin. I've told you how he made his reconnaissance flight, how he allowed kzinti aircraft to attack him, how he landed on the great ship and waited while they continued their attacks. The attacks lasted some six hours before Chmeee himself broke off and flew elsewhere. I wish I understood what he hoped to gain, Louis."

"I don't know either, really. Go on."

"The aircraft followed him some way, then turned back. Chmeee continued to search. He found a stretch of wilderness with a small, walled stone castle on the highest peak. He landed in the courtyard. He was attacked, of course, but the defenders had nothing but swords and bows and the like. When they were well assembled around the lander, he sprayed them with stun cannon. Then he—"

"Hold it."

A kzin sprinted out of one of the rounded arches and across the gray flagstones, moving toward the hologram window at a four-legged dead run. It had to be Chmeee; he was wearing impact armor. An arrow protruded from his eye, a long wooden arrow with papery leaves for feathering.

Other kzinti ran behind him, waving swords and maces. Arrows fell from the slit windows and glanced from his impact armor. As Chmeee reached the lander's airlock, a thread of light lashed from a window. The laser beam chewed flame from the flagstones, then focused on the lander. Chmeee had disappeared. The beam held . . . then snuffed out as the slit window exploded in red and white flame.

"Careless," the Hindmost murmured. "Giving such a weapon to enemies!" His other mouth nibbled at the controls. He switched to an inside camera. Louis watched Chmeee lock the airlock, then stagger toward the autodoc, struggling to take off his impact armor, dropping it as he moved. The kzin's leg was gashed beneath the armor. He heaved the lid of the autodoc up and more or less fell inside.

"Tanj! He hasn't turned the monitors on! Hindmost, we've got to help him."

"How, Louis? If you tried to reach him via stepping discs, you would be heated to fusion temperatures. Between your velocity and the lander's—"

"Yah." The Great Ocean was thirty-five degrees around the curve of the Ringworld. The kinetic energy difference would be enough to blast a city. There was no way to help.

Chmeee lay bleeding.

Suddenly he cried out. He half turned over. His thick fingers stabbed at the autodoc's keyboard. He heaved himself on his back, reached up and pulled the cover closed.

"Good enough," Louis said. The arrow had entered the socket at a sharp outward angle. It might have missed destroying brain tissue . . . or it might not. "He was careless, all right. Okay, go on."

"Chmeee used stun cannon to irradiate the entire castle. Then he spent three hours loading unconscious kzinti onto repulser platforms and taking them outside. He barred the gates. He went away, into the castle. For nine hours I saw nothing of him. Why are you grinning?"

"He didn't take any females outside, did he?"

"No. I think I see."

"He was tanj lucky to get his armor on fast enough. He got that slash on his leg before he finished."

"It does seem that Chmeee is no threat to me."

He'd be in the 'doc twenty to forty hours, Louis estimated. Now it was Louis Wu's decision alone. "There's something we ought to discuss with him, but I guess there's no help for it. Hindmost, please record the following conversation. Send it to the lander on a looped tape. I want it in Chmeee's ears when he wakes up."

The puppeteer reached behind him; he seemed to chew at the control panel. "Done. What is it we are to discuss?"

"Chmeee and I haven't been able to make ourselves believe that you'll take us back to known space. Or even that you can."

The puppeteer peered at him from two directions. His flat heads spread wide, giving him maximum binocular effect, the better to study his dubious ally and possible enemy. He asked, "Why should I not, Louis?"

"First, we know too much. Second, you don't have any reason to go back to any world in known space. With or without the magic transmuter, the place you want to be is the Fleet of Worlds."

Muscles in the puppeteer's hindquarters flexed restlessly. (That was the leg a puppeteer fought with: turn your back on the enemy, zero in with wide-spaced eyes, kick!) He said, "Would that be so bad?"

"It might be better than staying here," Louis conceded. "What *did* you have in mind?"

"We can make your lives very comfortable. You know that we have the kzinti longevity drug. We can supply boosterspice too. There is room in *Needle* for hominid and kzinti females, and in fact we have a City Builder female aboard. You would travel in stasis, so crowding is not a problem. You and your entourage may settle on one of the four farming worlds of the Fleet. You would virtually own it."

"What if we got bored with the pastoral life?"

"Nonsense. You would have access to the libraries of the home world. Access to knowledge humanity has wondered about since first we revealed ourselves! The Fleet is moving through space at nearly lightspeed, eventually to reach the Clouds of Magellan. With us you will escape the galactic core explosion. Likely we will need you to explore . . . interesting territories ahead of our path."

"You mean dangerous."

"What else would I mean?"

Louis was more tempted than he would have expected. How would Chmeee take such an offer? Vengeance postponed? A chance to damage the puppeteer home world in some indefinite future? Or simple cowardice?

He asked, "Is this offer contingent on our finding a magic transmuter?"

"No. Your talents are needed regardless. However . . . any promise I make now would be more easily carried out under an Experimentalist regime. Conservatives might not recognize your value, let alone Chmeee's."

That was nicely phrased, Louis conceded. "Speaking of Chmeee—"

"The kzin has defected, but I leave my offer open to him. He has found kzinti females to save. Perhaps you can persuade him."

"I wonder."

"And after all, you may see your worlds again. In a thousand years, known space may have forgotten the puppeteers. Mere decades will have passed for you, falling near lightspeed with the Fleet of Worlds."

"I want time to think it over. I'll put it to Chmeee when I get the chance." Louis glanced behind him. The City Builders were watching him. It was a pity he couldn't consult them, because he was deciding their fate too.

But he had decided. "What I'd like to do next," he said, "is move on to the Great Ocean. We could come up through Fist-of-God Mountain and go slowly enough—"

"I have no intention of moving the *Needle* at all. There may be threats other than the meteor defense, and surely it is enough!"

"I'll bet I can change your mind. Do you remember finding a rig for hoisting the Bussard ramjets on the rim wall? Have a look at that rig now."

For a moment the puppeteer remained frozen. Then he whirled and was out of sight behind the opaque wall of his quarters.

And that ought to keep him busy long enough.

* * *

At his leisure, Louis Wu moved to his pile of discarded clothing and equipment. He fished the flashlight-laser out of his vest. *Step four: coming up.* A pity his autodoc was in the lander, a hundred million miles out of reach. He might need it soon.

There was certainly flare shielding on the outer hull of *Needle*. Every ship had that, at least on the windows. Under the impact of too much light, flare shielding became a mirror, and maybe saved the pilot's eyesight.

It stopped solar flares, and it stopped lasers. If the Hindmost had set impervious walls between himself and his captive crew, surely he would have coated the entire flight deck with shielding.

But what about the floor?

Louis knelt. The hyperdrive motor ran the whole length of the ship; it was bronze-colored, with some copper and hullmetal. Puppeteer machinery, with all angles rounded, it looked half melted already. Louis angled the flashlight-laser into it and fired through the transparent floor.

Light glared back from the bronze surface. Metal vapor spewed. Liquid metal ran. Louis let the beam chew deep, then played it around, burning or melting anything that looked interesting. A pity he'd never studied hyperdrive system engineering.

The laser grew warm in his hand. He'd been at this for some minutes. He shifted the beam to one of the six mountings that held the motor suspended in its vacuum chamber. It didn't melt; it softened and settled. He attacked another. The motor's great mass sagged and twisted.

The narrow beam flickered, strobelike, then faded. Battery dead. Louis tossed the flashlight-laser away from him, remembering that the puppeteer could make it explode in his hand.

He strolled to the forward wall of his cage. The puppeteer wasn't in sight, but presently Louis heard the sound of a steam calliope dying in agony.

The puppeteer trotted around the opaque green sec-

tion and stood facing him. Muscles quivered beneath
his skin.

"Come," said Louis Wu, "let us reason together."

Without haste, the puppeteer tucked both heads beneath his forelegs and let his legs fold under him.

CHAPTER 24

Counterproposal

Louis Wu woke clearheaded and hungry. For a few minutes he rested, savoring free fall; then he reached out and killed the field. His watch said he'd slept seven hours.

Needle's guests were sleeping beneath one of the tremendous clamps that had held the lander in place during flight. The white-haired woman slept restlessly, tangled in her ponchos, with one bare leg sticking out. The brown-haired boy slept like a baby.

There was no way to wake them, and no point. The wall wouldn't carry sound, and the translator didn't work. And the stepping-disc link would carry no more than a few pounds. Had the puppeteer really expected some kind of complex conspiracy? Louis smiled. His mutiny had been simplicity itself.

He dialed a toasted-cheese handmeal and ate while he padded to the forward wall of his cell.

In repose the Hindmost was a smooth egg shape, covered in hide, with a cloud of white hair tufting the big end. His legs and his heads were hidden beneath him. He hadn't moved in seven hours.

Louis had seen Nessus do that. It was a puppeteer's response to shock: to tuck himself into his navel and make the universe disappear. Well and good, but nine hours seemed excessive. If the puppeteer had been driven into catatonia by Louis's shock treatment, that could be the end of everything.

The puppeteer's ears were in his heads. Louis's words must carry through a thickness of meat and

239

bone. He shouted, "Let me offer you several points to ponder!"

The puppeteer did not respond. Louis raised his voice in soliloquy. "This structure is sliding into its sun. There are things we can do about that, but we can't do any of them while you contemplate your navel. Nobody but you can control any of *Needle*'s instruments, sensors, drives, et cetera, and that's just the way you planned it. So: every minute you spend imitating a footstool, you and I and Chmeee come one minute closer to an opportunity no astrophysicist could resist."

He finished his handmeal while he waited. Puppeteers were superb linguists, in any number of alien languages. Would a puppeteer respond to a narrative hook?

And in fact the Hindmost exposed one head far enough to ask, "What opportunity?"

"The chance to study sunspots from underneath."

The head withdrew under the puppeteer's belly.

Louis bellowed, "The repair team is coming!"

Head and neck reappeared and bellowed in response. "What have you done to us? What have you done to me, to yourself, to two natives who might have fled the fire? Did you have thought for anything besides mere vandalism?"

"I did. You said it once. Some day we must decide who rules this expedition. This is the day," said Louis Wu. "Let me tell you why you should be taking my orders."

"I never guessed that a wirehead would lust for mere power."

"Make that point one. I'm better at guessing than you are."

"Proceed."

"We're not leaving here. Even the Fleet of Worlds is out of reach at slower-than-light speeds. If the Ringworld goes, we all go. We've got to put it back in position somehow.

"Third point. The Ringworld engineers have been

dead for at least a quarter of a million years," Louis said carefully. "Chmeee would say a couple of million. The hominids couldn't have mutated and evolved while the Ringworld engineers were alive. They wouldn't have allowed it. They were Pak protectors."

Louis had expected horror or terror or surprise. The puppeteer showed only resignation. "Xenophobes," he said. "Vicious and hardy and very intelligent."

He must have suspected.

"My ancestors," said Louis. "They built the Ringworld, and they built whatever system is supposed to hold it in place. Which of us has a better chance of thinking like a Pak protector? One of us has to try."

"These arguments would mean nothing if you had left us the chance to run. Louis, I trusted you."

"I wouldn't like to think you were that stupid. We didn't volunteer for this expedition. Kzinti and humans, we make poor slaves."

"Did you have a fourth argument?"

Louis grimaced. "Chmeee is disappointed in me. He wants to force you to his will. If I can tell him you're taking my orders, he'll be impressed. And we need him."

"We do, yes. He may think more like a Pak protector than you do."

"Well?"

"Your orders?"

Louis told him.

Harkabeeparolyn had rolled over and was on her feet before she saw Louis stepping out of the corner. Then she gasped, crouched, and disappeared into the ponchos. A lumpy poncho slithered toward a discarded blue robe.

Peculiar behavior. City Builders with a nudity taboo? Should Louis have worn clothing? He did what he considered tactful: he turned his back on her and joined the boy.

The boy was at the wall, looking out at the great

dismembered starships. The poncho he wore was too big for him. "Luweewu," he asked, "were those our ships?"

"Yah."

The boy smiled. "Did your people build ships that big?"

Louis tried to remember. "The slowboats were almost that size. We needed very big ships before we broke the lightspeed barrier."

"Is this one of your ships? Can it travel faster than light?"

"It could once. Not any more. I think the number four General Products hulls were even bigger than yours, but we didn't build those. They were puppeteer ships."

"That was a puppeteer we were talking to yesterday, wasn't it? He asked about you. We couldn't tell him much."

Harkabeeparolyn had come to join them. She had recovered her composure with her blue librarian's robe. She asked, "Has our status changed, Luweewu? We were told that you would not be allowed to visit us." It was an effort for her to look him in the face.

"I've taken command," Louis said.

"So easily?"

"I paid a price—"

The boy's voice cut in. "Luweewu? We're moving!"

"It's all right."

"Can you make it darker in here?"

Louis shouted the lights out. Immediately he felt more comfortable. The dark hid his nakedness. Harkabeeparolyn's attitude was contagious.

Hot Needle of Inquiry lifted twelve feet above the spaceport ledge. Quickly, almost furtively, with no display of pyrotechnics, the ship drifted to the edge of the world and off.

"Where are we going?" the woman demanded.

"Under the world. We'll end up at the Great Ocean."

There was no sensation of falling, but the spaceport ledge was falling silently upward. The Hindmost let them drop several miles before he activated the thrusters: *Needle* decelerated and began edging beneath the Ringworld.

The edge of blackness slid across to become the sky. Below was a sea of stars, brighter than anything a Ringworld native could have seen through depths of air and scattered Archlight. But the sky was essence of black. The Ringworld's sheath of foamed *scrith* reflected no starlight.

Louis still felt uncomfortable in his nudity. "I'm going back to my room," he said. "Why don't you join me? There's food and a change of clothing, and better beds if you want them."

Harkabeeparolyn flicked into existence, last in line on the stepping disc, and flinched violently. Louis laughed aloud. She tried to glare at him, but her eyes shied away. *Naked!*

Louis dialed for a falling jumper and covered himself. "Better?"

"Yes, better. Do you think I am foolish?"

"No, I think you don't have climate control. You can't go naked most places, so it looks strange to you. I could be wrong."

"You could be right," she said, surprised.

"You slept on a hard deck last night. Try the water bed. It's big enough for both of you and a couple more, and Chmeee isn't using it right now."

Kawaresksenjajok flung himself bodily onto the fur-covered water bed. He bounced, and waves surged outward beneath the fur. "Luweewu, I like it! It's like swimming, but dry!"

Stiff-backed with distrust, Harkabeeparolyn sat down on the uneasy surface. Dubiously she asked, "Chmeee?"

"Eight feet tall and covered with orange fur. He's ... on a mission in the Great Ocean. We're going to get him now. You may talk him into sharing with you."

The boy laughed. The woman said, "Your friend must find another playmate. I do not indulge in *rishathra*."

Louis chortled. (The underside of his mind thought: *tanj!*) "Chmeee's stranger than you think. He's as likely to want *rishathra* with a weenie plant. You'd be quite safe unless he wants the whole bed, which is possible. Be careful never to shake him awake. Or you can try the sleeping plates."

"Do you use the sleeping plates?"

"Yes." He guessed at the meaning of her expression. "The field can be set to keep two bodies apart." (*Tanj!* Did the boy's presence inhibit her?)

She said, "Luweewu, we have inflicted ourselves on you in the middle of your mission. Did you come simply to steal knowledge?"

The correct answer would have been *yes*. Louis's answer was at least true. "We're here to save the Ringworld."

Thoughtfully she said, "But how can I . . . ?" And then she was staring past Louis's shoulder.

The Hindmost waited beyond the forward wall, and he was glorious. Now his claws were tipped with silver, and he wore his mane in gold and silver strands. The short, pale hair over the rest of his body had been brushed to a glow. "Harkabeeparolyn, Kawaresksen-jajok, be welcome," he sang. "Your aid is urgently needed. We have traveled a vast distance between the stars in hope of saving your peoples and your world from a fiery death."

Louis swallowed laughter. Fortunately his guests had eyes only for the Pierson's puppeteer.

"Where are you from?" the boy demanded of the puppeteer. "What is it like?"

The puppeteer tried to tell them. He spoke of worlds falling through space at near lightspeed, five worlds arrayed in a pentagon, a Kemplerer rosette. Artificial suns circled four, to grow food for the population of the fifth. The fifth world glowed only by the light of its streets and buildings. Continents blazed yellow-white, oceans dark. Isolated brilliant stars surrounded by mist were factories floating on the sea, their waste heat boiling the water. Waste industrial heat alone kept the world from freezing.

The boy forgot to breathe as he listened. But the librarian spoke softly to herself. "He *must* come from the stars. He is shaped like no living thing known anywhere."

The puppeteer spoke of crowded streets, tremendous buildings, parks that were the last refuge of a world's native life. He spoke of stepping-disc arrays whereby one could walk around the world in minutes.

Harkabeeparolyn shook her head violently. Her voice rose. "Please, we don't have time. I'm sorry, Kawa! We want to hear more, we *need* to know more, but—the world, the sun! Louis, I never should have doubted you. What can we do to help?"

The Hindmost said, "Read to me."

Kawaresksenjajok lay on his back, watching the back of the world roll past him.

Needle ran beneath a featureless black roof in which the Hindmost had set two hologram "windows." One wide rectangle showed a light-amplified view; the other examined the Ringworld's underside by infrared light. In infrared the underside of day still glowed brighter than night-shadowed land; and rivers and seas were dark by day and light by night.

"Like the back of a mask, see?" Louis kept his voice down to avoid interrupting Harkabeeparolyn. "That branching river chain: see how it stands out? The seas bulge too. And that line of dents—that's a whole mountain range."

"Are your worlds like that?"

"Oh, no. On one of my worlds all that would be solid underneath, and the surface would be happening by accident. Here the world was sculpted. Look, the seas are all the same depth, and they're spaced out so there's enough water everywhere."

"Somebody carved the world like a bas relief?"

"Just like that."

"Luweewu, that's scary. What were they like?"

"They thought big, and they loved their children, and they looked like suits of armor." Louis decided not to say more about the protectors.

The boy pointed. "What's that?"

"I don't know." It was a dimple in the Ringworld's underside . . . with fog in it. "I think it's a meteor puncture. There'll be an eye storm above it."

The reading screen was on the flight deck, facing Harkabeeparolyn through the wall. The Hindmost had repaired the damage and added a braided cable that led into the control panel. As Harkabeeparolyn read aloud, the ship's computer was reading the tape and correlating it to her voice and to its own stored knowledge of Halrloprillalar's tongue. That tongue would have changed over the centuries, but not too much, not in a literate society. Hopefully the computer could take over soon.

As for the Hindmost, he had disappeared into the hidden section. The alien had suffered repeated shocks. Louis didn't begrudge him time off for hysterics.

Needle continued to accelerate. Presently the inverse landscape was speeding past almost too fast for detail. And Harkabeeparolyn's voice was becoming throaty. Time for a lunch break, Louis decided.

A problem emerged. Louis dialed filets mignons and baked potatoes, with Brie and French bread to follow. The boy stared in horror. So did the woman, but at Louis Wu.

"I'm sorry. I forgot. I keep thinking of you as omnivores."

"Omnivores, yes. We eat plants and flesh both," the librarian said. "But not *decayed* food!"

"Don't get so upset. There's no bacteria involved." Properly aged steak, milk attacked by mold . . . Louis dumped their plates into the toilet and dialed again. Fruit, *crudités* with a separate sour-cream dip which he dumped, and seafood, including sashimi. His guests had never seen salt-water fish before. They liked it, but it made them thirsty.

And watching Louis eat made them unhappy. What was he supposed to do, starve?

They might starve. Where would he get fresh red meat for them? Why, from Chmeee's side of the auto-kitchen, of course. Broil it with the laser on wide beam, high intensity. He'd have to get the Hindmost to recharge the laser. That might not be easy, considering the last use to which he'd put it.

Another problem: they might be consuming too much salt. Louis didn't know what to do about that. Maybe the Hindmost could reset the autokitchen controls.

After lunch Harkabeeparolyn went back to her reading. By now the Ringworld was streaming past too fast for detail. Kawaresksenjajok flicked restlessly from cell to cargo hold and back again.

Louis, too, was restive. He should be studying: reviewing the records of the first voyage, or of Chmeee's adventures to date on the Map of Kzin. But the Hindmost wasn't available.

Gradually he became aware of another source of discomfort.

He lusted after the librarian.

He loved her voice. She'd been talking for hours, yet the lilt was still there. She'd told him that she sometimes read to blind children: children without sight. Louis got queasy just thinking about it. He liked her dignity and her courage. He liked the way the robe outlined her shape; and he'd glimpsed her nakedness.

It had been years since Louis Wu had loved a strictly human woman. Harkabeeparolyn came too close. And she wasn't having any. When the puppeteer finally rejoined them, Louis was glad of the distraction.

They talked quietly in Interworld, below the sound of Harkabeeparolyn reading to the computer.

"Where did they come from, these amateur repairmen?" Louis wondered. "Who on the Ringworld would know enough to remount the attitude jets? Yet they don't seem to know that it's not enough."

"Let them alone," the Hindmost said.

"Maybe they *know* it's not enough? Maybe the poor bleeders just can't think of anything else to do. And there's the question of where they got their equipment. It could have come from the Repair Center."

"We face enough complications now. Let them alone."

"For once I think you're right. But I can't help wondering. Teela Brown got her schooling in human space. Big space-built structures are nothing new to her. She'd know what it meant when the sun started sliding around."

"Could Teela Brown have organized so large an effort?"

"Maybe not. But Seeker would be with her. Was Seeker in your tapes? He was a Ringworld native, and maybe immortal. Teela found him. A little crazy, but he could have done the organizing. He was a king more than once, he said."

"Teela Brown was a failed experiment. We tried to breed a lucky human being, feeling that puppeteer associates would share the luck. Teela may or may not have been lucky, but her luck was surely not contagious. We do not want to meet Teela Brown."

Louis shivered. "No."

"Then we must avoid the attention of the repair crew."

"Add a postscript to the tape you're sending to Chmeee," Louis said. "Louis Wu rejects your offer of sanctuary on the Fleet of Worlds. Louis Wu has taken command of *Hot Needle of Inquiry* and has destroyed the hyperdrive motor. That should shake him up."

"It did that for me. Louis, my sensors will not penetrate *scrith*. Your message will have to wait."

"How long until we reach him?"

"About forty hours. I have accelerated to a thousand

miles per second. At this velocity it takes more than five gravities of acceleration to hold us in our path."

"We can take thirty gravities. You're being overcautious."

"I'm aware of your opinion."

"You don't take orders worth a tanj," Louis said. "Either."

CHAPTER 25

The Seeds of Empire

Beyond the curved ceiling the Ringworld floor streamed past.

It wasn't much of a view, not from thirty thousand miles away, passing at a thousand miles per second, and cloaked in foam padding. Presently the boy fell asleep in the orange furs. Louis continued to watch. The alternative was to float here wondering if he'd doomed them all.

And finally the Hindmost told the City Builder woman, "Enough."

Louis tumbled off the shifting surface.

Harkabeeparolyn massaged her throat. They watched as the Hindmost ran four stolen tapes through the reading machine.

It took only a few minutes. "This now becomes the computer's problem," the puppeteer said. "I've programmed in the questions. If the answers are in the tapes, we'll have them in a few hours, maximum. Louis, what if we don't like the answers?"

"Let's hear the questions."

"Is there a history of repair activity on the Ringworld? If so, did repair machinery approach from any one source? Is repair more frequent in any given locale? Is any section of the Ringworld in better repair than the rest? Locate all references to Pak-like beings. Does the style of armor vary with distance from a central point? What are the magnetic properties of the Ringworld floor and of *scrith* in general?"

"Good."

"Did I miss anything?"

". . . Yah. We want the most probable source of the immortality drug. It'll be the Great Ocean, but let's ask anyway."

"I will. Why the Great Ocean?"

"Oh, partly because it's so visible. And partly because we've found one surviving sample of the immortality drug, and one only. Halrloprillalar had it. We found her in the vicinity of the Great Ocean." *And partly because we crashed there,* Louis thought. *The luck of Teela Brown distorts probability. Teela's luck could have brought us straight to the Repair Center that first time.* "Harkabeeparolyn? Can you think of anything we missed?"

Her voice was scratchy. "I don't understand what you're doing."

How to explain? "Our machine remembers everything on your tapes. We tell it to search its memory for answers to given questions."

"Ask it how to save the Ringworld."

"We have to be more specific. The machine can remember and correlate and do sums, but it can't think for itself. It's not big enough."

She shook her head.

"What if the answers are wrong?" the Hindmost persisted. "We cannot flee."

"We try something else."

"I have thought about this. We must go into polar orbit around the sun, to minimize the risk that a fragment of the disintegrating Ringworld will strike us. I will put *Needle* in stasis, to wait for rescue. Rescue will not come, but the risk is better than what we face now."

It could come to that, Louis thought. "Fine. We've got a couple of years to try to find better odds."

"Less than that. If—"

"Shut up."

The exhausted librarian dropped onto the water bed. Imitation kzin fur surged and rippled under her. She held herself rigid for a moment, then cautiously let herself fall back. The fur continued to ripple. Presently the stiffness left her and she let herself roll with the tide. Kawaresksenjajok murmured sleepy protest and turned over.

The librarian looked most appealing. Louis resisted an urge to join her on the bed. "How are you feeling?"

"Tired. Miserable. Will I ever see my home again? If the end comes—when it comes—I'd like to wait for it on the Library roof. But the flowers will be dead by then, won't they? Scorched and frozen."

"Yah." Louis was touched. Certainly he'd never see his own home again. "I'll try to get you back. Right now you need sleep. And a back massage."

"No."

Strange. Wasn't Harkabeeparolyn one of the City Builders, Halrloprillalar's people, who had ruled the Ringworld largely through sex appeal? Sometimes it was difficult to remember that the individuals within an alien species could differ as thoroughly as humans did.

He said, "The Library staff seemed more priests than professionals. Do you practice continence?"

"While we work in the Library, we are continent. But I was continent by choice." She rose on an elbow to look at him. "We learn that all other species lust to do *rishathra* with the City Builders. Is that the case with you?"

He admitted it.

"I hope you can control it."

He sighed, "Oh, tanj, yes. I'm a thousand *falans* old. I've learned how to distract myself."

"How?"

"Ordinarily I'd go looking for another woman."

The librarian didn't laugh. "What if another woman is not available?"

"Oh . . . exercise to exhaustion. Get drunk on 'fuel.' Go on sabbatical, off into interstellar space in a one-man ship. Find some other pleasure to indulge myself. Get involved in work."

"You should not be drunk," she said, and she was right. "What pleasure might you try?"

The droud! A touch of current and he wouldn't care

if Harkabeeparolyn turned to green slime before his eyes. Why should he care now? He didn't admire her . . . well, maybe he did, a little. But she'd done her part. He could save the Ringworld, or lose it, without more help from her.

"You'll have your massage anyway," he said. He stepped wide around her to touch a control on the water bed. Harkabeeparolyn looked startled, then smiled and relaxed completely as the sonic vibrations in the water enfolded her. In a few minutes she was asleep. He set the unit to switch off in twenty minutes.

Then he brooded.

If he hadn't spent a year with Halrloprillalar, he'd find Harkabeeparolyn unsightly, with her bald head and knife-edge lips and small flat nose. But he had . . .

He had hair where no City Builder had hair. Was that it? Or the smell of his food on his breath? Or a social signal he didn't know?

A man who had hijacked a starship, a man who had bet his life on the chance to rescue trillions of other lives, a man who had beaten the ultimate in drug habits, should not be bothered by so minor a distraction as an itch for a lovely roommate. A touch of the wire would give him the dispassionate clarity to see that.

Yah.

Louis went to the forward wall. "Hindmost!"

The puppeteer trotted into view.

"Run the records of the Pak for me. Interviews and medical reports on Jack Brennan, studies of the alien's corpse, everything you've got." He'd try work.

Louis Wu hovered in midair, in lotus position, with his loose clothing drifting around him. On a screen that floated motionless outside *Needle*'s hull, a man long dead was lecturing on the origin of humanity.

"Protectors have precious little free will," he was saying. "We're too intelligent not to see the right answers. Besides that, there are instincts. If a Pak protector has no living children, he generally dies. He stops eating. Some protectors can generalize; they can find a way to do something for their whole species, and it keeps them alive. I think that was easier for me than it was for Phssthpok."

"What did you find? What's the cause that keeps you eating?"

"Warning you about Pak protectors."

Louis nodded, remembering the autopsy data on the alien. Phssthpok's brain was bigger than a man's, but the swelling did not include the frontal lobes. Jack Brennan's head looked dented in the middle because of his human frontal development and the upward swelling of the back of the skull.

Brennan's skin was deeply wrinkled leathery armor. His joints were abnormally swollen. His lips and gums had fused into a hard beak. None of this seemed to bother the drastically altered Belt miner.

"All the symptoms of old age are holdovers from the change from breeder to protector," he was telling a long-dead ARM inquisitor. "Skin thickens and wrinkles; it's supposed to get like *this*, hard enough to turn a knife. You lose your teeth to leave room for the gums to harden. Your heart can weaken because you're supposed to grow a second heart, two-chambered, in the groin."

Brennan's voice was a rasp. "Your joints are supposed to expand, to offer a larger moment arm for the muscles. Increased strength. But none of this works quite right without tree-of-life, and there hasn't been tree-of-life on Earth for three million—"

Louis jumped when fingers tugged at his jumper. "Luweewu? I'm hungry."

"Okay." He was tired of studying anyway; it wasn't telling him much that was useful.

Harkabeeparolyn was still asleep. The smell of meat broiling in a flashlight-laser beam woke her. Louis dialed fruits and cooked vegetables for them, and showed them where to dump anything they didn't like.

He took his own dinner into the cargo hold.

It bothered him to have dependents. Granted that both were Louis Wu's victims. But he couldn't even teach them to get their own meals! The settings were marked in Interworld and the Hero's Tongue.

Was there any way to put them to work?

Tomorrow. He'd think of something.

The computer was beginning to deliver results. The Hindmost was busy. When Louis got the puppeteer's attention for a moment he asked for the records of Chmeee's invasion of the castle.

The castle occupied the peak of a rocky hill. Herds of piglike beasts, yellow with an orange stripe, grazed the yellow grass veldt below. The lander circled about the castle, then settled into the courtyard in a cloud of arrows.

Nothing happened for several minutes.

Then orange blurred from several arched doorways at once, too fast to see.

They stopped, flattened like rugs and clutching weapons, against the base of the lander. They were kzinti, but they seemed distorted. There had been divergence over a quarter of a million years.

Harkabeeparolyn spoke at Louis's shoulder. "Are these your companion's kind?"

"Close enough. They seem a little shorter and a little darker, and . . . the lower jaw seems more massive."

"He abandoned you. Why don't you leave him?"

Louis laughed. "Why, to get you a bed? We were in battle conditions when I let a vampire seduce me. He was disgusted. As far as Chmeee knows, *I* abandoned *him*."

"No man or woman can resist a vampire."

"Chmeee is not a man. He couldn't possibly want *rishathra* with a vampire, or with any hominid."

Now more of the great orange cats sprinted to posts beneath the lander. Two carried a rust-stained metal cylinder. The dozen cats crept to the far side of the lander.

The cylinder disappeared in a blast of yellow-white flame. The lander slid a yard or two. The kzinti waited, then crept back to study the results.

Harkabeeparolyn shuddered. "They seem more likely to desire me for a meal."

Louis was growing irritated. "They might. But I remember a time when Chmeee was starving, and he never touched me. What's your problem, anyway? Don't you get carnivores in the city?"

"We do."

"And the Library?"

He thought she wouldn't answer. (Furry faces showed at many of the slit windows. The explosion had done no visible damage.) Then, "I was in Panth Building for a time." She did not meet his eyes.

For a moment he couldn't remember. Then: Panth Building. Built like an onion floating tip down. Repairs to the water condenser. The ruler wanted to pay the fee in sex. Scent of vampire in the halls.

"You had *rishathra* with carnivores?"

"With Herders and Grass People and Hanging People and Night People. One remembers."

Louis withdrew a little. "With Night People?" Ghouls?

"The Night People are very important to us. They bear information for us and for the Machine People. They hold together what is left of civilization, and we do well not to offend them."

"Uh-huh."

"But it was the—Luweewu, the Night Hunters have a very keen sense of smell. The scent of vampire sends them running. I was told that I must have *rishathra* with a Night Hunter. Without vampire scent. I asked for transfer to the Library."

Louis remembered Mar Korssil. "They don't seem repugnant."

"But for *rishathra*? We who have no parents, we must pay society's debt before we can mate and make a household. I lost my accumulated fund when I transferred. The transfer did not come soon enough." She looked up into his eyes. "It was not joyful. But other times were as bad. When the vampire scent wears off, the memory does not. One remembers the smells.

Blood on the Night Hunter's breath. Corruption on the Night People's."

"You're well out of that," Louis said.

Some of the kzinti tried to stand up. Then they all fell asleep. Ten minutes later the hatch descended. Chmeee came down to take command.

It was late when the Hindmost reappeared. He looked rumpled and tired. "It seems your guess was correct," he said. "Not only will *scrith* hold a magnetic field, but the Ringworld structure is webbed with superconductor cables."

"That's good," said Louis. A great weight lifted from him. "That's *good*! But how would City Builders know that? I can't see them digging into the *scrith* to find out."

"No. They made magnets for compasses. They traced a gridwork of superconductor lines running in hexagonal patterns through the Ringworld foundation, fifty thousand miles across. It helped them make their maps. Centuries passed before the City Builders knew enough physics to guess what they were tracing, but their guess led them to develop their own superconductor."

"The bacteria you seeded—"

"It will not have touched superconductor buried in *scrith*. I'm aware that the Ringworld floor is vulnerable to meteorites. We must hope that none ever breached the superconductor grid."

"It's good odds."

The puppeteer pondered. "Louis, are we still searching for the secret of massive transmutation?"

"No."

"It would solve our problem very nicely," said the Hindmost. "The device must have operated on a tremendous scale. Converting matter to energy must be far easier than converting matter to other matter. Suppose we simply fired a . . . call it a transmutation cannon at the underside of the Ringworld at its farthest distance from the sun. Reaction would put the structure back in place very nicely. Of course there would be problems.

The shock wave would kill many natives, but many would live, too. The burned-off meteor shielding could be replaced at some later date. Why are you laughing?"

"You're brilliant. The trouble is, we don't have any reason to think there was ever a transmutation cannon."

"I don't understand."

"Halrloprillalar was just making up stories. She told us so later. And after all, how would *she* know anything about the way the Ringworld was built? Her ancestors weren't much more than monkeys when that happened." Louis saw the heads dip, and snapped, "Do *not* curl up on me. We don't have the time."

"Aye, aye."

"What else have you got?"

"Little. Pattern analysis is still incomplete. The fantasies involving the Great Ocean mean nothing to me. You try them."

"Tomorrow."

Sounds too low to interpret held him awake. Louis turned over in darkness and free fall.

There was light enough to see. Kawaresksenjajok and Harkabeeparolyn lay in each other's arms, murmuring in each other's ears. Louis's translator wasn't picking it up. It sounded like love. The sudden stab of envy made him smile at himself. He'd thought the boy was too young; he'd thought the woman had sworn off. But this wasn't *rishathra*. They were the same species.

Louis turned his back and closed his eyes. His ears expected a rhythmic wave action; but it never came, and presently he was asleep.

He dreamed that he was on sabbatical.

Falling, falling between the stars. When the world became too rich, too varied, too demanding, then there came a time to leave all worlds behind. Louis had done this before. Alone in a small spacecraft, he had gone into the unexplored gaps beyond known space, to see what there was to see, and to learn if he still loved himself. Now Louis floated between sleeping plates and

dreamed happy dreams of falling between the stars. No
dependents, no promises to keep.

Then a woman howled in panic, right in his ear. A
heel kicked him hard, just below the floating ribs, and
Louis doubled up with a breathy cry. Flailing arms
battered him, then closed round his neck in a death-grip
hug. The wailing continued.

Louis pried at the arms to free his throat. He called,
"Sleepfield off!"

Gravity returned. Louis and his attacker settled onto
the lower plate. Harkabeeparolyn stopped screaming.
She let her arms be pried away.

The boy Kawaresksenjajok knelt beside her, confused and frightened. He spoke urgent questions in the
City Builder language. The woman snarled.

The boy spoke again. Harkabeeparolyn answered
him at length. The boy nodded reluctantly. Whatever
he'd heard, he didn't like it. He stepped into the corner,
with a parting look that Louis couldn't interpret at all,
and vanished into the cargo hold.

Louis reached out for his translator. "Okay, what's it
all about?"

"I was falling!" she sobbed.

"It's nothing to be afraid of," Louis told her. "This is
how some of us like to sleep."

She looked up into his face. "Falling?"

"Yah."

Her expression was easy to interpret. *Mad. Quite
mad* . . . and a shrug. Visibly she braced herself. She
said, "I have made myself know that my usefulness is
over, now that your machines can read faster than I
can. I can do one thing only to make our mission easier, and that is to ease the pain of your thwarted lust."

"That's a relief," Louis said. He meant it as sarcasm;
would she hear it that way? Louis was tanjed if he'd
accept that kind of charity.

"If you bathe, and clean your mouth very thoroughly—"

"Hold it. Your sacrifice of your comfort to higher

goals is praiseworthy, but it would be bad manners for me to accept."

She was bewildered. "Luweewu? Do you not want *rishathra* with me?"

"Thank you, no. Sleepfield on." Louis floated away from her. From previous experience he sensed a shouting match coming, and that couldn't be helped. But if she tried physical force, she'd find herself falling.

She surprised him. She said, "Luweewu, it would be terrible for me to have children now."

He looked down at her face: not enraged, but very serious. She said, "If I mate now with Kawaresksenjajok, I may bring forth a baby to die in the fire of the sun."

"Then don't. He's too young anyway."

"No, he's not."

"Oh. Well. Don't you have— No, you wouldn't be carrying contraceptives. Well, can't you estimate your fertile period and avoid it?"

"I don't understand. No, wait, I do understand. Luweewu, our species ruled most of the world because of our command of the nuances and variations of *rishathra*. Do you know how we learned so much about *rishathra*?"

"Just lucky, I guess?"

"Luweewu, some species are more fertile than others."

"Oh."

"Before history began, we learned that *rishathra* is the way not to have children. If we mate, four *falans* later there is a child. Luweewu, can the world be saved? Do you *know* that the world can be saved?"

Oh, to be on sabbatical. Alone in a singleship, lightyears from all responsibility to anyone but Louis Wu. Oh, to be under the wire . . . "I can't guarantee anything at all."

"Then do *rishathra* with me, to let me stop thinking of Kawaresksenjajok!"

It was not the most flattering proposal of Louis Wu's young life. He asked, "How do we ease *his* mind?"

"There is no way. Poor boy, he must suffer."

Then you can both suffer, Louis thought. But he couldn't make himself say it. The woman was serious, and she was hurting, and she was right. This was not a time to bring a baby City Builder into the world.

And he wanted her.

He climbed out of free fall and took her to the water bed. He was glad that Kawaresksenjajok had retired to the cargo hold. What would the boy have to say tomorrow morning?

CHAPTER 26

Beneath the Waters

Louis woke under gravity, with a smile on his face, a pleasant ache in every muscle, and a grittiness in his eyes. He had slept very little last night. Harkabeeparolyn hadn't exaggerated her urgency. He had never known (despite his time with Halrloprillalar) that City Builders went into heat.

He shifted, and the big bed surged beneath him. A body rolled against him: Kawaresksenjajok, on his belly, spread out like a starfish and snoring gently.

Harkabeeparolyn, curled in orange fur at the foot of the bed, stirred and sat up. She said, perhaps in apology at leaving him, "I kept waking up and not knowing where I was, with the bed heaving under me."

Culture shock, he thought. He remembered that Halrloprillalar had liked the sleeping field, but not for sleeping. "There's plenty of floor. How do you feel?"

"Much better, for the moment. Thank you."

"Thank *you*. Are you hungry?"

"Not yet."

He exercised. His muscles were still hard, but he was out of practice. The City Builders watched him with puzzled expressions. Afterward he dialed breakfast: melon, soufflés Grand Marnier, muffins, coffee. His guests refused the coffee, predictably, and also the muffins.

When the Hindmost appeared he looked rumpled and tired. "The patterns we sought are not evident in the records of the floating city," he said. "All species build their armor in the shape of a Pak protector. Armor is not the same everywhere, not quite, but the

styling does not vary in any pattern. It may be we can
blame the spread of City Builder culture for that. Their
empire mixed ideas and inventions until we may never
trace their origins."

"What about the immortality drug?"

"You were right. The Great Ocean is seen as a
source of horrors and delights, including immortality.
The gift is not always a drug. Sometimes it comes without warning, bestowed by whimsical gods. Louis, the
legends make no sense to me, a nonhuman."

"Set the tape up for us. I'll get our guests to watch it
too. Maybe they can explain what I can't."

"Aye, aye."

"What about repairs?"

"There has been no repair activity on the Ringworld
in recorded history."

"You're kidding!"

"How large a region is covered by the city records?
How long a time? Small, and short. Aside from that,
I've studied the old interviews with Jack Brennan. I
gather that protectors have long lives and very long
attention spans. They prefer not to use servomecha-
nisms if they can do a job themselves. There was no
autopilot aboard Phssthpok's spacecraft, for instance."

"That's not consistent. The spillpipe system is certainly automatic."

"A very simple brute-force approach. We don't know
why the protectors died or left the Ringworld. Is it
possible that they knew their fate, that they had time to
automate the spillpipe system? Louis, we don't *need* to
know any of this."

"Oh, yah? The meteor defense is probably automatic
too. Wouldn't you like to know more about the meteor
defense?"

"I would."

"And the attitude jets were automatic. Maybe there
were manual overrides for all of that. But a thousand
hominid species have evolved since the Pak disappeared, and the automatics are still going. Either the

protectors always intended to leave—which I can't
believe——"

"Or they took many years to die," the Hindmost
said. "I have my own ideas on that." And he would say
no more.

Louis found fine entertainment that morning. The
tales of the Great Ocean were good stuff, with heroes
and royalty and feats of detection and magic and fearsome monsters, and a flavor different from the fairy
tales of any human culture. Love was not eternal. The
City Builder hero's (or heroine's) companions were
always of the opposite sex, their loyalty was held by
imaginatively described *rishathra*, and their conveni-
ently strange powers were taken for granted. Magicians
were not automatically evil; they were random dangers
to be avoided, not fought.

Louis found the common denominators he was looking for. Always there was the vastness of the sea and
the terror of the storms and the sea monsters.

Some of those would be sharks, sperm whales, killer
whales, Gummidgy destroyers, Wunderland shadowfish,
or trapweed jungles. Some were intelligent. There were
sea serpents miles long, with steaming nostrils (imply-
ing lungs?) and large mouths lined with sharp teeth.
There was a land that burned any ship that approached,
invariably leaving one survivor. (Fantasy, or sunflowers?) Certain islands were sea beasts of sedentary inclination, such that a whole ecology could establish
itself on a beast's back, until a shipload of sailors disturbed the creature. Then it would dive. Louis might
have believed that one if he hadn't seen the same legend
in Earth's literature.

He did believe the ferocious storms. Over that long a
reach, storms could build terribly, even without the
Coriolis effect that gives rise to hurricanes on any normal world. On the Map of Kzin he'd seen a ship as big
as a city. It might take a ship that size to weather Great
Ocean storms.

He did not disbelieve the notion of magicians, not

completely. They (in three legends) seemed to be of the City Builder race. But unlike the magicians of Earthly legend, they were mighty fighters. And all three wore armor.

"Kawaresksenjajok? Do magicians always wear armor?"

The boy looked at him strangely. "You mean in stories, don't you? No. Except, I guess they always do around the Great Ocean. Why?"

"Do magicians fight? Are they great fighters?"

"They don't have to be." The questioning was making the boy uneasy.

Harkabeeparolyn broke in. "Luweewu, I may know more of children's tales than Kawa does. What are you trying to learn?"

"I'm looking for the home of the Ringworld engineers. These armored magicians could be them, except they're too late in history."

"Then it isn't them."

"But what sparked the legends? Statues? Mummies pulled out of a desert? Racial memories?"

She thought it over. "Magicians usually belong to the species that is telling the story. Descriptions vary: height, weight, what they eat. Yet they have traits in common. They are terrible fighters. They do not take a moral stand. They are not to be defeated, but avoided."

Like a submarine beneath polar ice, *Hot Needle of Inquiry* cruised beneath the Great Ocean.

The Hindmost had slowed the ship. They had a good view of the long, intricately curved ribbon of continental shelf falling behind them. Beyond, the floor of the Great Ocean was as active as the land: mountains high enough to rise above the water; undersea canyons showing as ridges five and six miles high.

What was above them now—a pebbled roof, dark even under light amplification, that seemed obtrusively close even though it was three thousand miles above —should be the Map of Kzin. The computer said it was. Kzin must have been tectonically active when the

Map was carved. The sea beds bulged strongly; the mountain ranges were deep and sharp of outline.

Louis could identify nothing. Foam-shrouded contours weren't enough. He needed to see sunlight patterns and yellow-and-orange jungle. "Keep the cameras rolling. Are you getting a signal from the lander?"

From his post at the controls the Hindmost turned one head back. "No, Louis, the *scrith* blocks it. Do you see the nearly circular bay, there where the big river ends? The great ship is moored across its mouth. Nearly across the Map, the Y-shape where two rivers join—that is the castle where the lander now rests."

"Okay. Drop a few thousand miles. Give me an overview . . . or underview."

Needle sank beneath its carved roof. The Hindmost said, "You made this same tour in the *Lying Bastard*. Do you expect to find changes now?"

"No. Getting impatient?"

"Of course not, Louis."

"I know more than I did then. Maybe I'll pick up details we missed. Like—what's that, sticking out near the south pole?"

The Hindmost gave them an expanded view. A long, narrow, utterly black triangle with a textured surface, it dropped straight down from the center of the Map of Kzin. "A radiator fin," the puppeteer said. "The antarctic must be kept refrigerated, of course."

The Ringworlders were utterly bewildered. "I don't understand," Harkabeeparolyn said. "I thought I knew some science, but . . . what *is* it?"

"Too complicated. Hindmost—"

"Luweewu, I am not a fool or a child!"

She couldn't be much over forty, Louis thought. "All right. The whole point is to imitate a planet. A spinning ball, right? Sunlight falls almost level at the poles of a spinning ball, so it's cold. So this imitation world has to be cooled at the poles. Hindmost, give us more magnification."

The fin's textured surface became myriad adjustable horizontal flaps, silver above, black below. Summer and winter, he thought; and he heard himself say, "I can't believe it."

"Luweewu?"

He spread his hands helplessly. "Every so often I lose it. I think I've accepted it all, and then all of a sudden it's too big. Too tanj big."

Tears were brimming in Harkabeeparolyn's eyes. "I believe it now. My world is an imitation of a real world."

Louis put his arms around her. "It's real. Feel this? You're as real as I am. Stamp your foot. The world is as real as this ship. Just bigger. Way way bigger."

The Hindmost said, "Louis?"

A bit of telescope work had found him more fins, smaller ones, around the Map's perimeter. "Naturally the arctic regions must be cooled too."

"Yah. I'll be all right in a minute. Take us toward Fist-of-God, but take your time. The computer can find it?"

"Yes. Might we find it plugged? You said that the eye storm has been plugged or repaired."

"Plugging Fist-of-God wouldn't be easy. The hole's bigger than Australia, and clear above the atmosphere." He rubbed his closed eyes hard.

I can't let this happen to me, he thought. *What happens is real. What's real, I can manipulate with my brain. Tanj, I should never have used the wire. It's screwed up my sense of reality. But . . . cooling fins under the poles?*

They were out from under the Map of Kzin. Deep-radar showed nothing of pipes beneath the contoured sea bottoms. Which must mean that the meteor shielding was foamed *scrith*. The pipes had to be there, or else *flup* would fill the ocean beds.

Those ridges on the Ringworld's underside—those long, long undersea canyons. A dredge in each of the deepest canyons, an outlet at one end: you could keep the whole ocean bed clear.

"Veer a little, Hindmost. Take us under the Map of

Mars. Then under the Map of Earth. It won't take us too far out of our way."

"Nearly two hours."

"Risk it."

Two hours. Louis dozed in the sleeping field. He knew that an adventurer snatches sleep when he can. He woke well ahead of time, with sea bottom still gliding past above *Needle*'s roof. He watched it slow and stop.

The Hindmost said, "Mars is missing."

Louis shook his head violently. *Wake up!* "What?"

"Mars is a cold, dry, nearly airless world, isn't it? The entire Map should be cooled, and desiccated too, somehow, and raised nearly above the atmosphere."

"Yah. All of that."

"Then look up. We should be beneath the Map of Mars. Do you see a fin far larger than that beneath the Map of Kzin? Do you see a nearly circular cavity bulging twenty miles inward?"

There was nothing above their heads but the inverted contours of a sea bottom.

"Louis, this is disturbing. If our computer memory is failing us . . ." The Hindmost's legs folded. His heads dipped downward, inward.

"The computer memory is fine," Louis said. "Relax. The computer's fine. See if the ocean temperature is higher above us."

The Hindmost hesitated, half into fetal position. Then, "Aye, aye." The puppeteer busied himself at the controls.

Harkabeeparolyn asked, "Do I understand you? One of your worlds is missing?"

"One of the smaller ones. Sheer carelessness, my dear."

"These aren't balls," she said thoughtfully.

"No. Peeled like a round fruit, the peel spread flat."

The Hindmost called, "The temperatures in this vicinity vary. Ignoring the regions around fins, I find temperatures from forty to eighty degrees Fahrenheit."

"The water should be warmer around the Map of Mars."

"The Map of Mars is not in evidence, and the water is not warmer."

"Wha . . . at? But that's *weird*."

"If I understand you—yes, there is a problem." The puppeteer's necks arched out and curved around until he was looking into his own eyes. Louis had seen Nessus do that, and wondered if it was puppeteer laughter. It could be concentration. It was making Harkabee-parolyn queasy, but she couldn't seem to look away.

Louis paced. Mars *had* to be refrigerated. Then where? . . .

The puppeteer whistled an odd harmonic. "The grid?"

Louis stopped in midstride. "The grid. Right. And that would mean . . . futz! That easy?"

"We make progress of sorts. Our next move?"

They'd learned a good deal, looking at undersides of worlds. So— "Take us on to the Map of Earth, basement level, please."

"Aye, aye," said the Hindmost. *Needle* continued to spinward.

So much ocean, Louis thought. So little land. Why had the Ringworld Engineers wanted so much salt sea in two single bodies? Two for balance, of course, but why so large?

Reservoirs? Partly. Preserves for the sea life of an abandoned Pak world? A conservationist would call that praiseworthy; but these were Pak protectors. Whatever they did was done for the safety of themselves and their blood descendants.

The Maps, Louis thought, were a superb piece of misdirection.

Despite the contoured ocean floor, Earth was easy to recognize. Louis pointed out the flat curves of the continental shelves as they passed beneath Africa, Australia, the Americas, Greenland . . . fins under Antarctica and the Arctic Ocean . . . the Ringworlders watched and nodded politely. Why would they care? It wasn't *their* home.

Yah, he'd do his best to get Harkabeeparolyn and Kawaresksenjajok home, if there was nothing else he could do for them. Louis Wu was as close to Earth now as he would ever be.

More sea bottom passed above them.

Then shoreline: a flat curve of continental shelf bordering a maze of gulfs and bays and river deltas and peninsulas and island clusters and raggedy detail too fine for the human eye. *Needle* ran on to port of spinward. They passed beneath hollow mountain ranges and flat seas. A finely ruled line ran straight to spinward, and at its near end, a glint of light—

Fist-of-God.

Something huge had struck the Ringworld long ago. The fireball had pushed the Ringworld floor upward into the shape of a tilted cone, then ripped through. Pointing almost away from that great funnel shape was the track of a much later meteorite: a crippled General Products spacecraft, with its passengers frozen in stasis, had touched down at a horizontal seven hundred and seventy miles per second. Futz, they'd actually bent the *scrith*!

Hot Needle of Inquiry rose into a spotlight beam: raw sunlight flooding vertically through the crater in Fist-of-God Mountain. Shards of *scrith,* stretched thin when that old fireball broke through, stood like minor peaks around a volcano cone. The ship lifted above them.

Desert sloped down and away. The impact that made Fist-of-God had cremated all life over a region comfortably larger than the Earth. Far, far away, a hundred thousand miles away, the blue of distance became the blue of sea; and only *Needle*'s thousand-mile height let them see that far.

"Get us moving," Louis said. "Then give us a view from the lander's cameras. Let's see how Chmeee's doing."

"Aye aye."

CHAPTER 27

The Great Ocean

Six rectangular windows floated beyond the hull. Six cameras showed the lander's flight deck, lower deck, and four outside views.

The flight deck was empty. Louis scanned for emergency lights and found none.

The autodoc was still a great coffin, closed.

Something was wrong with the outside cameras. The view wavered and shifted and streamed with glowing colors. Louis was able to make out the courtyard, the arrow slits, several kzinti standing guard in leather armor. Other kzinti sprinted to and fro on all fours: blurred streaks.

Flames! The defenders had built a bonfire around the lander!

"Hindmost? Can you lift the lander from here? You said you had remote controls."

"I could take off," the Hindmost said, "but it would be dangerous. We are . . . twelve minutes of arc to spinward and a bit to port of the Map of Kzin—a third of a million miles. Would you expect me to fly the lander with a lightspeed delay of three and a half seconds? The life-support system is holding well."

Four kzinti streaked across the courtyard to throw open massive gates. A wheeled vehicle pulled in and stopped. It was larger than the Machine People vehicle that had brought Louis to the floating city. Projectile weapons were mounted on its four fenders. Kzinti emerged and stood studying the lander.

Had the castle's lord called on a neighbor for help?

Or had a neighbor come to claim rights to an impregnable flying fort?

The vehicle's guns swiveled to face the cameras, and spat. Flame bloomed; the cameras shuddered. The great orange cats ducked, then rose to study the results.

No emergency lights showed on the flight deck.

"These savages haven't the means to harm the lander," the Hindmost said.

Explosive projectiles sprayed the lander again.

"I'll just take your word for it," Louis said. "Continue monitoring. Are we close enough that I can get to the lander by stepping discs?"

The puppeteer looked himself in the eyes. He held the pose for several seconds.

Then he spoke. "We are two hundred thousand miles to spinward of the Map of Kzin, and a hundred and twenty thousand miles to port. The portward distance is irrelevant. The spinward distance would be lethal. It gives Needle and the lander a relative velocity of eight-tenths of a mile per second."

"Too much?"

"Our technology is not miraculous, Louis! Stepping discs can absorb kinetic energies of up to two hundred feet per second, no more."

The explosions had scattered the bonfire. Armored kzinti guards were building it up again.

Louis bit down on a bad word. "All right. The fastest way to get me there is to run us straight to antispinward until I can use the stepping discs. Then we can take our time running to starboard."

"Aye, aye. What speed?"

Louis opened his mouth and left it open while he thought. "Now, that is one fascinating question," he said. "What does the Ringworld meteor defense consider a meteor? Or an invading spacecraft?"

The puppeteer reached behind him, chewed at the controls. "I've cut our acceleration. We should discuss this. Louis, I don't understand how the City Builders knew it was safe to build a rim transport system. They were right, but how did they know?"

Louis shook his head. He could see why the Ring-world protectors might program the meteor defense not to fire on the rim walls. A safe corridor for their own ships—or maybe they found that the computer was firing on the attitude jets whenever the attitude jets fired a high-velocity plume of gas. "I'd say the City Builders started with small ships and built up. They tried it and it worked."

"Stupid. Dangerous."

"We already know they did things like that."

"You have my opinion. At your orders, Louis: what speed?"

The high desert sloped gradually down: a baked and lifeless land, an ecology shattered and heated to incandescence thousands of *falans* ago. What had struck that blow from underneath the Ringworld? A comet wouldn't normally be that big. There were no asteroids, no planets; they had been cleaned out of the system during the building of the Ringworld.

Needle's velocity was already respectable. The land ahead was beginning to turn green. There were silver threads of river.

"On the first expedition we flew at Mach 2, using flycycles," Louis said. "That'd take us . . . eight days before I can use the stepping discs. Too tanj long. I'm assuming the meteor defense fires on things that move fast relative to the surface. How fast is fast?"

"The easy way to find out is to accelerate until something happens."

"I do not *believe* I heard a Pierson's puppeteer say that."

"Have faith in puppeteer engineering, Louis. The stasis field will function. No weapon can harm us in stasis. At worst we will return to normal status after we strike the surface, and proceed henceforth at a lower speed. There are hierarchies of risk, Louis. The most dangerous thing we can do during the next two years is hide."

"I don't—if it was *Chmeee* saying,—but a Pierson's . . . give me a minute." Louis closed his eyes and tried to think. Then "See how this sounds. First we loft the ruined probe, the one we left in the Library—"

"I moved it."

"Where?"

"To the nearest high mountain with an exposed *scrith* crest. The safest place I could think of. The probe is still valuable, though it can no longer manufacture fuel."

"That's a good place. *Don't* try to fly it. Just turn on every sensor on the probe, and every sensor aboard *Needle* and the lander. Turn most of them in the direction of the shadow squares. Now, where else would you put a meteor defense? Bear in mind that it can't seem to fire at anything *under* the Ringworld floor."

"I have no ideas."

"Okay. We aim cameras all over the Arch. Cameras on the shadow squares. Cameras on the sun. Cameras on the Map of Kzin and the Map of Mars."

"Definitely."

"We stay at an altitude of a thousand miles. Shall we dismount the probe in the cargo hold? Set it to following us?"

"Our only source of fuel? No."

"Then start accelerating until something happens. How does it sound?"

"Aye, aye," said the Hindmost, and he turned to the controls. And Louis, who would have welcomed more discussion, more time to nerve himself up, kept his silence.

The cameras caught it, but none of *Needle*'s passengers did. Even if they'd been looking up, they wouldn't have caught it. They would have seen glare-white stars and the checkered blue Arch glowing against black space, and a black circle at the peak of the Arch, where *Needle*'s flare shielding blocked out the naked sun.

But they weren't even looking up.

Below the ruin of the hyperdrive motor, the land was green with life. Jungle and swamp and wild land prevailed, with an occasional ragged crazy quilt of cultivated farmland. Of the Ringworld hominids they'd seen so far, not many would make farmers.

There were covies of boats on flat seas. Once they crossed a spider web of roads half an hour wide, seven thousand miles wide. The telescope showed steeds carrying riders or pulling small carts. No powered vehicles. A City Builder culture must have fallen here, and stayed down.

"I feel like a goddess," Harkabeeparolyn said. "Nobody else could have such a view."

"I knew a goddess," Louis said. "At least she thought she was. She was a City Builder too. She was part of a spacecraft crew; she probably saw what you're seeing now."

"Ah."

"Don't let it go to your head."

Fist-of-God Mountain shrank slowly. The Earth's moon could have nestled in that vast shell. One had to see the mountain over such a distance, standing behind a landscape vaster than the habitable surfaces of all the worlds of known space, to appreciate its size. Louis wasn't feeling godlike. He felt tiny. Vulnerable.

The autodoc lid aboard the lander hadn't moved. Louis asked, "Hindmost, could Chmeee have had other wounds?"

The puppeteer was out of sight somewhere, but his voice came clear. "Of course."

"He could be dying in there."

"No. Louis, I'm busy. Don't bother me!"

The telescope view had become a blur. The bright land a thousand miles below was visibly moving now; *Needle*'s velocity had passed five miles per second. Orbital speed for Earth.

Cloud decks shone bright enough to hurt the eyes. Far aft, a checkerboard pattern of cultivation was thinning out. Directly below, the land dipped, then leveled off into hundreds of miles of flat grassland. The flatlands extended to right and left as far as the eye could see. Rivers that fed into the flats became swamps, suddenly green.

You could trace a ragged line of contoured bays, inlets, islands, peninsulas: the mark of Ringworld shoreline, designed for the convenience of boats and shipping. But that was the *spinward* border. Then several hundred miles of flat, salt-poisoned land. Then the blue line of ocean. Louis felt the hair stir on his neck at this fresh memento of the Fist-of-God impact. Even this far away, the shoreline of the Great Ocean had been lifted; the sea had receded seven or eight hundred miles.

Louis rubbed dazzled eyes. It was too bright down there. Violet highlights—

Then blackness.

Louis closed his eyes tight. When he opened them it was as if he had left them closed: black as the inside of a stomach.

Harkabeeparolyn screamed. Kawaresksenjajok thrashed. His arm struck Louis's shoulder, and the boy gripped Louis's arm with both hands and hung on. The woman's scream cut off abruptly. Then she said, in a voice with teeth in it, "Luweewu, where are we?"

Louis said, "I take a wild guess and say we're at the bottom of the ocean."

"You are correct," said the Hindmost's contralto. "I have a good view by deep-radar. Shall I turn on a spotlight?"

"Sure."

The water was murky. *Needle* wasn't as deep as it might have been. There were fish nosing about; there was even a seaweed forest anchored nearby.

The boy released Louis and pressed his nose to the wall. Harkabeeparolyn stared too, but she was shivering. She asked, "Luweewu, can you tell me what happened? Can you make it make sense?"

"We'll find out," said Louis. "Hindmost, take us up. Back to a thousand miles altitude."

"Aye, aye."

"How long were we in stasis?"

"I cannot tell. *Needle*'s chronometer stopped, of

course. I will signal the probe to send data, but the lightspeed delay is sixteen minutes."

"How fast were we moving?"

"Five point eight one miles per second."

"Then take us up to five even and hold us there while we see what we've got."

The signals from the lander resumed as *Needle* approached the surface. Fire still surrounded the lander. The autodoc was still closed. Chmeee should have emerged by now, Louis thought.

Blue light grew around them. *Needle* broke free of the ocean and surged upward into sunlight. The deck barely quivered as the ocean dropped away at twenty gravities of acceleration.

The view aft was instructive.

Forty or fifty miles behind them, huge combers rolled across the flat beach that had been an undersea continental shelf. A grooved line ran straight back from the shore. *Needle* had not struck water. The fireball had struck land and kept going.

Farther back, the beach became grassland. Farther yet, forest. It was all burning. Thousands of square miles of firestorm, flame streaming inward from all sides, pouring straight upward in the center, like the steam rushing in over a sunflower patch far, far away. *Needle*'s impact could not have caused all of that.

"Now we know," the Hindmost said. "The meteor defense is programmed to fire on inhabited territory. Louis, I am awed. The power expended compares to nothing less than the project that set the Fleet of Worlds in motion. Yet the automatics must do this repeatedly."

"We know the Pak thought big. How was it done?"

"Don't bother me for a while. I'll let you know." The Hindmost disappeared.

It was annoying. The puppeteer had all the instruments. He could lie his heads off, and how would Louis know? At this point the puppeteer couldn't even change the arrangement . . .

Harkabeeparolyn was tugging at his arm. He snapped, "What?"

"Louis, I don't ask this lightly. My sanity flinches. Forces batter me, and I can't even describe them. Please, what has happened to us?"

Louis sighed. "I'd have to tell you about stasis fields and the Ringworld meteor defense. Also about Pierson's puppeteers and General Products hulls and Pak."

"I am ready."

And he talked, and she nodded and asked questions, and he talked. He couldn't be certain how much she understood, and of course he himself knew a lot less than he wanted to. Mostly he was telling her that Louis Wu knew what he was talking about. And when she was sure of that, she became calmer, which was what he was after.

Presently she took him to the water bed—ignoring the presence of Kawaresksenjajok, who grinned at them over his shoulder, once, then went back to watching the Great Ocean move past.

In *rishathra* there was reassurance. Spurious, perhaps. Who cared?

There sure was a lot of water down there.

From a thousand miles up, one could see a long way before the blanket of air blocked the view. And for most of that distance, there wasn't a single island! The contours of sea bottom showed, and some of that was shallow enough. But the only islands were far behind, and those had probably been underwater peaks before Fist-of-God distorted the land.

There were storms. One looked in vain for the spiral patterns that meant hurricane and typhoon. But there were cloud patterns that looked like rivers in the air. As you watched them, they moved: even from this height, they moved.

The kzinti who dared that vastness had not been cowards, and those who returned had not been fools. That pattern of islands on the starboard horizon—you had to squint to be sure it was really there—must be the Map of Earth. And it was *lost* in all that blue.

A cool, precise contralto voice eased into his thoughts. "Louis? I have reduced our maximum velocity to four miles per second."

"Okay." Four, five—who cared?

"Louis, where did you say the meteor defense was located?"

Something in the puppeteer's tone . . . "I didn't say. I don't know."

"The shadow squares, you said. You're on record. It must be the shadow squares if the meteor defense can't guard the Ringworld's underside." No overtones, no emotion showing in that voice.

"Do I gather I was wrong?"

"Now, pay attention, Louis. As we passed four point four miles per second, the sun flared. I have it on visual record. We didn't see it because of the flare shielding. The sun extruded a jet of plasma some millions of miles long. It is difficult to observe because it came straight at us. It did not arch over in the sun's magnetic field, as flares commonly do."

"That was no solar flare that hit us."

"The flare stretched out several million miles over a period of twenty minutes. Then it lased in violet."

"Oh my *God.*"

"A gas laser on a very large scale. The earth still glows where the beam fell. I estimate that it covered a region ten kilometers across: not an especially tight beam, but it would not normally need to be. With even moderate efficiency, a flare that large would power a gas laser beam at three times ten to the twenty-seventh power ergs per second, for on the order of an hour."

Silence.

"Louis?"

"Give me a minute. Hindmost, that is one impressive weapon." It hit him, then: the secret of the Ringworld engineers. "*That's* why they felt safe. That's why they could build a Ringworld. They could hold off any kind of invasion. They had a laser weapon bigger than worlds, bigger than the Earth-Moon system, bigger than ... Hindmost? I think I'm going to faint."

"Louis, we don't have time for that."

"What caused it? Something caused the sun to jet plasma. Magnetic, it has to be magnetic. Could it be one function of the shadow squares?"

"I wouldn't think so. Cameras record that the shadow square ring moved aside to allow the beam to pass, and constricted elsewhere, presumably to protect the land from increased insolation. We cannot assume that this same shadow-square ring was manipulating the photosphere magnetically. An intelligent engineer would design two separate systems."

"You're right. Absolutely right. Check it anyway, will you? We've recorded all possible magnetic effects from three different angles. Find out what made the sun flare." Allah, Kdapt, Brahma, Finagle, let it be the shadow squares! "Hindmost? Whatever you find, don't curl up on me."

There was a peculiar pause. Then "Under the circumstances, that would doom us all. I would not do that unless there was no hope left. What are you thinking?"

"There is *never* no hope left. Remember."

The Map of Mars was in view at last. It was farther away than the Map of Earth—a hundred thousand miles straight to starboard—but unlike the Map of Earth, it was one compact mass. From this angle it showed as a black line: twenty miles above the sea, as the Hindmost had predicted.

A red light blinked on the lander's instrument board. Temperature: a hundred and ten Fahrenheit, just right for a spa. No lights blinked on the big coffin that held Chmeee. The autodoc had its own temperature controls.

The kzinti defenders seemed to have run out of explosives. Their supply of firewood seemed infinite.

Twenty thousand miles to go, at four miles per second.

"Louis?"

Louis eased himself out of the sleeping field. The Hindmost, he thought, looked awful. Mane rumpled, the garnets rubbed off along one side. He staggered as if his knees were made of wood.

"We'll think of something else," Louis told him. He was wishing he could reach through the wall, stroke the puppeteer's mane, give reassurance of some kind. "Maybe there's some kind of library in that castle. Maybe Chmeee already knows something we don't. Tanj, maybe the repair crew already knows the answer."

"We know the same answer. A chance to study sunspots from underneath." The puppeteer's voice was wintry-cool, the voice of a computer. "You guessed, didn't you? Hexagonal patterns of superconductor embedded in the Ringworld floor. The *scrith* can be magnetized to manipulate plasma jets in the solar photosphere."

"Yah."

"It may have been just such an event that pushed the Ringworld off center. A plasma jet formed to fire on a meteoroid, a stray comet, even a fleet from Earth or Kzin. The plasma impacted the Ringworld. There were no attitude jets to push it back into place. Without the plasma jet, the meteor itself might have been sufficient. The repair crew came later: too late."

"Let's hope not."

"The grid is not a backup for the attitude jets."

"No. Are you all right?"

"No."

"What are you going to do?"

"I will follow orders."

"Good."

"If I were still Hindmost to this expedition, I would give up now."

"I believe you."

"Have you guessed the worst of it? I compute that

the sun can probably be moved. The sun can be made to jet plasma, and the plasma can be made to act as a gas laser, forming a photon drive for the sun itself. The Ringworld would be pulled along by the sun's gravity. But even the maximum thrust would be minuscule, too little to help us. At anything over two times ten to the minus fourth power gravities of acceleration, the Ringworld would be left behind. In any case, radiation from the plasma jet would ruin the ecology. Louis, are you *laughing*?"

Louis was. "I never thought of moving the sun. I never would have. You actually went ahead and *worked out the math*?"

Wintry-cool and mechanical, that voice. "I did. It can't help us. What is left?"

"Follow orders. Hold us at four miles per second antispinward. Let me know when I can flick across to the lander."

"Aye, aye." The puppeteer turned away.

"Hindmost?"

A head turned back.

"Sometimes there's no point in giving up."

CHAPTER 28

The Map of Kzin

All the lights glowed green. Whatever the medical situation, the autodoc was handling it somehow. Chmeee was alive in there—alive, if not healthy.

But the flight-deck thermometer indicated a temperature of a hundred and sixty degrees Fahrenheit.

The Hindmost said, "Louis, are you ready to cross?"

The Map of Mars was a black dash below the line of hologram "windows," straight to starboard. The Map of Kzin was a good deal harder to see. Ahead of Mars by several degrees of arc, and fifty thousand miles farther away, Louis made out blue-gray dashed lines against a blue-gray sea.

He said, "We're not exactly opposite yet."

"No. The Ringworld's spin will still impose a velocity difference between *Needle* and the lander. But the vector is vertical. We can compensate for long enough."

It took Louis a moment to translate those words into a diagram. Then "You're going to dive at the ocean from a thousand miles altitude."

"Yes. No risk is insane now, given the position your insanity has put us in."

Louis burst out laughing (a puppeteer teaching courage to Louis Wu?) and sobered as suddenly. How else could an ex-Hindmost regain any of his authority? He said, "Good enough. Start your dive."

He dialed and donned a pair of wooden clogs. He stripped off his falling jumper and rolled it around the impact suit and utility vest, but kept the flashlight-laser in his hand. The empty seascape had begun to expand.

"Ready."

"Go."

Louis crossed a hundred and twenty thousand miles in one giant step.

Kzin, twenty years ago:

Louis Wu sprawled on a worn stone *fooch* and thought well of himself.

These oddly shaped stone couches called *foochesth* were as ubiquitous as park benches throughout the hunting parks of Kzin. They were almost kidney-shaped, built for a male kzin to lie half curled up. The kzinti hunting parks were half wild and stocked with both predators and meat animals: orange-and-yellow jungle, with the *foochesth* as the only touch of civilization. With a population in the hundreds of millions, the planet was crowded by kzinti standards. The parks were crowded too.

Louis had been touring the jungle since morning. He was tired. Legs dangling, he watched the populace pass before him.

Within the jungle the orange kzinti were almost invisible. One moment, nothing. The next, a quarter-ton of sentient carnivore hot on the trail of something fast and frightened. The male kzin would jerk to a stop and stare—at Louis's closed-lip smile (because a kzin shows his teeth in challenge) and at the sign of the Patriarch's protection on his shoulder (Louis had made sure it showed prominently). The kzin would decide it was none of his business, and leave.

Strange, how that much predator could show only as a sense of presence in the frilly yellow foliage. Watching eyes and playful murder, somewhere. Then a huge adult male and a furry, cuddly adolescent half his height were watching the intruder.

Louis had a tyro's grasp of the Hero's Tongue. He understood when the kzin kitten looked up at its parent and asked, "Is it good to eat?"

The adult's eyes met Louis's eyes. Louis let his smile widen to show the teeth.

The adult said, "No."

In the confidence of four Man-Kzin wars plus some "incidents"—all centuries in the past, but all won by men—Louis grinned and nodded. *You tell him, Daddy! It's safer to eat white arsenic than human meat!*

Ringworld, twenty years later:

The walls bathed him in heat. He started to sweat. It didn't bother him. He'd used saunas. One hundred and sixty degrees isn't hot for a sauna.

The Hindmost's recorded voice snarled and spat in the Hero's Tongue, offering sanctuary on the Fleet of Worlds. "Cut that broadcast!" Louis commanded, and it was done.

Upward-streaming flames screened the windows. The cannon-carrying vehicle had been moved away. A pair of distorted kzinti sprinted across the courtyard, placed a canister under the lander, sprinted back to a doorway.

These were not quite kzinti: not as civilized as Chmeee. If they got their paws on Louis Wu—but he should be safe enough here.

Louis squinted down through the flames. There were six of the canisters in place around the lander's base. Bombs, no doubt. They'd be set off any second now, before the flame could explode them individually.

Louis grinned. His hands poised above the control board while he fought temptation. Then: he tapped in instructions, fast. The buttons were uncomfortably hot. He braced his legs and gripped the chair back, with his falling jumper to pad his hands.

The lander rose from the flames. A ring of fireballs billowed below, and then the castle was a dwindling toy. Louis was still grinning. He felt virtuous; he'd resisted temptation. If he'd taken off on the fusion drive instead of the repulsers, the kzinti would have been *amazed* at the power of their explosives.

Hail clattered on the hull and windows. Louis looked up, startled, as a dozen winged toys curved down toward him. Then the aircraft were dropping away.

Louis pursed his lips; he reset the autopilot to halt his rise at five miles. Maybe he'd want to lose those planes. Maybe not.

He got up and turned for the stairs.

Louis snorted when he read the dials. He called the Hindmost. "Chmeee is fully healed and peacefully asleep in the 'doc. The 'doc won't wake him up and let him out because conditions outside are not habitable."

"Not habitable?"

"It's too hot. The autodoc isn't set to let the patient step out into a fire. Things ought to cool off now that we're out of the flames." Louis ran his hand across his forehead; water streamed to his elbow. "If Chmeee gets out, will you tell him the situation? I need a cold shower."

He was in the shower when the floor dropped under him. Louis snatched for a towel and was wrapping it around his waist as he ran up the stairs. He heard hail rapping on the hull.

Slowly and carefully, as if he still hurt, Chmeee turned from his place at the controls. He squinted oddly. Hair had been shaved away around the eye. Mock skin covered a shaved strip running up his thigh to the groin. He said, "Hello, Louis. I see you survived."

"Yah. What are you doing?"

"I left pregnant females in the fortress."

"Are they about to be killed this instant? Or can we hover for a few minutes?"

"Have we something to discuss? I trust you know better than to interfere."

"The way things stand now, your females will be dead in two years."

"They may ride home in stasis aboard *Hot Needle of Inquiry*. I still hope to persuade the Hindmost—"

"Persuade me. I have taken command of *Needle*."

Chmeee's hands moved. The floor surged savagely. Louis grabbed at a chair back and rode it out. A glance at the board told him that *Needle*'s descent had stopped. The rain of projectiles had stopped too, though a dozen aircraft still circled beyond the windows. The fortress was half a mile below.

Chmeee asked, "How did you arrange that?"

"I made slag out of the hyperdrive motor."

The kzin moved incredibly fast. Before Louis could do more than flinch, he was wrapped in orange fur. The kzin was pulling Louis against his chest with one arm while the other held four claws against Louis's eyebrows.

"Shrewd," said Louis. "Very shrewd. Where do your plans carry you from here?"

The kzin didn't move. Blood trickled past Louis's eyes. He felt that his back was breaking. Louis said, "It seems I've had to rescue you again."

The kzin released him and stepped back carefully, as if afraid to move on impulse. He asked, "Have you doomed us all? Or do you have some notion of moving the entire Ringworld back into position?"

"The latter."

"How?"

"A couple of hours ago I could have told you. Now we'll have to find another answer."

"Why did you do it?"

"I wanted to save the Ringworld. There was just one way to get the Hindmost's cooperation. His life's at stake now. How do I go about getting *your* cooperation?"

"You fool. I fully intend to learn how to move the Ringworld, if only to save my children. Your problem is to persuade me that I need *you*."

"The Pak who built the Ringworld were my ancestors. We're trying to think like them, aren't we? What did they build in that would do the job? Aside from that, I've got two City Builder librarians with a good knowledge of Ringworld history. They wouldn't cooperate with you. They already see you as monstrous, and you haven't even killed me yet."

Chmeee thought it over. "If they fear me they will obey. Their world is at stake. Their ancestors were Pak too."

The lander's temperature had become uncomfortably cool for a naked man, but Louis was sweating again. "I've already located the Repair Center."

"Where?"

Louis considered withholding that information, briefly. "The Map of Mars."

Chmeee sat down. "Now, that is most impressive. These displaced kzinti learned a good deal about the Map of Mars during their age of exploration, but they never learned that."

"I'll bet some ships disappeared around the Map of Mars."

"The aircraft pilot told me that many ships disappeared, and nothing of value was ever taken from the Map of Mars. The explorers brought home wealth from a Map further to spinward, but they never brought as much wealth as they put into making the ships. Do you need the autodoc?"

Louis wiped blood from his face with his falling jumper. "Not just yet. That Map to spinward sounds like Earth. So it wasn't defended after all."

"It seems not. But there is a Map to port, and ships that went there never returned. Could the Repair Center be there?"

"No, that's the Map of Down. They met Grogs." Louis swabbed at his face again. The claws hadn't cut deep, he thought, but a facial cut bleeds a long time. "Let's do something about your pregnant females. How many?"

"I don't know. Six were in their mating period."

"Well, we don't have room for them. They'll have to stay in the castle. Unless you think the local lord will kill them?"

"No, but he may very well kill my male children. Another danger . . . Well, I can deal with that." Chmeee turned to the controls. "The most powerful civilization is built around one of the old exploration ships, the *Behemoth*. If they track me here, there might be war against the fortress."

The aircraft burned like torches as they fell. Chmeee tested the sky with radar, deep-radar, and infrared. Empty. "Louis, were there more? Did any land?"

"I don't think so. If they did, they ran out of fuel, and there aren't any runways . . . Roads? Scan the roads. You can't let them radio the big ship." Radio would be line of sight, and the Ringworld atmosphere probably had a Heaviside layer.

There was one road, and tanj few straight patches on it. There were flat fields . . . It was some minutes before Chmeee was satisfied. The aircraft were dead, all of them.

"Next step," said Louis. "You can't just wipe out everyone in the fortress. I gather kzinti females can't take care of themselves."

"No . . . Louis, it's odd. The females of the castle are much more intelligent than those of the Patriarchy."

"As intelligent as you?"

"No! But they even have a small vocabulary."

"Is it possible that your own people have been breeding your females for docility? Refusing to mate with the intelligent ones for hundreds of thousands of years? After all, you cull the slave species."

Chmeee shifted restlessly. "It may be. The males here are different too. I tried to deal with the rulers of the exploration ship. I showed my power, then waited for them to attempt to negotiate. They attempted no such thing. They behaved as if there was nothing to do but fight until they or I were destroyed. I had to mock Chjarrl, to insult his pride in his ancestry, before he would tell me anything."

But puppeteers never bred these kzinti for docility, Louis thought. "Well, if you can't take the females out of the fortress and you can't kill off the males, then you'll tanj well have to deal with them. God Gambit?"

"Perhaps. Let us do it this way . . ."

* * *

Well above arrow range, just above the range of the cannon on the intruder's vehicle, the lander hovered. Its shadow covered the ashes of the fire in the courtyard. Louis listened to the voices from Chmeee's translator, and waited for Chmeee's signal.

Chmeee inviting archers to fire at him. Chmeee threatening, promising, threatening. Staccato thunder from a laser beam cutting rock, followed by a crash. Hissing, snarling, spitting.

No mention of Chmeee's *really* dangerous master.

Four hours he was down there. Then Chmeee stepped from one of the narrow windows and floated upward. Louis waited till he was aboard, then lifted.

Presently Chmeee appeared behind him, minus flying belt and impact armor. Louis said, "You never signaled for the God Gambit."

"Are you offended?"

"No, of course not."

"It would have gone badly. And . . . I could not have done it. This is my own species. I could not threaten them with a man."

"Okay."

"Kathakt will raise my children as heroes. He will teach them arms, and arm them well, and when they are old enough he will turn them loose to conquer their own lands. They will be no threat to his own domains, you see, and they will stand a good chance to survive if I do not return. I left Kathakt my flashlight-laser."

"Good enough."

"I hope so."

"Are we through with the Map of Kzin?"

Chmeee pondered. "I captured an aircraft pilot. They are all nobility, with names and comprehensive educations. Chjarrl told me much about the age of exploration after I mocked the accomplishments of his ancestors. We may assume that there is an extensive historical library within the *Behemoth*. Shall we capture it?"

"Tell me what Chjarrl told you. How far did they get on Mars?"

"They found a wall of falling water. Later generations invented pressure suits and high-altitude aircraft. They explored the edges of the Map, and one team reached the center, where there was ice."

"I think we'll just skip the *Behemoth*'s library, then. They never got inside. Hindmost, are you there?"

A microphone said, "Yes, Louis."

"We're heading for the Map of Mars. You do the same, but stay to port of us in case we have to flick across."

"Aye, aye. Have you anything to report?"

"Chmeee picked up some information. Kzinti explored the surface of the Map of Mars, and they didn't find anything un-Marslike. So we still don't know where to look for an opening."

"Perhaps from beneath."

"Yah, could be. That'd be annoying. How are our guests holding out?"

"You should rejoin them soon."

"Soon as I can, then. You see if there's data on Mars in *Needle*'s computer. And on *martians*. Louis out." He turned. "Chmeee, do you want to fly this thing? Don't exceed four miles per second."

The lander surged up and forward in obedience to the kzin's touch. A gray wall of cloud broke to let them through; then there was only blue sky, darkening as they rose. The Map of Kzin streamed below them. Then behind them.

Chmeee said, "The puppeteer seems docile enough."

"Yah."

"You seem very sure of the Map of Mars."

"Yah." Louis grinned. "It's a very nice piece of misdirection, but it couldn't be perfect, could it? They had too much to hide, by volume. We went under the Great Ocean on the way here. Guess what we found when we went under the Map of Mars?"

"Don't play games."

"Nothing. Nothing but sea bottom. Not even radiator fins. Most of the other Maps have radiator fins to cool the poles. Passive cooling systems. There has to be a system to cool the Map of Mars. Where's the heat going? I thought it might be going into the sea water, but it wasn't. We think the heat is pumped directly into the superconductor grid in the Ringworld floor."

"Superconductor grid?"

"Big mesh, but it controls magnetic effects in the Ringworld foundation. It's used to control effects in the sun. If the Map of Mars plugs into the grid, it has to be the Ringworld control center."

Chmeee thought it over. He said, "They could not pump heat into the sea water. The warm, wet air would rise. Cloud patterns would stream inward and outward from great distances. From space the Map of Mars would appear as a great target. Can you imagine Pak protectors making such a mistake?"

"No." Though Louis would have.

"I remember too little about Mars. The planet was never very important to your people, was it? It was no more than a source of legends. I do know that the Map is twenty miles high, to mimic the very rarefied air of the planet."

"Twenty miles high, and fifty-six million square miles in area. That's one billion, one hundred and twenty million cubic miles of hiding place."

"Urrr," said Chmeee. "You must be right. The Map of Mars is the Repair Center, and the Pak did their best to hide it. Chjarrl told me of the monsters and the storms and the distances of the Great Ocean. They would have made good passive guardians. A fleet of invaders might never have guessed the secret."

Louis rubbed absently at four itching spots across his eyebrows. "One point twelve times ten to the ninth cubic miles. I have to admit it, that number leaves me numb. What were they *keeping* in there? Patches big enough to plug Fist-of-God Mountain? Machinery big enough to carry those patches, and plant them, and weld them tight? That winching equipment we saw on the rim wall, for the attitude jets? Spare attitude jets? Tanj, I'd love to find spare attitude jets. But they'd *still* have room to spare."

"War fleets."

"Yah. We already know about their *big* weapon, but —war fleets, of course, and ships to carry refugees, too. Maybe the whole Map is one big refugee ship. It must have been big enough to evacuate the Ringworld before the population started filling every niche in the ecology."

"A spacecraft? Perhaps a spacecraft big enough to tow the Ringworld back into place? I have trouble thinking on this scale, Louis."

"Me too. I don't think it'd be big enough."

"Then what did you have in mind when you destroyed our hyperdrive motor?" Suddenly the kzin was snarling.

Louis chose not to flinch. "I thought the Ringworld might be set up to act on the sun magnetically. I was almost right. The trouble—"

The Hindmost's voice blared from a speaker. "Louis! Chmeee! Set the lander on autopilot and flick across to me now!"

CHAPTER 29

The Map of Mars

Chmeee reached the disc ahead of Louis, in one monstrous bound. The kzin could take orders too, Louis thought. He forbore to remark on the fact.

The City Builders were looking out through the hull, not at the passing seascape—which was nothing but blue sea and cloud-striped blue sky merging at the infinity-horizon—but at a movie-screen-sized hologram. As Chmeee appeared on the receiver disc they turned and flinched and then tried to hide it.

Louis said, "Chmeee, meet Harkabeeparolyn and Kawaresksenjajok, librarians from the floating city. They've been of great help in gaining us information."

The kzin said, "Good. Hindmost, what is the problem?"

Louis tugged at the kzin's fur and pointed.

"Yes," said the puppeteer. "The Sun."

The sun showed dimmed and magnified in the hologram rectangle. A brilliant patch near the center was shifting, twisting, changing shape as they watched.

Chmeee said, "Wasn't the sun doing that shortly before we boarded the spaceport ledge?"

"Right. You're looking at the Ringworld meteor defense. Hindmost, what do we do now? We can slow down, but I don't see any way to save the lander."

"My first thought was to save your valuable selves," the puppeteer said.

The sea threw back a highlight from directly below the fleeing *Needle*. Now it seemed to be growing brighter, with a violet tinge. Suddenly, momentarily, it

294

was unbearably bright. Then it was a black spot on the hull beneath their feet.

And a thread of jet-black, outlined in violet-white, stood upon the spinward horizon. A vertical pillar, reaching from ground to sky. Above the atmosphere it was invisible.

The kzin spoke words in the Hero's Tongue.

"All very well," said the Hindmost in Interworld, "but what is it firing on? I assumed we were the target."

Louis asked, "Isn't the Map of Earth in that direction?"

"Yes. Also a good deal of water and considerable Ringworld landscape."

Where the beam touched down, the horizon glowed white. Chmeee whispered in the Hero's Tongue, but Louis caught the sense. "With such a weapon I could boil the Earth to vapor."

"Shut up."

"It was a natural thought, Louis."

"Yah."

The beam cut off abruptly. Then it touched down again, a few degrees to port.

"Tanj dammit! All right, Hindmost, take us up. Take us high enough to use the telescope."

There was a glowing yellow-white point on the Map of Earth. It had the look of a major asteroid strike.

There was a similar glow farther away, at the far shore of the Great Ocean.

The solar flare had dimmed and was losing coherence.

Chmeee asked, "Were there aircraft or spacecraft in those directions? Fast-moving objects?"

"The instruments may have recorded something," the Hindmost said.

"Find out. And take us down to one mile altitude. I think we want to approach the Map of Mars from below the surface."

"Louis?"

"Do it."

Chmeee asked, "Have you knowledge of how that laser beam was produced?"

"Louis can tell you," the puppeteer said. "I will be busy."

Needle and the lander converged on the Map of Mars from two directions. The Hindmost held the two vehicles parallel so that it was possible to cross between them.

Louis and Chmeee flicked across to the lander for lunch. Chmeee was hungry. He consumed several pounds of red meat, a salmon, a gallon of water. Louis's own appetite suffered. He was pleased that his guests weren't watching.

"I don't understand why you picked up these passengers," Chmeee said, "unless it was to mate with the woman. But why the boy?"

"They're City Builders," Louis said. "Their species ruled most of the Ringworld. And I plucked these two out of a library. Get to know them, Chmeee. Ask them questions."

"They fear me."

"You're a soft-spoken diplomat, remember? I'm going to invite the boy to see the lander. Tell him stories. Tell him about Kzin and hunting parks and the House of the Patriarch's Past. Tell him how kzinti mate."

Louis flicked across to *Needle*, spoke to Kawaresksenjajok, and was back in the lander with him before Harkabeeparolyn quite realized what was happening.

Chmeee showed him how to fly. The lander swooped and did somersaults and darted skyward at his command. The boy was entranced. Chmeee showed him the magic of binocular goggles, and superconductor cloth, and impact armor.

The boy asked about kzinti mating practices.

Chmeee had mated with a female who could talk! It had opened new vistas for him. He told Kawaresksenjajok what he wanted to know—which Louis thought was pretty dull stuff—and then got the boy talking about mating and *rishathra*.

Kawaresksenjajok had no practice but a lot of theory. "We make records if a species will let us. We have archives of tapes. Some species have things they can do instead of *rishathra*, or they may like to watch or to talk about it. Some mate in only one position, others only in season, and this carries over. All of this influences trade relationships. There are aids of various kinds. Did Luweewu tell you about vampire perfume?"

They hardly noticed when Louis left to return to *Needle* alone.

Harkabeeparolyn was upset. "Luweewu, he might *hurt* Kawa!"

"They're doing fine," Louis told her. "Chmeee's my crewmate, and he likes children of all species. He's perfectly safe. If you want to be his friend too, scratch him behind the ears."

"How did you hurt your forehead?"

"I was careless. Look, I know how to calm you down."

They made love—well, *rishathra*—on the water bed, with the massage unit going. The woman might have hated Panth Building, but she had learned a good deal. Two hours later, when Louis was sure he would never move again, Harkabeeparolyn stroked his cheek and said, "My time of mating should end tomorrow. Then you may recover."

"I have mixed feelings about that." He chuckled.

"Luweewu, I would feel better if you would rejoin Chmeee and Kawa."

"Okay. Behold as I stagger to my feet. See me at the stepping disc? There I go: poof, gone."

"Luweewu—"

"Oh, all right."

The Map of Mars was a dark line, growing, becoming a wall across their path. As Chmeee slowed, microphones on the lander's hull picked up a steady whispering, louder than the wind of their passage.

They came to a wall of falling water.

From a mile distant it appeared perfectly straight and infinitely long. The top of the waterfall was twenty miles above their heads. The base was hidden in fog. Water thundered in their ears until Chmeee had to turn off the microphones, and then they could hear it through the hull.

"It's like the water condensers in the city," the boy said. "This must be where my people learned how to make water condensers. Chmeee, did I tell you about water condensers?"

"Yes. If the City Builders came this far, one wonders if they found the way inside. Do your tales tell anything of a hollow land?"

"No."

Louis said, "Their magicians are all built like Pak protectors."

The boy asked, "Luweewu, this great waterfall—why is there so much of it?"

"It must run all the way round the top of the Map. It takes out the water vapor. The top of the Map has to be kept dry," Louis said. "Hindmost, are you listening?"

"Yes. Your orders?"

"We'll circle with the lander, using deep-radar and the other instruments. Maybe we'll find a door under the waterfall. We'll use *Needle* to explore the top. How's our fuel supply?"

"Adequate, given that we won't be going home."

"Good. We'll dismount the probe and set it following *Needle* at . . . ten miles and ground-hugging altitude, I think. Keep the stepping-disc links and the microphones open. Chmeee, do you want to fly the lander?"

The kzin said, "Aye, aye."

"Okay. Come on, Kawa."

"I'd like to stay here," the boy said.

"Harkabeeparolyn would kill me. Come on."

Needle rose twenty miles, and red Mars stretched before them.

Kawaresksenjajok said, "It looks awful."

Louis ignored that. "At least we know we're looking for something big. Picture a blowout patch big enough to plug Fist-of-God Mountain. We want a hatch big enough for that patch plus the vehicle to lift it. Where would you put it on the Map of Mars? Hindmost?"

"Under the waterfall," the Hindmost said. "Who would see? The ocean is empty. The falling water would hide all."

"Yah. Makes sense. But Chmeee's searching that. Where else?"

"I must hide the lines of a gigantic hatch in a martian landscape? Perhaps an irregular shape, with hinges in a long, straight canyon. Perhaps I would put it beneath the ice, melting and refreezing the north pole to conceal my comings and goings."

"Is there a canyon like that?"

"Yes. I did my homework. Louis, the poles are the best gamble. Martians never went near the poles. Water killed them."

The Map was a polar projection; the south pole was spread out around the rim. "Okay. Take us to the north pole. If we don't find anything, we'll spiral out from there. Stay high and keep all instruments going. We don't care too much if something fires on *Needle*. Chmeee, are you listening?"

"I hear."

"Tell us everything. Chances are you'll find what we're after. Don't try to do anything about it." Would he obey? "We don't invade in the lander. We're burglars. We'd rather be shot at in a General Products hull."

Deep-radar stopped at the *scrith* floor. Above the *scrith* the mountains and valleys showed translucent. There were seas of marsdust fine enough to flow like oil. Under the dust were cities of a sort: stone buildings denser than the dust, with curved walls and rounded corners and a good many openings. The City Builders stared, and so did Louis Wu. Martians had been extinct in human space for hundreds of years.

The air was clear as vacuum. Off to starboard, well beyond the horizon, was a mountain taller than any on Earth. Mons Olympus, of course. And a splinter of white floated above the crater.

Needle fell, and pulled out of the fall just above the crescent dunes. The structure was still visible, floating fifty to sixty yards above the peak; and *Needle* must have been quite visible to its occupants.

"Chmeee?"

"Listening."

Louis fought a tendency to whisper. "We've found a floating skyscraper. Maybe thirty stories tall, with bay windows and a landing ledge for cars. Built like a double cone. It looks very much like the building we took over on our first trip, the good ship *Improbable*."

"Identical?"

"Not quite, but close. And it's floating above the highest mountain on Mars, just like a god-tanjed signpost."

"It does sound like a signal meant for us. Shall I flick through?"

"Not yet. Have you found anything?"

"I believe I've traced the lines of a tremendous hatch inside the waterfall. It would pass a war fleet or a patch to cover the crater in Fist-of-God. There may be signals to open it. I haven't tried."

"Don't. Stand by. Hindmost?"

"I have radiation and deep-radar scans. The building is radiating little energy. Magnetic levitation does not require large amounts of power."

"What's inside?"

"Here." The Hindmost gave them a view. By deepradar the structure showed translucent gray. It appeared to be a floating building modified for travel, with fuel tanks and an air-breathing motor built into the fifteenth floor. The puppeteer said, "Solid construction: walls of concrete or something equally dense. No vehicles in the carport. Those are telescopes or other sensor devices in the tower and the basement. I cannot tell if the structure is occupied."

"That's the problem, all right. I want to outline a strategy. You tell me how it sounds. One: we go as fast as possible to just above the peak."

"Making perfect targets of ourselves."

"We're targets now."

"Not from weapons inside Mons Olympus."

"What the futz, we're wearing a General Products hull. If nothing fires on us, we go to step two: we deep-radar the crater. If we find anything but a solid *scrith* floor we go to step three: vaporize that building. Can we do that? Fast?"

"Yes. We don't have power storage to do it twice. What is step four?"

"Anything to get us inside quick. Chmeee stands by to rescue us any way he can. Now tell me whether you're going to freeze up halfway through this procedure."

"I wouldn't dare."

"Wait a bit." It came to Louis that their native guests were scared spitless. To Harkabeeparolyn he said, "If there is a place in the world where the world can be saved, that place is below us. We think we've found the door. Someone else has found it too. We don't know anything about him, or them. Understand?"

The woman said, "I'm frightened."

"So am I. Can you keep the boy calm?"

"Can you keep *me* calm?" She laughed raggedly. "I'll try."

"Hindmost. Go."

Needle leapt into the sky at twenty gravities, and rolled, and stopped upside down, almost alongside the floating building. Louis's belly rolled too. Both City Builders shrieked. Kawaresksenjajok had a death grip on his arm.

Eyesight showed the crater plugged by old lava. Louis watched the deep-radar image.

It was there! A hole in the *scrith*, an inverted funnel leading up (down!) through the crater in Mons Olympus. It was far too small to pass Ringworld repair equip-

ment. This was a mere escape hatch, but it was roomy
enough for *Needle*.

"Fire," Louis said.

The Hindmost had last used this beam as a spotlight.
At close range it was devastating. The floating building
became a streamer of incandescence with a cometlike
head of boiling concrete. Then it was only dust cloud.

Louis said, "Dive."

"Louis?"

"We're a target here. We don't have *time*. Dive.
Twenty gravities. We'll make our own door."

The ocher landscape was a roof over their heads.
Deep-radar showed a hole in the *scrith*, dropping to
engulf them. But every other sense showed the solid
lava crater in Mons Olympus descending at terrible
speed to smash them.

Kawaresksenjajok's nails in Louis's arm were draw-
ing blood. Harkabeeparolyn seemed frozen. Louis
braced for the impact.

Darkness.

There was formless, milky light from the deep-radar
screen. Something else was glowing somewhere: green
and red and orange stars. Those were dials on the flight
deck.

"Hindmost!"

No answer.

"Hindmost, give us some light! Use the spotlight! Let
us see what's threatening us!"

"What happened?" Harkabeeparolyn asked plain-
tively. Louis's eyes were adjusting; he could see her
sitting on the floor, hugging her knees.

Cabin lights came on. The Hindmost turned from the
controls. He looked shrunken: half curled up already.
"I can't do this any more, Louis."

"We can't use the controls. You know that. Give us a
spotlight so we can see out."

The puppeteer touched controls. A white diffused
light bathed the hull in front of the flight deck.

"We are embedded in something." One head glanced
down; the other said, "Lava. The outer hull is at seven

hundred degrees. Lava was poured over us while we were in stasis and is now cooled."

"Sounds like someone was ready for us. Are we still upside down?"

"Yes."

"Then we can't accelerate up. Just down."

"Yes."

"Want to try it?"

"What are you asking? I want to start over from just before you burned out the hyperdrive motor—"

"Come on, now."

"—or from just before I decided to kidnap a man and a kzin. That was probably a mistake."

"We're wasting time."

"There is no place to radiate *Needle*'s excess heat. Using the thrusters would bring us an hour or two closer to the moment when we must go into stasis and await developments."

"Hold off for a while, then. What are you getting from deep-radar?"

"Igneous rock in all directions, cracked with cooling. Let me expand the field . . . Louis? *Scrith* floor some six miles below us, below *Needle*'s roof. A much thinner *scrith* ceiling fourteen miles above."

Louis was beginning to panic. "Chmeee, are you getting all this?"

He was answered in unexpected fashion.

He heard a howl of inhuman pain and rage as Chmeee burst from the stepping disc, running full out with his arms across his eyes. Harkabeeparolyn dove out of his path. The water bed caught the kzin across the knees and he rolled across the bed and onto the floor.

Louis had leaped for the shower. He flipped it on full blast, jumped the water bed, put his shoulder into Chmeee's armpit, and heaved. Chmeee's flesh was hot beneath the fur.

The kzin stood and followed the pull into the stream of cold water. He moved about, getting water over every part of himself; then he huddled with his face in the stream. Presently he said, "How did you know?"

"You'll smell it in a minute," Louis said. "Scorched fur. What happened?"

"Suddenly I was burning. A dozen red lights glowed on the board. I leaped for the stepping disc. The lander is still on autopilot, if it isn't destroyed."

"We may have to find out. *Needle*'s embedded in lava. Hindmost?" Louis turned toward the flight deck.

The puppeteer was curled up with his heads beneath his belly.

One shock too many. It was easy to see why. A screen on the flight deck showed a half-familiar face.

The same face, enlarged, was looking out of the rectangle that had been a deep-radar projection. A mask of a face, like a human face molded out of old leather, but not quite. It was hairless. The jaws were hard, toothless crescents. From deep under a ridge of brow, the eyes looked speculatively out at Louis Wu.

CHAPTER 30

Wheels Within Wheels

"It appears you've lost your pilot," the leathery-faced intruder told them. It floated outside the hull: the distorted head and melon-sized shoulders of a protector, a ghost within the black rock that enclosed them.

Louis could only nod. The shocks had come too fast, from the wrong directions. He was aware that Chmeee stood beside him, dripping water, silently studying a potential enemy. The City Builders were mute. If Louis read their faces right, they were closer to awe or rapture than fear.

The protector said, "That traps you thoroughly. Soon enough you must go into stasis, and we need not discuss what happens after that. I am relieved. I wonder if I could make myself kill you."

Louis said, "We thought you were all dead."

"The Pak died off a quarter of a million years ago." The protector's fused lips and gums distorted some of the consonants, but it was speaking Interworld. Why Interworld? "A disease took them. You were right to assume that the protectors were all dead. But tree-of-life is alive and well beneath the Map of Mars. Sometimes it is discovered. I speculate that the immortality drug was made here when a protector needed funding for some project."

"How did you learn Interworld?"

"I grew up with it. Louis, don't you know me?"

It was like a knife in the gut. "Teela. How?"

Her face was hard as a mask. How could it show expression? She said, "A little knowledge. You know the adage? Seeker was looking for the base of the Arch.

305

I paraded my superior education before him: I told him that the Arch had no base, that the world was a ring. He became badly upset. I told him that if he was looking for the place from which the world could be ruled, he should look for the construction shack."

"Repair Center," said Louis. A glance toward the flight deck showed the Hindmost as an elongated white footstool decorated in ruby and lavender gems.

"Of course it would become the Repair Center, and the center of power too," the protector said. "Seeker remembered tales of the Great Ocean. It seemed a likely choice, protected by the natural barriers of distance, storm, and a dozen predatory ecologies. Astronomers had studied the Great Ocean from vantages far along the Arch, and Seeker remembered enough to make us maps.

"We were sixteen years crossing the Great Ocean. There should be legends made from that voyage. Did you know that the Maps are stocked? The kzinti have colonized the Map of Earth. We could not have continued if we had not captured a kzinti colony ship. There are islands in the Great Ocean that are large life forms, their backs covered in vegetation, who dive when a sailor least expects it—"

"Teela! How? How could you get to be like this?"

"A little knowledge, Louis. I never did reason out the origin of the Ringworld engineers, not until too late."

"But you were *lucky*!"

The protector nodded. "Bred for luck, by Pierson's puppeteers meddling with Earth's Fertility Laws to make the Birthright Lotteries. You assumed it worked. It always seemed stupid to me. Louis, do you *want* to believe that six generations of Birthright Lottery winners produced a lucky human being?"

He didn't answer.

"Only one?" She seemed to be laughing at him. "Consider the luck of all the descendants of all the winners of the Birthright Lotteries. In twenty thousand years they must be well on their way out of the galaxy, fleeing the explosion of the galactic core. Why not aboard the Ringworld? Three million times the habitable surface area of the Earth, and it can be moved, Louis. The Ringworld is lucky for those unborn descendants of people bred for luck. If I can save the Ringworld, then it is luck for them that we came here twenty-three years ago, and luck for them that Seeker and I found the entrance in Mons Olympus. Their luck. Never mine."

"Did it happen to him too?"

"Seeker died, of course. We both went mad with the hunger for tree-of-life root, but Seeker was a thousand years too old. It killed him."

"I should never have left you," Louis said.

"I gave you no choice. I had none myself—if you believe in luck. I have little choice now. Instincts are very strong in a protector."

"Do you believe in luck?"

She said, "No. I wish I could."

Louis flapped his arms—a gesture of helplessness—and turned away. He had always known that he would meet Teela Brown again. But not like this! He waved the sleeping field on and floated.

The Hindmost had the right idea. Crawl into your own navel.

But humans can't bury their ears. Louis floated half curled up, with his arms over his face. But he heard:

"Speaker-To-Animals, I congratulate you on regaining your youth."

"My name is Chmeee."

"I beg your pardon," the protector said. "Chmeee, how did you come here?"

The kzin said, "I am thrice trapped. Kidnapped by the Hindmost, barred by Louis from escaping the Ringworld, trapped underground by Teela Brown. This is a habit I must break. Will you fight me, Teela?"

"Not unless you can reach me, Chmeee."

The kzin turned away.

"What do you want from us?" That was Kawaresk-senjajok, speaking diffidently in the City Builder tongue, echoed in Interworld by the translator.

"Nothing." Teela, in City Builder.

"Then what are we doing here?"

"Nothing. I've seen to it that you can do nothing."

"I don't understand." The boy was near tears. "Why do you want to bury us underground?"

"Child, I do what I must. I must prevent one point five times ten to the twelfth murders."

Louis opened his eyes.

Harkabeeparolyn objected heatedly. "But we're here to *prevent* deaths! Don't you know that the world is off center, sliding into the sun?"

"I know of that. I formed the team that has been remounting the Ringworld's attitude jets, reversing the damage done by your species."

"Luweewu says that it isn't enough."

"It isn't."

They had Louis Wu's complete attention now.

The librarian shook her head. "I don't understand."

"With the attitude jets in action we extend the life span of the Ringworld by as much as a year. An extra year for three times ten to the thirteenth intelligent beings is equivalent to giving everyone on Earth an extra thousand years of life span. A worthy accomplishment. My collaborators agreed, even those who are not protectors."

Louis could trace the lines of Teela Brown's face in the protector's leather mask. Bulges at the hinges of the jaw, a skull swollen to accommodate more brain tissue . . . but it was Teela, and it hurt terribly. *Why doesn't she go away?*

Habits die hard, and Louis had an analytic mind. He thought, *Why doesn't she go away? A dying protector in a doomed artificial world! She doesn't have a minute to spare talking to a collection of trapped breeders. What does she think she's doing?*

He turned to face her. "You formed the repair crew, did you? Who are they?"

"My appearance helped. Most hominids will at least listen to me. I gathered a team of several hundred thousand from various species. I brought three here to become protectors: from the Spill Mountain People and the Night People and the Vampires. I hoped that they would see a solution hidden to me. Their viewpoints would differ. The vampire, for instance, was nonsentient before the change.

"They failed me," said Teela. *She certainly behaved as if she had time. Time to entertain trapped aliens and breeders until the Ringworld brushed the shadow squares!* "They saw no better solution. And so we mounted the remaining Bussard ramjets on the rim wall. We have now mounted all but the last. Under the direction of the remaining protector, my team will gear the remaining Ringworld spacecraft to carry them to safety around some nearby star. Some Ringworlders will survive."

"We're back to the original question," Louis said. "Your crew is hard at work. What are you doing here?" *I'm right! She's trying to tell us something!*

"I came to prevent the murder of fifteen hundred thousand million intelligent hominids. I recognized the neutrino exhaust from thrusters built in human space, and I came to the only feasible scene of the crime. I waited. Here you are."

"Here we are," Louis agreed. "But you know tanj well that we didn't come to commit any murders whatever."

"You would have."

"Why?"

"I can't tell you that."

Yet she showed no inclination to end the conversation. It was a strange game Teela was playing. They would have to guess at the rules. Louis asked, "Suppose you could save the Ringworld by killing one and a half trillion inhabitants out of thirty trillion. A protector would do that, wouldn't she? Five percent to save 95 percent. It seems so . . . efficient."

"Can you empathize with that many thinking beings,

Louis? Or can you only imagine one death a time, with yourself in the starring role?"

He didn't answer.

"Thirty billion people inhabit human space. Picture all of them dead. Picture fifty times that population dying of, let us say, radiation poisoning. Do you sense their pain, their regrets, their thoughts for each other? From that many? The numbers are too large. Your brain won't handle it. But mine will."

"Oh."

"I can't make it happen. I can't let it happen. I knew I must stop you."

"Teela. Picture a shadow square sweeping down the width of the Ringworld at around seven hundred miles per second. Picture a thousand times the population of human space dying as the Ringworld disintegrates."

"I do."

Louis nodded. Pieces of a puzzle. Teela would give them as many pieces as she could. She couldn't make herself hand them a finished picture. So keep fishing for pieces. "Did you say the remaining protector? There were four, and now there's one plus you? What happened to the others?"

"Two protectors left the repair crew at the same time I did. They must have left separately. Perhaps they found the clues that announced your arrival. I felt it necessary to track them down and stop them."

"Really? If they were protectors, they could no more kill a trillion and a half thinking hominids than you could."

"They might arrange for it to happen, somehow."

"Somehow." Careful with the wording, now. He was glad that nobody was trying to interrupt. Not even Chmeee, the soft-spoken diplomat. "Somehow, let breeders reach the only place on the Ringworld where the crime can be committed. Would that have been their strategy, if you hadn't stopped them?"

"Perhaps."

"Let these carefully chosen breeders be protected from smelling tree-of-life, somehow." *Pressure suits!*

That was why Teela had been looking for an interstellar spacecraft. "Let them become aware of the situation, somehow. And somehow a protector has to double-think his way out of killing them before they see the solution and use it, killing astronomical numbers of breeders to save even more. Is that what you think you prevented?"

"Yes."

"And this is the right place?"

"Why else would I be waiting here?"

"There's one protector left. Will he come after you?"

"No. The Night People protector knows that she alone is left to supervise the evacuation. If she tries to kill me and I kill her, breeders alone might die en route."

"You do seem to kill very easily," Louis said bitterly.

"No. I can't kill 5 percent of the Ringworld populace, and I don't know that I can kill you, Louis. You are a breeder of my species. On the Ringworld you are alone in that regard."

"I thought of ways to save the Ringworld," said Louis Wu. "If you know of a large-scale transmutation device, we know how to use it."

"Certainly the Pak had none. That was not your cleverest deduction, Louis."

"If we could punch a hole under one of the Great Oceans, then control the outflow, we could use the reaction to put the Ringworld back in place."

"Clever. But you can't make the hole and you can't plug it. Furthermore, there is a solution that does less damage, yet it is too much damage, and I cannot permit it."

"How would you save the Ringworld?"

The protector said, "I can't."

"Where are we? What went on in this part of the Repair Center?"

A long moment passed. The protector said, "I may not tell you more than you know. I don't see how you can escape, but I must consider the possibility."

"I quit," said Louis Wu. "I concede. Tanj on your silly game."

"All right, Louis. At least you will never die."

Louis closed his eyes and curled up in free fall. *Pious bitch.*

"I will keep you company until you must go into stasis," Teela said. "I can do little else for your comfort. You, what are your names and where are you from? You are of the species that conquered the Ringworld and the stars."

Chattering. Why weren't people born with flaps over their ears? Was there a hominid with that trait?

Kawaresksenjajok asked, "What is a magician's position regarding *rishathra*?"

"That is important when you meet a new species, isn't it, child? My position is that *rishathra* is for breeders. But we do love."

The boy was enjoying himself immensely. His sense of wonder was stretched nowhere near its limits. Teela told of her great journey. Her band of explorers had been trapped by Grogs on the Map of Down, then freed by the odd inhabitants. On Kzin there were hominid animals imported long ago from the Map of Earth, bred for special traits until they differed as thoroughly as dogs do in human space. Teela's crew had hidden among them. They had stolen a kzinti colony ship. They had killed one of the krill-eating island-beasts for food, freezing the meat in an empty liquid hydrogen tank. It had fed them for months.

Finally he heard her say, "I must eat now, but I will return soon." And then there was quiet.

The few minutes of silence ended as blunt teeth closed gently on Louis's wrist. "Louis, wake. We have no time to indulge you."

Louis turned over; he killed the sleeping field. He took a moment to savor the interesting sight of a puppeteer standing next to a kzin in the prime of health. "I thought you were out of it."

"A valuable illusion that came too near reality. I was

tempted to let events take their own course," said the puppeteer. "Teela Brown spoke the truth when she said we will not die. Most of the Ringworld will break up and fly free, beyond the cometary halo. We might even be found someday."

"I'm starting to feel the same way. Ready to give up."

"The protectors must have been dead for a quarter of a million years. Who told me that?"

"If you had any sense you'd quit listening to me."

"Not quite yet, if you please. I have the impression the protector was trying to tell us something. Pak were your ancestors, and Teela is of your own culture. Advise us."

"She wants us to do her dirty work for her," Louis said. "It's doublethink all the way. Futz, you studied the interviews with Brennan after he turned protector. Protectors have very strong instincts and superhuman intelligence. There's bound to be conflict between the two."

"I don't grasp the nature of the dirty work."

"She knows how to save the Ringworld. They all did. Kill 5 percent, save 95—but they can't do it themselves. They can't even let someone else do it, but they have to *make* someone else do it. Doublethink."

"Specifics?"

Something about those numbers ticked at Louis's hindbrain. Why? . . . Tanj on it. "Teela picked that building because it looked like Halrloprillalar's floating jail, the one we commandeered on the first expedition. She picked it to get our attention. She left it where she wanted *us*. I don't know what this part of the Repair Center *does*, but it's the right spot, in a billion-cubic-mile box. We're supposed to figure out the rest."

"What then? Is she certain we're trapped?"

"Whatever we try, she'll try to stop us. We'll have to kill her. That's what she was telling us. We only have one advantage. She's fighting to lose."

"I don't follow you," said the puppeteer.

"She wants the Ringworld to live. She wants us to

kill her. She told us as much as she could. But even if we figure it all out, can *we* kill that many intelligent beings?"

Chmeee said, "I pity Teela."

"Yah."

"How can we kill her? If you are right, then she must have planned something for us."

"I doubt it. I'd guess she's done her best not to think of anything we can do. She'd have to block it. We're on our own. And she'll kill aliens by instinct. With me she might hesitate that crucial half-second."

"Very well," said the kzin. "The big weapons are all on the lander. We are embedded in rock. Is the stepping-disc link to the lander still open?"

The Hindmost returned to the flight deck to find out. He reported, "The link is open. The Map of Mars is *scrith*, but only centimeters thick. It does not have to stand the terrible stresses of the Ringworld floor. My instruments penetrate it, and so do the stepping discs. Our only good fortune to date."

"Good. Louis, will you join me?"

"Sure. What's the temperature aboard the lander?"

"Some of the sensors have burned out. I can't tell," said the Hindmost. "If the lander can be used, well and good. Otherwise gather your equipment and return in haste. If conditions are intolerable, return instantly. We need to know what we have to work with."

"The obvious next step," Chmeee agreed. "What if the lander is inoperable?"

"We'd still have a way out," said Louis, "but we've got to have pressure suits. Hindmost, don't wait for us. Find out where we are, and find Teela. She'll be in an open space, something suitable for growing crops."

"Aye, aye. I expect we are some distance beneath Mons Olympus."

"Don't count on it. She could have put a heavy laser beam on us to keep *Needle* in stasis, then towed us to where she had molten rock ready to pour. And that place will turn out to be the murder site."

"Louis, do you have any idea what she expects of us?"

"Barely an idea. Skip it for now." Louis dialed himself a couple of bath towels and passed one to Chmeee. He added a set of wooden clogs. "Are we ready?"

Chmeee bounded onto the stepping disc. Louis followed.

CHAPTER 31

The Repair Center

It was like flicking into an oven. Louis had his clogs, but the only thing protecting Chmeee's feet was the carpeting. The kzin disappeared down the stairs, snarling once when he brushed metal.

Louis was holding his breath. He hoped Chmeee was doing the same. It felt that hot: hot enough to sear the lungs. The floor was tilted four or five degrees. Looking out the window was a mistake: it froze him in disbelief. In the murky dark outside: a questing sand shark? *Sea water?*

He'd lost two or three seconds. He took the stairs more carefully than Chmeee had, fighting the need to breathe, snorting puffs of breath through his nose to clear the oven-hot air that worked its way in anyway. He smelled char, staleness, smoke, heat.

Chmeee was nursing burnt hands; the fur puffed up hugely around his neck. The handles on the lockers were metal. Louis wrapped the towel around his hands and began opening lockers. Chmeee used his own towel to heave out the contents. Pressure suits. Flying belts. Disintegrator. Superconductor cloth. Louis picked his pressure-suit helmet out of that and turned on the air feed, wrapped his towel around his neck for padding and donned the helmet. The wind that blew around his face was merely warm. He pulled in sweet air, his chest heaving.

Chmeee's suit didn't have a separate helmet; he had to put it on and seal it up. The rasp of his sudden panting was fearsome in Louis's earphones.

"We're underwater," Louis gasped. "Why is it so futzy hot?"

"Ask me later. Help me carry this." Chmeee scooped up his flying belt and impact armor, a spool of black wire and a healthy share of the superconductor cloth, and the heavy two-handed disintegrator. He made for the stairs. Louis staggered after him, with Prill's flying belt and flashlight-laser and two pressure suits and sets of impact armor. The meat of him was beginning to broil.

Chmeee stopped before the flight-deck instruments. Bubbling dark-green water showed through the windows. Small fish wove paths within an extensive seaweed forest. The kzin puffed, "There, the dials . . . record your answer. Teela poured heat at me in . . . a blast of microwaves. Life support failed. *Scrith* repulsers failed. The lander sank. Water stopped . . . the microwaves. Lander stayed hot because . . . heat pumps burned out first . . . insulation too good. We can't use the lander now."

"Futz that." Louis used the stepping disc.

He dropped what he was carrying. Sweat was streaming into his eyes and mouth. He pulled the hot helmet off and sucked cool air. Harkabeeparolyn had her shoulder under his armpit and was half carrying him toward the bed, murmuring soothing City Builder words.

Chmeee hadn't appeared.

Louis pulled himself loose. He dropped the helmet over his head and staggered back to the stepping disc.

Chmeee was working the controls. He pushed his own gear into Louis's arms. "Take this. Join you momentarily."

"Aye, aye."

Louis was half into his pressure suit when the kzin reappeared in *Needle*. The kzin stripped off his own suit. "We are in no great hurry, Louis. Hindmost, the lander is useless. I set it to take off on fusion motors and fly to Mons Olympus, purely as a diversion. Teela may waste a few seconds destroying it."

The microphone answered. "Good. I can report some progress, but I may not show it to you. We know that Teela can tap my communications."

"Well?"

The Hindmost flicked in from the flight deck. Now he could speak without mechanical aids. "Most of my instruments are useless, of course. I do know our orientation. There is a massive source of neutrino emission, probably a fusion plant, some two hundred miles to port of spinward. Deep-radar shows cavities all around us. Most are merely room-sized. Some are tremendous, and these hold heavy machinery. I believe I have identified the empty cavern that held the repair crew's scaffolding, from its size and shape and the cradles on the floor. Its exit is a massive curved door in the wall of the Map, hidden by the waterfall. I found storage for what must be patches for major meteor strikes, and another hatch. Small spacecraft, possibly warcraft—I can't tell—and yet another hatch. There are six hatches in all beneath the waterfall. I managed to—"

"Hindmost, you were to find Teela Brown!"

"Did I hear you counsel Louis Wu to patience?"

"Louis Wu is human; he knows patience. You, you grazing beast, you have far too much."

"And you propose to murder the human variant of a Pak protector. I hope you are not expecting some kind of duel? Scream and leap, and Teela will fight barehanded? We must fight Teela with our minds. Patience, kzin. Remember the stakes."

"Proceed."

"I managed to locate the mapping of Mons Olympus, eight hundred miles to antispinward of port of us. I surmise that Teela kept a heavy laser firing on *Needle*, or some such similar artifice, to keep us in stasis while she towed us eight hundred miles. I cannot guess why."

Louis said, "She towed us to where she had molten

rock ready to pour. That place will turn out to be the site of her hypothetical multiple murder. We still have to figure out how. Tanj, maybe she's overestimated our intelligence!"

"Speak for yourself, Louis. Likely it is below us." One puppeteer head arced upward. "Nearly above us, by ship's orientation, is a complex of rooms in which a good deal of electrical activity can be sensed, not to mention enough pulsed neutrino emission to indicate half a dozen deep-radar sets.

"I also found a hemisphere thirty-eight point eight miles in diameter, with another neutrino source partly up the wall. A moving source. Output is random, as with a fusion plant. It hasn't moved far during the few minutes you've been gone, but it might traverse the full one hundred and eighty degrees of dome in fifteen hours plus or minus three. Meat-eater, warrior, does that suggest anything to you?"

"An artificial sun. Agriculture. Where?"

"Twenty-five hundred miles toward the starboard edge of the Map. But since you will be invading through Mons Olympus, you must search twelve degrees to antispinward of starboard. There may be walls to penetrate. Did you bring the hand disintegrator?"

"Not being totally nonsentient, I did. Hindmost, if the lander should reach Mons Olympus, then we may exit through the stepping discs and straight out the lander's cargo door. But Teela will shoot it down first."

"Why should she? We are not aboard yet. She has deep-radar; she will know that."

"Uurrr. Then she will track the lander, wait until we appear, and destroy us then. Is this the sapience that aids your people to sneak up on a leaf?"

"Yes. You will enter Mons Olympus hours before the lander arrives. I set the probe to follow us. There is a stepping-disc receiver in the probe. Of course you will have no way to return to *Needle*."

"Uurrr. It sounds workable."

"What equipment will you use?"

"Pressure suits, flying belts, flashlight-lasers, and the disintegrator. I also brought this." Chmeee indicated the superconductor cloth. "Teela doesn't know of it. That may help us. We can sew it into garments to cover our pressure suits. You, Harkabeeparolyn, can you sew?"

"No."

Louis said, "I can."

"So can I," said the boy. "You have to show me what you want."

"I will. It need not be elegant. We must hope that Teela will use lasers rather than projectiles or a war ax. Our impact armor will not fit over pressure suits."

"Not quite true," Louis said. "For instance, Chmeee, your impact armor would fit over my pressure suit."

"Swaddled like that, you could not move fast enough."

"Maybe not. Harkabeeparolyn, how are you holding up?"

"I'm confused, Louis. Are you battling with or against the protector?"

"She's fighting us, but she's hoping to lose," Louis said gently. "She can't say so. The rules she plays by are built into her brain and glands. Can you believe any of that?"

Harkabeeparolyn hesitated. Then "The protector acted like—like somebody it feared was supervising everything it said and did. It was like that in Panth Building when I was being trained."

"That's the way it is. The supervisor is Teela herself. Can you fight a protector, knowing that the whole world could die if you lose?"

"I think so. At worst I may distract the protector."

"Okay. We're taking you with us. We've got equipment that was meant for another City Builder woman. I'll teach you as much as I can about what you'll be wearing. Chmeee, she'll have your impact suit between her pressure suit and the superconductor cloth."

"She may have Halrloprillalar's flashlight-laser. I lost mine through carelessness. I will carry the disintegrator.

I also know how to rig spare batteries to release their power in a millisecond."

"These batteries are my people's. We designed them for safety," the Hindmost said dubiously.

"Let me see them anyway. Next you must close off all avenues of communication. We must expect Teela to eat and return before we finish here. I wish we had more time. Louis, show Kawaresksenjajok how to sew our covering garments. Use superconductor for thread."

"Yah, I thought of that. Tanj, I wish we had more time."

They bounced toward the stepping discs, swaddled in gear.

Harkabeeparolyn was shapeless in layers of cloth. Her face within the helmet was tense with concentration. Pressure suit, flying belt, laser—she'd be lucky to remember how to work what she was wearing, let alone fight. From a distance it might be Louis Wu under all that cloth. Teela might hesitate. Anything might count.

She was gone. Louis followed, switching on his flying belt.

Chmeee, Harkabeeparolyn, Louis Wu: they floated like balls of black tissue paper above the rust-colored slope of Mons Olympus. The probe wasn't floating. It must have hovered until it ran out of fuel, then dropped and rolled. It was badly battered. The stepping disc had survived.

The dials below Louis's chin told him that the air was very thin, very dry, rich in carbon dioxide. A good imitation of Mars, but this was nearly Earth's gravity. How had the martians survived? They must have adapted, buoyed by the sea of dust they lived in. Stronger than their extinct cousins . . . *Stick to business!*

The crater rim was forty miles upslope. It took them fifteen minutes. Harkabeeparolyn trailed. Her flying was jerky; she must have been constantly fiddling with the controls.

The hatch at the bottom of the crater was rock-and-rust-colored and rough-surfaced. It had exploded inward, downward.

They dropped into darkness.

Their flying belts held them. That shouldn't have worked. The repulser units were repelling flat *scrith* plates overhead and underneath. But the *scrith* ceiling was not load-bearing. It was much thinner than the Ringworld floor below them.

Louis switched to infrared (hoping Harkabeeparolyn would remember; otherwise she'd be blind). Heat radiated from below—a small, bright circle. Their surroundings were vast, indistinct. Columns of discs, and slender ladders alongside, along three walls. And rising up the middle of the great room, a tilted tower of toroids. They fell past it, ring by ring. A linear accelerator, aimed up through Mons Olympus? Then those discs could be one-protector fighting platforms waiting to be launched into the sky.

A hole had been punched downward through the floor. They dropped through. Harkabeeparolyn was still with them. The warm spot was still below, growing large.

Twelve floors, close together, each with a hole punched through. *Needle* had cut quite a swath. Even the last of the ruptures was a big one . . . and infrared light glared through it. The chamber below was just short of red-hot. Chmeee dropped into it well ahead of Louis. A moment later he floated back up, then settled on the floor above.

They were maintaining radio silence. Louis imitated Chmeee: he dropped through the last hole and found himself in a blaze of infrared. Enormous heat had been released here. And the tunnel leading away glowed more brightly still.

Louis rose to join Chmeee. He waved at Harkabeeparolyn, and she settled beside him with a thump.

Yah. Needle had been towed away through that tunnel, with enough heat played on the ship to trigger the stasis field. Easy to follow . . . except that they'd broil. Now what?

Now follow Chmeee, who was floating away at speed. What did he have in mind? If only they could talk!

They were moving through residential space. It was confining for people trying to fly at speed. Cubicles with no doors, or else doors like the doors on a safe; never a curtain for mere privacy. How did Pak protectors live? Glimpses into cubicles showed spartan simplicity. On the floor of a cubicle, a skeleton with swollen joints and a crested skull. One great room was full of what must have been exercise equipment, including a jungle gym that looked a mile high.

They flew for hours. Sometimes there were miles of straight corridor. They could take these at high speed. At other times they had to pick their way.

Doors blocked them. Chmeee dealt with that: the doors sprayed away from the disintegrator beam in a cloud of monatomic dust.

Dust puffed from one big door, and then the dust stopped coming and the door was still there. A blank rectangle. It must be *scrith*, Louis thought.

Chmeee took them left, around whatever that door guarded. Louis dropped behind Harkabeeparolyn and flew backward, watching for Teela Brown to emerge. The big door remained closed. If it hid Teela Brown, she couldn't detect them through *scrith*. Even protectors had limits.

They could have been following the tunnel to *Needle*, moving above it, but they weren't. With *Needle*'s position to establish their orientation, Chmeee was leading them about twelve degrees to antispinward of starboard . . . toward a great hemispherical cavity with a moving neutrino source halfway up one wall. Good enough.

They veered right when they could. They passed another *scrith* door, but it wasn't blocking their path. Whatever they had circled, it was big. An emergency control room? They might want to find it again.

Fourteen hours had passed, and almost a thousand miles, before they stopped to rest. They slept in a kind of waist-high metal doughnut centered in a vast expanse of floor. Purpose unknown—but nothing could sneak up on them. Louis was getting hungry for something besides nutrient syrup. He wondered: had Teela eaten and gone about her business and had time to grow hungry again?

They flew on. They were out of the residential section now, though there were still cubicles here and there, with empty food storage bins and plumbing and nice flat floors for catnaps. But these were tucked away in huge chambers that might hold anything or nothing.

They flew around the perimeter of what must have been a tremendous pump, judging from the racket that pounded their eardrums until they had left it behind. Chmeee led them left, and blasted through a wall, and took them into a map room so large that Louis shrank within himself. When Chmeee blasted the far wall the huge hologram blazed and died, and they moved on.

Close now. They slept on top of a fusion generator that wasn't running. Four hours; then they moved on.

A corridor, and light beyond, and wind blowing them onward.

They emerged into the light.

The sun was just past zenith in a nearly cloudless sky. An endless sunlit landscape stretched before them: ponds, groves of trees, fields of grain, and rows of dark green vegetables. Louis felt like a target. A coil of black wire was taped to his shoulder. Now he pulled it free and flung it away. One end was still attached to his suit. It would radiate heat if she fired now.

Where was Teela Brown?

Not here, it seemed.

Chmeee led them across a range of small hills. He arced down beside a stagnant pond. Louis followed, with Harkabeeparolyn behind him. The kzin was opening his spacesuit. As Louis touched down, Chmeee held both palms outward, then mimed holding his suit tightly shut.

Don't open your suit. He meant it for Harkabeeparolyn. She'd been warned, but Louis watched her till he was sure she wouldn't.

Now what?

The land was too flat. Hiding places looked scarce— groves of trees, a handful of soft-edged hills behind them: too obvious. Hide underwater? Maybe. Louis began reeling in the superconductor wire he'd thrown away. They probably had hours to prepare, but when Teela came, she'd come like lightning.

Chmeee had stripped himself naked. Now he put the suit of superconductor cloth back on. He went to Harkabeeparolyn and helped her remove his own impact armor, and donned it. Leaving her that much more helpless. Louis did not interfere.

Hide behind the sun? The small, fusion-powered, neutrino-emitting sun—at least it was no obvious hiding place. Could it be done? With superconductor wire trailing into a pond, he'd only be at the boiling point of water. Tanj, that was clever! It would even have worked, nearer the martian surface, where water would boil at some reasonable temperature. But they were too near the Ringworld floor; air pressure was nearly at sea level.

They might wait for days. The water in the suits would hold out, and the sugar syrup, and Louis Wu's patience, probably. Chmeee was already out of his suit. There might even be prey for him.

But what of Harkabeeparolyn? If she opened her suit she'd be sniffing tree-of-life.

Chmeee had reinflated his pressure suit. Now he pulled his flying belt over it. He set a rock on each toe, then fiddled with the flying belt until it was straining upward. Now, *that* was clever. Kick the rocks away and flip the thruster on, and an empty suit would fly to the attack.

Louis hadn't thought of anything comparable.

Maybe Teela came here only every couple of weeks. Maybe she stored tree-of-life roots elsewhere.

What did tree-of-life look like, anyway? These glossy clumps of dark-green leaves? Louis pulled one up. There were fat roots underneath, vaguely like yams or sweet potatoes. He didn't recognize the plant, but he didn't recognize anything that lived here. Most of what lived on the Ringworld, and everything here, must have been imported from the galactic core.

Teela laughed in Louis's ear.

CHAPTER 32

Protector

Louis didn't just jump; he screamed inside his helmet.

There was laughter in Teela's voice, and a slurring of consonants that she couldn't help: lips and gums fused into a hard beak. "I never want to fight a Pierson's puppeteer again! Chmeee, do you think you're dangerous? That puppeteer almost got me."

Somehow she was activating their dead earphones. Could she track them by the same means? Then they were dead. So assume she couldn't.

"There were no signals from your ship. Communications dead. I had to know what was happening inside. So I rigged something to hook into the stepping discs. I can tell you that wasn't easy. First I had to guess that a puppeteer might bring stepping discs from his home planet, then I had to deduce how they worked, and build it . . . and when I hooked in and flicked over, the puppeteer was reaching for the stasis field switch! I had to guess where the transmitter disc was, and tanj fast! But I got out, and your ship must be in stasis, and nobody's coming to help you. I'm coming for you now," said Teela, and Louis heard the regret in her voice.

Nothing to do but wait now. The Hindmost was out of the picture, with all of the equipment aboard *Needle*. Nothing left but what was in their hands.

It sounded like she'd be a while, though—if she wasn't lying. Louis lifted on his flying belt.

A mile, two miles, and the roof was still far above. Ponds, streams, gentle hills: a thousand square miles of garden turned to wilderness. Lacy-leaved, bell-shaped trees formed a spreading jungle to port. Hundreds of

square miles of yellow bushes to spinward and starboard still retained traces of the rows in which they'd
been planted.

He found one big entrance to spinward, and at least
three smaller ones, including the tunnel to antispinward, the one that had brought them here.

Louis dropped to near the surface. They'd have to
defend from all four directions. If he could find some
kind of bowl shape . . . there, off center, a stream with
low hills around it. Why *not* the middle of a stream? He
studied it from above, with the feeling that he was missing some crucial point.

Yah.

Louis streaked back to where Chmeee had taken
cover. He shook Chmeee's arm and pointed.

Chmeee nodded. He ran toward the corridor they'd
entered by, towing his pressure suit like a balloon.
Louis lifted via his flying belt and waved Harkabeeparolyn to follow.

A notched ridge of low hills, with a pond behind.
Might make a nice ambush. Louis settled on the crest.
He stretched out flat, where he could watch the entrance. He turned for a moment to hurl his coil of
superconductor wire toward the pond, and watched to
be sure it reached the water.

*There was only one way out of Needle. The only step-
ping disc Teela could have reached led to a probe on
the slope of Mons Olympus. Teela's route was the route
they'd followed, and it led here.*

Several swallows of sugar syrup; several swallows of
water. Try to relax. Louis couldn't see Chmeee; he
hadn't any idea where the kzin had gone. Harkabeeparolyn was looking at him. Louis pointed at the
corridor, then waved her away. She got it. She slid
around the curve of a hill. Louis was alone.

These hills were too tanj flat. The thigh-high clumps
of dark, glossy green leaves would hide a motionless
man, but would impede movement.

Time passed. Louis used the sanitary facilities in his

suit, feeling helpless and hurried. Back to his post. *Stay ready. With her knowledge of the Repair Center's interior transport systems, she'd come fast. Hours from now, or now . . .*

Now! Teela came like a guided missile, just under the corridor's roof. Louis glimpsed her as he rolled to fire. She was standing upright on a disc six feet across, hanging on to an upright post with handles and controls on it.

Louis fired. Chmeee fired from wherever he hid. Two threads of ruby light touched the same target. Teela was squatting by then, hidden by the disc. She'd seen all she wanted, placed their positions to the inch.

But the flying disc flared ruby flame, and it was falling. Louis had a last glimpse of Teela before she dropped behind the strange, lacy trees.

She had spread a tiny paraglider.

So assume she's alive and unhurt, and move away fast. Economically, Louis went over the crest of the hill and watched from the other side. It could work, and his tail of superconductor thread was still in the pond.

Where was she?

Something leaped from the crest of the next hill over. Green light speared it in midair, and held while the thing flamed and died. So much for Chmeee's spacesuit. But a flight of hand-sized missiles flew toward the base of the green laser beam. Half a dozen white flashes from behind the rise, and the *snap!* of lightning striking close, showed that Chmeee had succeeded in turning puppeteer-made batteries into bombs.

Teela was close, and she was using a laser. And if she was circling the pond, just beyond the crest . . . Louis adjusted his position.

Chmeee's burnt suit had fallen too slowly. A protector would know it was empty. Cthulhu and Allah! How could anyone fight a lucky protector?

Teela popped up, lower down the hillside than Louis had expected, speared Louis on a lance of green light, and was gone before Louis's thumb could move. Louis

blinked. The flare shielding in his helmet had saved his
eyes. But, instincts or no, Teela was trying to kill Louis
Wu.

She popped up again elsewhere. Green light died on
black cloth. This time Louis fired back. She was gone;
he didn't know whether he'd hit her. He'd glimpsed
pliant leather armor a little loose on her, and joints
swollen hugely: knuckles and finger joints like walnuts,
knees and elbows like cantaloupes. She wore no armor
except her own skin.

Louis rolled sideways and down the hill. He started
crawling, fast. Crawling was hard work. Where would
she be next? He'd never played this game. In two hundred years of life, he'd never been a soldier.

Two puffs of steam drifted above the pond.

To his left, Harkabeeparolyn suddenly stood and
fired. Where was Teela? Her laser didn't answer. Harkabeeparolyn stood like a black-robed target; then she
ducked and ran down the hill. Flattened out and started
to crawl left and upward.

The rock came from her left, and how could Teela
have been there that fast? It smacked Harkabeeparolyn's arm hard enough to smash bone and to rip the
sleeve open. The City Builder woman stood howling,
and Louis waited to see her cut down. *Futzfutzfutz! but
track the beam—*

No beam came. And he shouldn't be watching; he
should be acting. He'd seen where the rock came from.
There was a cleft between two hills, and he crawled as
fast as he dared, to put hillside between himself and
Teela. Then around . . . Tanj, where was Chmeee now?
Louis risked a glance over the crest.

Harkabeeparolyn had stopped screaming. She sniffed.
She dropped her flying belt and tore the black cloth
away, one-handed. Her other arm flapped loose, broken.
She began trying to take off her suit.

Teela had been *there*. Where would she move? She
was ignoring Harkabeeparolyn.

Harkabeeparolyn's helmet wouldn't come loose. She

reeled down the hill, straining to rip the fabric one-handed, then smashing at the faceplate with a rock.

Too much time was passing. Teela could be anywhere by now. Louis moved again, to a notch carved by a brook now dry. If he tried a hilltop, she'd be watching it.

Could she actually guess his every move? Protector! Where was she now?

Behind me? Louis felt spiders on the back of his neck. He spun around, for no good reason, and fired at Teela as a small metal tool slashed along his ribs. The missile ripped his suit and flesh, and jarred his aim. He clasped his left arm across the torn fabric while playing the ruby beam where Teela had last been. Then she popped up and was gone before the beam could reach her, and a dense metal ball sprayed chips from his helmet.

He rolled downhill, holding his suit shut with his left arm. Through the starred helmet he saw Teela coming at him like a great black bat, and he held the ruby beam on her faster than she could dodge.

Tanj dammit, she wasn't dodging! And why should she? Harkabeeparolyn's suit of black superconductor cloth was now worn by Teela Brown. He held the beam on her with both hands. She'd get warmer than she liked before she killed him. The armored demon bounded toward him with black cloth shredding around her like wet tissue.

Shredding. Why? And *what was that smell?*

She veered and threw the laser like a missile, sideways, at Chmeee. Disintegrator and flashlight-laser spun away from Chmeee's hand. They crashed together.

The smell of tree-of-life was in Louis's nose and in his brain. It was not like the wire. Current was sufficient unto itself, an experience that demanded nothing further to make it perfect. The smell of tree-of-life was ecstasy, but it sparked a raging hunger. Louis knew what tree-of-life was now. It had glossy dark-green leaves and roots like a sweet potato, and it was all

around him, and the taste—something in his brain remembered the taste of Paradise.

It was all around him, and he couldn't eat. He
couldn't eat. He couldn't eat because of his helmet, and
he tore his hands away from the clamps that would
release his helmet, because he couldn't eat while the
human variant of a Pak protector was killing Chmeee.

He steadied the laser with both hands, as if it might
recoil. The kzin and the protector were inextricably
tangled and rolling downhill, leaving shreds of black
cloth. He followed them down with a thread of ruby
light. *First fire, then aim. You're not really hungry. It
would kill you, you're too old to make the change to
protector, it would kill you.*

Tanj, the smell! His brain reeled with it. The strain
of resisting it was horrible. It was every bit as bad as
not resetting his droud every evening of his life for
these past eighteen years. Intolerable! Louis held the
beam steady and waited.

Teela missed a disemboweling kick. For an instant
her leg stuck straight out. The red thread touched it,
and Teela's shin flashed eye-searing red.

He saw another clear shot that disappeared as he
fired. Part of Chmeee's nude pink tail flared and fell
away, writhing like an injured worm. Chmeee didn't
seem to notice. But Teela knew where the beam was.
She tried to throw Chmeee into it. Louis moved the
wand of red light clear and waited.

Chmeee had been slashed; he was bleeding in several
places; but he was on top of the protector, using his
mass. Louis noticed a sharp-edged rock nearby, like a
carefully flaked fist ax, that would crush Chmeee's skull.
He released the trigger and aimed at the rock. Teela's
hand flashed out for it and burst into flame.

Surprise, Teela!

*Tanj, the smell! I'll kill you for the smell of tree-of-
life!*

A hand gone and a lower leg: Teela should be handi-
capped by that, but how badly had she damaged
Chmeee? They must have been tiring, because Louis

caught a clear glimpse of Teela's hard beak in Chmeee's thick neck. Chmeee twisted, and for an instant there was nothing behind Teela's misshapen skull but blue sky. Louis waved the light into her brain.

It took Louis and Chmeee pulling together to open Teela's jaws where they were locked in Chmeee's throat. "She let her instincts fight for her," Chmeee gasped. "Not her mind. You were right, she fought to lose. Kdapt help me if she had fought to win."

And then it was over, except for the blood leaking into Chmeee's fur; except for Louis's bruised and possibly broken ribs, and the pain that twisted him sideways; except for the smell, the smell of tree-of-life, and that went on and on. Except for Harkabeeparolyn, now standing in pond water up to her knees, mad-eyed and frothing at the mouth as she fought to pound her helmet open.

They took her arms and led her away. She fought. Louis fought too: he fought to keep walking away from the rows and rows of tree-of-life.

Chmeee stopped in the corridor. He undogged Louis's helmet and pulled it away. "Breathe, Louis. The wind blows toward the farm."

Louis sniffed. The smell was gone. They took Harkabeeparolyn's helmet off to let the smell out of her suit. It didn't seem to matter. Her eyes were mad, staring. Louis wiped foam from her mouth.

The kzin asked, "Can you resist? Can you hold her from returning? And yourself?"

"Yah. Nobody but a reformed wirehead could have done it."

"Urrr?"

"You'll never know."

"I never will. Give me your flying belt."

The straps were tight. They must have hurt, cutting across Chmeee's wounds. Chmeee was gone only a few minutes. He came back with Harkabeeparolyn's flying belt, his own disintegrator, and two flashlight-lasers.

Harkabeeparolyn was calmer, probably through exhaustion. Louis was fighting a terrible depression. He barely heard Chmeee say, "We seem to have won a battle and lost the war. What shall we do next? Your woman and I both need treatment. It may be we can reach the lander."

"We'll go through *Needle*. What do you mean, lost the war?"

"You heard Teela. *Needle* is in stasis, and we are left with nothing but our hands. How can we learn what any of this machinery does without *Needle*'s instruments?"

"We won." Louis felt awful enough without the kzin's pessimism. "Teela isn't infallible. She's dead, isn't she? How would she know if the Hindmost was reaching for the stasis switch? Why should he?"

"With a protector in his ship, just a wall away?"

"Didn't he have a kzin trapped in that same room? That wall is General Products hull. I'd say the Hindmost reached to turn off the stepping discs. He was a little slow."

Chmeee thought it over. "We have the disintegrator."

"And only two flying belts. Let's see, how far are we from *Needle*? Around two thousand miles, almost back the way we came. Futz."

"What does a human do for a broken arm?"

"Splint." Louis got up. It was not easy to keep moving. He found a length of aluminum bar and had to be reminded what he wanted it for. They had nothing for bindings but superconductor cloth. Harkabeeparolyn's arm was swelling ominously. Louis bound her arm. He used the black thread to sew stitches where Chmeee had been most deeply gashed.

They could both die without treatment, and there wasn't any treatment. And Louis might sit down and die, the way he was feeling. *Keep moving. Futz, it won't hurt any less if you stop moving. You've got to get over this sometime. Why not now?*

"Got to rig a sling between the flying belts. What can we use? Superconductor isn't strong enough."

"We must find something. Louis, I am too badly wounded to scout."

"We don't need to. Help me get this suit off Harkabeeparolyn."

He used the laser. He cut away the front of the pressure suit. He sliced the loose fabric into strips. He punched holes around the edges of what was left of the suit, and threaded strips of the rubberized fabric through it. The other ends he tied to the straps of his flying belt.

The suit had become a Harkabeeparolyn-shaped sling. They put her back into it. She was docile now, but she wouldn't speak.

Chmeee said, "Clever."

"Thank you. Can you fly?"

"I don't know."

"Try it. If you have to drop out and you feel better later, you'll still have a flying belt. Maybe we'll find a landmark big enough that I can come back for you and find you again."

They set off down the corridor that had brought them here. Chmeee's gashes were bleeding again, and Louis knew he was hurting. Three minutes into their journey they came to a disc six feet across, floating a foot in the air and piled with gear. They settled beside it.

"We might have known. Teela's cargo disc, by another of those interesting coincidences," Louis said.

"Another part of her game?"

"Yah. If we lived, we'd find it." Everything on the disc was strange to the eye, alien, except a heavy box whose bolts had been melted off. "Do you remember this? It's the medical kit off Teela's flycycle."

"It won't help a kzin. And the medicines are twenty-three Earth years old."

"Better than nothing, for her. You, you've got allergy pills, and there's nothing here to infect you. We're not close enough to the Map of Kzin to get kzinti bacteria."

The kzin looked bad. He shouldn't have been standing up. He asked, "Can you learn these controls? I don't trust myself to try them."

Louis shook his head. "Why bother? You and Harkabeeparolyn get on the disc. It's already floating. I'll tow it. You sleep."

"Good."

"Get her attached to the pocket 'doc first. And tie yourselves to the control post, both of you."

CHAPTER 33

1.5 X 10 EXP 12

Both of them slept through the next thirty hours while Louis towed the disc. His ribs on the right side were one great red-and-purple bruise.

He stopped when he saw that Harkabeeparolyn was awake.

She babbled of the terrible compulsion that had gripped her, of the horror and delight of the insidious evil that was tree-of-life. Louis had been trying not to think about it. She waxed poetic as hell, and she wouldn't shut up, and Louis wouldn't tell her to. She needed to talk.

She wanted the comfort of Louis's arms around her, and he could give her that too.

He also hooked Teela's old 'doc to his own arm for an hour. When the agony in his ribs had receded a little, and when he felt a little less woozy, he gave it back. There was still enough pain to distract him from a smell that was still with him. His flying belt might have brushed against tree-of-life. Or else . . . perhaps it was in his head. Forever.

Chmeee had grown delirious. Louis made Harkabeeparolyn wear Chmeee's impact armor. Teela had torn it open in the fight, but it was better than skin for a woman who planned to lie next to a delirious kzin.

The armor probably saved her life at least once, when Chmeee slashed at her because she looked too much like Teela. She tended the kzin as best she could, feeding him water and nutrient from her pressure-suit helmet. By the fourth day Chmeee was rational, but

still weak . . . and ravenous. The syrup in a human's
pressure suit wasn't enough.

It took them four days in all to reach the approxi-
mate position of *Needle*, and another day cutting
through walls until they found a solid block of fused
basalt.

A week after it had solidified, the rock was still
warm. Louis left his floating disc and passengers far
down the tunnel down which Teela had towed *Needle*.
He had his pressure-suit helmet on, with clean air blowing into it, when he held the disintegrator two-handed
and pressed the trigger.

A hurricane of dust blew back at him. A tunnel
formed ahead of him, and he walked into it.

There was nothing to see, and no sound but the howl
of basalt disintegrating and blowing past him, and
lightning somewhere behind him where the electron
charges were reasserting their prerogatives. Just how
much lava had Teela poured? It seemed he'd been at
this for hours.

He bumped into something.

Yah. He was looking through a window into a
strange place. A living room, with couches and a floating coffee table. But everything looked soft, somehow;
there wasn't a sharp edge or a hard surface anywhere—
nothing that any living thing could bump a knee against.
Through a further window he could see huge buildings, and a glimpse of black sky between. Pierson's
puppeteers swarmed in the streets. Everything was upside down.

That which he had taken for one of the couches
wasn't. Louis used his flashlight-laser at low intensity.
He flicked it on and off. For a good minute nothing
happened. Then a flattish white head and neck, emerg-
ing to drink from a shallow bowl, jerked in amazement
and darted back under its belly.

Louis waited.

The puppeteer stood up. He led Louis around the
hull—slowly, because Louis had to make his path with

the disintegrator—to where he had placed a stepping-disc transmitter on the outside of the hull. Louis nodded. He went back for his companions.

Ten minutes later he was inside. Eleven minutes later, he and Harkabeeparolyn were eating like kzinti. Chmeee's hunger was beyond description. Kawaresk-senjajok watched him in awe. Harkabeeparolyn hadn't even noticed.

Ship's morning, for a spacecraft buried in congealed lava, tens of miles beneath the sunlight.

"Our medical facilities are crippled," the Hindmost said. "Chmeee and Harkabeeparolyn must heal as best they can."

He was on the flight deck, speaking via the intercom system; and that might or might not have been signifi-cant. Teela was gone, and the Ringworld might survive. The puppeteer suddenly had a long, long life span to protect. Rubbing shoulders with aliens was contraindi-cated.

"I have lost contact with both the lander and the probe," the puppeteer said. "The meteor defense flared at about the time the lander stopped sending, for what-ever significance that may have. Signals from the dam-aged probe stopped just after Teela Brown tried to invade *Needle*."

Chmeee had slept (on the water bed, quite alone) and eaten. His restored pelt would bear interesting scars once again, but the wounds were healing. He said, "Teela must have destroyed the probe as soon as she saw it. She could not force herself to leave a dangerous enemy behind her."

"Behind her? Who?"

"Hindmost, she called you more dangerous than a kzin. A tactical ploy, to insult us both, no doubt."

"Did she indeed." Two flat heads looked into each other's eyes for a moment. "Well. Our resources have dwindled to *Needle* itself and a single probe. We left that probe on a peak near the floating city. It still has working sensors, and I have signaled it to return, in case we think of a use for it. We should have it available in six local days.

"Meanwhile we seem to have our original problem back, with additional clues and additional complications. How to restore the Ringworld's stability? We believe that we are in the right place to begin," the Hindmost said. "Don't we? Teela's behavior, inconsistent for a being of acknowledged intelligence . . . ?"

Louis Wu made no comment. Louis was quiet this morning.

Kawaresksenjajok and Harkabeeparolyn sat cross-legged against a wall, close enough that their arms were touching. Harkabeeparolyn's arm was padded and in a sling. From time to time the boy glanced at her. She puzzled and worried him. She was running on painkillers, of course, but that wasn't enough to account for her torpor. Louis knew he ought to talk to the boy . . . if he knew what to say.

The City Builders had slept in the cargo hold. Fear of falling would have kept Harkabeeparolyn out of the sleeping field in any case. She had offered *rishathra*, without urgency, when Louis joined them for breakfast. "But be careful of my arm, Luweewu."

Refusing sex took tact in Louis's culture. He had told her that he was afraid of jarring her arm, which he was. It was equally true that he couldn't seem to work up an interest. He wondered if tree-of-life had affected him so. But he sensed no lust in himself for yellow roots, nor even for a wire trickling electric current.

This morning he seemed to have no strong urges at all.

Fifteen hundred billion people . . .

The Hindmost said, "Let us accept Louis's judgment regarding Teela Brown. Teela brought us here. Her intent matched our own. She gave us as many clues as she could. But what clues? She was fighting both sides of a battle. Was it important for her to create three more protectors, then kill two of them? Louis?"

Louis, lost in thought, felt four sharp points prick his skin above the carotid artery. He said, "Sorry?"

The Hindmost started to repeat himself. Louis shook his head violently. "She killed them with the meteor defense. She fired the meteor defense, twice, at targets other than our vitally necessary selves. We were allowed to watch it without being in stasis at the time. Just another message."

Chmeee asked, "Do you assume that she could have chosen other weapons?"

"Weapons, times, circumstances, number of operating protectors—she had considerable choice."

"Are *you* playing games with us now, Louis? If you know something, why not tell us?"

Louis's guilty glance at the City Builders showed Harkabeeparolyn trying to stay awake, Kawaresksenjajok listening intently. A pair of self-elected heroes waiting their chance to help save the world. *Tanj.* He said, "One point five trillion people."

"To save twenty-eight point five trillion, and ourselves."

"You didn't get to know them, Chmeee. Not as many, anyway. I was hoping one of you would think of this. I've been thrashing around in my head trying to see some—"

"Know them? Know who?"

"Valavirgillin. Ginjerofer. The king giant. Mar Korssil. Laliskareerlyar and Fortaralisplyar. Herders, Grass Giants, Amphibians, Hanging People, Night People, Night Hunters . . . We're supposed to kill 5 percent to save 95 percent. Don't those numbers sound familiar to you?"

It was the puppeteer who answered. "The Ringworld's attitude jet system is 5 percent functional. Teela's repair crew remounted them over 5 percent of the arc of the Ringworld. Are these the people who must die, Louis? The people on that arc?"

Harkabeeparolyn and Kawaresksenjajok stared in disbelief. Louis spread his arms, helpless. "I'm sorry."

The boy cried, "Luweewu! Why?"

"I promised," said Louis. "If I hadn't promised, maybe I'd have a decision to make. I told Valavirgillin I'd save the Ringworld no matter what it took. I promised I'd save her, too, if I could, but I can't. We don't have time to find her. The longer we wait, the bigger the force pushing the Ringworld off center. So she's on the arc. So's the floating city, and the Machine People empire, and the little red carnivores and the Grass Giants. So they die."

Harkabeeparolyn beat the heels of her hands together. "But this is everyone we know in the world, even by reputation!"

"Me too."

"But this leaves nothing worth saving! Why must they die? How?"

"Dead is dead," said Louis. Then, "Radiation poisoning. Fifteen hundred billion people of twenty or thirty species. But only if we do everything exactly right. First we have to find out where we are."

The puppeteer asked reasonably, "Where do we need to be?"

"Two places. Places that control the meteor defense. We have to be able to guide the plasma jets, the solar flares. And we have to disconnect the subsystem that causes the plasma jet to lase."

"I have already found these places," the Hindmost said. "While you were gone, the meteor defense fired, possibly to destroy the lander. Magnetic effects scrambled half my sensor equipment. Nonetheless I traced the origin of the impulse. The massive currents in the Ringworld floor that make and manipulate solar flares derive from a point beneath the north pole of the Map of Mars."

Chmeee said, "Perhaps the equipment must be cooled—"

"Futz that! What about the laser effect?"

"Activity there came hours later: smaller electrical effects, patterned. I told you of this source. It is just over our heads, by ship's orientation."

"I take it we must disconnect this system," Chmeee said.

Louis snorted. "It's easy. I could do it with a flash-light-laser or a bomb or the disintegrator. Learning how to make solar flares will be the hard part. The controls probably weren't designed for idiots, and we don't have too much time."

"And afterward?"

"Then we put a blowtorch against inhabited land."

"Louis! Details!"

He would be speaking a death sentence for a score of species.

Kawaresksenjajok wouldn't show his face. Harka-beeparolyn's face was set like stone. She said, "Do what you must."

He did. "The attitude jet system is only 5 percent operational."

Chmeee waited.

"Operating fuel is hot protons streaming from the sun. The solar wind."

The puppeteer said, "Ah. We flare the sun to multiply the fuel intake by a factor of twenty. Life forms beneath the flare die or mutate drastically. Thrust increases by the same factor. The attitude jets either take us to safety or explode."

"We don't really have time to redesign them, Hind-most."

Chmeee said, "Irrelevant unless Louis is totally wrong. Teela inspected those motors while mounting them."

"Yah. If they weren't strong enough, she talked herself into adding an overdesign safety factor. Guarding against the mischance of a large solar flare. She knew that was possible. Doublethink."

"To guide the flare is not necessary to us, merely convenient," the kzin continued. "Let the laser-generating subsystem be disconnected. Then, if need be, *Needle* may be placed where we want the flare to fall, then used as a target: accelerated until the meteor defense fires. *Needle* is invulnerable."

Louis nodded. "We'd like something a little more accurate. We'd do the job faster and kill less people. But . . . yah. We can do it all. We can do it."

The Hindmost came with them to inspect the components of the meteor defense. Nobody talked him into that. The sensor devices they dismounted from *Needle* had to be operated by a puppeteer's lips and tongue. When he suggested teaching Louis how to manipulate the controls using a pick and tweezers, Louis laughed at him.

The Hindmost spent some hours in the blocked section of *Needle*. Then he followed them out through the tunnel. His mane was dyed in streaks of a hundred glowing colors, and beautifully groomed. Louis thought, *Everyone wants to look good at his own funeral*, and wondered if that was it.

It wasn't necessary to use a bomb on the laser subsystem. Finding the off switch took the Hindmost a full day and a disc-load of the dismounted instruments, but it was there.

The web of superconductor cables had its nexus in the *scrith* twenty miles beneath the north pole of the Map of Mars. They found a central pillar twenty miles tall, a sheath of *scrith* enclosing the cooling pumps for the Map of Mars. The complex at the bottom must be the control center, they decided. They found a maze of huge airlocks, and each had to be passed by solving some kind of design puzzle. The Hindmost handled that.

They passed through the last door. Beyond was a brightly lighted dome, and dry-looking soil with a podium in the center, and a smell that sent Louis spinning around, running for his life, towing a bewildered Kawaresksenjajok by his thin wrist. The airlock was closed before the boy started to fight. Louis batted him across the head and kept going. They had passed through three airlocks before he let them stop.

Presently Chmeee joined them. "The path led across a patch of soil beneath artificial sunlights. The automated gardening equipment has failed, and few plants still grow, but I recognized them."

"So did I," said Louis.

"I knew the smell. Mildly unpleasant."

The boy was crying. "I didn't smell anything! Why did you throw me around like that? Why did you hit me?"

"*Flup*," said Louis. It had finally occurred to him that Kawaresksenjajok was too young; the smell of tree-of-life wouldn't mean anything to him.

So the City Builder boy stayed with the aliens. But Louis Wu didn't see what went on in the control room. He returned to *Needle* alone.

The probe was still far around the Ringworld, light-minutes distant. A hologram window, glowing within the black basalt outside *Needle*'s wall, looked out through the probe's camera: a dimmed telescopic view of a sun somewhat less active than Sol. The Hindmost must have set that up before he left.

The bone in Harkabeeparolyn's arm was healing slightly crooked; Teela's old portable 'doc couldn't set it. But it was healing. Louis worried more about her emotional state.

With nothing of her own world around her, and flame about to take everything she remembered—call it culture shock. He found her on the water bed watching the magnified sun. She nodded when he greeted her. Hours later she hadn't moved.

Louis tried to get her talking. It wasn't good. She was trying to forget her past, all of it.

He found a better approach when he tried to explain the physical situation. She knew some physics. He didn't have access to *Needle*'s computer and hologram facilities, so he drew diagrams on the walls. He waved his arms a lot. She seemed to understand.

On the second night after his return, he woke to see her cross-legged on the water bed, watching him thoughtfully, holding the flashlight-laser in her lap. He met its glassy stare, then swung his arm in circles to turn himself over and went back to sleep. He woke up next morning, so what the tanj.

That afternoon he and Harkabeeparolyn watched a flame rise from the sun, licking out and out and out. They said very little.

Epilogue

One *falan* later: ten Ringworld rotations.

Far up the arc of the Ringworld, twenty-one candle flames glowed brightly, as brightly as the corona of the hyperactive sun showing around the edges of a shadow square.

Needle was still embedded in basalt beneath the Map of Mars. *Needle*'s crew watched in a hologram window, courtesy of the probe's cameras. The probe had been brought to rest at the cliff edge of the Map of Mars, on carbon dioxide snow, where martians were not likely to tamper with it.

Between those two rows of candle flames, plants and animals and people would be dying. In numbers that would make human space look empty, the plants would be withering or growing strangely. Insects and animals would breed, but not according to their kind. Valavirgillin would be wondering why her father had died and why she was throwing up so often and whether it was part of the general doom and what was the Star People man doing about it all?

But none of that showed from fifty-seven million miles away. They saw only the flames of the Bussard ramjets burning enriched fuel.

"I am pleased to announce," the Hindmost said, "that the center of mass of the Ringworld is moving back toward the sun. In another six or seven rotations we can set the meteor defense as we found it, to fire on meteors. Five percent of attitude jet efficiency will be enough to hold the structure in place."

Chmeee grunted in satisfaction. Louis and the City

Builders continued to stare into the hologram glowing in a depth of black basalt.

"We have won," the Hindmost said. "Louis, you set me a task whose magnitude compares only to the building of the Ringworld itself, and you set my life at stake. I can accept your arrogance now that we have won, but there are limits. I will hear you congratulate me or I will cut off your air."

"Congratulations," said Louis Wu.

The woman and boy on either side of him began to cry.

Chmeee snorted. "To the victor belongs the right to gloat, at minimum. Do the dead and dying bother you? Those worth your respect would have volunteered."

"I didn't give them the chance. Look, I'm not asking *you* to be guilt-ridden—"

"Why should I be? I mean no offense, but the dead and dying are all hominids. They are not of your species, Louis, and they are certainly not of mine, nor of the Hindmost's. I am a hero. I have saved the equivalent of two inhabited worlds, and their populations *are* of my species, or nearly so."

"All right, I see your point."

"And now, with advanced technology to back me, I intend to carve out an empire."

Louis found himself smiling. "Sure, why not? On the Map of Kzin?"

"I thought of that. I believe I prefer the Map of Earth. Teela told us that kzinti explorers rule the Map of Earth. In spirit they may resemble my world-conquering people more nearly than the decadents of the Map of Kzin."

"You know, you're probably right."

"Furthermore, they of the Map of Earth have fulfilled an ancient daydream of my people."

"Oh?"

"Conquering Earth, you idiot."

It had been long since Louis Wu laughed. Conquering plains apes! "*Sic transit gloria mundi.* How do you plan to get there?"

"It should be no great feat to free *Needle* and guide it back to Mons Olympus—"

"My ship," the Hindmost said gently, but his voice cut through Chmeee's. "My controls. *Needle* goes where I will it."

An edge in Chmeee's voice. "And where might that be?"

"Nowhere. I feel no strong urge to justify myself," the Hindmost said. "You are not my species, and how can you harm me? Will you burn out my hyperdrive motor again? Yet you are allies. I will explain."

Chmeee was up against the forward wall, giving the puppeteer his full attention. Claws extended. Fur fluffed around his neck. Naturally.

"I have violated tradition," said the Hindmost. "I have continued to function when death might touch me at any second. My life has been at stake for nearly two decades, with the risk rising almost asymptotically. The risk is over, and I am exiled, but I live. I want to rest. Can you empathize with my need to take a long rest? In *Needle* I have as many of the comforts of home as I will ever see. My ship is safely buried in rock, between two layers of *scrith*, which compares in strength to *Needle*'s own hull. I have quiet and safety. If later I feel the need to explore, a billion cubic miles of the Ringworld Repair Center is just outside. I am just where I want to be, and I will stay."

Louis and Harkabeeparolyn did *rishathra* that night. (No: they made love.) They hadn't done that in some time. Louis had feared that the urge was gone. Afterward she told him.

"I have mated with Kawaresksenjajok."

He'd noticed. But she meant permanently, didn't she? "Congratulations."

"This is not the place to raise a child." She had not bothered to say *I'm pregnant*. Of course she was pregnant.

"There must be City Builders all over the Ringworld. You could settle anywhere. In fact, I'd like to come with you," Louis said. "We saved the world. We'll all be heroes, assuming anyone believes us."

"But, Louis, we can't *leave!* We can't even breathe on the surface, our pressure suits are in shreds, and we are in the middle of the *Great Ocean!*"

"We're not desperate," said Louis. "You talk as if we'd been left naked between the Clouds of Magellan. *Needle* isn't our only transportation. There are thousands of those floating discs. There's a spacecraft so big that the Hindmost could pick out the details on deep-radar. We'll find something in between."

"Will your two-headed ally try to stop us?"

"Contrariwise. Hindmost, are you listening?"

The ceiling said, "Yes," and Harkabeeparolyn jumped.

Louis said, "You're in the safest place imaginable on the Ringworld. You said so yourself. The most unpredictable threat you face has to be the aliens aboard your own ship. How would you like to get rid of us?"

"I would. I have suggestions. Shall I wake Chmeee?"

"No, we'll talk tomorrow."

Just at the cliff edge was where the water began to condense. From there it streamed downward. It became a vertical river, a waterfall twenty miles tall. The bottom was a sea of mist reaching hundreds of miles out to sea.

The probe camera that looked down the side of the Map of Mars showed them nothing but falling water and white mist.

"But in infrared light the picture is different," the Hindmost said. "Observe—"

The mist hid a ship. A narrow triangle of a ship, oddly designed. No masts. Just a second, thought Louis. Twenty miles down . . . "That thing must be a full mile long!"

"Nearly that," the Hindmost agreed. "Teela told us she had stolen a kzinti colony vessel."

"Okay." Louis had already decided, that quick.

"I detached an intact deuterium filter from the probe

Teela later destroyed," the Hindmost said. "I can fuel that ship. Teela's journey was grueling, but yours need not be. You may take floating discs for exploring, and for trade goods when you reach shore."

"Good idea."

"Will you want a working droud?"

"Don't ever ask me that again, okay?"

"Okay. Your answer is evasive."

"Right. Can you dismount a pair of stepping discs from *Needle* and install them in the ship? It'd give us something to fall back on if we hit real trouble." He saw the puppeteer eye to eye with himself, and he added, "It could save *your* life. There's still a protector around, and he won't have to leave the Ringworld now, thanks to us."

"I can do that," the Hindmost said. "Well, is this an adequate means to reach the mainland?"

Chmeee said, "Yes. A long voyage . . . a hundred-thousand-mile journey. Louis, your people suppose a sea voyage to be restful."

"On this sea, it's more likely to be entertaining. We wouldn't have to head straight to spinward. There's the Map of an unknown world to antispinward, and it's less than twice as far." Louis smiled at the City Builders. "Kawaresksenjajok, Harkabeeparolyn, shall we check out some legends for ourselves? And maybe make a few."

Glossary

ANTISPINWARD: Direction opposite to the Ringworld's direction of spin.

ARCH: The Ringworld as seen from the surface. Some natives believe their world is a flat surface surmounted by a narrow parabolic arch.

ARM: The United Nations police. Jurisdiction is limited to Earth-Moon system.

BELTER: Citizen of the asteroid belt, Sol system.

CONTROL CENTER: See REPAIR CENTER.

CZILTANG BRONE: A City Builder device, a beamer that allows solid objects, freight, passengers, etc., to penetrate *scrith*.

DROUD: A small device that plugs into the skull of a current addict. Its purpose: to meter the current flow to the pleasure center of the addict's brain.

EYE STORM: The pattern of winds that form around a meteor puncture in the Ringworld floor.

ELBOW ROOT: Ringworld plant grown for fences.

FLEET OF WORLDS: The five puppeteer planets.

FLYCYCLE: Single-seater vehicle used for exploration on the first Ringworld expedition.

FLUP: Seabottom ooze.

FOOCH (FOOCHESTH): Stone couches set throughout the kzinti hunting parks.

HUMAN SPACE: The cluster of stellar systems inhabited by mankind.

KNOWN SPACE: The stellar region known to humanity through the explorations of human or other species.

LANDER: General term for a ground-to-orbit craft.

LONG SHOT: See QUANTUM II HYPERDRIVE.

MAKE HIS (HER) DAY: Use a tasp on him (her), especially from concealment.

OUTSIDER: Intelligent life form whose biochemistry is based on liquid helium and the thermoelectric effect. Outsider ships roam the stars at sublight speeds, trading in information.

OUTSIDER HYPERDRIVE: Faster-than-light drive never used by the Outsiders themselves, but used extensively by the star-traveling species of known space.

PORT: To the left as one faces spinward.

QUANTUM II HYPERDRIVE: Developed by Pierson's puppeteers, a mode of travel is enormously faster than the Outsider hyperdrive. *Long Shot* was the prototype spacecraft, the first to visit the galactic core.

REPAIR CENTER: (Hypothetical) Center of Ringworld maintenance and controls.

RISHATHRA: Sex practices outside of one's own species (but within the hominids).

SCRITH: Ringworld structural material. *Scrith* underlies all of the terraformed and contoured inner surface of the Ringworld. The rim walls are also of *scrith*. Very dense, with a tensile strength on the order of the force that holds atomic nuclei together.

STEPPING DISKS: Teleportation system used on the Fleet of Worlds. (Other known races use a less sophisticated method, the enclosed transfer booths.)

SPILL MOUNTAINS: Mountains standing against the rim wall. They have their own ecology. One stage in the circulation of *flup*.

SPAGHETTI PLANT: Ringworld plant, description obvious. Edible.

SPINWARD: In the direction of rotation of the Ringworld.

STARBOARD: To the right as one faces spinward.

STASIS: A condition in which time passes very slowly. Ratios can be as high as half a billion years of real time to a few seconds in stasis. An object in stasis is very nearly invulnerable.

TANJ: Slang acronym formed from "There Ain't No Justice." Used as an expletive.

TASP: A hand-held device to tickle the pleasure center of a human brain from a distance.

TERRAFORM: Operate on an environment to render it Earthlike.

THRUSTER: Reactionless drive; has generally replaced fusion rockets on all spacecraft save warcraft.

WEENIE PLANT: Ringworld plant similar to melons or cucumbers, but growing in links. Clusters of roots spring from the nodes. Grows in damp areas. Edible.

Ringworld Parameters

30 hours = 1 Ringworld day

1 turn = 7½ days = A Ringworld rotation

75 days = 10 turns = 1 falan

Mass = 2 × 10exp30 grams

Radius = .95 × 10exp8 miles

Circumference = 5.97 × 10exp8 miles

Width = 997,000 miles

Surface area = 6 × 10exp14 square miles = 3 × 10exp6 times the surface area of Earth (approx.)

Surface gravity = 31 feet/second/second = .992 G

Rim walls rise inward, 1000 miles high.

Star: G3 verging on G2, barely smaller and cooler than Sol

About the Author

Larry Niven is one of today's leading science-fiction authors, recognized particularly for his mercurial scientific imagination as exercised in his "Tales of Known Space," short fiction published in several collections, and the prize-winning novel, *Ringworld*. His other recent books include the mainstream best-seller, *Lucifer's Hammer*, written with Jerry Pournelle.